Also Available from Jolly Horror Press

Betwixt the Dark & Light

Don't Cry To Mama

Accursed

Coffin Blossoms

Edited by Jonathan Lambert, Lori Titus, & Autumn Miller

Jolly Horror Press

Copyright © 2020 Jolly Horror Press

All Rights Reserved. No portion of this book may be reproduced without written consent of Jolly Horror Press.

This is a work of fiction. Names, characters, places and incidents are either the product of the authors' imagination or are used fictitiously, and any resemblance to any person or persons, living or dead, events or locales is entirely coincidental.

Cover design by Eloise J. Knapp based on original artwork by Amanda Crum

CONTENTS

- FOREWORD 1
- THERE'S SOMETHING ABOUT BLOODY MARY By Richard Lau 7
- THE GOLDEN FALCON By Angelique Fawns 21
- AXE-MURDERERS' GORGE By Alex Colvin 35
- BUMPER-TO-BUMPER By Kevin M. Folliard 47
- CARL THE FORTUITOUS By John Kiste 65
- THE DOOM THAT CAME TO 1347 BEECHWOOD AVENUE By Mark McLaughlin 77
- HOW THE OTHER HALF LIVES By R. A. Clarke 83
- A GHOST NAMED GRADY By Robert P. Ottone 103
- HEEBIE JEEBIES By John Wolf 119
- JIANGSHI By Judith Baron 141
- VACATION INTERRUPTUS By Mya Lairis 151
- THE STAGES OF MONSTER GRIEF By Carina Bissett 175
- DRACULARRY By Lin Morris 181
- THE DARKER SIDE OF US By Clarence Carter 193
- HIGH TECH CLOTHES RACK By Mark McLaughlin 215
- RETAIL HELL By Amanda Crum 227
- BEST INTENTIONS By Columbia Stover 249
- POTION By Timothy C. Hobbs 263
- AN OLDER LADY By Nicole M. Wolverton 291
- JACK IN THE MORNING By Wade Hunter 301
- AGNES AND THE GHOST IN WHITE By George Tsirakidis 323
- TV SPIRITUAL GUIDE By Zachariah Stanfield 337
- ALL THE DEVILS ARE SINGING By E.J. Sidle 347
- A VEGGIE TALE By Richard Lau 371
- ABOUT THE AUTHORS 389
- ACKNOWLEDGEMENTS 399

FOREWORD

Horror has been a part of my life since I was a kid. Not true horror, I had a loving childhood, wonderful parents, and no tragedies. But I had a grandmother that loved to watch horror movies and had two TV's going all the time, each playing one horror movie or another. She also had horror figurines, and models. The wolfman, Frankenstein's monster, you name it. Her attic was also haunted apparently. I never went up there, but I heard stories.

I was in my junior year of college, living in a townhouse. My girlfriend at the time was with me and we popped on the movie *Evil Dead 2* expecting to be scared silly. Only I wasn't. Not sure about her. I found it hilarious. Full of one-line zingers. When Ash cut off his possessed hand, and put a bucket over it, weighted down with the book *A Farewell to Arms*, I howled. Then, when it got loose and flipped him the bird, I fell on the floor laughing. I never saw a movie like that before.

We didn't have the internet back then, we had big

hair. It was the 1980s. Couldn't Google the movie and find out all about it. But as time went on we did get internet, IMDB, Evil Dead Facebook groups, *Army of Darkness* and 3 seasons of *Ash vs. Evil Dead* on Starz (and oh yeah, one bad reboot of *Evil Dead*). It's still my favorite movie of all time. Turns out, horror/comedy is my thing. There have been a number of horror/comedy movies over the years. *Tucker and Dale vs. Evil* and *What We Do In the Shadows* are two of my favorites. Yet, they are few and far between. *Mom and Dad* was a good one too, with Nicholas Cage going batshit crazy as a possessed father. I love this stuff.

When I began writing my own stories. I wanted to write horror. But every single one detoured at some point into horror/comedy. I'm pretty sure I'm the only author that has ever used a fart to bring about the demise of a vampire, or ended a coven of neighborhood witches in a giant sized kabob. Those stories didn't start out that way. But that's what they became. Horror/comedy is my favorite genre, and it's the reason I started Jolly Horror Press. To give a home for these stories which are often hard to place. Most publishers want comedy, or pure horror. A funny horror story is lucky to find a home. Until now.

So, funny horror is the mission of Jolly Horror Press. What we have found however, throughout three anthologies, is not a lot of authors write horror/comedy. I think it's easier for a comedy writer to dip into horror, than it is for a horror writer to dip into comedy. Time will tell.

We received a lot of story submissions for this anthology. The most we've received yet. Many were very good. They just weren't that funny. We had to reject them. I'm sure they will find a home as good stories are always wanted. We held tight to our mission on this one however, and if we didn't at least chuckle once, the story wasn't getting in. So I'm very proud of this book. It's our first true horror/comedy anthology. And that's what we at Jolly Horror Press are all about.

I'd like to also point out that we get stories from across the globe. Even though we publish in the USA, we made a decision with this anthology, as well as future ones, to leave the original spellings of words when written by authors in other countries where word usage and spelling are slightly different. In other words, in some stories you might see favourite instead of favorite, or lorry instead of truck. We like the original flavour (get it?)

Not many people reads forewords (I know I usually don't), so I'll close this now, but here for your reading pleasure are 24 stories that made us both chuckle and nearly $hit our pants. I hope you enjoy reading them as much as I did.

-Jonathan Lambert

I usually write supernatural horror. I love monsters, spirits, and creatures that don't fit easy classification. I also love to write about the darker side of human nature, the parts we wish weren't there. It can be a safe way to explore the uglier side of humanity.

If you've watched or read the news lately, you're quite aware that this new millennia is already full of the same kind of horrors as the last. People find a way to create or worsen the suffering of other humans time and time again. Werewolves and vampires have nothing on dictators and serial killers.

In these very serious times, stepping away from darker subject matter can give one a chance to breathe. Or in this case, maybe looking at a crazed world through the softer lens of humor.

When Jonathan Lambert asked me to partner up with him as an editor at Jolly Horror, I wasn't sure if I was the right choice for the gig. I am more horror than humor oriented. And I didn't know for sure how I would like working with stories that blend funny and frightening.

The one thing I was sure of was that the few examples I could point out of combining the two genres, when done right, is sublime.

Now, here comes the part that's hard. Horror comedy is a small cross-section of stories for a reason. First, they're not the easiest thing to write. It takes a very thoughtful, careful bit of writing to balance out what's scary with downright silly. Once writers craft these stories, they don't have a lot of places to go for publication. This has been one of Jolly Horror's missions to begin with—give these stories a platform and people will write them.

For the first two anthologies, we focused on getting Jolly Horror on its feet as an imprint. We didn't want to turn away some of the straight horror stories we were getting, as there were a lot of high-quality work among the submissions.

With Coffin Blossoms being our third anthology in print, we wanted to return to the original purpose of Jolly Horror: only horror/comedy stories that make you laugh and give you the chills. I've found a new love of these stories myself and I hope that if you haven't yet, by the time you finish this collection you'll be a fan.

-Lori Titus

To me, the dark times are better when tempered with light, even if it's just a scant bit. It gives you something to focus on while you stumble about. The bitter bite before will make your next taste sweeter.

I've had a lifetime of pain that is suffered through while laughing. My own personal horror/comedy if you will, so of course I enjoy horror stories that make me laugh.

I immediately loved the name Coffin Blossoms when I heard it because it's a reminder that hope does spring eternal, and even in death there is beauty, and life.

Picking out the stories for this anthology wasn't always an easy feat. There were so many amazing tales, but we tried to pick ones that had a certain tone to them. I hope that you enjoy reading this as much as I loved reading all of these stories.

I'd like to thank Jon for giving me this wonderful opportunity and being a great person to work with, and having a method to the madness. Also, thanks for the kind words about my work and the appreciation.

Thanks to all of the authors (both accepted and rejected) for letting me pore over your labors. And thank you to my boyfriend Lanty for his understanding when I had my nose in my tablet reading more than usual and was checked out of life.

-Autumn Miller

FOREWORD

THERE'S SOMETHING ABOUT BLOODY MARY

BY RICHARD LAU

The trouble began where trouble usually begins: in a bar after eleven-thirty at night.

I was sitting on my usual stool at Salvadore's, staring mournfully at the bottom of my empty glass, my tongue burning from the vodka that had apparently evaporated.

I looked up and saw my reflection in the large mirror behind the bar. My non-existent twin brother hadn't shown up yet, so I knew I could down a few more Bloody Marys.

Now some people, going only by the name, might think a Bloody Mary is a sissy drink. But if she's made properly, or at least the way I like, those experiencing her salty kiss would know she's strong enough to kick your ass down the stairs, fast enough to arrive at the bottom before you, and mean enough to kick you back up them again.

Most folks have a Bloody Mary after a long night of drinking to cure hangovers. Me? I say, "Why wait?" I glanced at my watch and saw it was about a few minutes before midnight. I wasn't that interested in the time, as much as seeing if I could still read the numbers clearly. Yup, there were a few more shots in my future.

"Petey!" I called, waving my hand to get the old bartender's attention. He was eighty-three, or at least looked it for the past ten years. He was also at the other end of the twenty-foot bar and hard of hearing even when the place was empty. Tonight, the joint was packed with the usual Thursday night crowd.

The place probably needed a second bartender, but Salvadore was too cheap to get Petey some help, especially when the regulars didn't mind the wait. Plus, Petey didn't want the competition or the division of the tips.

So, it wasn't unusual for me to have to repeat my order. "Petey! Another Bloody Mary!" He looked at me and put his age-spotted hand to his white-fuzzed ear. I hoisted my glass. "Bloody Mary! Bloody Mary!"

Petey gave me a thumbs-up, meaning I was in his queue. I grabbed a handful of salted peanuts from a nearby communal bowl and tossed my head back to pop a few into my mouth.

That's when I saw her. In the mirror. Sitting on the stool next to me. Her face was an inverted teardrop, wide at the forehead, narrowing to a pointed chin, damp dark hair, falling limply from either side of a center part. Her scowl made me shiver and feel guilty at the same time.

I pulled my gaze away from the glare of her baleful, black-circled eyes and looked at the stool next to me. It was empty. I closed my eyes, counted to ten, and looked at my reflection again. She was gone. Perhaps I had had more to drink than I thought. Petey, who appeared before me, seemed to agree. He held out the glass in his hand and abruptly pulled it back.

I reached for the glass instinctively, and he shook his wispy head. "You know in all the years we've known each other, I've never cut you off once, George."

"So why start now?" I asked, thinking it was some sort of new witty bartender banter he had recently picked up.

Petey nodded to the stool next to me. "You've never pulled something like this before, George. Salvadore could lose his license. I could get fired. What the hell are you thinking bringing your daughter in here?"

"What daughter? I don't got no daughter!" The protest never escaped my lips, for there on the stool next to me was the girl I had seen in the mirror.

She looked to be about twelve-years old. She was dressed in a frilly, white, knee-length gown covered with reddish brown splotches, like the result of a really bad tie-dye job.

A woman a couple of seats over said, "The poor thing. Look at the bags under her eyes. You've been depriving her of sleep while you're out drinking! Don't you know it's a school night?"

"It's child abuse, that's what it is!" her friend chimed in shrilly, attracting even more unwanted attention.

"Whatcha trying to do?" A beefy guy approached me from his spot holding up one of the walls. "Get the place shut down? I haven't had my fill yet, mister."

The scene was getting uglier than a morning-after lover. I grabbed the girl's thin arm and pulled her outside. She fluttered behind me, almost weightless like a kite.

I found a quiet spot in the parking lot under a streetlight. "Okay, sweetie, where's your parents? Who brought you into Salvadore's, because it sure as hell wasn't me!"

Ever since she had appeared, her expression had been one of pure hatred. I watched as the glare melted into sorrow

"I don't have any parents. I am an orphan spirit. But I'm with you now."

"With me? How the hell can you be with me?"

"You invoked me."

"Well, you're provoking me!" Under stress, I admit, I can get a little defensive.

"Invoked, not provoked."

Just my luck. She was probably a spelling bee winner with a huge vocabulary.

My head was spinning, and I was pretty sure it wasn't just the alcohol.

At that moment, I saw another of Salvadore's regulars getting out of her car.

"Dorie!" I called, running over to her. "There's this girl I met in the bar…"

"Brag, brag, brag," grumbled Dorie, pocketing her keys and heading toward the entrance.

"But you don't understand! I got a girl I can't get rid of!"

"Don't we all?" muttered Dorie, pushing me aside. "Outta my way, George. I need a drink!"

It was then that I remembered Dorie was currently going through a bad break-up with her girlfriend. I was about to follow her inside to explain further, when I felt a tug on my sleeve.

It was the little girl, standing right behind me. No wonder Dorie hadn't seen her. "Petey said you are not allowed to go back in there."

In spite of everything, my temper flared. "Well, Petey is not my boss!"

"Okay," said the girl, shrugging her bony shoulders. "Just remember, where you go, I go."

I took one step forward and so did she. I took a step back and so did she. I took another step forward and two steps back. She did the same.

An exiting patron noticed our crazy game of hopscotch. "Hey, buddy, what do you call that fancy dance?" Laughing loudly to himself, he headed for his car.

I retreated again to a less busy part of the parking lot, and she, of course, followed.

"Okay, let's start over. My name is George. What's your name?"

"Bloody Mary," came her reply.

"Well, Mary," I started to continue to ask about who brought her to Salvadore's.

"*Bloody* Mary, stupid!" she repeated sternly, in that unfiltered way kids have.

"Like the drink?"

"I was around long before that so-called drink," she said with a hint of pride.

"Look, you can insult me, but leave my favorite drink alone!" I tried to look as intimidating as possible, but from the little girl's bubbling giggle, I failed miserably. I tried to cover my failure by moving on the offense. I adopted what I thought was a sufficient British accent. "What's so bloody about you anyway? Your bloody attitude? Are you English?"

"Naw, guvnor," she said, with a very respectable British accent that made my attempt sound like it was from Dixie, "but I can do *this*!"

Her hair immediately grew more damp. In moments, it was soaked with dark liquid. Against the pale skin of her face, I could see the liquid was blood. Scarlet rivulets ran down from her hairline, like perspiration from a stint in a sauna. Thicker oozings spilled from her eyes, nose, and mouth. Soon, her face was a crimson mask, her previously white gown turned Hollywood carpet red.

I gasped and stumbled backward in surprise.

"No point in running, mate," said Mary, still doing her British thing. "You're stuck with me."

I recovered my balance and my nerve. "I'm not trying to run! I'm trying not to get blood all over my work clothes! Do you know how much the company will take out of my pay for a new uniform?"

She squinted, trying to read the faded logo on my company shirt. "What do you do?"

"I'm a lineman," I replied. "I work for the utility company. Wait a minute! Why are we talking about me? What about you? Don't we need to take you to the hospital or something? All that blood!"

"Oh, this?" Mary said casually, as if she was talking about an old dress she had just tossed on. She made a quick wave of her skinny arm, and I could swear I saw flecks of blood flying toward me in slow motion.

I was about to yell something rude when the droplets and all the other blood just disappeared, no residue, no stain, no nothing.

"I can easily undo my puddles," Mary said by way of explanation.

"Neat trick, unpuddling," I said, greatly relieved. "I wish the cat I used to have could do that."

"What's wrong with you?" Mary demanded, suddenly exasperated.

"What's wrong with me?" I asked, insulted once again. "What's wrong with *me*? *You're* the one who can bleed from head to toe at will and act like nothing's wrong!"

"That's because that's what I am! I am an apparition. I'm an undead spirit that lives on the other side of the mirror. You say my name three times into a mirror at midnight, and I pass through to this side of reality and haunt you. I bleed profusely without injury because I'm supernatural!"

She paused to catch her breath. Apparently, being supernatural gives you unlimited blood but not infinite oxygen. "But you! You're just a human. You've just seen a girl appear out of a mirror. You've just seen her gush blood! And all you can think of is dirtying your uniform and your cat?"

"Former cat," I corrected. "Very territorial. Peed a lot. My ex-wife took the cat with her when she left. And as for getting bloodstains out of clothes, I'm really not that good at laundry. My ex-wife, now *she* was good at laundry, but as I said, she's gone now."

My quite reasonable explanations only seemed to infuriate the girl further. She started spraying the red stuff again. Mary's eyes turned upwards until only the whites showed, and then even the whites turned bloodshot with exploding arteries until there were no whites at all, only reds. Her mouth became a hydrant, spewing such a forceful gush of projectile tomato juice, it was as if her name was Bloody Niagara. Every strand of hair on her head was a tiny pressurized hose, whipping about crazily, jet-streaming out the plasma.

Bloody Mary had turned herself into a literal hemorrhaging geyser, water sprinkler, and Medusa combined. The flood of blood covered everything: nearby cars, the streetlamp post, and me.

Eventually, she stopped, stood there dripping, and glared at me with her normal eyes. I got the impression she was waiting for me to say something or expecting me to have some sort of reaction.

I reached deep inside, searching for the right words. "Whoa! That was incredible! I've only seen something similar with the dancing fountains in Las Vegas and Disneyland! Can you synchronize to music, too?"

"Are you intentionally trying to piss me off? No! Don't answer that!" She took a deep breath and tried a different approach. "Did you hear what you just said? You've made my point! You're human, yet you're more dead inside than I am! I've been horrifying people for hundreds of years! Why aren't you scared?"

"Uh, maybe I'm a tough guy? Maybe I'm drunk?" I replied, pulling guesses out of the air that didn't sound convincing even to me. I wished I was hallucinating or passed out and dreaming. But I knew I wasn't. Apparently, a Bloody Mary, the apparition not the drink, can sober someone up faster than ten cups of coffee. "Uh, maybe I don't scare easily?"

"Bollocks!" she cursed back at me, reminding me that she hadn't forgotten my cultural slight. "Remember when you grabbed my arm and dragged me out here? Very few people ever touch me, but when they do, I learn things about them from the contact. You're scared all right. But not of me! Because you've got an even bigger fear!"

"I do?" I honestly didn't know what she was talking about, but I was willing to listen.

"Yeah, you're afraid of being alone."

"No, not true."

"Really? You come to Salvadore's every night after work. And you take extra shifts at work, hoping that by keeping busy, you won't have to face how empty your life has become. You can't stand returning to your apartment except to sleep."

No little kid was going to get the better of me. "First of all, I like coming to Salvadore's to unwind, see some friendly faces that don't bleed unless they're punched, catch up on the news, and maybe take in a ball game. As for my work, maybe I'm just conscientious. Maybe I'm ambitious and want a raise or a promotion."

"Go ahead, lie to yourself," said Mary, wringing the blood out of her soaked gown, looking as if she wished the cloth was my neck instead but couldn't reach it. "Try to explain it away. There's one thing you can't explain, though."

"What's that?" I asked, rising to the challenge.

"Why you're standing here having this long conversation with a ghost. Are you really that desperate for someone to talk to?"

I patted my pockets for a cigarette and then remembered I quit smoking fifteen years ago. "What does a precocious twelve-year-old girl know about life anyway?"

"I may look twelve, but I'm hundreds of years old. I have seen much of life, on both sides of the mirror. And I was alive once, too."

I barely heard those last few words. I stubbornly and sulkily slumped on a parking block, letting her words sink in along with the blood seeping into my work clothes. I was a mess, both in appearance and emotionally.

There *was* something deep inside eating away at me. After prolonged reflection and careful introspection, I realized the angst was not *all mine*.

With me sitting, I could look Bloody Mary eye-to-eye. "You know what? I'm not the only one with issues. I may be scared of being alone, but you're scared of people!"

"I'm not scared of people," Bloody Mary protested. "I *scare* people."

Her retort was stiff and flat, and I knew I had struck a nerve. "You may scare people, but it's the reason why that interests me.

"You mentioned how you learned about me when we touched. Maybe that hasn't happened to you enough for you to realize that the contact works both ways. You learned about me. Well, I also learned about you!"

"What do you think you learned?" she asked, pretending not to care. She moved in a small circle, gesturing and causing the dripping and pooled blood to disappear.

"The real reason you like to scare people."

"Because I'm evil?"

"Yeah, I try to play the bad ass, too. And we both know how well that works out."

Mary said nothing, so I continued. "You like scaring people because it keeps them at a distance. Terrifying them is an easy way of pushing them away. And you do so because you're afraid of letting any of them get near you, and of *you* getting emotionally close to them. "You've always been painfully shy. Even when you were alive, you avoided situations where you had to interact socially. As a matter of fact, if you hadn't run off from a family gathering..."

I stopped. I wasn't being fair. I was being cruel. I tried to quickly change the subject.

"Have you ever wondered how you ended up in the situation you're in? Trapped behind a mirror until someone calls you? And then you scare them away, and you're trapped behind the mirror again? Have you thought that maybe you pushed away so many people in life that maybe somehow you're continuing to do so in death?"

Her eyes were leaking again, but this time with tears not blood. "I don't like you, George."

"I don't think that's true, either. Because this whole time I haven't been sitting here talking to myself. The whole time I've been talking to you, you've been talking to me, too. Explain that, Mary."

"Fortunately, I don't have to. I have to go."

"Wait! What?"

"I only haunt each person for an hour. There's always another midnight coming up in another time zone. Someone else who calls for Bloody Mary, either on a dare or out of curiosity. No one ever calls me for me, though. No one ever calls for Mary. Always, Bloody Mary."

And like the ghost she was, she faded before my eyes.

Then she reappeared, and a smile graced her face as she pointed. I was still covered in blood, looking like I had just pulled a double-shift at a slaughterhouse. With a sweep of her hand, I suddenly looked and felt as if I had just stepped out of a shower and a dry cleaner's.

"What do you think, George?" Mary said, hinting for a word of approval.

But she was leaving, and I was back to emotionally shutting down. "I think I'm glad I didn't order a White Russian."

Her giggling lasted longer than her image as she faded again.

***

The next day, I staggered into work with the worst hangover I've ever had. Maybe it wasn't actually a hangover, but it felt like one. I moved like a zombie, my head clouded with fog and filled with two-penny nails. I spent the day making rookie mistakes, getting lost on country roads, and almost fell off a pole several times.

I felt so guilty about my poor performance, I volunteered for a second shift, figuring I would wake up by then and at least make up for what I had lacked earlier in the day.

Nope. It was just another seven hours of crap, and I left the company lot feeling worse than when I had arrived.

Rush hour had long since passed, and there were few cars on the road this late in the evening. I glanced at my watch. It was eleven-thirty. Enough time to swing by Salvadore's and hopefully shave off some of the hair of the dog. Or at least comb it back a bit.

Instead, to my surprise, my hands steered my truck toward home.

I wearily stomped up the steps to my apartment, opened the door, went inside, and closed the door again without bothering to turn the lock.

I headed straight for the bathroom and closed the door. Ignoring the light switch, I washed my hands in the dark, tossed some water in my hangdog face, and dried it with a towel.

When I felt somewhat presentable, I said the magic words: "Mary. Mary. Mary."

The face that greeted me wore a smile that lit up the pitch-dark room. "Hey George! How are you?"

THE GOLDEN FALCON

BY ANGELIQUE FAWNS

There is nothing more satisfying than taking a shower in someone else's bathroom. Especially when the owners don't know you're enjoying their Body Spa Shower System, natural stone flooring, and unlimited hot water. Two hipsters, Suzette and Fergus, owned this McMansion on the good side of Mud Lake and worked in the city. I walked their Labradoodle Django for them every weekday.

I lived with my ma in her Winnebago on the other side of the lake. Her plumbing was rusty and the water hardly worked in the tiny lav. I'd left Django in the backyard with a piece of deer antler, so he wouldn't whine and bug me. Stepping out of the enormous glass stall, I wrapped myself in the little beach towel I brought and would take with me. No evidence.

I'd left my leopard print onesie in the master bedroom, and was toweling off my hair walking down the hall, when I saw a tall man with a rat-tail mullet leaning over the dresser and sorting through Suzette's jewelry. I screamed and tried to cover myself with the little towel. He whirled and pointed a BB gun at me.

"Whoa put that away. Earl! Is that you? Whatcha doing here? When'd you get out?" I said.

He grinned as his eyes skirted my naked body, like a starving man. For being on the other side of thirty I still looked pretty good. Bit of a pot belly but my C cups were still holding up.

"Whooo wee, a nude Tammi! Whatcho doin' here, girl? Moved to the rich side of the lake? And ya, I got probation."

Prison had done Earl some good. I don't remember him being such a hunk two years ago. Thick bicep muscles flexed under his Soundgarden t-shirt. He'd grown a thick mullet, and added mutton chops over his acne-scarred cheeks. My knees were feeling a little weak.

"Put away for robbery, and you're out and at it again? You can't roll these folks. They're my clients!"

Earl put down his BB gun, and sauntered over to pull my towel away. I could feel my breath speeding up in a funny way.

"Clients? What kinda work you doing naked in this big ole house?"

I pulled his wife beater tank over his head. Fair is fair.

"I walk dogs, speaking of, how'd you get in? Django didn't yowl bloody hell?"

Earl leaned down and gave me a kiss, his mutton chops tickling my lips. He drew back and stroked my blonde perm.

"Came in the front door, didn't even know about no

doggie. Dog walkin' pay well?"

"I make forty, even fifty bucks most days," I said, tugging down his camo pants.

"Oh, a sugar mama. You my dream come true Temptin' Tammi."

We tumbled onto the king bed, and it was even more satisfying than stealing a shower. I knew I was gonna spend the rest of my life with Earl by the end of those amazing ten minutes. Getting dressed, I told him how it was gonna be.

"Earl, you gotta put back the jewelry and make it look like we weren't never here. You can't be damaging my business."

At first he looked a little disappointed, but then gave me a little salute and sexy smile. I helped him put back everything, and straightened up the place. I still had a couple more dogs to walk, so Earl and I made plans to get together in the evening.

***

That night I put on my best tube top, feather earrings and Daisy Duke shorts where the pockets stick out on my upper thighs. We drove his scooter down to Mud Lake and spent the night under the stars. It was magical. I had beard rash on my face that would last for days. We cuddled up on a picnic bench.

"Tammi, you're my woman now," he said, puffing on a cigarillo.

I got a warm gooey feeling inside. I finally hooked myself a soul mate.

"I don't think Ma's going to let me move you into the Winnebago. It's not even a double-wide."

"And I'm bunking in with one of my roofer buds, it's not good for a class woman like you. We need to get our own place."

***

The next morning, I did the walk of pride back to my mom's trailer and changed into a spandex dog walking outfit. My body wanted to climb into my queen pullout. But Earl didn't have a job yet, and I had to keep earning the dough. I rushed through my walks that morning, not even bothering to steal a shower anywhere. Luckily, I had a few dollars saved up in an egg carton under my bed. Almost a G-note.

Earl was meeting me at the trailer dealer on the highway.

"A few guys owe me, so I'll collect and then we'll do some shopping," he promised.

My ma had a fair chunk of land, like an acre or two, and there was a patch down by the lake that would fit another trailer perfect. And far enough away, that if it got rockin', my ma wouldn't hear the talkin'.

Around 3 p.m., I put on my fanciest mini-dress, red with rib cut-outs, swiped on some pit stick, and shook some baby powder in my hair to degrease it. I borrowed Mom's old pickup truck with the bumper hitch (she was gone for the day, probably Bingo) and drove to Dick's Hitches and Homes to take a look.

Earl was already there, devastating smile on his face. Man he cleaned up good. "Here comes Temptin' Tammi."

His scooter was parked to the side and his fine dark mullet hung in a braid down his back. He had on grey sweatpants and a nice denim cut-off vest.

With his shades on, you wouldn't even know he was walleyed. My heart fluttered.

"Let's find ourselves a castle, Prince Charmin."

We walked down the strip of dead grass between the rows of trailers. There were pop-ups, tear drops, fifth wheels, but they all had one thing in common. All way too much moola. Like over ten thousand dollars for a tiny one. Earl brought a wad of cash, and between the both of us we had seventeen hundred. I started to cry a bit, which wasn't good news for my blue mascara.

"Hey, I think I see a used bunch over there," Earl said.

I squinted though the makeup burning my eyes, and saw a hand-painted sign "Pre-Loved." We went to take a look at the three trailers sitting in the back. One was on blocks. One looked like it had lost a fight with a semi. The third looked good with road-worthy tires. Dirty, a bit lopsided, but not bad. Earl walked over to the hulking trailer.

"We've found ourselves a gem here."

He was right. Golden Falcon written on the front in fancy lettering, shoebox size windows everywhere and only a few broken bits. We walked around the side. There were two doors, a single solid one at the back and huge sliding ones with a duct-taped screen at the front.

"Look at the bump outs! There's already a kitchen table in here," I said, pushing open the front screen.

Earl knocked me aside in his excitement to have a look. I rubbed my ear where his elbow had accidentally whacked me, following him into the trailer. He was eager. I like that. The smell of dust, mold, and long dead mouse hung in the air. Faded linoleum and stained carpet covered the floor. Fake wood paneling made the insides shadowy and dark.

"I wonder what sort of stories this lady has to tell?

Almost hear the porn and smell the weed," I said.

The way Earl ran his hand over the melamine counter in the mini-kitchen, he was sold. The best part? There was a full-sized bathroom in the back with a fine-looking shower.

"Yup babe, we found our new home. The Golden Falcon is gonna fly again," he said.

With that, we hopped out and went to find the owner of the yard. He'd seen us drive in and limped his way over from the office trailer at the front. A big belly, eight or nine strands of hair greasily plastered to his head and jaundiced skin.

"Hi! I'm Dick and I see you checking out our finest used trailers. So you folks wanna take this beaut home? Good deal! Just for today."

He stuck out a hand with dirty fingernails and I let Earl do the negotiating.

"Dick what's your best price? We'll take this baby off your hands right now."

"The only thing I gots to warn you about is the bedroom back door is jammed. But the rest of her works perfect." Dick said.

One thousand dollars and a few enthusiastic handshakes later, we were the proud new owners of the Golden Falcon. That left us seven hundred whole dollars to fix her up!

We hooked the trailer to the back of the pickup and hauled back. Thank goodness there were no cops out because the load was definitely illegal. The trailer rocked and shuddered as we slowly navigated the back roads. Luck was on our side and we managed to unhitch our new home in the dirt by the river.

My ma stood in the driveway bellowing "Tammi,

what in tarnation! You can't park that ugly thing on my lot! Don't think you're hooking up to my hydro!"

Earl slouched down and pretended he didn't hear. He was a smart man.

She stomped down to the lake edge. My ma let me do what I wanted most of the time. I'm her mini-me with the same long blonde hair, permed just right.

"Better keep it clean outside," she said, climbing into her truck.

Well, those first days were plain bliss. We dragged my sofa bed down the hill, and Earl and I got down to the serious work of setting up our new home. Listening to our favourite hard rock bands, we ripped out the stinky carpet and bought a lime green shag from the thrift store. Earl managed to find a generator second-hand somewhere, so the beer fridge was humming. Plus the shower worked perfect once we put an old pump into the lake. My ma gave us a TV and VCR as a house-warming gift. After I found some vintage XXX movies on tape at a yardsale, we were partying like it was 1970!

Things didn't start going wrong until a week after we moved the Golden Falcon in. That day started as usual, I got up hungover from cheap box wine and staggered to the other side of the lake to walk my dogs. Thank goodness the owners are normally at work. Django the Labradoodle and his designer breed friends never judge me for red-rimmed eyes. I survived the morning and went back home, looking forward to tumbling into Earl's arms (he hadn't found work yet) and perhaps having a beer to shake the cobwebs.

I stopped outside the duct-taped door. Terrible music blaring. I'm not a classical music fan but I could hear piano, string instruments, and horns. The Golden Falcon was pulsing with it. We listened to Slayer, not Chop chop or Beathaven or whatever. Storming in, I got my second shock.

"Earl! What have you done to your hair?"

Instead of drooling in bed with one hairy leg sticking out of the sheets, my lover was sitting at the kitchen table writing on a pad of paper. His mullet was gone. All that lovely hair. He raised one hand to it, and stroked the neat business-like cut.

"I decided it was time for a new look. I don't want to stay a degenerate thief forever, my darling."

Darling? New look? Earl called me Temptin' Tammi. Not darling.

"What is this? We wake up to Metallica or Nirvana."

He kept writing on the pad of paper in front of him. I noticed he shaved. The mutton chops were gone, he wasn't half the sexy guy anymore.

"I find it inspirational; I had an idea for a story. Something re-envisioning the world with minimal light pollution and sustainable agricultural practices."

Sustainable what? Who was this guy?

"I'm going to go visit my mom, okay? Let you do your writing thing in peace."

He hardly acknowledged me, bending back over his notepad, grooving to his old-folk music. I grabbed two beers out of our fridge and walked the two hundred metres to my mom's trailer. Stopping to look back at the Golden Falcon, I squinted my eyes. Did she look shinier? There was no way Earl had time to cut his own hair, shave and scrub the exterior of the trailer.

Instead of sitting down for a breakfast beer, I hopped into my mom's pickup truck and drove back to Dick's Hitches. The proprietor was out inspecting his mobile homes. Walking over to him, I noticed with disdain he was wearing a stained wife-beater tank top with a pair of dual-purpose swim trunks.

"Mr. Dick, may I have some discourse with you on the history and past ownership of our fine Golden Falcon?"

"Come again?" He squinted at me.

Come again was right. What verbiage was spewing out of my mouth? I always hated people who spoke with high falutin' language. Thinking they were better than everyone else.

First my beloved Earl and now me! I concentrated and tried again,

"Who used to own that there trailer we bought from y'all a couple weeks ago?"

"Oh, some rich kids from a farm the next county brought 'er in. It'd been rotting in the field. They had a great-grandfather used to write poetry in it."

"And what happened to this author?" I asked.

Dick looked at me a moment, trying to access some dark compartment of his memory.

"If I remember rightly, they said the old geezer died in the trailer. He took to spending more and more time in there with his music and his typewriter and didn't come out for days. Was the smell that made them finally check on him."

Alright, thank you Mr. Dick. Your time and consideration is much appreciated," I said, giving his gnarly hand a shake.

Now, I generally don't indulge in superstition or believe in ghosts, but I had to do some thinking. I liked Earl the way he was before we started living in that trailer. No business haircuts and dumb ideas about writing stories about pollution or whatever. We were real down-to-earth folks, not the pretentious sort that lived on the other side of Mud Lake. I drove back to the Golden Falcon and noticed the screen was fixed. No duct tape. I could hear some Mozart playing from the boom box. (How did I know that name? Mozart?) My man was standing in the kitchen with a big garbage bag. I saw him tossing out my Cheetos, Mac n' cheese, frozen pizzas and cola.

"What are you doing?" I asked in horror.

He didn't even turn and look at me. His preppie haircut made him almost unrecognizable.

"This is all garbage food, we are going to start eating organic and healthy. Farmer's markets, fresh produce. No more of this."

My jaw dropped open. This had to stop. The writing and haircut were bad enough, but an entire lifestyle change?

"I'm going out, Earl. My Cheetos better be back in that cupboard when I get home."

This time I drove into town to the hardware store. Turning up the radio loud, I tried to drown out crazy thoughts of going back to school and continuing my education. Perhaps as a vet tech? Or even a fully licensed vet? What a terrible idea! I hadn't even finished high school, there was no way I'd even get in.

Making sure I kept deranged thoughts at bay, I finished procuring what I needed from the hardware store. Then I drank a few beers and indulged in some fries at the pub until closing time.

Driving back to the Golden Falcon, I turned the truck lights out, the radio off, and drove up quietly. I needed to get my man back. The hot one with the mullet. I quietly opened the screen door and splashed gas over the green shag carpet. Then I lit it with a barbecue starter.

With a whoosh, flames roared up immediately. I stood back, the heat singeing my face. Like a bonfire. I could envision Earl and I warming ourselves, maybe roasting some marshmallows... Oh my God, Earl. What was I doing? I wanted to get rid of this cursed trailer, not him! It was the Falcon's fault everything was changing between us. I ran down to the bedroom door at the other end of the trailer and pounded.

"Come on out Earl! Fire!"

Nothing. I couldn't hear him inside. The fire was growing rapidly. The curtains and shag carpet went up like diesel fuel.

"Earl, you gotta get out!"

I wrenched on the door, but it didn't open. In a panic, I pulled and yanked harder.

"Fire, get outta there!"

The metal of the door was burning my fingers, I had to let go. It hadn't moved an inch. I could hear Earl now and he was screaming.

Even though my skin was turning red from the heat, a cold wave of memory washed over me. Didn't Dick say something about the door needing to be fixed? The second one was jammed? My God, I just found the man of my dreams, I couldn't lose him now. I rushed over to the sliding glass door, but its handles were glowing red. No touching them. The trailer was really flaming now.

Sitting on a lawn chair beside me, I noticed one of my super long dog leashes. Grabbing it, I ran to the truck and hooked one end to the hitch. Then hopped in the truck and backed it up as close as I dared to the trailer. I got out, looped the handle over the doorknob until it was tight, then returned to the truck and gunned it.

The truck jerked when it ran out of dog leash and I felt the tires dig in. It only took a second or two before the whole bedroom door flew off the trailer body. Slamming on the brakes, I threw it in Park and got out. Earl staggered out of the trailer, coughing up a lung from all the smoke he'd inhaled and red welts coming up on parts of his arms.

I almost knocked him over running into him with a huge hug.

"Oh my Gad, Earl, you were almost barbecued. I love you so much."

He leaned over me and gave me a huge squeeze back, the smell of ash and fuel stinging my nose.

"My Temptin' Tammi, you saved my life woman."

We stood back a few metres from the blazing trailer, now not much more than a burned-out shell, and watched the flames slowly die down. We didn't have much in the Golden Falcon to burn. Soon, my ma came up to stand beside me.

"Is there even a point of calling the fire department now? Looks like that she's gonna be nothing more than cinders and a shell before they'd even get it," she said pointing her cigarette at Earl and I. "You two are gonna have to pay to get what's left of that eyesore towed out of here.'"

Earl hugged me tighter, he was okay, done coughing, and the red arm spots just needed some aloe.

"Yes Ma'am. Tammi and me, we'll clean up this

mess. We ain't got no insurance so I guess we back to where we done begin," he said. "I must have fallen asleep smokin' or something."

His words were like music to my ears. I wasn't sure if he knew the fire was my fault and he was taking the blame—or if he genuinely didn't know. No matter, I was his Temptin' Tammi again and my Earl would grow his mullet back if I asked nice. I reached up and gave his scarred smoky cheek a kiss.

"Guess you're both spending the night with me then. Y'all have to look for a rental in the morning. I think my cousin might have a basement apartment in town he'd put you in for a good price," my ma said, turning and walking back up to her place.

I grabbed Earl's hand and smiled at him. We both needed to clean up, and I guess we were going to have to make do with my mom's tiny bathroom. But Earl and I had our whole future ahead of us. Who knew? Maybe this basement apartment would have a nice big shower with room for two.

AXE-MURDERERS' GORGE

BY ALEX COLVIN

If you go to high school or college in Merrittville and you haven't made out with someone in Merrittville Gorge, you're probably a loser. All the cool kids make out there. They don't care about the legend that the place is haunted by a bloodthirsty axe-murderer. In fact, that makes it hotter and a better place to make out on Halloween, and it's still popular on Valentine's Day too.

I've noticed all this because I spend a lot of time in the Gorge. You see, I'm the legendary axe murderer who hunts in it.

Yes, I'm a serial killer, but I'm also a great guy. I volunteer at an animal shelter. I recycle. As in, I sort my recycling and wash all my containers out first. I just have uncontrollable urges to kill people sometimes and this place is really secluded. I try to only kill people who seem like jerks. Like the guys I overhear asking for naked pictures from a girl they've just fooled around with. People who talk about *The Bachelor*. Or how their Instagram account is practically community service since it's helping and inspiring so many people around them. Most of my victims deserve it.

Yet, being an axe-murderer in the Gorge isn't as solitary and relaxing as you might think it is. Let me explain.

***

One night, I was out there hunting as usual, when I came across a couple sitting on a log in the moonlight. The city lights winked in the distance. The boy was so busy talking about his band that he was unaware the girl wanted to make out. She was wearing a "CALL HER DADDY" t-shirt. I knew this would be easy pickings.

Yet I didn't want to get ahead of myself. I crouched behind a stump and surveyed the scene. Taking the right amount of time is important in this line of work. If you made a move too soon you might get spotted. If you waited too long, they'd be doin' it and there was no thrill in sneaking up on them. I was going to wait for their first kiss and go in for the homerun swing. Easy does it, I cautioned myself. They were looking in each other's eyes… just about…

Oh, goddamn it!

I heard tremendous thunderous footsteps from the underbrush to the east. Terrible luck, plain and simple. Dante was on the hunt and he found my target. I had to beat him to it! The kids leapt up at the commotion and were both looking in the direction Dante's racket was coming from. The guy didn't hesitate, he grabbed the girl's hand and ran like hell into the woods. I leapt out from my hiding spot and took a wild swing at where they were sitting, but I was far too late. They were gone and didn't look back. That meant I hadn't been seen. Thank God. Getting caught would suck. I'd rather lose my prey than have to move again. The commotion also meant I had to talk to Dante. Which was never fun. So, I braced for him as I wrenched my axe from the fallen log.

Sure enough, Dante burst through the brush, his axe hanging languidly in his hand, his tattered overalls grimy and stinking fiercely, and with his trademark potato sack over his head, tied around the neck with twine. Dante's lumbering slowed as he saw me standing alone by the log. He stopped and stared down at me through the holes in his sack. "STEALER!" he rumbled; his roaring voice muffled slightly by his potato sack.

"Hello Dante," I said, wrenching my axe out of the fallen log. "And no. I saw them before you even got here. But I really need this and this is a huge gorge, so you can find another couple for yourself."

Dante growled. "VICTOR STOP STEALING FROM DANTE. THIS DANTE'S HUNTING GROUND."

"I've been hunting here for years. It's because of my legendary reputation that so many idiot teenagers come here to make out. Go hunt in the bog or the quarry or something."

"VICTOR NOT SHARE. GREEDY. NOT KILL PROPERLY."

"And how do I not kill properly, exactly?"

Dante jutted out his chin and rested his axe on his massive shoulder. "VICTOR FOLLOW PEOPLE LIKE LITTLE PUPPY. NO REAL HUNT. NO REAL KILL."

"Well you're 'real' hunting is getting in my way!

Your crashing around through the woods scares off the people I'm trying to hunt!"

"DANTE HERE FOR REVENGE. VICTOR KILL FOR FUN. REVENGE BETTER REASON."

"And why do you want revenge?"

"DANTE LOST EVERYTHING."

"Sorry you went through that. Did you want to talk about it?"

"NO. IT WEIRD YOU WOULD OFFER."

"Fuck you! I'm just trying to make you feel better!"

"THEN VICTOR STOP STEALING WITH HIS WEAK LITTLE-GIRL-STYLE KILLS!"

I threw my hands up. "I'm not! You're the one being a pain in the ass!"

"DANTE FIGHT VICTOR FOR GORGE."

"Try it"

We didn't end up fighting, and we've never wanted to since that night. We stopped because we heard a rustling in some leaves to my left.

"By the increasing volume and decreasing vocabulary in this conversation, I suspect there will be an altercation in the next thirty seconds if I don't intervene," a silky and almost songlike voice called from the foliage.

Oh balls.

Sure enough. The third axe-murderer of the evening, Dr. Hermann Bell, stepped through the brush as delicately as if he were walking on a ballroom floor. He was carrying his straitjacket over his shoulder as if it were a dinner jacket and was carrying a wickedly sharp axe in his other hand.

"Escaped again, have you?" I asked.

"My dear boy, I leave my confines most evenings.

This evening, I felt like a walk in the woods. But as long as neither of you draw attention to us being here..." his eyes narrowed, although he continued smiling as he said this. "I'll come and go as I please for the rest of my days."

"VICTOR STEALING," Dante said.

"I heard your conversation, thank you." Dr. Bell said. "I agree it is getting crowded around here. Whatever you two work out between yourselves, I would like to be able to stay. This is the easiest secluded place to get to from the asylum."

"Why should we accommodate you?" I asked.

"If anyone realizes I've left, then there will be a manhunt, and things will be far less peaceful and secluded around here. People might not venture out, even after they give up on the manhunt. There goes your hunting ground."

"DANTE KILL YOU BOTH. DANTE BEST AXE KILLER IN GORGE!"

Please. Between you and I, Dante is an appalling axe-murderer. I get along with him well enough now, but I'm pretty sure his axe isn't even sharp. He might as well be using a club. I'm the reason people fear the Gorge, by the way. Not him. I've been killing people and leaving their corpses hidden in swamps around here since Obama was president.

Meanwhile, Dante's whole shtick with bursting through shrubs and lumbering at people was a great opening, but it always gave his victims tons of time to run away. I doubt he's killed more than five people in the year he's been hunting here.

The combination of Dante's stubbornness and Dr. Bell's silky arrogance finally made me lose my cool. I turned and chucked my axe at a nearby tree, where it stuck fast in the trunk.

"Okay! Enough! If you two think you're better than me and deserve this grove, we should figure out who should have it, fair and square."

"Are you suggesting we all try to kill each other?" Dr. Bell asked, already planning the fight in his head like a chess game, I figured.

"DANTE WINS!"

"No," I snapped. "We make tonight a contest. A free-for-all. Whoever catches and kills the most people tonight gets exclusive use of the Gorge. In two hours, we meet at Merritt Lake-"

"It's technically a pond, my boy, but continue."

I scowled at Dr. Bell. It was tempting to just kill him right there. But he was probably ready for me. Axe-murderers are hard to trust. Especially when they're being competitive. Before I could retort, Dante decided to chime in, "WHAT DIFFERENCE BETWEEN LAKE AND POND?"

I wasn't sure if I was more annoyed by the question or the fact that I didn't know the answer. Dr. Bell's grin widened. "I will tell you, my good man, when we toast Victor getting relegated to another hunting ground. Good evening gentleman, see you in two hours!"

He turned and strode off into the darkness. I left without a word.

I combed the forest for the next hour and didn't find anyone. I also didn't hear any screams or see any blood anywhere, so I figured Dante and Dr. Bell were having terrible luck as well.

With ten minutes to go, I was ready to just give up. All I'd found was some poor Christian girl praying in the forest for her brother to recover from cancer. I couldn't bring myself to kill her. Actually, I consoled her and advised her to get the hell out of there since there might be an axe-murderer at large and I called her an Uber. After that, I wandered around, looking for movement in the moonlight and listening for prey. Nothing.

Suddenly, I got an unnerving feeling. The sense that I was being hunted. I couldn't shake it no matter where or went or how fast I walked. I went off the trails and tried to move silently through the brush. I could still feel someone's eyes on me. I had a very good idea whose eyes they were. Once I was well-hidden in the brush, I stopped in my tracks and listened in the dark to see if my suspicions were correct.

It turned out they were.

After a few moments of waiting, Dr. Bell slipped through the forest, axe in hand, scanning the darkness for me. He wasn't hunting for teenagers to win the contest. He was hunting me. He followed my trail up to where I was hiding and stopped. "Well, Victor," he said. "This is checkmate. Will you surrender like a gentleman?"

I tightened my grip on my axe. No way in hell I'd surrender to that lunatic. I stood perfectly still and waited. He was arrogant. He'd make a careless mistake. He had to. He took a step toward where I was hiding and was in striking distance. I tensed and sprang.

He was waiting for it. He raised his axe just as I swung mine down and managed to block the blow. He twisted his hand and yanked my axe from my grip. It landed somewhere in the darkness and I knew I was finished. The only thing left to do was turn and run. Dr. Bell knew it too, and he lunged forward, swinging his axe in a wide arc. It passed less than an inch from my face as I stumbled backwards. Dr. Bell snarled as he staggered after missing me and I ran as fast as I could.

"I will kill you, Victor!" Dr. Bell's screams echoed through the trees. "I will catch you and I will kill you!"

My heart thundered in my chest as I ran, and I realized that I believed him. He would catch me and kill me before the night was up. He was a killing machine and was unstoppable. I ran anyway, my legs aching and my lungs on fire. Aware he could only be a few steps behind me.

My luck had to run out soon, running in the dark off the path. I had to trip or collide with something sooner or later. Sure enough, I tripped over a root and was sent sprawling, hitting my head on a rock as a bonus. My vision swam, but I could hear Dr. Bell moving through the brush towards me. I looked up and saw two of him, weaving between each other. I was going to die. I was sure of it.

Then I heard a rumbling in the distance.

Dante!

He crashed through the brush and saw me lying on the ground and Dr. Bell standing over me, axe raised for the killing blow. Everyone was still for a moment. "CHEATER!" Dante boomed. "DOCTOR MAN CHEAT AT GAME!"

Before Dr. Bell could reply, Dante swung his enormous axe with blinding speed and cut Dr. Bell down. I guess his axe was sharp after all. I tried to stagger to my feet, but I was too much of a mess to manage it. Dante surprised me once more by grabbing me with his free hand and hauling me to my feet. I managed not to throw up and leaned against a tree while the world settled down around me.

"I don't know how to thank you," I said.

"GIVE GORGE TO DANTE."

Oh. I mean, I suppose. "We can talk about that," I said. "Sure."

I picked up Dr. Bell's axe. He wouldn't need it anymore. "Let's get back to the trail," I said. "We can talk more there."

We'd only gone a short way when we found a couple cuddling in the darkness. They were talking and didn't notice us. Dante and I hid behind a tree and strained to hear their conversation.

"I mean, I could never go down on a guy who likes Star Wars. It's just not a sexy thing to like. Guys who like Star Wars just can't turn me on."

"Oh, yeah, that's totally cool," The guy nodded like a bobble head. "I don't know anything about Star Wars and I, like, couldn't tell you how many parsecs it takes to do the Kessel Run. I just don't know anything about Star Wars, you know?"

"After we bang, can you take some pictures of me down by the lake after to post on Instagram? I think I could get as many likes as the engagement photos that Kadence posted last week."

"Yeah, sure, whatever! Let's do this! Mad Money Mike is gonna be so jealous when I tell him about this!"

Oh, they would be perfect.

I looked at Dante and whispered, "We can take these two out. You and me."

I wasn't sure if Dante had any volume other than

shouting, and maybe he wasn't sure either, because he just nodded. "I'll go around them. When I whistle, charge at them and we'll box them in."

Dante nodded again and I crept around the couple, keeping my distance.

I clutched my axe and tip-toed to the other side of the clearing. Not that I needed to be stealthy. The girl was busy, and the boy was yelling out into the night that he was getting action from the hottest waitress at Texas Johnny's Bar and Grill. I rose from my crouched stance and waved at Dante.

Dante charged.

Dante's racket made the girl stop and the boy panic. The couple stumbled away from their log and away from Dante, luckily, heading for me.

Dante's lumbering was awful for giving away his location, but it was brilliant when used correctly. We'd just discovered the magic formula. I waited and listened for their footsteps and once I could hear their breathing, I stepped out from behind my hiding spot and swung my axe. I caught the man in a clean swing. The woman screamed, and scrambled away from Dante and I. Her screams faded away into the night. At least we still got one.

Actually, the guy was still alive, if only just, so Dante walked over and gave a final chop that did the job. Both of us stood there in the silence, savouring the moment. I looked at him and said, "That was terrific."

"VICTOR HELP DANTE. MAKE LITTLE MAN STOP MOVING."

"I gotta say, this was pretty slick with both of us. Dante, you sent them right to me! That was a class act."

"DANTE GOT TO CHOP LITTLE MAN. DANTE'S

DEAD MOM WILL BE PROUD."
"I'm sure she will be."
"DANTE LIKE VICTOR NOW THAT HE STOP STEALING AND LEARNED TO SHARE."
I was kind of touched. "Thanks," I said. "We make a good team. Want to team up again some time?"
"DANTE AND VICTOR BEST TEAM!"
We hid the body and walked back to the main trail, axes over our shoulders and springs in our steps. We stopped by a bridge with some crude graffiti on it. Just under the lip of the bridge, someone had scrawled "AXE MURDERER'S GORGE".
"Hang on a second," I said. "I want to fix that."
Dante wasn't following what I was on about. I doubt he can read, and he had other things on his mind.
"DANTE HUNGRY," he said, rummaging around in the front pocket of his filthy overalls. "VICTOR WANT TO SHARE SNACK WITH DANTE?"
The snacks were burnt chunks of meat. Squirrel, I think. He lived in an abandoned shack near the old campground and that was probably all he could get. I appreciated the effort but didn't try it. I got to work touching up the graffiti. It only took a moment, and the scrawl now read: AXE MURDERERS' GORGE
"WHY YOU MOVE LITTLE LINE?" Dante asked.
"To show that we share this place," I said. "To show we're friends."
I wasn't sure Dante got it, but he really liked the last part of that explanation.
"FRIENDS!" he boomed. "FRIEND HELP DANTE KILL TO AVENGE DANTE'S MOM!"
"Well, I'm sure she's very proud of you and everything you've done," I said.

"FRIEND COME MEET HER. DANTE KEEP HER UNDER FLOORBOARDS IN SHACK."

"Oh, gosh, no." I said, alarmed. "Sounds like she's earned some rest. Company might be a bit much."

Dante polished off his snacks and we were left standing together in the moonlight. "DANTE GO HOME AND SLEEP. SEE NEW FRIEND SOON?"

"Yep! Sound good."

Dante skipped out of the Gorge and off towards his shack. We've been friends ever since that night. And you can take it from me, the friends you go on midnight axe-murdering rampages are the best kind of friends.

***

Having said all that, I imagine you're not keen to meet up with us. I don't blame you. If you're out in the Gorge and you see Dante and I on the hunt...

Run.

BUMPER-TO-BUMPER

BY KEVIN M. FOLLIARD

For millennia, the magician's urn silenced me. Until at last, flesh hands pressed against ancient ceramic. My screams erupted from the skull of man. Reborn at last within a filthy, human shell. Meat that would suit my purposes.

My screams gave way to laughter. All the knowledge of this human, this man, Jasper Carmichael—37-year-old schoolteacher from United States of America, Chicago, Illinois—filled my consciousness. This kingdom of United States, I knew now, had risen in the time since Mesopotamia fell into obscurity. That meant the magician who had sealed me in the urn was long gone. No longer an obstacle.

My host Jasper Carmichael was smart. Within a few seconds, his years of scholarly knowledge, great tomes of history, compiled into my memory.

A bald, angry man in a tan uniform shouted at Jasper Carmichael, "Sir! Do *not* touch the artifacts!"

I cowered for a moment. Perhaps this man was a descendant of the magician, guarding the urn. But Jasper's knowledge assured me he was a mere meat-bag security guard.

Jasper Carmichael, I understood now, was not always smart. He should have obeyed the posted sign. He touched the urn. Now he was gone forever, and in his place, I—a being of eternal hatred—walked once more among the flesh and bone creatures of the earth.

I smiled.

Carmichael's muscle and joints were functional enough. He had an achy knee, but after cramped ages in a magician's jar, I bounded free as a hungry locust.

The urn had traveled far to this Field Museum, a place of antiquity. To restore my true power, I would have to return to the cradle of civilization, to sacred Mesopotamian grounds, and resume the ritual the magician had thwarted all those centuries ago.

This museum was in a city on another continent, but Carmichael's knowledge assured me of cars, trains, and great airplanes that soared the sky. It would be a simple matter, a mere day of travel, to cross the earth in this age of miracles. A heartbeat compared to my time imprisoned in the urn.

I struck off toward blazing red exit signs, appreciating the blocky simplicity of this civilization's language. How their words glowed like blood in sunlight above doors and tunnels. As I left the museum exhibit, eager children trotted alongside me.

"Mr. Carmichael! Where are you going? Our field trip's not over yet!" I raised my hand to smack the nearest human brat, and the sniveling weakling cowered before I struck. Then I sneered at it and continued toward the main hall.

The bones of ancient lizards towered over me. The museum interested me, as it had Carmichael, but why waste time? I had the human's knowledge of the artifacts and history contained there. Besides, if a magician indeed lurked nearby, I should stay far away from the urn that trapped me.

Knowledge surfaced of the long yellow vehicle—*the school bus*—that transported Carmichael's 5th grade classroom to the museum. It was parked nearby. Carmichael knew the driver. He knew how to operate the vehicle. I would commandeer this vehicle and take it to the airplane port—*the airport*.

My host's knowledge, language, and customs continued to stitch together like puzzle pieces as I exited into bright day. Ships lined a harbor and great obelisks of steel, stone, and glass—packed no doubt with human-meat workers—carved a line across the sky.

Yellow buses lined the curb beside the museum's pillared entrance. Carmichael knew that ours was the bus whose sign read George Washington Carver Math and Science Academy.

I climbed aboard.

A burly mustached man sat in the driver's seat of this bus, bopping his head, a wire hooked to a rectangle, supplying music. *A phone.* He glanced up. "Jasper! It's not 4 o'clock yet. The hell are you doin'..."

I grabbed this man—a friend named Ty—and lifted him by the throat. Ty was much larger than Carmichael. Without my mystical essence inhabiting this body, Jasper could never have moved this man. But effortlessly, I threw Ty onto the grass. Heat surged through Carmichael's arms, into his heart. Smoke seeped from my host's pores.

I had nearly forgotten the effect my spirit has on human flesh. Perhaps it was my time in the urn, perhaps it was something about the humans of his era, but I was burning through this host faster than I had anticipated. I would have to be more careful. It would arouse unwanted attention for my host body to decay, and I could not be without another host to transfer into if Carmichael gave out completely.

I used a lever to seal the door and drove away.

The man Ty shouted and ran alongside the bus. He slapped the window with a bloody hand. He was bothering me. I should have killed him, but he was of no consequence now.

The names of the roads were all there in Carmichael's mind. I maneuvered the school bus away from the museum, operating the bus with only slight motions of hands and feet on wheel and pedal.

The streets teemed with such vehicles, and this school bus, it seemed, was one of the larger, clumsier ones. For now, it behooved me to obey this city's regulations, so I stopped at blazing red lights, and accelerated at green ones, making my way to the I-55 roadway which would eventually connect to the airport zone called Midway—the closer of two such complexes which Carmichael knew were capable of intercontinental travel.

As I waited at a red light, skin on Carmichael's hand blistered, bubbled. I should have transferred my essence into the stronger man, Ty. That host may have lasted longer.

The light turned green. I made a sharp turn toward

the interstate's entrance ramp. Tires screeched. Other humans honked their vehicles as I cut in front of them.

I sped up the ramp, pulled onto the I-55—a special road where humans were allowed to drive fast—and immediately the school bus slammed into the back of another vehicle. Carmichael's frail body jolted. Glass broke. Metal crunched. A hard, white cushion exploded from the steering wheel.

Air bag—my new knowledge assured me.

I looked up. A stout, bald man screamed at Carmichael and exited his vehicle. I ignored that man and instead surveyed the terrain behind him. The entire I-55 road was completely occupied by vehicles, packed so tight they moved at a snail's pace.

It's a traffic jam, I knew. *Of course.* This was the time of day that many humans tried to use the I-55 all at the same time. Carmichael's brain was not surprised by this. My immortal wisdom, on the other hand, knew this to be ludicrous.

Why have a special road to drive fast and allow so many humans on it at once?

"Hey!" The red-faced man approached my bus. "You just rear-ended... Jesus!" he shouted. "What's wrong with you?"

I glanced into the mirror. Jasper Carmichael's face was melting. Perhaps the stress of the collision had accelerated his decay. Perhaps this man was stronger than I had assumed, and his soul was rejecting me. My human host's skin quivered, cooked.

I had to act fast, before the eyes went.

"Holy shit!" the man in the street yelled. "This guy's melting."

I glanced at the angry, now frightened man. "Look

at me." I commanded. I locked eyes with this man. Focused.

Within three shared human heartbeats, my essence transferred into the other man. I now stared up at the black, sizzling eye-sockets of Jasper Carmichael's corpse. My new human's name was Martino Lopez. He was on his way home from working at an insurance office. He hated his job, and on top of that, he now had to deal with a traffic accident on fucking I-55, but of course none of those thoughts mattered anymore.

Martino Lopez was just a vessel now. A vehicle of no more consequence than the school bus which had become useless to me.

I prepared to return to Martino Lopez's Dodge Charger, but when I saw the shattered rear window and dented bumper, I opted to find another vehicle.

"Dude! Get back in your car. Wait for the cops," a human shouted.

The traffic, this rush hour, would only be aggravated by the disturbance I had caused. I would have to bypass the stalled vehicles.

Ignoring the shouts and honks of the other humans, I ran forward, between cars, and searched for a better vehicle, a place where the traffic lessened. Martino Lopez was neither young nor athletic. His heart strained. I could continue running, but the ocean of stalled vehicles stretched to the horizon.

It would do me no good to have my host expire. Already his blood boiled. His skin crackled. I slapped the window of a nearby vehicle. A beautiful woman with deep brown eyes and ebony skin gasped.

Martino Lopez's vision blurred, and I realized that I had strained him further than I had intended. But he held together enough to make eye contact with the woman.

Chanise Jones was my new host's name. I smiled and breathed through her lungs while I watched Martino Lopez shudder, stumble back against the opposite vehicle, and cook. The cars in front of me started moving again, unaware of the dead man. A commotion stirred behind Jones's Jeep Cherokee as I left my former host dead on the highway.

Jones was younger, stronger, and healthier than either of my previous hosts. She would last—hopefully long enough to reach the Midway facility and board a plane back to the cradle of civilization.

Smooth, sensual music poured from the radio of the Jeep Cherokee. It relaxed me. Allowed me to focus. Distant wails echoed—*ambulances, emergency vehicles.* In the rearview mirror, red and blue lights flashed near the spot where I had abandoned the school bus. Soon they would make their way up to find Martino Lopez's corpse.

I was being careless. Although none of my three hosts seemed to know, it was still entirely possible that magicians existed in this society. They could notice my pattern and block my goal.

Traffic on the I-55 eased. Then an enormous truck halted in front of me. I slammed the brakes. I waited, listening to the smooth music—the jazz that this woman loved. I could understand why she loved it, especially in such frustrating circumstances.

I had waited for millennia as a dark essence sealed in an urn, but there was something uniquely annoying about being a meat bag, trapped in a car, trapped in a line of cars on a road that was far too narrow, too unaccommodating, for so many accursed cars, each pumping noxious fumes onto the vehicle behind them. *Why don't you just get off and take the side streets?* came an idea that surely belonged to Chanise Jones.

Side streets. Yes. There are other routes besides the expressway—which was not as express as my original host had promised. The off ramp neared. We jostled, braked, and waited our way toward the exit. But many other humans seemed to have a similar idea. They were all pulling into the right-hand lane, attempting to get off the I-55.

For several long minutes, I waited for gridlocked cars to move. I attempted to steer Jones's vehicle right, and cursed as human after human refused to slow down to let me over. I attempted to signal with the flashing rear light—*turn signal*—but sour-looking meat-sacks rolled by as if they did not even notice.

"You must have seen the flashing light!" I screamed in the woman's shrill voice. The opportunity to get over onto the ramp was running out.

I yanked the wheel, slammed my host's high-heel on the acceleration pad—*gas pedal*—and shot into the other lane. In that moment, a driver from behind had the same plan.

The fronts of our vehicles crunched against each other.

Glass shattered.

An enormous, bearded warrior slammed his horn.

"Why!" I unbuckled Chanise Jones's safety strap—*seat belt*—and opened her door. "Why could not you wait, you pathetic bag of flesh!"

The man's face was as blood-red as a battlefield. He emerged from his truck, muscles bulging from a dirty, torn shirt. "You came out of nowhere, lady!" he said.

"You are the one who came out of nowhere! I should obliterate your immortal soul for such insolence!"

The man's jaw dropped. I yanked open the back seat of my vehicle and searched for a weapon, assuming surely in such a situation, the humans must duel for honor. I found a bag full of paint for the woman's face, minty-tasting chalk, paper currency.

I glanced back. The man, too, rummaged through his car.

"This woman has no weapon!" I yelled. "We duel with fists, human!"

But the enormous warrior held only slips of paper and a small card. *License and registration*, my host's memories explained. *There's no duel.* With his other hand, my human enemy held his glowing phone to his head. "This crazy woman just hit me," he said. "She's screaming about a duel."

Again, I had attracted undue attention. I kicked off the woman's ridiculous high-heeled shoes, walked barefoot through broken glass, and advanced along the side—*shoulder*—of the highway.

"Hey! Get back here!" the burly coward shouted.

I screamed back, "Chase me and kill me if you must!"

Rage boiled my host's blood. Her meat cooked. I had minutes to transfer my essence into another human. Fortunately, plenty were available.

I slapped my hand on the hood of another girl's car, made eye contact, and within moments I was Rachel West, a 21-year-old art student who had gotten off school early and regretted heading home in traffic.

I should have gotten coffee downtown and done some

drawing in the park, she had been thinking before I possessed her. She was right. That would have been a preferable fate.

I maneuvered all the way to the left shoulder, then I accelerated past other vehicles at 40, 50, 60 of the units on the speed-dial.

Horns blared. I cackled. By now, the human authorities, the magicians, must be hunting me. My best bet was to transfer, soul-to-soul, through this insufferable mess called a traffic jam.

I yanked Rachel West's car right when an enormous truck attempted to block me. I swerved and crashed into a blocky purple car — *a van.* Rachel's skin boiled against the airbag that erupted from her steering wheel.

I realized that perhaps my own demonic rage was the problem. The traffic was inciting such intense anger that I was burning through these humans faster than I was accustomed. Only the calm woman, with her jazz music, had managed to stabilize the decay.

When I glanced up, many of Rachel West's fellow motorists were already back. I saw their eyes, in mirrors, out open windows. Some exited their vehicles to check on my bubbling, burning husk. I focused on the furthest human. In spite of the technological innovations of this era, soul transfer remained my fastest route through this traffic.

I concentrated on a set of rugged eyes, focused, and soon I occupied investment banker Scott Harginson. Harginson was on an important business call, and a very frustrated superior was telling him about a deadline for a project.

"Contract a disease and die, human!" I shouted at

the glowing screen on the dash.

"Excuse me?"

I punched the screen, leaving a spider-web crack. The man's glowing rectangle continued to shout. "Scott? Is everything okay?" I tossed the device out the window.

Suddenly, it occurred to me that humans used those rectangle phones to speak over long distances. *You need them to book tickets,* Scott Harginson's memories explained. *To enter airplanes.*

I almost exited the vehicle to retrieve the phone, but I now understood that every human had one of these devices. Furthermore, the phone ticket would need to match the human host. I could not book a plane ride as Scott Harginson and expect to board that plane as a different human.

Why was everything so complicated in this time?

I leaned into my host's leather seat. I stared at the icon of a trumpet on the center of the wheel and recalled how the others had made noises to gain attention or vent frustration.

I punched Scott Harginson's fist against the wheel and the horn blared. Instantly, pairs of eyes glanced back to meet my gaze in rear-view mirrors. Again, I found the furthest pair of eyes from my own. Focused.

I burned my way down the I-55 from one human host to the next. Emily Johnson. Nathan Martin. Martin Lim. Kirk Lam. Jason Hernandez. Lila North.

All disposable.

All blips in my spiritual continuum.

Vessels to deliver me back to the sacred grounds and bring about my apocalypse.

I left dozens of blistering, melting corpses in stalled

vehicles, knowing full well the gambit of leaving a trail.

And yet, not one of these humans knew the dangers of my kind.

Not one feared dark spirits, nor practiced the magic necessary to recapture me.

Soon they would know again.

At last, I found myself in the sleek vehicle of a wealthy fat businessperson, Omar Nassar. The traffic was clearing. My spirit relaxed. Wind washed over my host's face, and I glided down the I-55 at the intended speed.

My frustration subsiding, I neared the Cicero Avenue exit that Omar Nassar assured me led to the Midway Airport. Nassar knew much about traveling and purchasing tickets. He had immigrated to this land as a young boy and become successful owning many businesses that helped maintain and refuel the humans' vehicles.

He had access to funds through his phone using a series of numbers—*credit card numbers*. As I waited in my host body at red traffic lights, I thumbed across his glowing rectangle, allowed him to open up a special interface to the airline and order a ticket. The flight would not take me directly to Mesopotamia, but very, very close. From there, I would jump host-to-host until I reached the sacred grounds.

I would complete the ritual, reproduce, and my dark brethren would be reborn in the husks of every human on Earth.

Approaching Midway Airport, my rage vanished entirely. This City of Chicago would puzzle over the sudden deaths, the charred corpses littering the insufferable I-55 for days.

By then, I would have left this land behind me in one of their planes. I spotted one such vessel careening from the sky like an enormous steel eagle. It was beautiful.

I finalized and purchased the ticket that would bring me to the shores of the Mediterranean. Perhaps my host body would not last the entire journey. However, Nassar's experience assured me that once we were halfway across the ocean, even his dramatic death as I transferred into another passenger would fail to ground or reroute the flight.

I parked Nassar's Lexus in a stone shelter behind the Midway Airport and entered a maze-like fortress, bustling with humans, coming, going, waiting in lines, arguing about blocky bags on wheels and whether or not they would fit into small compartments.

I bypassed all of this. Nassar required no baggage, for he would not survive the flight.

A large clock displayed blazing red numbers which told the time of day: 4:57 p.m. Excellent. The flight I had booked was scheduled to leave at 5:20 p.m., and the terminal, I knew, was just beyond a security checkpoint. Nassar had a driver's license, passport, and phone ticket.

The humans would allow me to slip past, oblivious to their impending doom.

I descended a mechanical staircase, followed the sign for "All Terminals," and stopped suddenly in my tracks. My host's guts twisted with surprise. A horde of human meat wound through long ribbons, corralled like livestock. Hundreds of them, blocked up, packed tight as cars on the I-55.

My first instinct was to shout at the crowd of humans, draw their eyes toward me, and burn through the crowd as I had down the I-55. But Nassar's knowledge gave me pause. *The airport is different,* I began to understand. *If you burn through human after human, they will assume the facility is under attack. They might ground every flight. Wait until you are far over the ocean.*

I shook my human head. Surely there was some other way past this throng of listless travelers. I showed the glowing screen of my phone with the electronic ticket to a uniformed agent. "I have booked passage onto an airplane flight," I explained. "Allow me through."

"Sir," the woman said. "Get in line with everyone else."

"How swiftly will these lines of humans progress?"

She glared. "As swiftly as people like you cooperate."

"How long, exactly!" I demanded. "I scheduled the flight for 20 of your minutes from this moment."

"Well, we recommend that you allow from one to two hours to pass through security, sir," the woman said. "We are not responsible for your punctuality."

"Unacceptable—"

"Get in line!" she yelled. "The longer you complain, the more likely you will miss your flight, sir."

I filed in line with the other humans, stewing in the flesh of my human meat, frequently checking the minutes displayed on my host's phone. I kept my breaths controlled. The ticket was for Omar Nassar, so I had to maintain my composure and make this host last. They would not permit a different human to use his ticket.

"Insufferable," I muttered. We crept at the pace of a desert tortoise.

A sour-faced human scrutinized travelers one-by-one. Beyond him, was yet *another* line, where machines with moving carpets scanned and processed human belongings. The agent eventually motioned for me to step forward. He took the phone with the electronic code, then carefully studied the passport and Omar Nassar's face.

"I'm him," I snapped. "Permit me to pass."

The agent glared. "Be patient, sir."

I glanced at the time on Nassar's phone when he returned it to me. In five minutes, my airplane was scheduled to depart. "Must I wait in the next line?" I asked. "I have no bags for your machines to examine."

"Everyone has to pass through the scanner, Mr. Nassar." He handed back the passport. "You'll need to empty your pockets, remove your belt, anything that will set off the metal detector, just like every other passenger here."

I could not suppress a growl of anger. The line inched forward. An ancient hag of a woman and her shriveled husband blocked the moving carpet—*conveyor belt*. With slow, shuddery movements, they stooped and untied their shoes one lace at a time. They slowly emptied their pockets—one item at a time. They meticulously arranged metal garments and possessions across five bins.

"Why does it take you so long to remove your shoes?" I snapped. "Watch how quickly I do it!" I yanked off my human host's belt, kicked off my shoes and shouldered my way in front of an insipid teenage girl. "Scan me, so that I can be done with this process!"

"Excuse me, sir!" an agent shouted. "Pick up your shoes and put them in a bin."

"I will not require them on the plane," I shouted. "My flight leaves in minutes. Scan me!"

"Pick up your possessions and place them on the belt!" the agent commanded.

"You human sheep! How do any of you stand the indignity of these processes?" My host's head throbbed. His blood at last boiled with my ancient rage. "Shoved into metal coffins on wheels! Forced through corrals like goats to slaughter!"

More agents approached.

"Let me pass, or I will unleash my wrath on the lot of you!"

Suddenly a large man tackled me from behind. He slammed me against the filthy Midway Airport floor. More human agents forced me down.

"Remove your filthy human paws from this vessel or—" I started to lift the burly agent off me, growling in rage. Again, I failed. Nassar's body would not last long enough. Whatever the consequences, I needed to transfer into another human.

I opened Nassar's eyes wide and scanned the crowd for a suitable host, when suddenly, a female agent sprayed burning mist at my host's face.

I screamed in rage. "What magic is this?" Some kind of potion? A concoction to ward off demons?

"It's pepper spray, Mr. Nassar. Now cooperate."

I opened my eyes to a red blur of pain. "No!" I screamed. Without eye contact, I could not bewitch and enter another human. Metal shackles clamped Nassar's wrists together.

"You have the right to remain silent," came the agent's voice. "Anything you say—"

"Curse your feeble species!" I screamed. Omar Nassar's skin cooked and blistered. Without another host, without an urn or other magical object to contain my essence, where would I go?

For countless millennia, I occupied the flesh of mortal things, occasionally hibernating in objects imbued with mystic power.

But there was no magic in this modern world.

People shouted and screamed.

Omar Nassar's tongue swelled and burst. I could only make gurgling noises. The human filth had bested me without even trying.

My host's eyes melted. Stone-cold darkness gripped me.

And then.

Nothing.

CARL THE FORTUITOUS

BY JOHN KISTE

"Well, is he a vampire or what?" asked Carl as he tentatively rubbed his throat. Carl was always exhibiting one tic or another, depending on the conversation. Some days he was hard to watch.

"No, idiot, you saw him," I retorted. "Did he look like Dracula?" He shook his head. "Or Count Yorga?" He shook his head again. "Did he shimmer?"

Carl held up a finger. "He could be one of those European-ugly Klaus Kinski vampires. He did kinda look like that."

"He's not a vampire!" I insisted. I walked around to the back of the rusting Vega and began filling the trunk with my duffels. Late afternoon had crept upon us as we gathered supplies—I really didn't want to do things too long after dark.

Carl wouldn't let it go. "What is he, Gerry?" he whined. "Best guess."

I shrugged as I reached for his bag. "I dunno.

Clearly dangerous. He growled something almost intelligible last night as he fed, you heard that. So, not a zombie. But some kind of ghoul. Definitely an undead sort. Why the hell is your bag so light?" I opened his tattered gym bag, looked inside, turned to Carl in disgust, and dumped the contents in the road. "Geez, dude..." I bent and picked up a small rubber hammer and a foot-long, hand-carved pine stake. I shook them in his face.

"What?" he moaned, running his hand through already wild hair. "You said stakes were essential for anything dead and yet not dead."

I unzipped my duffel and extracted from the trunk a four-foot long sharpened piece of white ash. And a huge wooden mallet. "Like this. I've told you, like this. Real hunters of Nosferatu and their like use ash, and stakes long enough to pin the bastards to the ground. Some legends say you need to leave plenty of ash outside the body to drain their unholy power to the earth and the elements. Then you cut off the top of the stake when they are dispatched. That's probably crap. You use long stakes because hitting the heart doesn't always snuff them, since their hearts aren't actually beating, and many often writhe and reach for you until you can decapitate them—so a long stake keeps you from the fangs and fingers. Then you fill their mouths with garlic and burn the whole kit and kaboodle. Voila! These tinker toy weapons of yours are a recipe for finding our throats torn out. Get in the car."

I started teaching Carl this nonsensical but necessary trade seven years ago. You could call him a quick study—in that anyone would see quick he was incapable of study. I have since seen his high school transcript; it was written like a masterwork in someone stuttering 'F's. Still, he had a knack for staying alive, which was more than my three partners before him had managed. I don't know if I had come to trust the instincts of my greasy little sidekick or if I had simply come to rely on his remarkable good luck. Many a black night in an even blacker mausoleum or backwoods or sewer, Carl had inexplicably happened upon exactly the weapon we required in order to see another morning.

One midnight a couple of years back, we were stumbling among grass-grown graves in a deserted cemetery, attempting and failing to stay ahead of a reanimated zombie that a pissed-off voodoo priest had unleashed on us, and my buddy Carl literally kicked a bag of rock salt that some caretaker had forgotten against a tombstone after the winter freeze. A few handfuls tossed into this resurrected thing's face and mouth gave us time to encircle him with it and sew his lips together.

Another time, a lesser demon was in close pursuit down the stone steps of a Scottish castle when poor Carl lost his footing and smashed against a wooden framework at the foot of the stairway. The toothy imp was only three steps from the bottom which meant curtains for us, but the rigging my partner rammed was the trigger some ancient laird had installed to guard against marauders. The stone step under the demon fell away like a trap door and the beastie plunged two hundred feet into the sea.

It was crazy, but that kind of shit happened to Carl all the time. It would be hard to reconcile with reality, but so were ghosts, werewolves, and kelpies. I figured if my life's work had to be letting the populace sleep soundly by wiping out unfathomably evil things before they made their horrible presence known to the general public, it was only fair that we had some inexplicable good fortune occasionally on our side. So I'd take the luck. If only he wasn't both dense and irritating. Both. That duo nearly negated the luck.

Tonight would be not so much a running to ground of a monster as a "let's drive out to a farmhouse and stake him." We had trailed this undead fellow, whom I was still betting was a ghoul, from a dairyman's field of three dead cows to a lonely dilapidated frame house far back in Ramsey's Woods. His pattern repeated the next night when we tracked him from a couple of dug up graves in an overgrown old churchyard back to the same house. He fed just after dark and then went home.

So tonight, we would stake out the farmhouse (forgive the inadvertent pun), and then head inside once he left. We would be awaiting him with revolvers, knives, stakes, and Carl's preternatural ability to stay alive, along with the element of surprise, when he returned. He clearly had not attacked any living humans to date; my only concern was that this could be the night he made that inevitable leap. Most ghouls these days emulated serial killers; after attacking livestock and other animals and mutilating corpses, they eventually graduated to murder.

My job, and Carl's, was to nip things in the bud. If civilized man ever became cognizant of the creatures of the nether world, beyond the sightings and encounters that could be attributed to crazy talk, who would sleep soundly again? Carl believed our mandate and funding for dealing with devils and demons came straight from the Vatican, and he was far too naive to question why we holed up in fleabag hotels, drove a rusty antediluvian Vega, and whittled our own stakes. I *had* been given an edict a decade ago by a parish priest who understood the horrors of the night, and I would wave it beneath Carl's nose periodically to steel his resolve. He would not have gotten wise to the ploy even if he had studied the document for a fortnight. As to our funding, I received a small inheritance many years before, which was nearly depleted by the time of this assignment. Perversely, I would fall asleep each night picturing my own bankruptcy coinciding with Earth being overrun by monsters.

Rosy twilight greeted us as we parked the car off the unused lane at the edge of Ramsey's Woods. Middle autumn had arrived, and crisp leaves like multicolored scales stretched in all directions, but plenty of their brothers still clung tight to their branches overhead. We had flashlights in our belts, but they were not yet necessary, so we slung our bags across our shoulders and tried to make as little noise as possible on the crackling carpet. In ten minutes, the farmhouse came into view. It was a small frame dwelling with walls and gables that had once been white, broken shutters that had once been black, and a roof that had no discernible color or material because of the abundance of moss that had overspread it. To the right of the house was an unpainted tool shed, and still farther right sat a tiny smokehouse.

We could see the front door on the small porch clearly, even though the sun had gone and dimness flooded the tiny clearing. Carl and I crouched behind wide tree trunks and waited. And waited. The forest grew dark. I checked my watch and found we had spent more than an hour on our vigil. My legs ached. I was about to signal Carl that we must have missed the creature's exit when I heard a crash inside the house. Shortly after the door opened and a pale head peered into the woods. The hunched, gangly body followed tentatively, and for a moment I was convinced he could smell us fifty yards away. Some things like him could. Then suddenly he scuttled down the steps and loped away in the opposite direction.

We waited ten more minutes—we didn't know if ghouls were capable of forgetting their keys—and then we dashed to the porch. Of one thing I was certain: no other fiends were within. Years of dispatching such ghoul-like beings had taught me that they never shared a building with anyone or anything—even if they had known them in life. There would be no threats inside. Frankly, however, I wasn't completely certain of what kind of ghoul we were dealing with, and Carl was less than useless on this score, so we still entered the farmhouse carefully, watching each other's backs. The place was empty. Dust-laden furniture dotted the rooms, and cobwebbed pictures hung askew upon the walls, but we encountered nothing alive or dead—or undead.

It had grown very dark. The tables and chairs and old sofa merged into groups of black blobs. We could not risk the flashlights, so knowing Carl's propensity for tumbling over things—and seeing no advantage to it in this instance—we took up locations on either side of the front door. I had wandered into the kitchen to survey the rear but the back door was barricaded, whether intentionally or unintentionally, by a stack of chairs and trash. Our prey would be returning through the front. I stood at the ready, four-foot white ash stake before me, every muscle tense and quivering in anticipation. Carl had dragged a chair through the dust to the other side of the door jamb. His muscles were decidedly not aquiver. Once I had to hiss at him to stop snoring.

Just before midnight, something rustled without. An owl cried, the wind rose, and momentarily the crunch of feet on dry leaves echoed about the farmhouse. I risked a rapid glance through a leaded glass side window of the door—the beast returneth. I nodded to Carl, who rose lethargically. Reflexes like a panther, that one. Then came a heavy stomping on the porch steps. I stiffened. The door opened. The thing stood outlined in the slightly brighter outside light. I was set to strike, but the actual appearance of the ghoul caused an imperceptible delay. Though hunched forward, he was well over six feet. Sinewy muscles shorn of much flesh stood out on the clutching arms that reached through the doorway. The clothes were the tattered bloody remains of bib overalls. But the face—in the half-light the shriveled cheeks and sunken eye sockets were still visible, and somewhat more than off-putting. Blood and some kind of bile dripped from thick lips, but I could still see fangs. Our foe sported characteristics of ghouls, zombies, and vampires. I had no clue as to his classification. The stake should dispatch him, though. I swung it toward his heart, when suddenly he bent to pull off a muddy boot before entering, and the stake skidded down his back.

What kind of unholy beast removed his shoes when he came home? We never figured that out. He snarled as he discovered our presence, and I was bodily lifted and hurled against an interior wall. My stake clattered to the wooden floor, kicking up eddies of dust. When I had shaken my head to clear it, I saw Carl being throttled just inside the door. He was gurgling and gesturing at me and then at the clawed hands about his throat. He was irritating like that. Some days he was hard to watch.

The attacking ghoul growled something in his chest that sounded like "Assholes!" as he pinned Carl high up the front wall. Before I could rise to assist, my partner clutched a framed picture on the wall and shattered it over the monster's head. The clawed grip slackened and gave me time to grab the stake and impale him from behind. He shrieked and dropped Carl, who scrambled for my big mallet and started pounding. In ten seconds, the fiend was pinned to the wall like an epileptic butterfly, raging and spitting wildly as we set to work with the hacksaws. I filled the mouth with salt, garlic, and poppy seeds for good measure and tossed the head from the porch. My watch read 12:21 a.m.

I reentered the house and rifled the pockets of the denim overalls that stood upright like a Duluth Trading manikin facing the wall. I found a wallet and flipped through its contents. "His name was Chester Livingstone in life," I said to Carl. He was sitting in the dust and grime on the floor, holding the broken picture frame—only I saw as he read it that it was not a picture but a document.

"Yep," replied my helper as he wiped his nose on

his bloody sleeve. "He must have owned the place. This is his marriage license."

All I could manage was "Shit!"

For all the rot and corruption of the thing we had just slain, I could tell he had been a man of about thirty before his transformation. And he had had a wife. So what had become of her? It was possible he had eaten her. It was more than possible he had not. Whatever had affected him might very well have affected her. But, as I said, they would not be together. It was imperative that we search the toolshed.

Gathering our tools of the trade into our bags, we left the farmhouse and crept around to the door of the shed. It was partly ajar. I flicked on my flashlight and surveyed the interior. There was just one open space, and a long table across the back wall was covered with hammers and wrenches and vises and jars of bolts and nails. Hanging from a beam were a variety of rakes, shovels, scythes and sickles. A long pitchfork hung askew beside them, attached to its spike by a timeworn strip of leather. Cobwebs layered everything. Nothing moved within. I switched off the light and got a shock at how completely dark it now was in the depth of the woods.

"Shall we wait inside?" I whispered to Carl. He only gurgled in reply. I thought nothing of this for a moment; after all, it was Carl, and I still felt his breath on the back of my neck. Then the hairs on the back of that same neck roiled—this breath was far more fetid than Carl's, it smelled like the grave. I turned just as he was hurled past me into the depths of the shed. Sharp nails raked my face in the blackness; I felt the blood well to the surface. Then a powerful hand clutched the breast of my jacket and a second twisted my arm. I heard and felt the bone snap. I screamed.

Though my eyes had filled with tears of pain, they had adjusted enough to the dark to make out a white smock from which pale arms flailed and beat at me. A gray head bobbed beneath a great mass of black hair. Mrs. Livingstone, I presumed. This post-death incarnation of her lifted me from the ground and I was dashed roughly to the dirt floor of the toolshed. As she stood over me, Carl shot his flashlight beam directly at her face. Even consumed by the agonizing pains in my arm and elsewhere, I found the wherewithal to gag as I stared at it. The features had clearly once been those of an attractive woman, but the skin now clung like yellow tissue paper to the cheekbones, one eye was gone from beneath a sharp, jutting brow, and maggots danced in the empty socket. Orange saliva ran over pointed teeth and dripped onto my face. I yelled in horror and tried to shield my head with my good arm as she—it—bent over me.

Carl fired his revolver three times, hitting her twice in the chest and once in the forehead, but she only stared at him with baleful eye before crouching on top of me. Then, as so often happened, Carl tripped on a crate on the ground and fell backwards, the gun going off for a fourth time as he did. The bullet struck the rotten leather hanging strap of the pitchfork above us, and the thing that had once been a farmer's wife was impaled on the three tines. She shrieked in surprise and fury and fell onto her side, and my serendipitous little partner snatched a scythe from its post and cleaved her head from her shivering shriveled neck.

I lay half sobbing while he bound my arm and fitted

a makeshift sling; then I crawled across to examine this second dead ghoul. The struggle had torn away much of the midriff of the smock, and I sighed as I shined my flashlight on the exposed belly. I pointedly touched the caesarean scar on her blackened gut. "Clearly, you had better check out the little smokehouse, Carl," I said. "You can probably use your own small stake and mallet."

He shook his head in agreement. "Okay," he replied. "What am I looking for?" Some days he was hard to watch.

THE DOOM THAT CAME TO 1347 BEECHWOOD AVENUE

BY MARK MCLAUGHLIN

The brain is a wonderfully resilient and flexible organ. And, of all the brains of living things on Earth, the most advanced brains belong to those animals known as humans. Certainly, humans depend on their brains to make sense of the universe, successfully interact with other creatures, determine viable sources of sustenance, and if necessary, order takeout.

But sometimes, the malevolent powers that inhabit the most poorly lit corners of the universe can surge forth with obscene gusto to perpetrate unspeakable mischiefs. They delight in focusing upon the minds of easily confounded human organisms, tossing their collective sanities into the Stygian depths of a veritable laundry hamper of universal madness.

Such was the abysmal fate of the Maplinger family of 1347 Beechwood Avenue. The brains of this family were driven to the very brink of madness and despair, while their carbon-based bodies later suffered from intermittent nausea and occasional itching.

The Maplinger family, like most common, everyday, traditional American families, was composed of a father, a mother, a teenage son, and ten-year-old conjoined twin daughters. The father, Roderick, was a certified public accountant who enjoyed wholesome pursuits, like stamp-collecting and scrutinizing insects. The mother, Tammy, was a homemaker and freelance colonic hydrotherapist in her spare time. The son, Vincent, was an A-student and an avid tap dancer. The girls, Clara and Mabel, were surprisingly adept at jumping rope, considering that they were joined at both the shoulders and hips.

Why should such an ordinary family be plagued by the cruel intentions of a diabolical cosmos? Who can say? Fate does not play favorites. Destiny can be a twisted force that delights in herding the pure and innocent down the primrose path to hell. Truly, the members of the Maplinger family were mere pawns in the eternal soccer match between the forces of healthy goodness and pustulent evil.

Unlike a dark winter evening, the horror began on a sunny summer morning. The children, Vincent and Clara/Mabel, were on break from school, and the parents, Roderick and Tammy, had both decided to take a week of time-off from their careers so they could enjoy some family-bonding time. Little did they know that the entire family would soon be bonding via the maddening glue of pure terror.

At the breakfast table, Tammy happily loaded the plates of her children with bacon, breakfast sausages, and servings of apple pie topped with cheddar cheese slices and fried eggs. "Did all my darlings sleep well last night?" she asked.

"I dreamed of oceans of blood, filled with giant frogs and screaming orphans," Vincent said, cramming his eager mouth with sausage meat.

"Just like your old man when I was your age!" Roderick said warmly, nodding with fond nostalgia. "How are my two little precious, perfectly normal princesses?"

"I dreamed of inventing a wonderful drug that cured cancer and made ugly people beautiful!" Carla said. "I gave it to the ugly hospital patients with cancer and they all became healthy supermodels."

"I dreamed I was a crazy guy who put on his dead grandmother's dress at night," Mabel said. "I wandered through the night, stabbing people in the eye, and—"

"Boooring!" Vincent said. "You had that same dream last week!"

It was then that a force of primordial evil disrupted their pleasant, normal middle-class lives.

Someone—or something—knocked sharply four times on the kitchen door.

"Four sharp knocks? On our back door? At this hour? 7 a.m.?" Tammy cried. "I'm reluctant to see who it is! Maybe if we ignore he or she or it, the knocker will just go away."

Roderick just laughed. "Don't be silly! The residents of the Maplinger house have never turned down a back-door knocker!" With that, he rose from his chair, crossed to the back door, twisted the little handle on the knob that disengaged the lock assembly, and then gave the knob a quick turn, so that the door instantly—

—opened.

Terror of terrors! Horror of horrors! A split-second later, Roderick Maplinger found himself staring into the grotesque depths of damnation.

Just outside of the back door swirled the open maw of a transdimensional gateway. It grew as it revolved, and while it started at five feet wide, it soon grew to at least fifteen feet wide. The rim of the gateway was lined with small, sharp, yellowed teeth, like the mouth of a hungry lamprey. Apparently the door had been knocked upon by the long, leathery tongue that extended out of the gateway. A single blood-red eye protruded from the top of the tongue's thick, knobby tip.

"Great sizzling Jesus!" Roderick cried. "What do you want from us, you unspeakable phantasm from out of the realm of nightmares? And why did you knock upon our back door, instead of the front door? Most entities use the front door."

"I will answer your second question first," intoned a deep, male voice that issued from the hideous vortex. "As I approached your house from the rear, and through the kitchen window, I could see you all at the table. So I knocked. As for your first question: I came to your house to learn one vitally important fact. I need to know: Are you the occupants of 1346 Beechwood Avenue?"

Roderick shook his head. "No, O mighty and fearsome vortex! This is 1347 Beechwood Avenue. 1346 Beechwood Avenue is on the other side of the street. This side of the street is for the odd-numbered houses. The other side is for the even-numbered houses."

The leathery tip of the alien tongue nodded. "My

bad! Thank you so much, my friend. Have a nice day. Bye!"

With that, the long, leathery tongue quickly withdrew into the spinning lamprey mouth. The vortex began to shrink, and then suddenly, it shrank down to nothing. It disappeared with a slight but still audible pop!

Roderick turned and saw that his family members were all staring at him, mouths agape. A bit of sausage fell out of Vincent's mouth.

"It was nothing," Roderick said. "Some guy had the wrong house number. No big deal. Go back to your breakfasts."

He rushed through the house to his own front door, opened it, and looked outside. He could see the transdimensional gateway, opening at the front door of 1346 Beechwood Avenue—the gateway looked totally different from the back. Across the street, he heard four sharp knocks.

Upon seeing and hearing this otherworldly spectacle, Roderick gasped—and then whispered to himself, in a hushed tone of ineffable sadness.

"What's so special about *them*?"

HOW THE OTHER HALF LIVES

BY R. A. CLARKE

"Tell me why we're doing this again?" Zagan asked.

Lilith hid her eye roll as they strolled hand-in-hand down the sidewalk. Several feet ahead, their curious son bounded his way toward a two-story house excessively slathered with bloody window decals and wafting ghostly figures. Not only was this the very first house on the cul-de-sac, but it was also Damien's first-time trick-or-treating.

"Because it's nice to do something as a family for once, that's why," she replied evenly. "It's always *end-of-the-world* this, and *Hell-spawn* that! And we never spend quality time together anymore."

"Sure, we do."

"Oh really? Name one time in the last hundred years?"

Zagan faltered for a moment, brows furrowed. "Ah... we went to that place, to do the thing that time."

Lilith thrust a hand out. "See? You can't even come up with *one.*" She shook her head while noticing Damien pacing uncertainly atop the residence's overly decorated doorstep. He waved to get their attention.

"Damien, you just ring the doorbell buddy," Zagan instructed.

"And say trick or treat!"

"Ughh hughh," Damien muttered, turning back to the door.

Lilith glanced at another parent walking past wearing a furry bear costume. Zagan was busy miming to little Damien exactly how he should ring the doorbell. The lady shared a supportive smile.

"It's his first time," Lilith explained with a nervous chuckle.

"Ah yes, well we all have to learn somehow!" An amused laugh emphasized the bear-lady's words before she disappeared, hurrying to catch up to her older children a few houses down.

Lilith's smile brightened. *What a friendly human.*

After finally ringing the doorbell, Damien received a handful of candy from a portly woman into the flimsy pumpkin bag he carried. He bounced back down the steps, and Lilith beamed with pride.

"Oooh, isn't he adorable in his costume?" Lilith beamed.

"Did he choose it, or did you?" Zagan asked.

"He did."

Zagan's brows raised, glancing over at his son dressed head to toe in blue and white. He looked back; skepticism written all over his face.

"He did! *The Smurfs* is his favourite show. He dreams of eating one someday. If you were home a little more, you'd know that." Lilith didn't make eye contact, smoothly continuing, "You should see his little mouth water whenever we watch it. It's so cute." She giggled, watching Damien make his way across the lawn to the next house.

Zagan ignored her overly obvious dig. "I think a Dinosaur or Godzilla would've been more appropriate, don't you? I mean, his tail is sticking out." He pointed to the snake-like appendage hanging down from the hole they'd cut in the rear of his costume.

"Oh, it's Halloween. Nobody will notice." Lilith waved it off.

Zagan zipped ahead a few steps, snapping his fingers at their smurfy son who'd suddenly halted by a row of bushes separating two yards. "Damien, leave it alone," he said.

Lilith looked past her husband to see his source of concern, eyes widening. "Oh Hell. Just go to the next house sweetie." She pointed emphatically to the next-door residence. Damien stared back blankly.

A small group of kids skipped up the driveway to the house Damien had just departed, the same portly woman answered the doorbell.

"Bhuut me wanna eaad da cat." Damien grumped, pointing to a fluffy calico cat winding itself around his legs.

"No, you can't eat the cat."

The lady handing out candy did a double take. "Pardon? Did he say *eat*?"

"No, no. So sorry ma'am," Lilith smiled apologetically. "When he says eat, he really means pet. You see, when our boy gets really excited, he just loses all his words." Feigning a casual smile, Lilith jogged across the lawn to shoo the cat away, but Damien shook his head.

"Nuh uh. I wannit." He picked it up and the furry feline started affectionately rubbing its face against his mask, purring, oblivious to any danger.

Lilith stared into her son's eyes and held her hands out. "Give it over."

He refused, snarling back.

Hiding her frustration, Lilith slapped on another smile. Adjusting her body to hide the following action, she clutched one of her son's hands. Beyond anyone's view, she blazed white-hot fire from her fingertips.

"No eating cats," she whispered, deathly serious.

Damien growled defiantly, but released the furry creature.

Lilith cradled the kitty, turning around to present how perfectly unharmed it was, before letting it go. The fuzzball meowed and scurried away.

Damien shook out his singed hand as Zagan appeared by their side.

"Good boy, now go to the next house." He sent Damien on his way, pointing.

"Thaad one?"

"Yes, that one."

As their son trudged to the next garishly decorated home, Lilith pondered him with a head tilt. "You know, we should really take Damien to a speech pathologist sometime soon. I've been wondering if he needs some help. I mean, he's three hundred years old already. His sister knew way more words and had no trouble with pronunciation by this age."

"Yeah, but Jezebel is *Jezebel*. She broke the mould in every way. We can't really use her as an accurate measure," Zagan shot her a lopsided smile. "I think our little monster's doing fine. He may be a late bloomer, but it'll come."

"You're probably right. I just worry. I can't help it."

"You're doing everything right," Zagan took hold of his wife's hand and squeezed. "You're a great mom." Lilith smiled, their gazes locking. "Thanks. It means a lot to hear you say that." Zagan leaned in close to kiss her lips, his horns twitching, but a familiar raspy giggle interrupted the moment. She turned toward the sound, seeing Damien holding onto two jack-o'-lanterns beside the neighbouring porch.

"Damien! No! Put those down."

"Bhuut me wanna taykem. Bring em ta life." Damien admired the horror-carved faces, swaying with them as a human child might rock a baby doll.

"No, we can't," Lilith said matter-of-factly. "Pumpkins aren't minions. They can't come with us."

An elderly man appeared on the porch, swinging the screen door open. "You there! Hands off the pumpkins!" His eyebrows touched in the middle, the wrinkles appearing to run away from his eyes.

Zagan swooped in to help. "And we are putting the pumpkins down *now*." He placed both of the robust round vegetables back onto the ground beside the others lining the rickety old porch. "Yep, there we go. Sorry sir. He just loves pumpkins so much." Zagan patted Damien's slumping shoulders and led him away.

A few sets of curious eyes swung in their direction because of the ordeal. Lilith held her cheerful facial expression in place.

"Everything is right as rain! The innocence of kids, hey?" Lilith laughed, shrugging at the sheer silliness of it all. She expected a chuckle in return, but the man's scowl stayed put, perhaps even deepening.

"Kids got no respect these days. Don't touch what doesn't belong to ya, plain and simple. Here," the man grumbled, tossing a couple mini-bars in Damien's direction.

Damien grumbled as he snatched them up, smelling the chocolate with a sour face. Zagan shushed his son's complaints, moving him along faster.

"Sorry again," Lilith added, waving politely from the sidewalk. Without another word, the old man turned on his heels and slammed the door.

As her family rejoined her on the sidewalk, she muttered into Zagan's ear, "Well, that human wasn't so friendly." Lilith encouraged Damien to continue trick-or-treating at the next house. Watching him go, she felt disappointed they'd caused a stir, and also slightly irritated by that man's reaction. It wasn't like her son had damaged his precious pumpkins. All kids were curious creatures. There was no reason for him to be so rude.

"No, he wasn't," Zagan agreed with a nod. "You know, I hear the grumpy ones make the tastiest hellhound treats."

Lilith smacked her husband's shoulder as if scandalized, yet was unable to stifle a giggle.

He grinned. "Just wait until he finds his pumpkins running around the yard later. Ha!" he burst out. "Damien already put the animation curse on them."

Lilian's hand flew to her mouth. "Oh, my goodness. We should go back and counteract it." She turned, but Zagan stopped her.

"Naw, c'mon, live a little. It'll be fun." He wrapped an arm around his beloved, eyes twinkling mischievously. "We'll circle back to watch the chaos."

"I don't know. I really wanted us to do something normal for once." Lilith pulled away from him, levelling her gaze.

"Normal how? Like boring ol' Earth? Why would you want that?" Zagan's face belied his disgust. "We're Demons."

"Don't you ever wonder what life is like for these humans? Most of them seem so happy... well, except that old man."

He pulled her back to his side. "Happiness is for weaklings. Mooning about all the time. Being *kind* to one another. What a waste of energy," he scoffed. "I mean, I'm doing this 'outing' because you wanted me to. Believe me, I'm on my best behaviour here, but it isn't easy."

They walked in silence for a moment, monitoring as Damien skipped across another yard to a tall house sporting dangling witches and skeletons. Lilith looked down, contemplating her next words.

"Zagan, don't you ever tire of living in the same old hellhole, day in and day out?" she asked quietly, staring at her shoes. Taking a deep breath, she straightened her shoulders and met her husband's gaze once more. "I was thinking, maybe it would be nice to spend more time here."

"Here? Seriously?" A rush of air escaped his lips. He stopped walking, and turned to face Lilith. "I happen to like our little hellhole. What's come over you?"

"I just want something different. A change of pace." She paused beside him, placing a hand on his forearm. "Perhaps even try being good for a while?"

"*Good?*" Zagan recoiled dramatically, holding his head as if he'd just been subjected to an angel's song. "I can't believe I'm hearing that word come out of your mouth. Where's the evil creature I married?"

Lilith placed her hands on his lapels, her eyes urging him to keep his voice down. "You wouldn't even consider giving it a try? For me? I think we need this."

An errant candy bag smacked into their sides as a group of kids ran past. Neither Lilith nor Zagan spared them a glance, laser-focused on each other.

"We need this, or *you* need this?" Zagan's words were sharp.

Lilith's eyes narrowed. "Listen, your work has consumed our lives these last few hundred years. We need a nice long vacation. We really do. One where we can focus on being a family again."

Somewhere up ahead, Damien's gleeful giggles rang out. He was clearly enjoying the outing. *At least somebody was.*

Zagan sighed, resting his hands on his hips. "Okay, yes, a vacation does sound nice, but not *here*. Regardless, I don't think anybody could easily take over for me at Hell's gate. It takes thousands of years of experience and training to coordinate all the comings and goings properly." He ran a hand through his hair, exposing his stubby horns for a split-second. "The legions aren't exactly easy to schedule."

"Yeah..." Lilith inspected her hands, feeling deflated.

Damien's giggles morphed into something more menacing.

"Sweet sin, Damien! Put that child down!" Zagan cried.

Lilith's eyes snapped up, breaking from her thoughtful fog. Her husband was already in full motion, running toward a growing commotion two yards over. She gave chase, catching sight of Damien holding a child dressed as the Devil up off the ground. *Oh, no!* They'd been too consumed by their discussion, and not keeping a watchful eye.

"That kid's got Michael by the neck! Call the police!" a trick-or-treater shouted.

Within seconds, Zagan and Lilian were there, urging Damien to put the child down. Their son had a powerful grip, and had no trouble holding the kid aloft.

"Bhuut he nod supposed ta be oudda Hell. He nuh allowwed." Notes of anger heightened Damien's trademark drawl as he turned the kid upside down, shaking him by the feet. When nothing fell to the ground, he said, "No passs."

"Don't shake him!"

Damien idolized his father, knowing how serious his dad's job as Hell's gatekeeper was. Damien was so upset his scaly skin began to glow like embers, its fiery light emanating through the thin fabric of his costume.

Lilith inched forward. "I know, sweetie. No pass, no travel; that's the rule." All Hallows Eve was the underworld's only official day off, a heavily enforced mandate. "But that's not a real demon."

"It's only a human child dressed up as a Demon, buddy," Zagan chimed in, nodding.

"Wha?"

"Let him go," Lilith cooed softly, motioning for her son to hand the human over. More eyes were turning their way now. This couldn't be any worse. So much for blending in.

"I don wanna." Damien flipped the kid upright again, squeezing the boy's neck.

"Let go, *now*." Her voice grew in intensity.

"Nuh uh."

The subject of Damien's fury barely rasped out the word 'help' as he struggled to get air beneath Damien's iron fist.

"Let Michael go! You're hurting him!" A random child in a cowboy outfit cried.

As more onlookers yelled for help, the parents in the area swarmed like a zombie apocalypse. Lilith would've almost preferred the undead at this point. Lovely creatures. Surprising conversationalists.

Luckily there weren't many trick-or-treaters in this cul-de-sac, but it was still plenty more attention than Lilith wanted to have tonight. She'd just wanted a simple and wholesome family outing.

So much for that idea.

"Everybody, settle down! The child is fine. Our son just doesn't know his own strength sometimes. He's just playing." Zagan splayed his arms out and encouraged calm from everybody present.

"Goodness no, he doesn't mean any harm." Lilith laughed it off for the benefit of their audience, pretending it was all a big joke. She turned back to her son with a scowl. "Damien, put him down, or we're going home."

"Me no wanna go hoome. Dis 'lil Satan need ta go hoome."

"That's not a little Satan!" she hissed, noting the boy's face turning a deep red, bordering on purple.

"Stop it, son!" Zagan snapped his fingers, pointing down.

Damien shook his head. "Nuh uh."

"He's a freak!"

"Look, his skin is glowing!"

"What is he?"

"Is that a *real tail?*"

Lilith cringed. She had to come up with a way to salvage this situation, else these people would figure out they weren't exactly human.

"It's gonna be okay, Michael!" The human boy's mother blazed forward, shooting an icy look at Zagan and Lilith. "I've called the cops, you crazies. You get your freaking kid off of mine right now!"

Zagan shot her a warning glare, and for good measure, he flashed a glimpse of his true teeth in all their jagged glory. The woman froze, terror-stricken. It was best that she keep her distance.

"Hey Mam, look! He no 'lil Satan ad all." Damien pulled off the tiny human's devil mask, jumping up and down excitedly. "Now me wanna eead him."

"EAT? Oh God, Michael!" The little Satan's mother cried. Despite her fear, the woman darted forward to save her son.

Damien pushed off his own mask, revealing his glowing alligator-like scales. He snapped his teeth at the woman, causing her to recoil once more.

Michael's bloodshot eyes widened with fresh terror, gasping and limbs flailing anew.

Lilith groaned, exasperated. *Really? Did he seriously have to take his mask off?* There was no salvaging this situation now. Their cover was officially blown.

Damien licked his reptilian teeth. He'd gotten his looks from his great-grandfather; His wildness, too. Certain characteristics tended to skip generations in the demon realm.

The mournful wail of a distant siren filled the once-quiet cul-de-sac. Lilith threw her hands in the air. "Oh perfect, that's just what we need right now."

"Thank God, the police are coming! Michael, it'll be okay!"

"Everybody just calm down! He's not going to eat anybody," Zagan snapped, losing patience, his muscles taut. Lilith was surprised he'd held onto his calm as long as he had.

The troubling truth was that their son could very likely try to eat the kid. She remembered their trip to see the Salem witch trials exhibit at a museum last year. Damien thought he could be sneaky and take a quick bite out of a Puritan child, which—much to his surprise—turned out to be a period-appropriate wax sculpture.

He'd been so disappointed.

Damien's little jaw was visibly unhinging, and saliva dripped from his mouth. Lilith was chiding herself now for thinking a year's time might've tempered his urges.

Zagan nodded to her, his irises aglow. With a flick of his head, he indicated to Lilith he'd grab the kid. Understanding his signal, Lilith tensed, preparing to launch toward Damien. But first, there was one last tactic left in her playbook.

Lilith spat out, "Damien, no more watching Smurfs for you if you *eat that child!*" Now if that didn't work, she'd have no choice but to tackle her son. There was no more time to waste.

"Buhht Mam!" Damien whined, his scales dimming as he looked at his mom. His focus was finally broken, his jaw shifting back to its normal position. He lowered the child in a huff.

Oh, thank Lucifer.

Zagan capitalized on the opportunity, swiftly removing the boy from Damien's clutches. He practically tossed the whimpering child into his mother's waiting arms.

"There's your kid! Now be happy," he grumbled with a scalding eye roll.

Lilith patted her visibly disappointed son on the head, ignoring all the sniveling humans. Poor guy must feel so confused, not understanding why he couldn't eat that human. To him *everything* was a possible food source, and his particular affinity for fleshy things didn't help matters.

The sirens grew louder.

"That's my good boy," Lilith soothed. "C'mon, let's just go home. We can finish trick-or-treating at Hades' place instead." Her shoulders sagged along with her spirits, but she kept her voice light for Damien's benefit. What a horrible ending to what she'd hoped would be a lovely evening. Placing a guiding hand on her son's back, she led him away.

"There, you see folks?" Zagan's arms spread wide as he addressed the crowd. "Everything's just fine.

Nobody was harmed. Everybody can go back to celebrating the *wondrous* joy of Halloween now."

Lilith detected a note of sarcasm in her husband's tone. The smirk on his face suggested he was clearly amused. Of course, this would be funny to him. He loved chaos. Lived for it. She glared, and Zagan mouthed the word 'what'?

"It's not funny," Lilith growled. He shrugged.

"Mam, look!"

Damien slipped from her grasp, darting forward on a dead run. "Ooop!" She lunged, but couldn't catch his tail. "Come back here, Damien!"

She gave chase. *What now?*

Her eyes scanned ahead for possible attractants as she ran. Zagan's footsteps pounded behind her.

Then she saw it. Just entering the cul-de-sac, a familiar blue and white costume was merrily skipping down the sidewalk.

Oh Hell…

With renewed vigour, Lilith shouted at the top of her lungs, "Damien—stop now! Listen to your mother!"

No response. Not even a backward glance.

"Oh, no. Lilith, there's a—"

"A Smurf, I know!" she yelled back at Zagan over her shoulder. "Run faster!"

He appeared at her side then, smiling proudly. "Gosh, he's a quick little demon, isn't he?"

"Is that *really* what you're thinking now?" Lilith glared, incredulous.

"Takes after his old man."

"Eead Smmuurrffff!" Their son's jubilant voice wafted back to them.

"Damien, get back here! I swear, they do NOT taste good!"

Zagan's face broke into a wider smile. "Yes, run away, humans! Run away!" He waved his arms wildly, not taking the matter seriously at all.

"I can't believe you. This isn't funny! Cut it out." Lilith shot a bolt of fire at him.

He let out a ragged sigh. "Fine. I'll be serious."

Damien's adorable little legs were really churning. He was only thirty feet from his target. The Smurfette was up and running, but stood no chance.

Twenty feet.

"DAMIEN! Stop!"

Ten feet.

"We're not kidding! No means no!" Lilith screamed.

The sirens were not so distant anymore, their wails piercing the air. Police cars would be appearing any minute.

Lilith's fingertips glowed as she focused all her energy and thrust her hands forward. A wall of flame burst forth from the earth to block Damien's path.

He didn't even flinch, simply bent his knees and launched his powerful body over top of the flames. Right onto the Smurfette. His jaw opened wide before clamping down on the little girl's hand, and with a violent shake, the Smurfette was relieved of a few fingers.

"Oh!" Lilith exclaimed, arms lowering. Her wall of flame extinguished in a whoosh, its flickering remnants evaporating into the crisp October air.

"Ah shit," Zagan slowed up, catching his breath amidst the cacophony of screams that erupted all around them. Such chaos was music to his ears, a beautifully intricate symphony of pain and anguish, albeit, not quite the desired result at this exact moment.

Lilith snatched the fingers from Damien's bloody mouth, carefully placing them onto the ground for the wailing child's parents to collect. They were a little chewed up, but perhaps salvageable. Unable to control her seething anger, Lilith's raven hair burst into flame as she yanked her son away.

"Buut Mam, me jus wanned a tayste," Damien whined, his thick feet plodding after her.

"Shh! I don't want to hear it," she scolded.

Two police cars careened around the corner, lights flashing. The vehicles veered in their direction once they caught sight of the spectacle. And what a sight it would've been. A distinctly lizard-like boy, with a mother whose head was fully engulfed in white-hot flame.

Oh yeah, and a slightly disfigured human child too.

"What a mess," Zagan groaned. "I'm going to have so much paperwork to fill out now. Damn it." It wasn't forbidden, but strongly discouraged to damage or kill humans while travelling on a pass for All Hallows Eve.

The police cars skidded to a stop, strategically angled to provide themselves cover.

Lilith snapped her fingers, looking to Zagan. "Time to go."

"Bhuut Maa!" Damien stomped his feet, disgruntled.

Police officers jumped out of their vehicles and aimed their guns at the oddball family.

Zagan roared and revealed his real face, his knotted horns sprouting to full size. Eyes sizzling, his molten skin cracked like the desert earth. All eyes were on him, exactly as he wanted.

Just then, a couple newly animated pumpkins came skittering past the police officers' feet, flailing their spindly sprouted arms. They chittered away to each other like drunken chipmunks. Startled officers cried out in alarm, jumping out of their way.

Damien squealed with delight, "Minyons!" Another one ambled close by and he tried to chase after it, but Lilith held onto her son with iron fists. He wouldn't be slipping away this time.

"Transport us now, Zagan!"

Spinning into a fiery tornado, Zagan sucked his family up into a searing vortex of flame and ashen smoke. A barrage of shots rang out from beyond the hellish funnel, their destructive capability rendered ineffective against Zagan's power. As Earth disappeared from view, he steered them toward home.

Only briefly did he stop to check in at Hell's gates. Zagan confirmed he'd swing by later to fill out the required forms, and then they carried onward.

The landscape grew darker and hotter as they went. Lilith smiled. It felt nice to be back in a place where they could feel completely normal and accepted again.

"And we're outta there," Zagan announced as their motion finally ceased, the turbulent cyclonic air receding around them. "Whew! That was tense." He patted out any lingering vortex embers singeing his suit jacket, then planted his hands on his hips.

"It was," Lilith said with a haggard sigh. She brushed similar embers off of Damien, and then herself.

"Now, what were you saying about being *good?*" He chuckled, shaking his head.

"Real funny," Lilith shot back. "That certainly didn't go as planned."

"What did you expect?"

"I don't know. Definitely not *that.*" Lilith licked her thumb and wiped a splatter of blood from her son's face, but it didn't do much good.

"Yes, it was unfortunate. But you have to admit, it was also pretty funny. A little Smurf on Smurf action." Zagan wiggled his eyebrows up and down.

"Shh!" Lilith clapped her hands over Damien's ears, but her glare morphed into a smirk. "Oh, you're bad."

"Isn't that why you married me?" He gave Damien a belly a quick tickle, while pulling Lilith into his arms.

He spun her around and dipped her low, eyes smoldering while the corners of his mouth curled. Lilith giggled. "Don't look at me like that, Zagan. You know I can't resist the dimples."

"Come here," he murmured, moving in for a kiss.

"Mam... Daa! Thaad's gross," Damien complained, nose scrunching.

Lilith disengaged herself from her husband's embrace with a laugh.

Zagan tossed Damien over his shoulder playfully. "Okay, okay. Let's go get you cleaned up."

Walking through the jagged-edged front door of their humble hellhole, Lilith and Zagan shed what remained of their human disguises. Lilith smiled, happy to be in her own skin again.

It's good to be home.

Zagan said, "You know, it *was* quite nice to spend a day as a family today. I'm happy you planned it,

Lilith." Zagan paused to close the door and set Damien down. "And for pushing me into doing it. Maybe a real vacation could do us some good."

Lilith was quiet, stunned.

"So, listen, I'll try my best to arrange that, okay?"

"Really?" Lilith's face lit up, her charred heart swelling inside her chest. He'd finally heard her. *Finally.* "Oh, that would be lovely. And perhaps we can even make it into an annual thing?"

He put his hands up. "Let's not get crazy. It'll be hard enough for me to organize *one*. We'll try that first, then go from there, okay?" There was softness in his eyes as he smiled.

"Oh, thank you," Lilith beamed, hugging him. Their lips touched. Perhaps this disaster of a day had been good for something after all.

The sound of snorting, ripping and grinding interrupted the precious moment, drawing their eyes to its source.

Damien, who'd made a bee-line into the kitchen upon arrival, was now actively chomping on a chunk of bloody carcass. He watched them impassively as he viciously stripped the bone clean.

"Maybe not to Earth though," Lilith and Zagan said in stereo, bursting into laughter.

Shaking her head, Lilith announced, "Okay, kiddo. It's bath time." She prodded her son to drop his snack and move along. Damien groaned in response, dragging his heels down the hall.

"You know, that was a mighty good bite tonight, son," Zagan commented with a nod, ruffling the scraggly strands of hair on Damien's scaly cowl. "But we need to work on your listening skills. *Big time.* No means no."

"Bhuut Daa!"

"No arguing, Damien," Lilith decreed, capitalizing on the teachable moment. Restraint was an important skill for all demons to master. "Your father's one-hundred percent right. Trick-or-treating is for candy *only.*" She sat on the edge of the cleansing pool. Maybe in a couple years, they could give trick-or-treating on Earth another try.

"Candy... Oookay." Damien ripped off his costume and slouched into the pool, bloody tendrils swirling off his skin. Crossing his arms, he grumbled, "Bhuut me stil tink da Smurf taysted bedder."

Or maybe not.

A GHOST NAMED GRADY

BY ROBERT P. OTTONE

Grady sat in his usual spot, on his favorite bench, watching the other monsters playing. Some were playing soccer, and kicking wildly at each other. Others were racing down the track, elbowing each other along the way. Grady wasn't up for that. He even had a note that excused him from participation in gym class, where the other kids were doing *trust-falls*. Grady knew they would let him drop to the floor, even if he *did* try, so he was happy to be excused from all activities.

"Heads up!" he heard from a group of werewolves nearby. He looked just in time to see a ball flying directly at his face. He quickly became intangible. The ball flew right through him, passing with a slight tickle. He turned and spotted Bebe. Immediately, the tickle from the passing ball changed to warmth in his cheeks.

Bebe, a ghost just like Grady, was one of the few

kids at the school he talked to from time to time. Since they were both ghosts, they had a lot in common. She had even died in a car accident like Grady. They would talk sometimes while waiting for the Spectral Express, their shared bus, each morning before school. Grady would've liked talking to her *after* school too, but Bebe walked in the opposite direction, heading north on Lampkin Lane. Grady headed south.

At the moment though, none of this mattered, as the ball was soaring with incredible speed at Bebe's backside. Thinking quickly, Grady reached out and stopped the ball in mid-air using an advanced skill called telekinesis. This wasn't something ghosts would learn until much later, but Grady had already mastered it, practicing by making things float around his room late at night before bed.

Bebe turned and saw the ball floating. She looked past it and saw Grady.

"Sorry, it was gonna hit your bu... I mean, your back," Grady said nervously. He never knew how to talk to Bebe. Sometimes he planned his responses in advance, but she always left him speechless, even if he did enjoy their interactions when they occurred.

"Thanks, Grady," she smiled, brushing a strand of nearly-translucent gray-blue hair behind her ear. One could always tell a ghost from any of the other creatures at the school. The ghosts were nearly see-through most of the time and looked like they were covered in a smattering of dust. Grady practiced transfiguration, normally a tool of the vampires, to add color to his body using the spectral magic that now coursed through his being, but he was met with middling results.

Bebe was nice. Pretty, with a slightly upturned nose that she was teased about from time to time by the vampire girls. Grady loved it. She was funny, too. Played handball, despite being a ghost, and could easily keep up with the possessed dolls. She was also in the mock United Nations, representing Finland. Bebe talked a lot. Grady liked listening to her and liked answering her questions. She seemed very sure of herself, for a ghost. Grady noticed that most ghosts really leaned into their roles as invisible nuisances to the living. Bebe, however, had goals of becoming the first spectre to practice law for both humans *and* ghosts. Her mom, who also died in the car accident, was also a lawyer and well-known in the monster community for handling a famous land dispute between the werewolves and wolf-men, who one should never, *ever* confuse with one-another.

Grady marveled at how fast the werewolves were. He could never be that fast. Also, he could never be that hairy. The vampires were fast, but they had a height advantage that made them perfect for the basketball team. The possessed dolls were great at handball. What was Grady good at? He had been at this middle school for a year now and didn't fit in with the other ghosts. They socialized. Gossiped. Joked around. Perfectly normal things for young teens to do. But not for Grady. He felt like an outsider.

Instead, he sat, every day, on the same bench. In the same spot. Watching others have fun during lunch. He'd eat his usual peanut butter and banana sandwich, left for him on the counter by his mom, who, though still alive, was able to see him and talk to him. For that, he was grateful. Grady didn't need to eat, nor did he feel hunger, but he didn't want to break that to his mom. She loved the routine of preparing meals for the two of them, even though the food just seemed to absorb into his body once he ate it. Grady felt it kept a level of normalcy between them, so every morning he made sure to grab the small paper bag with little hearts drawn in marker.

Grady wasn't fond of talking about his loneliness at school, or how he wasn't making any friends, even though his mom asked regularly. He didn't want to bore her with his teenage angst. Seventh grade was *supposed* to be like this, right? This is what all the movies Grady watched told him. Being a teenager wasn't easy, so Grady just assumed this was normal.

He took a bite of his sandwich and continued watching the other kids. After lunch he only had Undead Literature 1 and Spectral Travel remaining for the day. He liked Spectral Travel. He was good at it. He found mastering his new range of motion easy. Grady could fly if he wanted to. He wasn't sure if any of the other ghosts could yet, certainly none that were in his Spectral Travel class anyway. He didn't fly often though, but when he did it was usually at night, over the town. He didn't want anyone to think he was a freak that could fly already, nor deal with the questions that would generate. Most kids in his grade wouldn't be flying until senior year, so Grady kept it to himself.

***

After school, Grady stepped off the bus, followed by Bebe. He smiled and waved to her, and she did the same, before heading in their opposite directions. Grady took his time walking home, manifesting enough energy to kick some rocks along the side of the road. He didn't notice when it started raining, since he couldn't get wet any longer. A car sped past him, kicking up mud and a splash from a puddle, which passed right through him. Grady didn't notice that, either.

At home, Grady threw his bookbag on the kitchen table, and his mom turned from the stovetop, with a jump. "I didn't even hear you come in, you scared me half to death!"

His mom was wearing a black t-shirt, ripped jeans, and had streaks of green in her hair. Grady didn't remember any streaks in her hair when she tucked him into bed the night before. She was listening to music, as usual, with a record spinning on her vintage turntable.

"Sorry, Mom," he said, sheepishly, sitting down and taking out his homework.

"Well no, silly, that's a good thing, right? You're getting good at haunting," she smiled, giving him a kiss on the forehead.

"Mom, I'm a teenager now. You can't give me kisses like that," he said. He felt the familiar heat in his cheeks from embarrassment, but because he was no longer among the living, there was no redness to his face.

"And *you* can also *not* manifest when I do it. So if you don't want to kiss your dear old mother, you can just let me pass through you next time," she said, teasing him. "How much homework do you have?"

"Not much, just an outline for an essay on *The Amityville Horror*," he said. "I have to talk about the techniques the ghosts used to get the family out of the house and decide if they were effective or not."

"Well, obviously they *were* effective, right? They got them out of the house. Seems easy enough," his mom said, cutting carrots and dropping them into a large pot.

"I suppose," Grady said, reading his textbook, the cover of which depicted a graveyard with a transparent hand emerging from the dirt. Grady gestured to her hair. "New color?"

She smiled, "Yeah, I wanted to try green this time. You like?"

Grady nodded.

"Well, we're having stew tonight, my little spooky-boy. Should be ready by the time you're done outlining." She finished with the carrot and moved onto a potato.

"Moooommmm," Grady groaned. He hated being called her "little spooky-boy."

"Sorry," she said, smiling.

***

Dinner was delicious. Grady scarfed down two bowls of stew, and even had room for an ice cream sandwich. Rather, he *always* had room since he never felt hunger. *At least I can still taste things*, he mused, chomping down on the ice cream sandwich. A banner night, as far as dinner was concerned.

Grady reviewed his essay outline. *This is too easy*, he thought, analyzing his reasoning for why the haunting in Amityville had been a rousing success. *They even got the dog to run out of the house. This is expert haunting.*

Once finished, Grady turned on his television and grabbed a videotape from his mom's vintage VHS collection. He settled on an old favorite—*The Changeling*. A creepy story about a child ghost, like him, haunting a huge mansion, Grady perfected the scares from that movie early in his afterlife as a ghost. Banging on the walls of a bathtub? *Check.* Tossing a red rubber ball down the steps? *Check.* Projecting his voice out into the halls of a house, causing it to echo and sound super-creepy? *Double check.*

Grady watched the entire movie, and by the time it was over, he wanted to practice his technique a bit. He opened his bedroom window and floated out into the night sky. Moonlight passed through his body, and he swung by his mom's window, just to make sure she was asleep.

Once outside her window, he peeked in and saw her head to the side, glasses hanging off her face, and a copy of John Langan's *The Fisherman* resting on her chest. Grady was glad she was asleep. She worked hard. Losing him was difficult for her. Finding him again, more so. She thought she was going crazy when he manifested to her the first time. Grady thought she might have a heart attack. They warned him about that at school.

Grady soared above the clouds, soaking in the moonlight. The town below looked beautiful. Some folks sat outside around bonfires, some on their back porches. He'd peek through windows, spotting folks in their homes, watching television. Grady didn't like haunting the neighbors much, but he realized he'd have to settle on someone eventually if he was going to exercise his abilities.

"Revealing one's self to the living for the first time is a terrifying ordeal, Grady, you must be cautious," his teacher, Dr. Aickman told him.

It was almost like Grady hadn't died in the accident.

His mom was uninjured, thankfully, and it was the other driver's fault. Returning to her and helping mend her broken heart was the first thing on Grady's mind once he learned he was able to reveal himself to the living.

He continued floating through his neighborhood, spying on his neighbors. Eventually, he found his usual haunting spot. He felt bad about always settling on this one house, but in the end, he knew deep down why. Inside was Richie Bachman, the bully who used to shoulder-check Grady in the hallways of the middle school he went to when he was still alive. He also pantsed Peter Saul during his report on *The First Amendment*. Richie was a first-class bully with a capital "B."

Smiling to himself, Grady floated through the wall and walked around Richie's bedroom. The kid had good taste. Lots of Justice League stuff on the walls, and a huge fish tank that, instead of fish, held turtles. Richie was snoring in bed, probably dreaming of being a terror to the kids in his school, and Grady wondered what to do to scare him.

In the past, Grady would throw books around the room, turn the television on and off, hide the cell phone, and perform other mischievous tricks. One time, Grady conjured enough energy to produce ectoplasm, something most ghosts aren't able to do until tenth grade, and essentially glued Richie's clothes to the ceiling.

Grady paced around Richie's room, trying to think of a good way to terrify his former tormentor. Eventually, he looked at the turtles. *Wish I had turtles*, Grady thought, tapping the glass lightly. Then it hit him. *That's it!*

Slowly, Grady reached into the tank and pulled the turtles out, one by one. There were three smaller turtles, easily liftable with a single hand, and big one. Grady would've named it "Monstro" or "Godzilla" or something cool like that. He imagined Richie named it "Gary" or something stupid. The big one required two hands to lift, and Grady placed it, along with the others, right on Richie's chest.

Grady waited as the humongous turtle moved a little bit on the boy's slowly rising chest. Eventually, Richie began to stir. Grady froze and watched carefully.

Richie's eyes fluttered at first, and after rubbing them, he looked down at his chest. Face-to-face with the enormous turtle, the boy's eyes went wide and he screamed louder than anything Grady had ever heard before. He also noted the pitch of Richie's scream was alarmingly high, which made Grady crack up. Richie could easily star in any number of horror movies as a scream queen with a bellow like that.

Grady laughed loudly and made sure his laugh could be heard by Richie, who immediately burst into tears. He flailed around in bed with complete disregard for the turtles. Grady caught them in mid-air using his telekinesis skill. He floated the turtles around the room, using additional tricks to make the turtles do a variety of aerial maneuvers like barrel rolls and figure eights.

Grady carefully placed the little ones back in their tank, but held onto the big one, flying it at Richie's face as he cowered in bed. Richie continued to scream, and Grady could hear the boy's parents running down the hallway toward the bedroom and their screaming son.

Grady placed the huge turtle back into the tank and turned back to Richie as his parents opened the door and flipped on the light. Grady noticed an enormous wet spot between Richie's legs. The boy continued to tremor and cry in bed, and Grady felt a pang of guilt for causing him to piss the bed.

Collecting his thoughts, Grady flew through the wall of Richie's bedroom into the night, smiling that he finally made someone pee their pants, even though he still felt a little bad about it. Yet Richie was a bully. He didn't just make Grady's short life a nightmare, he made a bunch of kids' lives at school a nightmare. Reveling in this accomplishment, Grady did numerous barrel rolls in the sky, laughing, and smiling proudly to himself.

Eventually, he floated through his own window and tucked himself into bed, satisfied with the night's work. He wondered if Richie would sleep at all.

Grady wondered if there were ghost pet stores and if they had any turtles he could adopt.

***

The next day was largely the same, minus the late-night terrifying of the neighborhood bully. That morning, at the bus stop, Grady could hardly contain his excitement, and let it slip to Bebe that he made a human lose control of their bladder.

She stared at Grady, her brow furrowed. Then she softened, giggled and said "That's gross, but awesome. You should tell Dr. Aickman!"

"No, no, I wouldn't want to brag, you're the only one I've told," he said, suddenly worried he might get into trouble for his extracurricular activities.

"Well, I'm honored, Grady," she smiled, looking at her shoes. "So, you're pretty good at spookin', huh? Where'd you learn how to do that stuff?"

Grady didn't know which question to answer first, Bebe was always so rapid-fire when talking. "I guess so, and I watch a lot of scary movies."

"Oh my gosh, me too!" she exclaimed, slugging him in the chest. He stepped back a few feet. "Oh! Sorry! What's your favorite movie?"

"It's all good," Grady said, rubbing his chest. "I really like *The Haunting*. It's old. Black and white, but it's really scary. My mom calls it a classic."

"I've never seen that one. I like *The Exorcism of Emily Rose*," she said, excitedly.

Of course she does, it's about lawyers and demons. "I like that movie, too."

"We should hang out and watch one you like sometime," Bebe said.

The bus was coming down the road and rolling up slowly. Loaded with ghouls and other teenage monsters, anyone could hear it coming a mile away. Howls, roars, and shrieks pierced the air as the bus made its way toward Grady and Bebe. A trail of green, spectral smoke plumed behind it, and its wheels floated a few inches *above* the ground.

"For sure," Grady said, watching the bus approach.

"How about Friday night?"

Is this happening? he wondered, amazed. "Uhh, I mean, that should—"

"Oh wait!" she exclaimed, cutting him off. "The dance is Friday, I can't believe I forgot. You're going, right?"

Dance? "Totally, yeah, should be a great time,"

Grady lied. He knew nothing about the dance. He certainly didn't buy a ticket or have a date, so he imagined his Friday night would go as it usually did: scary movie with his mom, pizza, bedtime.

The bus rolled up, and Grady followed Bebe aboard.

Sitting alone, staring out the window of the bus as it rolled down the street, Grady knew that he had to go to the dance. If for nothing else, to see Bebe, talk to her, and maybe, *just maybe*, ask her to dance.

***

School went as it usually did, but Dr. Aickman decided to throw in a pop quiz on spectral manifestation as it relates to ectoplasm. Though it was for extra credit, Grady watched as each of his classmates attempted to conjure the slick, sticky fluid, and failed. Bebe came the closest, but instead of ectoplasm, a thin mist appeared.

"Grady, your turn," Dr. Aickman announced.

Being in front of his classmates always made Grady anxious. He swallowed hard, and even though he had conjured ectoplasm hundreds of times at home, he never did it in school. Certainly not in front of the *whole class*. With relative ease, however, he gestured to Dr. Aickman's desk. The light mist from Bebe's attempt was still drifting among the teacher's various knick-knacks. In a flash of light, the mist scattered and the entire desk was covered in thick, green slime. Dr. Aickman's eyes went wide and the class gasped when they saw Grady's ability on full display. Bebe smiled, blown away by the feat.

Slowly, Dr. Aickman started clapping and the rest of the class joined in. There were even a few howls from the werewolves in the back row.

***

That night, at dinner with his mom, Grady was particularly quiet. He was feeling guilty for buying a ticket to the dance behind his mom's back, knowing that their usual ritual of movies and pizza would take a back seat that week.

"Kiddo, you've barely touched your taco lasagna, what's going on?"

Grady wasn't hungry, but he had loved taco lasagna when he was alive. He was happy not to have to deal with the usual result of racing to the bathroom thirty minutes after eating though.

"I have something to tell you, but I feel bad," Grady said, quietly.

"Did *you* make the Bachman boy piss his pants?"

He looked at her. "Of course not, that's just crazy, how could I?"

"Easy, killer, I'm teasing, I *know* you did that," she said, smiling. "He's a bully, and *sometimes* it's okay for a bully to learn a lesson."

Grady sighed, relieved. "I bought a ticket to the dance on Friday. There's a girl going that I know, and she really likes scary movies, and—I just wanted to go and see her. I'm sorry."

His mom smiled. "Sweetie, don't apologize. I wish you would've told me, I would've given you the money."

"Really? You're not mad?"

"Grady, how could I ever be mad at you? You're the coolest kid I know," she said, with a wink.

"I'm the *only* kid you know," he said, smiling.

"Other than Richie, who pisses himself and talks about floating turtles," she said, stuffing a piece of taco lasagna in her mouth.

***

Friday came. *Doomsday*, he thought. Then, as he went through the school day, he realized *it's not like I can die twice, right? What's the worst that can happen?*

Grady only had his grandfather's suit jacket to wear, and a pair of khakis he wore to weddings and family gatherings. His mom surprised him with a tie that had skulls on it. "To give you some edge," she said. "Girls like edgy boys."

At the dance, Grady was amazed by the decorations, colorful streamers hanging from the ceiling, and a shiny disco ball which seemed to float in the center, casting light around the room.

Students kept asking Grady about his conjuring skills. Grady indulged them, telling them how he approached it, and offered to show them during lunch the following week. Truth be told, the only thing on Grady's mind was Bebe. He looked around the gym, craning his neck to find her.

The eyes of the monsters around him went wide suddenly, and Grady registered why. He had started floating in his search for Bebe. Eventually, he saw her. She looked up at him, smiled, and brushed her gray-blue hair from her face. Grady floated back to the ground, the monsters around him gasping with "Ooohs" and "Ahhhs," amazed by his abilities.

He straightened his tie unnecessarily and walked through the crowd toward Bebe. A million things ran through his mind. Pangs of insecurity, the kind he always felt. She looked lovely, in a floral-patterned dress, a black rose tucked in her hair.

Nervously, he locked eyes with her. "Magic" by

Mick Smiley floated over the sound system. "I love this song," she said, looking at Grady.

Here goes nothin', he thought.

HEEBIE JEEBIES

BY JOHN WOLF

Something clung to the chilly air, something harsh and spiced like the smoke from burning leaves. It might have come from the golden remains of the harvest blown from the turned soil, rich and ripe as graveyard earth. But there was something else. An unseen dry charge lingered, only growing stronger as the reddening sun shrank bit by bit below the horizon like a party guest refusing to leave. It tingled on the nose of every princess, monster, and superhero running out of their homes and into the street. Halloween had come, staking its sugary claim on this special night.

Margie hated it.

"You gonna be alright?" Herb struggled with Ryder's Buzz Lightyear costume.

Margie tried giving a reassuring smile. It seemed to do the trick. Ryder, ready for Space Command, dashed out into the growing evening.

"You two just go have fun." Margie hefted the

candy bowl in her arms. "I won't starve. Go on now."
Hurrying Herb out the door didn't help. It only reminded him.
"Wait a minute. Wait just a minute."
He reached behind the door and fished out the skeleton. CVS had a sale the day before, one Herb declared "Too good to pass up." This particular paper skeleton, a real steal for only five bucks, glowed ghoulish green in the dark and came with crazy googly eyes.
Ryder had approved. "Cool!" Between him and Herb there was no negotiation. Never mind how Margie's heart fluttered and stomach turned at the sight.
"Lemme just," Herb muttered to no one in particular while he fiddled with the tape. "There." He stood back to admire the handiwork. A cool breeze rustled down Ohio Street and sent the skeleton into a demented jig, eyeballs waggling on tissue paper optic nerves, bony mouth grinning at the street.
If anything, the single skeleton was a welcome de-escalation. There was always one decoration. Margie Roberts would never let herself be deemed a sourpuss or party-pooper. A few years back, there was a cemetery of plastic gravestones. Last year, a fog machine and spooky sounds CD. The porchlight stayed off every year, fat load of good that did. Children could sniff out a candy bowl blocks away. Margie thought it must be instinctual, like geese flying south for the winter.
"Grandpa!" Ryder called from the sidewalk. Witches, no more than third grade height, ran past him. "It's starting!"

Herb zipped up his jacket, patted the front pocket. "Got my phone." That was hardly a comfort. Herb still hadn't quite figured out how to work the darn thing. Even with the bigger buttons.

"Go on," Margie urged, "bring me home a Caramel Apple!" Her laughter cracked like peanut brittle, and she couldn't ignore the worried face Ryder wore. It said it all:

Grandma was weird.

Herb always tried to make light of it, called it her "Heebie Jeebies." It had another name before they married: Nerves. Doctor Ramsey had a more formal name; something somebody could scratch onto a prescription pad: "General Anxiety Disorder."

The knob shook a little as she closed the door. Then it was just Margie, her candy, and the whiteboard on the entryway table. On the plain white surface were columns for "Homemade" and "Store-bought." Neither Margie nor Herb had decided on stakes, but Herb thought it might be something fun to pass the time.

Margie knew he really meant, "Keep the nervous wife occupied." Herb already had one point for Store-bought. Margie didn't think that was very fair, him buying Ryder's costume and all, but she let it slide. It wouldn't be such a bad idea to keep score and worry less about being alone.

She thought of those witches: lumpy, green faces, pointy hats, and flowing cloaks. One cloak sparkled with sequined moons and stars. On the other, a black cat's glowing, green eyes. No way those came from CVS.

"Ha!" She quickly slashed two points beneath

Homemade. Now the evening could get interesting. Margie looked at the clock. A measly five minutes had passed. Worry quickly gnawed at her backbone again. Cocoa.

She took the steaming mug from the coffee table and took an eager sip. The sweetness pushed away any and all trouble like a magic spell. Cold, lonely weather was never a problem so long as Margie had a working stove, cocoa powder, and milk. She took another sip, breathed. The clock chimed half past five. It always ran slow no matter how carefully Herb wound it. Running slow wasn't the problem.

It will be fine, she told herself. *It will all be fine.* Herb and Ryder would soon be past Ohio, down Broad Street, and at the Fun Fair. They'd trick-or-treat, laugh, win a few prizes, bob for apples even. Laughing too much and moving too fast to think about their kooky old lady back home.

The doorbell rang. Margie started, spilling some of her drink. She stood there, sucking on her finger and struggling to decide what best got cocoa stains out of carpet.

The doorbell rang again. Margie put down her mug on the entryway table and picked up the candy bowl. Mountains of Whatchamacallits, Hershey bars, and others crinkled in their wrappers. One more breath to steady her hands, and she opened the door.

Margie choked on her scream. The peeling face on her doorstep oozed fluids nearly every color in the rainbow while a single, fat gray worm wriggled out from one punctured socket. The other held a ruined, jellied eye glowing like a dying coal within the bony face.

Princess Elsa and the zombie held up their pillowcases and sang, "Trick-or-treeeeat!"

"Oh," was all Margie could say. The children held their cases up a little higher. They had started early. The pillowcases already bulged with an entire treasure trove of candy.

"Oh," Margie said again and plunged her free hand into the candy bowl. A good fistful of candy went into Elsa's bag, and then another for the zombie.

They sang out again, "Thank you, Mrs. Roberts!"

The zombie lifted his mask. A wide, living grin spread across his face. He lisped between incoming adult teeth, "Ith juth a mathk, Mithuth Roberth! We made it in clath!"

"Yes," she replied. Margie was surprised by her even tone, especially with her heart hammering in her chest. "Very nice, Jake. Go catch your sister now." Jake Talbot whirled to find Elsa halfway down the sidewalk, spinning around and belting out verses of "Let It Go."

"Crap! Bye, Mithuth Roberth!"

Margie slammed the door shut. The wind howled against it, sending Herb's paper skeleton into another horrid dance. She plucked out a Jolly Rancher and puckered up at the sour taste. She wished she hadn't requested a caramel apple. Even if Ryder remembered through the sugar high, it wasn't like Margie's teeth could really take that kind of punishment. It really wasn't fair. Kids and grown-ups seemed to always get such a big kick out of Halloween. The kids with their candy, the adults laughing and hollering at parties.

Only, Margie never liked dressing up to scare people, and having company over as an adult just stressed her to the breaking point. She could have candy whenever she wanted, why did the rest of the town have to lose its mind for twenty-four hours?

Margie set the candy bowl down and breathed. It was all just a stupid holiday. A stupid, stupid holiday! But there was the scoreboard to think about. Sure, Elsa had come straight from Target or Walmart. Margie gave a point to Store-bought. Jake's mask had really been something. Just what was Miss Lyman teaching them in art class? Margie slashed a point beneath Homemade. Still in the lead. Margie helped herself to a celebratory sip of cocoa.

***

Wind whistled a pitiful tune as the clock kept time. The paper skeleton found the beat and boogied. Every time its limbs scratched and scrabbled at the door, Margie thought of giant spiders, hands caked in grave dirt, or other abominations.

She turned up the volume on *Seinfeld*. The clock kept ticking. She finished her cocoa, got up for a refill, and suddenly remembered the cherry brandy tucked away above the fridge. When had they last opened it? The big storm last summer? Or getting snowed in that one winter?

It didn't matter. Margie decided a little zip in her Halloween treat was better than a caramel apple or Jolly Rancher. It was a long reach to the top of the fridge, and Margie thought she really ought to use a footstool instead of going on tiptoe. While fumbling around for the brandy and thinking of footstools, an oil-black shape slithered across the glass face of a nearby cabinet.

Margie spun, thin hand on her chest, and stared out

into the living room. The brandy momentarily forgotten, her mind raced with possibilities: an intruder, Satanists, burglars, kids with an armory of toilet paper. The living room beyond the breakfast nook remained empty.

Something outside, probably. Definitely. All the doors and windows were locked. How could it be anything inside? It had to be outside. What was outside? A leaf probably, there were tons blowing around. It was autumn!

No, it was Halloween when all kinds of things bumped in the night. Fine, so it was some bratty kid having fun scaring an old woman half-to-death. Maybe it was Ryder? No, they'd never come home early.

Audience laughter boomed off the living room walls, echoing throughout the house, mocking Margie. Just a big old scaredy cat. Couldn't take a trick, couldn't ever have fun. A family passed on the sidewalk, clearly visible through the large living room window. A now much too big and far too fragile living room window.

She went to it, flicking on every single light switch she passed. She didn't care if the electric bill shot a hole through the roof. She imagined each cluster of swirling shadows dropping dead with a flick of the switch. The lights would probably draw more trick-or-treaters, but that was fine. Suddenly, Margie could do with a little company. It might even help her score a few more points on the costume board.

The shape flashed by the living room window again. Margie yelped and ducked back from the glass. She raised her hands in defense and only struck cold window. The pull cord felt slick in her sweaty hands, but she finally yanked it back and Halloween night vanished from view.

Should have gone with them, should have gone with, Margie thought over and over in time with her buzzing heart. With the blinds down she could breathe a little better. Now it seemed entirely possible she hadn't really seen screeching monsters intent on devouring her whole fly by her window. It now seemed plausible it was just another family going by, or an overexcited trick-or-treater rushing across her lawn. But whatever was outside had been dark. Darker than night, swifter than any third grader hopped up on sugar.

That settled it. No more trick-or-treaters tonight no matter how much they pounded on the door. Margie would only open it for Herb and Ryder. Those two wouldn't mind the candy surplus. The three of them could live off of Dots and Mr. Goodbars till the sun came up on November when the world made a little more sense.

Seinfeld gave way to *Wheel of Fortune* where Pat and Vanna were ready to help the contestants win Spooktacular prizes. Margie clicked off the television on her way back to the kitchen. The lukewarm chocolate still lacked for an adult beverage. A little of that to calm her nerves, maybe a little phone chat to pass the time, and Margie could relax.

Only without the television's racket, the *scritch scratch* of paper skeleton arms crawled right inside Margie's ears. It sounded as loud as Mr. Dickinson's marching band. She decided next year it would be only jack-o-lanterns. Herb could fight her all he wanted, but Margie would put her foot down. And that horrid little thing hanging on her door tonight? Straight. In. The.

Trash.

Margie let her mind wander to sadistic thoughts as she went to open the door. Maybe the skeleton would fit in her paper shredder. Maybe it was safe to burn. She opened the door and a screeching piece of the night sky came alive and flew at her face. There wasn't time to be scared or scream. The best Margie could do was let out a strangled, "What?"

She caught the candy bowl on her way down, rear end and bowl connecting with the tiled floor at the same time. The bowl wobbled crazily for a few seconds, then went silent and still as the grave.

Margie kicked the door shut with her legs and turned her back to it. Her eyes danced from one living room corner to the next. All she saw was eggshell white paint and a startling amount of dust bunnies. There weren't many hiding places left with almost every light in the house blazing. What shadows remained crawled to life. Margie watched through wide eyes as the dark patch beneath Herb's easy chair writhed across the carpet on thousands of smooth, shiny legs. The meager bits of shadow lurking in the fireplace dangled and swung from the ashy bricks like tentacles.

Then just like that, Margie couldn't breathe. Simple as someone flipping a switch in her lungs from "ON" to "OFF." Margie gasped, dry tongue heavy as lead in her mouth. White dots grew over her vision. It didn't matter if what she saw wasn't real. She couldn't afford to think that way. She couldn't understand how it could be so cold inside while pools of sweat formed in her armpits.

Doctor Ramsey's voice came to her: *"This is just*

fight-or-flight dialed up to 11. Fight-or-flight. Nothing wrong with your nerves. 'Nerves' isn't a real condition. You just need to breath. Breathe. Count. Count. Breathe."

God, she could kill Ramsey. A jury of her peers couldn't possibly convict.

Margie finally caught a stray gasp of air, clutched it and held on for dear life. She counted, turning the release and intake of air back into a regular rhythm. At least that worked. It didn't change her feelings on Ramsey though, or chase away the raw panic carving a ragged hole in her chest.

What the heck had flown in? What had she let into her house?

Those creepy bits of living shadow still lurked in the corner of Margie's vision. She didn't dare close her eyes and wish them away, not if there was a real something lurking in her house. But she could look up at the ceiling. Her perfectly average, off-white ceiling with a black, quivering square folded up into one corner.

Now Margie screamed.

The bat screamed too. It wasn't much, but it let loose all the same. Its fuzzy head unsheathed from beneath rubbery wings and frantically scanned the room. Jittering, black eyes landed on Margie. Her hand shot up to her mouth and capped any more noise. They waited there, Margie and her evening caller, just the two of them in a staring contest. Margie kept staring and reached back over her shoulder for the door knob.

It all played perfectly in her mind: Open the door, shoo out the little bugger, let it fly, fly, fly far away from her house. If it didn't Margie would fly, fly, fly far away across the street. Let Herb find her at the neighbor's.

Margie sang under her breath, "Shoo bat, don't bother me, shoo bat, don't bother me, smelly, smelly rat don't—"

The bat dove off the ceiling and swooped overhead, a flurry of bristly hair and wings. Margie met floor and scrambled back towards the kitchen. Halfway to the living room carpet, she turned and crab walked till she hit the opposite wall. There would certainly be a goose egg on the back of her head tomorrow.

Some of the neighbors teased Margie and Herb for keeping a rotary dial. Margie didn't know what a hipster was and she certainly didn't care. All she cared about was the way her shaking fingers fit into each wheel, allowing her to smoothly dial Herb's number. She could dial it from memory. That was one thing old age hadn't begun its assault on.

Her eyes never left the bat. It perched atop the doorframe like a living gargoyle. Every second number or so her finger dialed, it would stick a tiny pink tongue out from between jagged fangs and hiss. The thought of hurling the phone at the bat had some appeal. But common sense asked Margie, how would she make a call?

Finally, Herb picked up.

"Hello?" Along with Herb came cartoony howls and moans from the Fun Fair's haunted house. He shouted again, "Hello?" Someone or something on the other end screamed in fear or delight. Margie could spit.

"Herb!" She rasped, "You need to come home. Right. Now!"

The connection cleared a little as Herb put some

distance between himself and the Halloween hijinks.

"Margie? What's wrong?"

The bat hissed again.

"Herb! Come home now!"

"What happened? Are you alright?"

"A... bat." She choked out the last word. The plastic handset crackled in Margie's grasp. "A bat got in the house. Come get rid of it!"

The next laugh wasn't from a school spook house or excited kid. That it came from Herb hurt more than the back of Margie's bruised head. The sounds of good-natured ghouls, ghosts, and monsters grew over the phone.

"Is it trying to bite?"

Margie's brain nearly short-circuited with irritation while Herb went on:

"It's probably just as spooked as you are, hon. Leave the door open and I'm sure it'll leave. Probably."

"It's right over the door," she meant to say but all that came back was an angry croak.

"Gotta go, Margie. I don't want to lose Ryder in all this. Home soon!"

The click echoed over anything else. The bat bobbed its head up and down, cackling from its safe perch above the door as the old lady cowered in the corner of her own house on Halloween Night.

Cold tingled around Margie. Solid, ugly, cold rage. Her back stopped aching. She forgot all about the goose egg on her head. The bat's beady eyes met hers again, only this time Margie met them with a scowl. She laid the phone back in its cradle like it really was the antique the neighbors teased her for. The mug of hot chocolate next to it had grown cold as Margie. This observation only threw more kindling on the strange, icy flames billowing up inside of her.

"You," she finally spat out from behind her teeth. The bat quit bobbing and laughing. It crawled a little further up the wall, putting just a little more distance between them. As if afraid. Margie smiled, really smiled, for the first time that evening. The bat's puckered snout drew back for a full reveal of its needled teeth and wicked fangs. Margie kept smiling.

If Herb wouldn't be back anytime soon, then what? Margie Roberts didn't enjoy Halloween, but liked crouching helpless in a corner even less. Her heartbeat rose with her.

"You just get out."

The bat cocked its head from side-to-side. Good. Maybe it could understand.

"You little stinker." Margie moved forward till her aching knees struck the coffee table. She walked past it and the up-ended candy bowl, willing each step closer and closer to the door. The bat never left her sight. Another few steps. Then her feet touched the tile floor of the entryway. Just another few steps. One hand crept out and slowly came to rest just over the door knob. The bat still studied her with its unblinking, black gaze.

So close to the door knob, but Margie's hand refused to come down on it. The cold metal repelled her like a magnet. Margie tried breathing and counting again, tried looking away from the bat, tried inner criticism.

"Come on, just do it, you wiener."

In the end, another of the bat's jeering hisses did it. Margie glanced back up, grit her teeth, and slapped her hand down. The bat responded by unfurling its wings, filling the white wall like a bank of monstrous thunderheads. Only this time, Margie didn't scream. She backed away and launched her mug before common sense could intervene. The crash of ceramic against wood and splatter of cocoa did better than any exercise Doctor Ramsey could come up with.

The thought of the future mess never even registered. Or the fact that she missed her target by a mile. There was little time for that. Margie's nighttime caller flew overhead and made a beeline straight for the kitchen. Tiny claws ran ragged trails across wood cabinets. Muted thuds and crashing glassware came soon after. The little bat was still having a grand old time on Halloween night.

Margie kicked the candy bowl again. She dived, surprising even herself with her speed and flexibility. Maybe those yoga classes really did help. Shiny tin foil wrappers and cardboard boxes were crushed underfoot. The crunch of breaking Heath Bars and Butterfingers was like heaven. It made Margie think of snapping bones. The bat screeched out in delight from the kitchen. Margie answered with a howl of rage and charged towards the kitchen, empty bowl in front of her like a shield.

A vase lay tipped over and cracked on the kitchen counter, dripping stagnant water onto the floor. The cabinets, shined and polished for company, now bore crazy zigzags of claw marks. Torn open cocoa packets lay scattered on the counter like miniature body bags. Tiny chocolate-dusted tracks led to the fridge. Margie went hunting.

"Come on," she cooed and rapped her knuckles against the bowl. The hollow *GONG* echoed over the

ticking clock, the spooky wind, everything.
"Come on."
GONG.
"Come on."
GONG.
Something rustled in the cabinet atop the fridge. The door up there hung open just a crack. Had she forgotten that? Margie raised her candy bowl and readied to pounce. The cabinet door creaked and she leapt back. The red cap of the brandy bottle appeared, and then, bit by bit, the fuzzy head crawled into view.
"Get down from there!"
The bat obliged. But this time Margie was ready. The bowl let out another GONG as the bat collided inside it. Margie had no time to celebrate. She rushed the bowl straight into the wall. No satisfying crunch of bone, no horrific squeal of pain. The bat had wisely tucked inside and remained safe from impact. It sure wasn't having fun anymore. Claws scraping on metal made Margie's skin break out into gooseflesh. She looked to the nearby mudroom door and suddenly the plan became so simple.
"Fly around in there all you want." She held the bowl firm against the wall and drug it across to the door. Herb had planned on using the dim, concrete mudroom as a workshop. If by work he meant store boxes and dust, it was a home-run success. It also made a fine cage.
Margie flung the bowl and its contents into the mudroom and slammed the door shut.
"Keep it!"
And like that, it seemed she was cured of Heebie Jeebies or "Nerves" or whatever Ramsey felt like

calling it. She thought that was a pretty great deal. No pills, no classes, just an arrogant, flying rat laying siege to your house and flung into the mudroom. Boom! Problem solved.

Margie leaned against the fridge door and gave silent thanks for the cool surface. It felt so good, she barely heard the bat's angry squeaks or rustle and thud of falling boxes.

"Fly around in there all night, fella." Margie reached up on tiptoe and found the brandy without looking. The bottle's contents lapped against the cap like breakers on the lake. Her first swig went down easy as water. A shiver of a completely different kind swung through her on the second one. She slid down the wall and kept sliding till rear end hit floor. On the third swig, Margie finally understood why she and Herb had kept the same bottle of booze in nearly the same place since moving in almost twenty-five years ago. The stuff tasted less like brandy and more like cherry-tainted motor oil. By the fourth, it wasn't so bad.

It did nothing to make the messy kitchen disappear though. As dread left her body, weariness crawled in. Herb and Ryder would think she'd gone mad nuts. The squeaks faded away behind the door. Margie shut her eyes.

They sprang back open as the mudroom door shook with a dreadful impact. Then a wild series of blows followed, like someone throwing baseballs one after another. The bat's squeaks of protest rose over the thuds, and kept rising till they reached a high-pitched wail. Margie wailed back and ran for the front door, catching a shard of broken mug on her heel.

The merry chimes of the doorbell sang out before

Margie could clear the living room. The chimes put an end to the chaos in the mudroom and Margie's near heart attack. Someone else was finally here. Herb and Ryder back already maybe. A lost trick-or-treater. The darn census taker. Margie didn't care, so long as she could get help from a real live flesh and blood person. Someone else could deal with all the crazy nonsense happening tonight.

The doorbell rang again. The strange cries from the mudroom door came with them.

"Coming!" Margie limped to the door. "Please wait!"

She hoped there was at least one adult on her doorstep. God only knew how a bunch of little kids would react to a bleeding, limping woman swinging open the door.

"Good evening," the man answered.

"Oh my!" The woman extended a manicured hand to Margie's shoulder. "You look awful!"

Margie took the observation and hand without a moment's resistance. She did not shake, only let her hand rest in the woman's like a piece of roadkill. The woman's ruby lips twitched and gave a try at smiling. The man did about as well as the woman.

"Are you alright, ma'am?" That at least sounded sincere coming from him.

Margie cleared her throat and gave a strangled clicking sound instead of words.

The man quickly added, "May we come in?"

The "yes" that finally escaped Margie was meant for the man's first question, but did for the second one as well. A real two-for-one like at CVS. The woman pointed one long, black fingernail at the skeleton as she

passed through the doorway.
"Spooky!" She laughed, "Oh, I love it!" She quit laughing when one of her high-heels speared a Heath bar. "Oh dear!"
"It, it..." Margie slowed. The clock counted for her. Once. Twice. Then the events of the night poured out in a mad rush. She ended the story by leading the man and woman to the mudroom door.
"I locked it in here."
The man held up a slender hand. "Yes, we know."
"Huh?"
Something heavy crashed onto the mudroom floor. Margie jumped, clutching her shirt with white knuckles. The woman patted her shoulder, gave it a strong, gentle squeeze.
"It's alright, ma'am. It's alright. We will have a talk with him."
Before Margie could muster another mighty "huh" or ask who or what, the woman pounded on the mudroom door.
"Toby!" The cries stopped as soon as she spoke. "Tobias Matheson! Are you decent?"
She rolled her eyes with impatience as feet shuffled on the concrete floor.
Margie's injured foot throbbed while her mind spun and spun. She wasn't really sure which bothered her more. The man offered her a jelly glass of water. Margie took it and immediately discovered it was not water, but instead more brandy. On the rocks even. The ice did little to help the taste, but the brandy did wonders for her spinning head.
"Tobias." The man joined the woman by the door. Side-by side again, they reminded Margie a little of the

American Gothic family.

"You've done quite enough, son. Come now." A whimper came from beyond the door. The man continued: "No, we're not mad. Your mother and I were just scared. You scared this nice lady too." The last word came out as a placating, "Toooooo." It did the trick.

The door opened a crack. Wide, dark eyes stared out at them. Then the child stepped into full view. He shivered before them despite his thick, black sweater and trousers. Margie guessed he was no more than six or seven. Just about Ryder's age. Perfect for a little trick-or-treating.

Doctor Ramsey's voice crept back in, telling Margie to *breathe* and *think logically*. Margie told Doctor Ramsey to shove a sock in it.

"Toby, Toby, Toby," the boy's mother moaned and rocked him back and forth. He climbed into her arms and nestled his head in her neck. "There, there my love," she sang. "Thank goodness you're safe." Her placations faded as she left with her boy.

The man sighed, shrugged at Margie. He looked into the mudroom and sighed again.

"His first Halloween." The man shook his head, ran a hand through his dark hair. "We never counted on the sugar rush! Goodness gracious!"

Margie's stomach turned at the man's wide, red grin and too-white teeth. It was like he had chomped down on a big pair of wax candy lips. He placed a chilly hand into the small of Margie's back and led her into the living room.

"All we wanted was a nice night out." Margie wasn't so shocked at the man's hairy palms or overly long ring finger. It even had black nails too.

Margie glanced out the door into the front yard. Toby's feet, and the rest of him, hovered just off the ground. The evening mist swirled in little pools beneath him. His mother tugged on one arm of his sweater.

"Come down! People might see!" That sugar rush really was something.

The man smiled wider still and orange streetlight glittered off twin sets of curved canines.

"Holy. Shit." Margie said before fainting onto a pile of spilled candy.

***

"Shh, let's go unpack it in the kitchen."

The words passed through a tangle of poisonous cobwebs thrumming in Margie's skull.

Oh God, I have a hangover. At 72.

There was a true holiday miracle. The back of Margie's throat was slick with cherry aftertaste and her tongue felt like it needed a good shave. She groaned and creaked open one eye and then the other.

Herb came to the recliner and took her hand. "You alright, hon?" She tried to nod. "Can I get you something?"

"Coffee." The word escaped her in a growl. Herb hustled back to the kitchen quick as a nurse in the ICU. Ryder stood nearby. His plastic pumpkin wore a crown of candy, another successful Halloween night.

"Watch out for broken glass," Margie croaked without thinking. Then it all came back. The bat flying. The American Gothic couple. Toby. Fangs. Each memory more harsh than the last.

"Herb! Herb!"

It hadn't been a dream. It couldn't be. The instant Margie's heel touched the floor, a warm jet of pain traveled up her leg. Only, the bloody sock was gone, replaced with clean slippers. Tight bandages secured her injured foot.

"What glass, Grandma?" Ryder's Space Command boots stood on unblemished tile.

"What you hollering about?" Herb returned from the kitchen, two mugs of coffee in hand. Margie took the offered one, hoping the bitter warmth could shock her back to reality and was soon disappointed. She went back to the living room window and tried not to limp. Something fluttered down as Margie lifted the blinds, and for a single instant the bat was back. The bat that could be a boy if it wanted. A boy with sharp teeth, pale skin, and nothing on his mind tonight but tricks and treats. Like a million other children out there in the world tonight. Mostly like them anyway.

Then it was just a fluttering piece of folded paper again.

"See you took care of the bat, huh?" Coffee delivered and job done, Herb wandered back into the kitchen. "Where's the brandy, darling?"

Margie ignored him and unfolded the paper. It wasn't any kind she or Herb kept around the house. A rich, dense cream-colored parchment. No one putting a grocery list on this. The blue cursive embedded in the paper was just as fancy.

Ma'am,

My family and I, Tobias in particular, extend our deepest apologies. We try to teach him our days of home invasions and other such deeds are things of the past, but children can be so difficult. As further apology, we have mended what

mess our son made. Any irreparable damages will be paid for in full. However, I must insist that you in return keep this unpleasant business to yourself. Privacy is very important to our family. Rest assured, we will not trouble you again. I expect you to extend us the same courtesy.
Gratefully yours,
D.

"What is it, Grandma?" Ryder's face turned the color of off-cheese. Margie bet she resembled a similar shade.

She tucked the note away in her back pocket. "Trick-or-treaters, sweetie."

Later, Margie would cuddle with her grandson beneath blankets and watch *Frankenstein* and *Dracula* back-to-back. They didn't seem so scary anymore. Before the movie marathon though, Margie took down that silly skeleton. She was through with both tricks and treats for another year. She also locked the doors and windows, double checking for good measure. Then there was only one last thing to do before settling in to wait for November's first light.

Margie took the marker and added three blood-red slashes beneath Homemade.

JIANGSHI

BY JUDITH BARON

Ming was exhausted after spending eighteen hours on the plane. It had been one bus ride after another since; at times, he felt like he was doomed to travel forever but never arrive at his destination—his grandmother's home in northern China. He parked his suitcase at the bus stop, and waited for the last bus of the night.

The bus came five minutes late; it was empty except for the driver and a uniformed conductor. The conductor approached Ming to ask where he was going, and collected a pro-rated fare from him before issuing a ticket.

Ming sat down at the back of the bus. He was dozing off when an old woman boarded and sat right next to him. *Why, of all the seats, did she choose to sit next to me?* he thought. He hated it when people did that in theaters, and hated it on the bus even more. The road was bumpy and the bus was going a bit too fast, so he decided to wait till the next stop to change seats.

The next stop came, and he quickly moved and sat down in the middle of the bus close to the doors. He looked at the window to his left to steal a glance at the reflection of the old woman, wondering if his move had angered her. He rubbed his eyes to check again. The woman did not appear on the glass, yet when he looked at the window, he found his reflection right away. *Did she move?* He turned around to look. She was still there, but somehow her reflection did not register on the window.

Before he had a chance to think what this meant, two men with muddy clothes boarded the bus and sat down three rows behind him.

The bus moved; strangely enough, the conductor never came to collect fare from the old woman or the two muddy men. *Why?* Ming wondered. He looked over at the two men, and then at the window next to them, checking their reflections on the glass.

There were none.

A chill went down his back. He could see his own reflection on both sides of the windows, but the woman and the two men simply weren't there.

He took out his phone and searched the internet. He vaguely remembered a long-standing practice of some routes running one last bus of the night meant for the dead. He searched for his bus route, time and number; his heart skipped a few beats when he read that his bus was one of them.

Ten more minutes to go. He wondered if he should get off now and walk twenty minutes to the village or take his chances on the bus. Neither the driver nor the conductor seemed able to see these entities. The driver was pausing at every stop even though there was no one waiting. Ming wondered if this was just routine for the last bus of the night not meant for the living.

He fidgeted in his seat, holding the handle of his suitcase, his limbs loaded with tension in case he needed to move quickly. He didn't know what he was facing. To his relief, no one else boarded the bus after the two men. Still, it would be three against one, if it came to that; he wasn't counting on the conductor to come to his aid.

He looked over his shoulder; the old woman had moved one row closer. His nerves jumped to the next level. When he looked a second time, all three were sitting right behind him.

He scurried to get off at the next stop, nearly tripping and falling from the steps on his way down. As the bus drove off, the three entities stared at him from inside the bus. *Jesus!* he thought. At least they didn't follow him.

He looked at the dirt road in the dark and grimaced. *Now what?*

***

Ming looked at the map on his phone; it would still take him fifteen minutes to walk to the village since he exited the bus early. It was cold; he could see his breath shoot out in front of him like white puffs in the moonlight. He missed his home in New York already. He dragged his suitcase as he walked and looked ahead at the faint outline of a village in the distance.

His eyes came to rest on a hazy green image just up ahead. It was getting closer as he walked on, obviously approaching him. It was bopping up and down, coming toward him at a rhythmic pace. He strained to see clearly, and thought it looked like a green orb bouncing in the air. He could hear a series of metronomic stomping noises along with the movement too. He used his phone as a flashlight to try to further illuminate the orb.

A man in drab clothing was hopping stiffly toward him with his arms outstretched. Ming focused the light on the man's greenish-gray face, and he didn't even flinch. He just kept on hopping. Hopping directly toward Ming.

Old memories surfaced in Ming's mind. The hopping figure reminded him of the old jiangshi movies he watched when he was a kid. A hopping vampire, the jiangshi was a myth in Chinese culture. *Wasn't it?*

What the hell? Was this some kind of cosplay? Jiangshis were so eighties! He chuckled thinking about those movies. *Maybe they were still popular here?* At any rate, Mind thought it strange that someone had dressed up as a stiff corpse hopping around in the middle of nowhere at this time of the night, and two days before Chinese New Year no less.

The man looked at Ming with glassy white eyes, as if he had cataracts, or was wearing colored contact lenses. He opened his mouth, baring yellow, serrated teeth. *Prosthetics?* His rotten breath, which nearly knocked Ming unconscious, smelled very real though.

"Dude, you need a mint!" Ming said, covering his nose.

Two stiff hands with long, sharp black fingernails grabbed Ming by his arms.

"Hey, don't get physical!" Ming said, trying to shake the stranger's hands off.

The man did not respond, or loosen his grip. Ming's

breath was still steaming outward in the cold, but Ming noticed the odd man was expelling no breath at all. Suddenly, he pulled Ming close.

"Yo! We just met!" Ming said, trying to free himself from the stranger. "Too soon!"

The man did not respond. Instead, he gingerly inched his face close and started sucking from Ming's open mouth. Ming squirmed, but the stranger only tightened his grip; his sharp fingernails dug even deeper, breaking the fabric of Ming's coat and nearly piercing his flesh underneath.

Ming began to get dizzy. *What's happening?* he thought. *Was this a #himtoo moment?* It was beyond a kiss; it was as if the stranger was feeding on Ming's vital life force—his *chi*. The realization hit him hard. This was no ordinary creep; this was a *real* jiangshi.

Ming did the first thing that came to mind, the one trick that worked on these creatures in the movies—he held his breath. The jiangshi immediately loosened its grip on Ming, moving its head left and right as if it were searching for something; its bones crackled with each move it made.

Ming stood very still. The jiangshi stuck its face close to him again, grazing Ming's face. Ming shuddered, but dared not move or breathe. He realized he could not just stand there all night holding his breath. *What to do?*

He racked his brain to think of other counter measures he had seen in the movies. Talisman, rooster's call, adzuki beans, wood from a peach tree, the sound of handbell, black donkey hooves—any of these could thwart a hopping vampire. He couldn't help but dwell on the donkey hooves. As if he would have some with him like a pack of mints.

He did have something similar to a handbell. Thanks to his laziness, he never emptied his suitcase completely after his last trip. A trip to Los Angeles to see Blue Oyster Cult in concert. He quickly unzipped the outer pocket of his suitcase and took out a cowbell. *More cowbell? Gotta have more cowbell!* He laughed through his terror at the thought of the Saturday Night Live skit. He gave it a ring, thrusting his pelvis wildly, doing his best Will Ferrell impression.

The jiangshi froze upon hearing the cowbell. Before Ming could switch to a victory dance, however, the undead creature hopped toward him again.

Oh, come on! Ming lamented. *Did it really have to be a handbell? Wasn't a cowbell close enough?*

He rummaged through his suitcase as fast as he could, holding his breath again. Somewhere inside, he did have one exact item from the list. His fingers clasped around the bag of adzuki beans he had bought for his grandmother, tore it open and poured the contents on the ground.

This should work, he thought. Jiangshis were notorious for their obsessive-compulsive disorders; anything identical in multiples would cause them to stop what they were doing and count. In some legends, he remembered, gold coins would do the trick as well. *But who had those anymore?* The jiangshi looked at the ground, but did not count the small red beans. Most of them had rolled into the grass. It would be hard to find them in daylight, let alone in the dark.

"For fuck's sake!" Ming cursed aloud. *Could anything go right tonight?* He didn't have any of the other ridiculous items he recalled.

He inhaled, and the creature hopped toward him; He held his breath, and the jiangshi kept on looking around him. Ming wondered if perhaps he could continue to do this while moving slowly toward the village. Eventually he would arrive. To test this out, he held his breath on and off, and managed to move a few steps. At this rate, he might reach the village by sunrise, when the rooster crowed. *What a shitty plan!*

The jiangshi hopped toward him, as if sensing his presence again. After feeding on Ming's chi, it seemed as if it had gained some new abilities. *Holding my breath might not work for long*, Ming suddenly thought.

He wondered what else he had in his arsenal? *Wait, I do have "gold" coins!* he realized. He took out the coin-shaped chocolates wrapped in gold foil from his suitcase, scattered them in the middle of the road, and shone his flashlight to make sure the jiangshi saw them. "Tada!" he said, completely optimistic that this time it would work better than his "not handbell" cowbell, or those uncooperative adzuki beans.

The jiangshi bent over to count the coins with some difficulty because it was stiff from rigor mortis. Seizing the opportunity, Ming ran and left his suitcase behind.

***

The twenty chocolate coins did not keep the jiangshi occupied for long. Thirty seconds in, Ming heard that hopping cadence again, though it sounded sparser. *What was going on?* He turned around to look, and was terrified when he saw how big a hop the jiangshi made compared to before; its horizontal leaps had quadrupled, and it could jump three times as high now.

His initial burst of energy—powered by adrenaline—was short-lived as well. He was losing steam from his chi being drained; his head start was shrinking by the second. He would not be able to outrun the hopping corpse for much longer, and it was still another ten minutes before he would reach the village. He had to think fast.

Jiangshis were not invincible, he knew. In fact, they had lots of weaknesses. Right now, it had more energy than he did, but it was inflexible as hell. He had to exploit that weakness if he wanted to survive this strange turn of events.

He turned around, watching the jiangshi hop toward him. It was a big gamble and a little insane, but he thought it might just work. He had no other choice. Sometimes, he realized, you just have to face your problem head on.

"Here I come!" he said aloud, charging toward the hopping vampire with his eyes closed. He was hoping to knock the jiangshi to the side into the ditch, but the jiangshi was in midair when he reached it. Ming ended up going right under it before it landed back on its feet. For a moment, they were back to back against each other.

Shit! Ming fretted, his plan derailed by a miscalculation. He wished he had kept his eyes open, but it was too late now. The jiangshi hopped vertically and rotated around at the same time as Ming. They were face to face now, as if they were in some synchronized dance performance.

Give me a break! This was looking more and more like the jiangshi movies he had watched, except it wasn't funny because the one facing him was the real deal.

The jiangshi made its move and tried to feed on Ming's chi again. Yet this time, Ming reacted quickly enough to strike first. He ducked to avoid that dreadful kiss of death, and headbutted the jiangshi in its stomach. Using all his might, he pushed the jiangshi to the side of the road in one fell swoop.

The stiff corpse fell into the ditch on its back. Like a wind-up toy that had fallen over, it struggled to right itself. Its arms were outstretched upward, but it couldn't hop its way out of the ditch. Not yet, anyway.

Ming burst out laughing; it was the funniest thing he had seen in a long time. He went back and picked up his suitcase and power walked toward the village. He looked back a few times to make sure there was no jiangshi in pursuit.

Five minutes later, he arrived at the village.

***

A familiar figure stood in front of the house where he was heading. Feeling immensely relieved that he finally made it, Ming ran to hug his grandmother.

"I'm sorry I'm so late," Ming said, looking at his watch. "I had to walk a long way."

"You look a fright, dear!" she said, feeling the torn sleeves of his winter jacket. "What happened? Did you miss the bus? Were you robbed?"

"You shouldn't have waited up for me, Grandma," Ming said, checking his arms and feeling relief that the jiangshi hadn't injured him. "Let's get inside!"

There were yellow talismans on the short double doors at the entrance. Ming and his grandmother lowered their heads and climbed over the tall threshold to enter the house.

"You used to trip over the threshold and bang your

head at the top," she said sheepishly.

He looked back at the tall threshold and short doors, and finally understood what they were meant for.

VACATION INTERRUPTUS

BY MYA LAIRIS

While I was gawking at the monstrosity that had just emerged from the ocean, blocking out a perfectly brilliant and unobscured sun, the person next to me was laughing so hard that tears were coming out of his eyes. He was exceedingly animated by that deep-belly cackling that should only be allowed at comedy clubs with way too much cigarette smoke and a fucking two-drink, minimum.

Mind you, the emergence of what looked like an "Old God" on a perfectly sunny day, from the crystal blue waters of the Caribbean Sea, was like an oxymoron within itself. One would expect monstrosities to appear only on days with thunder, lightning, and black skies. Not while I was on vacation in Jamaica and the Jerk Chicken man was less than fifty meters away and headed in my direction. For fuck's sake.

The behemoth could have been easily four hundred

feet tall—possibly taller because he was at least a mile out in the ocean and I had no idea of the depth, so getting an accurate measurement was beyond my abilities. I didn't think it was really an "Old One," partly because I believed that Lovecraft had a hefty imagination, racism-propelled mania notwithstanding as fuel. Still this gigantic anomaly wading in the azure waters was certainly the kind of horror that demanded respect, just not from my companion.

Phalanx—his mother thought highly of her child as well as Greek warfare—was reacting as if the random appearance of the beast was a National Lampoon sketch. He wasn't normally the type prone to humor, yet his olive complexion had taken on a rosy hue and his silver eyes were glittering with tears.

I looked from his rollicking form on the beach chair next to me then back at the imposing organism whose movement caused the calm waters around it to become surf-board worthy, and I had to ask. "What's so damn funny?"

He was still laughing. His tone had gone from raucous to squeaking and onto fits of gasping. "Poseidon. It's fucking Poseidon, Kaylee," he said pointing wildly with the neck of his beer bottle. "Maybe the Kraken. Could be Cthulhu. Could be—"

"Could be 'not the time for this bullshit,' maybe," I interjected, still not getting the humor of the situation.

It... the being that was several hundred feet tall, possessed of many limbs, some tentacles, some claws and a mouth that looked mighty similar to a crab's— replete with several mandibles whose job it could be to shovel food into said mouth—had a dark, bluish, humanoid shape. It had four sets of muscular arms tipped with claws, one of which plucked a freight ship out of the water as easily as a bathing kid might pick up a rubber ducky. While people all around us were screaming, gasping, and chatting furiously about what was happening, Phalanx's comedic responses were a burgeoning irritation.

"Oh fuck," he blurted out before sitting up and taking a swig of his beer. He leaned forward. "I just know they're having a bad day on *that* boat."

"You think?" I offered, imagining how I would have felt as a captain just coming out of port with my goods all loaded up, looking at a bright, clear day on crystal blue waters and then being lifted into the air by a cosmic horror, or an ocean horror, or *whatever* it was. No doubt it could instill madness, but with the way its tentacles swirled around the ship, invading open spaces and pulling out screaming sailors, the madness wouldn't have lasted long.

Not to mention the freighter exploded *before* it was tossed it aside.

Taking deep breaths in order to quell his own laughter, Phalanx placed his empty bottle into the cooler sitting between our two lounge chairs, before retrieving a fresh one. He used the arm of his beach chair to pop off the cap and immediately took two healthy gulps.

"Dumbasses. Just standing there watching," he said, using the neck of the beer to indicate the people far too close to the surf, observing the fate of the boat as if what was before them was a car crash and not a threat to their very existence. "Shit, it's not like they don't have time. I'd be hightailing my ass out of fucking

Dodge if I were them."

I had to agree. It sounded like good advice to me, and apparently to the police officers flooding the beach around us trying to convince people not everything needed to be filmed for YouTube and Instagram. The authorities were valiant, brave, and wise souls, I felt as they yelled, "Get back," "Get Off the beach," and "Get outta here, now!" The captivated spectators' words however consisted of such foolishness as "I'm putting this on my live feed!"

Law enforcement targeted those closest to the surf, yet many of the spectators refused to budge or acknowledge the warnings being yelled their way. *Were they deaf?* I wondered. Then Mountainous Mass of Ocean Terror roared, and even the deaf would have felt the vibrations of that thunderous sound in their bones. I knew I sure as shit did.

Heroics were swiftly thrown to the winds, as even the police began to move back from the angry whitewash of the ocean surf. The hysteria-spurred running didn't really start however until The Beast with No Name tossed the flaming tanker and took a stride—I assumed it had feet but really I had no fucking clue. The rushing waves that came barreling toward the beach were just as inspiring as the shockwaves traveling beneath the sands and bringing most of the now-sprinters to their knees.

I had to move fast to grab my rum punch in a pineapple before it fell over on the little table next to my beach chair. Subsequent shaking occurred but at least my beverage was safe. When I turned back to look at the ocean, the situation was getting worse. I saw what looked to be scales or some type of armor, falling off the giant's body and into the ocean. It didn't take me long to figure out that scales didn't swim, certainly not faster than cigarette boats smuggling coke.

Heaving a sigh of irritation, I scanned the beach and the spectators that were seeing the exact same fuckery I saw. I was not a scientist and didn't know Jack or shit about symbiotic or parasitic life forms but what I did know was that as the *scales* emerged from the ocean and leapt onto fleeing beachgoers (who really should have left so much earlier) was that their intent was not entirely to eat and maim but to immobilize.

Two of the skittering lice-looking creatures started toward me and my companion, churning up puffs of sand with their many feet and glaring at me with dead, black eyes that would have made a Great White envious.

Within five feet of my beach chair, Phalanx put an immediate halt to their progress.

The murder mites froze in mid-scuttle; their every limb locked by his will before they exploded in a shower of greenish blue ichor. Phalanx was still chuckling, non plussed by their failed attempt at attack.

I decided then that I had had enough. Swinging my legs over the side of the beach chair, I finished off my drink and placed it on the mini-table. It fell off as Godfather of the Sea took another step, but I didn't care. It, the mountain of terror and flesh, was now less than a mile away and I could see that it did have legs, many of them, and a tail. With the monolith pressing onward, I realized there was a lot I needed to learn about its biology.

My companion on the other hand had relaxed back

in his chair.

"Um. Are you just gonna lay there?" I asked.

Phalanx's attention moved from his beer bottle to me and surely the look he must have seen on my face killed any remnants of humor he had left. "Hey, I... we're on vacation, remember," he scowled.

I could have used the phrase, "People are dying," but I knew that he held people in only the level of esteem and importance that their money could provide. Hell, exorcisms started at twenty grand and he never budged on that price. More than a few people had been left to deal with their disgruntled and downright evil poltergeists, phantoms and wraiths, alone.

With the sound of shrieks, terror-tinged vocals, and scuttling minions around us, my companion sat up and cocked his head at me as if I should take some pity... on him. "Hey. Look," he said. "I don't think Big Boy is gonna stay out of the water long. I mean dehydration, pressure sickness, the bends, full stomach. Something. It'll go back home eventually."

The idea of the monstrosity shuffling back beneath the waves was more irritating than his emergence in the first place. My concern hadn't been born out of the need to save those who were running for their lives. My need to act was so much more primal.

It was a scene that caught both my attention as well as my companion's, as much larger and more menacing Foot Soldiers of the Kraken sprung upon a fleeing man's back and pierced him with a stinger at the end of its tail. The man—correction—the victim fell face forward onto the boardwalk. He began to convulse. Apparently, this beast's toxin had more than just paralysis in its nature. The victim's skin began to swell and bubble, hemorrhaging blood from places I couldn't even see. His formerly pale skin shimmered crimson as blood began to blossom from every pore.

I winced in disgust. My anger, my need to act and to do something began to burn brighter.

I expected Phalanx to be as amped up as I was. Instead he looked at me with a wrinkled nose. "You wanna to try another beach?" he asked.

It took me several minutes to even form my response. "No. I don't, you ass!"

The vibrations from the elder god coming toward land were getting much worse, causing us to stand. I snatched up my belongings while he stood there with a perturbed look on his face. "I'm sorry, Kaylee. Have you ever taken on anything that size? You been doing work that I don't know about?"

Okay so the biggest thing I had ever taken on *personally* was maybe fifty feet shorter and not nearly as functional and menacing as the approaching Behemoth of the Sea. It had been more of a blob of phantasmal energy trying to manifest into flesh. Hadn't quite made it. The key to that one however was the proactive approach, stopping shit like that from occurring in the first place. Not that I had known what kind of demon it wanted to be, but I was pretty sure then that it would be ten times more vulnerable in gelatinous, blob form. Sure, it was a little late to use that tactic with The Grand Whale Destroyer but I was never one to back down from a fight. "You're pathetic and a coward. We should definitely get in on the action."

Phalanx's humor returned as if it was a drag queen

bursting from a closet with a feather boa and a shower of glitter. The only thing he was missing were sequins, but I'd be damned if his eyes weren't sparkling.

"And you're rich," he blurted out. "I'm not getting caught on camera and being sent to Area 51 or any shit like that. Humans are not weaklings. Somebody has to have the phone number of the Army, or maybe the Air Force. Hope no one called the Navy though. Shit. They probably wouldn't do so well. Nope. I came here for sun, drinks, the ocean and a spa treatment or two. Definitely not to deal with the same shit I have to deal with back on the continents, and I thought you did too. Besides, you're the one that picked Jamaica."

I *had* picked the location, but how was I to know that an Eldritch horror would decide to emerge from the depths and take a leisurely jaunt to the shore. Clenching my fists, I was ready to take it on. "Area 51 is for aliens, smart ass."

"Well, Area 52 then," he balked. "No. Nope. Not going." He reached down and closed the cooler before grabbing the handle. "Come on."

I stood my ground as he began to trudge through the sand, choosing to turn around and face The Summoned. It had to be from another dimension. There was no fucking way anything of that size could have maintained its bulk out of the sea if it were natural, just as Mr. Apathy had said. "The least we can do is find out who summoned this thing."

I doubted that Phalanx could hear exactly what I said, as the Kaiju Extraordinaire continued to roar out the song of his fucking people. Taking my crocheted beach coverup off of the back of the chair, I slipped it over my head. If I was going to get into a fight, somehow I felt I would be more dignified in a coverup rather than a one-piece. Okay, so maybe I was a just a bit self-conscious about my pot belly.

"How do you know it was summoned?" Phalanx asked.

I looked over my shoulder to see that Phalanx hadn't gone far. Glaring between me and the Kraken, which was now a measly thousand feet out at best, he said, "We know more about space then we do about what's in our own oceans."

"Really, National Geographic?" I didn't even try to hide my sarcasm.

"I'm just saying, Rambo. You don't know."

"But *you* would," I snapped back at him. Hell, I was not the psychic one or the wisest one. I was the brawn, and I was eager to delve into some seafood!

Just then, the Towering Crustacean cum Demigod fell forward, easily closing half of the distance to the surf of the beach. What was once standing tall, became a beast of locomotion that would have made a millipede pissed.

I guarantee those brave souls who still lingered on the beach thought better of their decisions as they realized what a good idea running would be… albeit too late. As Lobster-Cthulhu scuttled past me and my companion, we both shook with the might of its movements. Far longer than it had been tall, the creature charged forward, squishing some of its minions along the way. Less than a hundred feet away from me and my companion, it was headed straight toward the resort, our resort, that luxury 5-star establishment that had lively Bob Marley tributes at midnight, a Fondue buffet, pool aerobics at two and a real quality salon with mud and sea salt wraps. In its path of destruction, I noted a familiar sight. Over turned, the rolling grill attached to a mobile cutting station and change drawer lay decimated. Chicken, marinated in jerk seasonings and grilled to perfection lay strewn across the sand and ruined wooden walkway. "Oh shit. The chicken cart..."

Phalanx let go of the cooler's handle and he followed my gaze to the horrific sight. "What? Oh, Hell no! No."

There were people in the second level of one of the resort's buildings, screaming their heads off as the Monolith used one of its tentacles to pluck them, one by one, out of the window, but that was just background noise. Kicking and screaming as they were carried toward the jaws of destruction, the humans really didn't stand much of a chance, but then neither did anyone else who thought hiding in their rooms was a good option. Still the travesty of all of that delicious chicken being wasted hurt both of our souls. Me and Phalanx.

"Oh, so you're upset? Now? Maybe?"

"We can't go anywhere. Shit!" Truly pissed, his features were a stormy mask with nostrils flaring. He closed his eyes and went tense. It might have seemed to a passerby that he was straining to take a shit standing up even though he still wore his pineapple printed swim trunks and hadn't spread his knees, but I knew exactly what he was doing. That and the only passerby was a mite that scrambled by giving us a wary and wide berth.

Phalanx's eyes snapped open and he pointed to the

right at a villa that was far away enough to still be safe, but also close enough to see the action on the beach. It looked very posh. "There, on that hill. It's a fucking coven. They summoned this shit show."

"Then we should definitely pay them a visit." I walked to his side, slapping a hand on his shoulder and trying to convince him with my best attempt at charm. "Look here, if they summoned the denizens of the deep then by my dad's balls, they summoned us too."

"Fine, Kaylee. Fine." Acquiescing, he placed his hand over my belly and pressed firm, connecting with the core of my essence. Hey, you had to have a connection to someone if you were going to teleport them. Getting lost in the mists between realities and dimensions was no picnic.

Phalanx grinned eagerly as he propelled us both from the blood covered sands to the white stone balcony of the villa. Huge vases filled with exotic flowers in colors I couldn't even begin to describe framed the circumference of a balcony big enough to hold a 20-member band and a wedding party, but instead just held dumbasses, in white robes and turquoise blue sashes. All save one who wore a turquoise robe with a gold sash. I assumed he was the leader. He was standing over a crackling fire pit piled high with body parts and had a leader-like look.

As soon as we appeared on the balcony just beside the Grand Poohbah, all of the chanting came to a stop and all eyes focused upon us. Those gazes included the poor, sobbing naked woman who was probably going to provide additional limbs for the crackling fire. If I had ever seen a silent plea for help, there it was in dark brown eyes, and it actually touched a nerve.

"Hi. Hello there," I said, greeting the surprised cult members. Phalanx took his hands off my stomach and stepped back, being the brains as it were.

I walked up to the wide-eyed cult leader who was holding a fucking scimitar. I didn't give two shits as I continued to address the gathering. "You fuckers summoned something? The Kraken's Phantasmal Pops, maybe?"

No one answered me, which I would have attributed to the fact that it wasn't everyday people experienced *two* mind-blowing manifestations. Okay so, I wasn't a few hundred feet tall nor did I reek of brine. I didn't have claws, tentacles, and scales. I was rather unimposing at five foot eight. I had what most would call an ample figure. Big Beautiful Woman. I had a dark cinnamon complexion and my dreadlocks were pulled up high by a scarf. Yet I did just suddenly manifest, thanks to Phalanx.

I continued, "Well the thing you're doing this whole ritual for showed up. He's outside, wreaking havoc on the beach, but I'm guessing he's on his way here. He's currently killing poor souls with his minion gang as he lumbers on, causing all kinds of destruction to one of my fucking favorite vacation spots. I don't know what you were promised or what kind of rewards you think you're gonna get in this life or the afterlife, but I'm here to tell you that you're shit outta luck today."

The High Priest looked me up and down, and not because I was drop dead gorgeous with an hourglass figure. Hefting his scimitar up to his shoulder, he rested the flat edge there and grinned with a wickedness a starving shark would envy. "I don't know where you came from, sorceress, and I don't care. You will not stop us."

"Sorceress? Sorceress... Did you hear what he just called me?" I cocked my head toward Phalanx, in disbelief of the absurd claim. I suppose it was an easy mistake to make, but still. Sure, I had a little magic in me, but it paled in comparison to Phalanx. "Oh, no, no, no." Gesturing with a thumb back to my companion, I said, "He's the sorcerer, not me."

The High Priest wasn't bad looking, in a menacing, gray fox type of way. Tanned skin so gold it almost gave him an exotic look with the pale blue eyes he had. Not as good looking as that old dude that reps for Dos Equis, but still easy on the eyes. With the confidence emanating from him, I wondered if he was capable of any real magic. The average summoner either had no powers or had powers granted through demon whimsy. No matter...

Silver Summoner turned his attention to my companion and raised an eyebrow questioningly, before swinging his blade back down to his side at the ready. "So, sorcerer, are *you* here to stop me?"

Phalanx huffed as if the idea was an absurdity. He held out his hand and in a puff of purple smoke, a beer appeared. He popped the cap off and took a swig before replying. "Not really. I'm just here to watch. I'm voyeuristic that way."

"Well, then, I shall try to give you both a show. Children of the Depths," he called out to his followers. "Subdue her!"

I didn't move a muscle as two of the burliest males in robes rushed to my side and seized me by the arms, while another came up behind me and wrapped his log of an arm around my throat. Held so firmly by the three men, I had to admire whatever oils or spices they were wearing. It certainly wasn't any cheap cologne as it didn't have a tinge of alcohol underneath the scents of sea, lavender oil and honeysuckle. In any other circumstance, I might have considered myself one lucky chick, but Summon Daddy was determined to put an end to my budding fantasies.

"Foolish. Foolish, woman." He tsked, waving his Sinbad sword at me. "Our God will destroy you, tear you apart and suck the marrow from your bones! We will feed you to him personally."

I burst out laughing, finally finding the humor in the whole situation. "Your... your—Fuck your god," I snapped, framing my words with air quotes. "Your god ain't nothing but another triflin' ass, overweight, crab-squid freak from the nether realms who promised you fucking ponies that your mommas wouldn't get you. Hell, I don't know why you jackasses can't just be happy with yourselves and regular reality. Always willing to serve, be it a cosmic horror, interdimensional monstrosity or hell born citizen, as if they wouldn't straight out lie to get what they want and then eat your ass later. Well you know what... I'm not here to fix stupid. I'm gonna be the Dumbass Whisperer today and you will pay for ruining my fucking vacation!"

The High Priest of Foolishness began to laugh maniacally as he took a step toward me with the blade of dismemberment raised. I could see a mad fire in his eyes, and perhaps it came from the knowledge that Gargantua had begun his ascent up the mountain that led to the villa. He seemed to be in no rush as he scoured every house in his path for morsels his tentacles could drag out into any one of his mouths, but still he was coming. I could see most of his creepy bulk from my high vantage point on the balcony.

"Yes. He comes for you and all others who do not know his name," said the priest who noted me looking out off the balcony. "But you will."

I had about forty-five names for the fucker, but I doubted if any were actually his true name. Still, I was always giddy to meet new and interesting entities, so I smiled too.

"Hold out her arms. Those I shall add to the pyre so that she may live to see—"

I understood what he wanted to do and had to give him extra credit points for the sheer creativity of my proposed dismemberment, but I had heard enough. As he raised the blade, the two men holding my arms forced them away from my side.

He would have been able to make two very clean slices and was about to part me from my right arm first, if I hadn't pulled free of my suit. I yanked my true arms out of their human sleeves, leaving the two men holding nothing but the floppy cloth of my skin… and my torn one piece and crocheted cover up. For the fool holding me around the throat, I left him with the human hood I wore over my true face, easily craning my blue-black head around and stretching my jaws wide—wide enough to bite off his face from forehead to chin.

I was chewing vigorously, having to deal with what little skull and jaw bone I had managed to take in my ambitious bite, when I set my eyes on the stunned priest, arm frozen in the air with the scimitar still held in mid-swing.

Stepping out of the remainder of my suit, I exposed my three tails, talon-tipped feet and my four arms, one of which I used to backhand the priest halfway across the room. With all thoughts of remaining hidden, appearing normal or even being civil, thrown to the wayside, I observed the smorgasbord around me.

I grabbed one of the men who had formerly held me by the arms, bringing him to me in order to demonstrate *my* brand of embrace. Body to body, I stretched my mouth wide again and fastened my lips onto his throat. Some might have imagined I was giving my best impression of a vampire, but then vampires didn't take so much that there was only the slightest sliver of flesh left to hold the head onto the shoulders. Hells yeah, I took the neck bones too, crunching them down to wet, bloody crumbs as I spun around to face another of the guards. This one had picked up the scimitar that his priestly lord had dropped mid-flight and was rushing toward me with murder in his eyes. I scoffed. As he rushed at me, I dropped low on my haunches, ducking the swing of the blade. As it passed over my head, I sprang into his personal space with an uppercut to his jaw. Before he could even register what had happened, I snatched the sword from him and used it to slice his body in half. I switched the blade to my other hand and sliced again. My lower arms held the trunk tightly as first the top half of Mr. Morsel fell away... then the bottom half. Holding tight to a chunk of midsection, I pressed it into the line of my abdomen where my second mouth swiftly consumed it.

I looked for more brave souls, but chaos was surrounding me. Robes were being cast aside, cult members were screaming, shrieking in fright. The High Priest was picking himself up off of the floor but hate and defiance still burned a little too brightly still, in his eyes. As for Phalanx, he was standing beside the archway, holding a bowl of fruit from which he was taking the odd morsel here and there. I might have doubted his conviction to the cause, his willingness to provide help if I hadn't seen the shimmering oil-like shield before him, the one preventing the cult members from fleeing safely. Nope, if they wanted to escape my wrath, they would have had to jump over the balcony to a death of some fifty-odd feet.

As I leapt upon one of the female cult members, too stunned to have released the naked woman who was to be the final sacrifice, I pinned her to the floor. To the crazed sacrifice, I turned my head and promised her. "You will survive this, but do not get in my way."

She nodded errantly but I knew that her mind was half-shattered, not completely broken but still, she would have difficulty sleeping without aid for a long time.

I turned my attention back to the woman beneath me, the one who was so willing to sacrifice another just for her *God's* pleasure. An equal opportunity creature of destruction, I seized her by the arms and conveyed the punishment her priest would have given me. I tore both of her arms out of their sockets before standing up and slapping her with one of them.

The other limb, I ate with my face-mouth before stepping on her head and driving my foot to the floor beneath it.

I attacked only two more cult members, disemboweling one and yanking the spine out of another, before I realized that the light around me, that formerly beaming sunshine, was gone and that Triton 2020 was looming just over the precipice of the balcony. He looked down at me with well over fifty eyes, six large and the others much smaller, kinda like a spider. The beast had a leering sort of feel to him. I noticed out of the corner of my eye, one of his tentacles coming toward me. Wondering how I'd nearly missed that advance, I looked down at the tip of the two-foot thick appendage and spat upon it. The length of flesh swiftly pulled back but the damage had already been done. It was time for this creature's flesh to start bubbling and dissolving, just like those poor humans who had been stung by its minions. The massive, sun-blocking creature gave out an ululating shriek before taking a step back as if he all of a sudden understood exactly what the fuck I was. And I couldn't resist gloating, not in least, as I turned my gaze upon the High Priest and grinned.

I have no idea where all of the bravado and scorn crawled off to, but I ran forward and captured the priest mid-flee. He attempted to fight me, crying, jerking and kicking, swearing and throwing spittle, but he had no chance against the grip of all four of my arms. "Thought you wanted to meet Bob over here," I asked rhetorically. "You summoned him, so obviously you wanted to meet him."

"Please! Please. I'll do anything. I'll worship you! I'll bring you sacrifices, offerings, money, jewels, whatever you want," the priest stammered on.

Using my left upper hand, I grasped his head and turned him to face me as he received my message. "You're giving me what I want and you don't even know it. Fuck worshipping... I'll take your fear," I whispered to him, knowing that my companion couldn't hear anything. Well, hoping.

Casting him across the room as if he weighed no more than a bag of beans, I heard the thud as he hit the column of stone closest to the open space of the balcony... right in full view of his deity. He got in a few more pleas, promises and oaths before becoming a snack of the worst sort. The "saved for later" type. I gawked with wonder as I witnessed what I had thought were nubby growths on Big Man's carapace, open up. A tentacle snatched up the terrified priest and carried him to one of the nodules. The flesh split apart exposing a fleshy chamber into which the priest was placed before a fibrous membrane closed over the opening.

How could I have missed that? There were hundreds of *pockets* on the creature and I quickly realized that many of them were filled.

I called Sacrifice—What else was I gonna call her—to me and scared shitless or no, she immediately ran over to my side. Maybe it was a lesser of two demons kinda situation, but she couldn't have really known which one I was. Taking her hand in one of mine, I turned and gave a nod to my companion who had somehow passed the exit for bored and was making his way to irritation.

He held up his hands, magenta tinged fingers, moving ever so slightly as he pushed the forcefield he had created back, then back again. I walked toward it to the symphony of cries, the sounds of vomiting and wails of despair. I heard a couple of prayers to the Christian god, the Jewish deity, Allah and even one for

Buddha, but I kept forward. "Oh no. You can't cry now. None of you," I smirked as I passed one miserable soul. "I'm sure that your man over there ate up folk that were crying just like you. It's called comeuppance and you picked the wrong team motherfuckers."

Laughter bubbled up in my stomach—just below my abdomen-mouth and came rushing out. By the time I passed through my companion's barrier with Sacrifice, I was a hysterical, laughing mess. Phalanx led the way from the balcony, through the villa and up to the rooftop terrace. This villa was way more swankier than the hotel I was staying at, with a roof top, inground swimming pool, framed with seating and tables and a panoramic view of at least our part of the island.

Phalanx found a lounger close to the edge of the roof, where he plopped down his Bermuda-shorts covered ass and stretched out flip-flopped feet.

I took the lounge chair right next to him and it was almost like it had been on the beach. With the absence of our cooler and my skin suit. Gesturing for Sacrifice to pull up a chair, I didn't have to lean over the rail to see the head of Crab Gargantua as he was devouring some and packing away meals for later. *Unda Da Sea...* I chuckled again.

Monstrosity of the Ages must have finished his buffet, as he eventually backed away from the villa. He raised his head but none of the multitude of eyes remained on me and my companions for very long. Hell, this thing was smart, I had to give him that, as he moved backward first, giving the villa a wide berth as he crushed a smoke shop, a curry restaurant and a small hotel in the effort. Heading back to the sea, its back was a polka dot display of boils containing anguished beings. The priest being one of them. I swear I felt like waving.

My companion turned to me and waved a finger around. "Alright, Cap'n Save Em," he said. "What are you waiting for? There's more work to be done. Minions still foraging. You need to get on down there."

Stretching out on my lounger, I put my feet up mimicking his relaxed state. "Fuck you. I'm ready for a nap. A drink maybe."

"I... I can get you one. A drink," Sacrifice offered shakily, getting up from her seat and stepping toward me. Eager to serve.

I wanted to tell her no. I was serious when I said that I didn't need any worshippers, but the young woman seemed so sincere, the look in her eyes seemed so appreciative, or was that madness? I was in no mood to find out, but then I figured—I didn't command her, and she *had* offered. "Thank you," I said, accepting her proposal. "Anything with rum will do."

As she departed, I caught Phalanx glaring at me with narrowed, suspicious eyes. "I knew it. I fucking knew it!"

"Knew what?"

"You," he scoffed just as an explosion shook the ground even more so than the footsteps of Lord Sea Dweller, who had apparently smushed a gas station by the sight of the huge black and red fireball mushrooming into the sky. "You," he continued. "Pretending like you were all concerned for the safety of humans. You just wanted some action, you psychopath."

"I was... You know it just wasn't right that—. There's a natural order of things..." I groaned finally, unable to find a bullshit excuse but knowing that he was telling the truth. I warmed a little, with just the smallest modicum of shame before demanding a new skin and cover up from his magic hands.

"Aww fuck it," I gave up. "Every vacation needs activities."

"Kaylee... activities and albeit warranted slaughter are two different things. We were scheduled for the glass-bottom boat at five."

I may have been a psychopath, but at least I wasn't scraping the barrel of apathy, I thought. "You're acting like it was *me* that summoned Godzilla's cousin."

"Whatever."

By the time Sacrifice returned from the bar with two very elaborate cocoanuts with straws and fruit, I was back to my humanoid best with a new crocheted coverup and one-piece swimsuit. Phalanx had even magicked up some flower-topped flip flops for me. Okay so he wasn't totally devoid of the ability to care, which was the reason we were married in the first place.

I accepted my drink graciously and took my cocoanut. Inside of it was some mixture of rum and pineapple, a bit of mango and sours. Turned out Sacrifice was a pretty damn good bartender and the hospitality coordinator at a chain hotel on the other side of the island... the undamaged side that hadn't encountered hellspawn horrors.

She promised us snorkeling adventures, river boat tours, five-star restaurants with private tastings, even a VIP booth at the Reggaeton Bash.

I may have been a psycho and a demon but even Phalanx had to admit that we ended up having one of the best vacations ever and it was all because I hadn't stood idly by while evil—Ha! Okay, I *had* only acted because I was jonesing for action! Not every solution required money for an incentive and vacation or no, a demon has still got to demon.

THE STAGES OF MONSTER GRIEF

BY CARINA BISSETT

(A Guide for Middle-Aged Vampires)

Ladies, you may have dreamed of a day when you no longer have to "age gracefully" or are forced into obscurity by a wardrobe filled with basic neutrals. You look in the mirror only to be confronted with sagging skin, pebbled cellulite, and wrinkles in places you never expected. You start to wonder if you'll be old and alone forever. A little bit of blood is worth the price to drink at the fountain of youth, isn't it?

1. Denial

And then it happens: some figure seduces you from the shadows, and you fall lovingly into their arms with your throat bared by a torn turtleneck. You think you've beaten the odds. Only, death is never as romantic as it is in the movies, and rebirth is downright disgusting. That two hundred dollar cut and color is reduced to a dirt-matted mop, and your nails are broken from digging your way out of a shallow grave. Don't even get started on the state of your skin. And *they* say mud makes a magical facial. Call bullshit on that one.

You blow it off, decide you were slipped a mickey, and some teenage asshat buried your passed out body in a mound of moldy leaves as a joke. No Prince Charming dressed like Bela Lugosi. No sexy interlude behind the cocktail lounge. No throb of the forbidden. You refuse to acknowledge the truth. So you rub at the bruise on your neck and search through the closet for an even higher collar to hide the arterial bloom.

The next day, you call in sick. After all, you've been working at the college, wearing your nicest smile for twenty fucking years. Don't you deserve some time off for good behavior? You've never acted on the impulse to fail a student just because they are a monster in the classroom. But no one has ever thanked you—not once. Screw that.

When you wake up, the day has disappeared and September's Harvest Moon squats low on the horizon. You've been eating vegan in an attempt to lose belly fat and to reduce cholesterol, but all you can think about is a nice, juicy steak. Rare. And why shouldn't you treat yourself? You only live once, right?

2. Anger

Okay, so maybe you didn't make it to the restaurant on your walk from campus to downtown. And those belligerent frat boys probably had it coming anyway.

Back at home, you take a shower and toss your blood-soaked clothes in the bin. No more beige for you. From here on out, you will only wear velvet and lace, cut seductively to show off the new you. But, when you look in the mirror, nothing has changed. That crepey skin is still visible on your neck, your breasts sag without the support of an underwire, and the cellulite on your thighs appears even more dimpled than it did before.

You go out the next night looking for answers from your vampire progenitor. You figure they have some explaining to do. Why can you see yourself in a mirror? Better yet, where's the God-damn fountain of youth? You wouldn't have wanted the cursed blessing if you knew that you'd have to spend the rest of your presumably immortal days alone at the resting age of fifty-five. What kind of sick fuck would damn you to that particular purgatory?

3. Depression

You think about walking outside and ending it all with a little vitamin D, but you've never liked the sun—skin cancer and all of that. You didn't wear wide-brimmed hats, long sleeves, and your weight in SPF 100 for thirty years to go out in a blaze of glory.

Instead, you go on a binge of boys and booze.

It could be worse.

4. Acceptance

You invest in corsets, light your home with candles. Still, it takes some time to let go of modern perceptions of youth and beauty, even though you know from experience there's more to life than that.

After all, you can deadlift a family sedan. You've gotten out of the academic grind with a few well-placed casualties. And snapshots of your new "I don't give a fuck" stylings turned you into an Instagram hit. Sure, those pictures are mistakenly titled "Sexy at Sixty," but whatever.

It doesn't take long before your memoir is sold as fiction for six-figures, and you start the popular blog "So You Want to Write a Vampire Novel." In between readings and convention appearances, you stalk the streets looking for one of your own kind. Even though you never found the vampire who turned you, or any other vampire for that matter, you crave a companion. So, when you see the foxy woman astride a black beast of a motorcycle, silver hair streaming out behind her, you act on impulse.

You pretend you didn't notice it was a full moon, or that the howls dogging her trail sounded like wolves.

It's your nature after all, you tell yourself as you dig a shallow grave with a broken fender. You tell yourself that she'll love you forever even as you push the dirt over her drained body. She'll forget her lover with the moon-bright eyes. She'll forget the spat that sent her far from her pack. Your blood will triumph; you're sure of it. But when she rises, the silver-haired woman looks right through you.

She stumbles away and leaves you behind to stare at an empty hole filled with nothing more than moonlight and frost.

Over the distant sounds of traffic and sirens, a wolf howls.

5. Betrayal

Overhead, January's Wolf Moon watches with an amused grin. The silver-haired woman breaks into a lope.

You don't need a magic mirror to tell you how this will play out. The movies are full of stories about romantic triangles and unrequited love. If nothing else, you'll no longer be alone. You gather your cape. And follow.

DRACULARRY

BY LIN MORRIS

I'd never heard that thing about how a vampire can't enter your home uninvited, or believe me I never would have let Larry in the front door.

But, y'know, you meet a guy at a casino; you get a flirtatious banter-y thing going; blah-blah-blah, he says, "Seth, I'd love to teach you how to gamble sometime" (which, since he's a professional gambler, wasn't *just* a come-on); it's only polite to ask him over for dinner so he can teach you to gamble, right?

Who knew about that whole "inviting a vampire inside" thing?

Wait, really? Everyone knows this?

Everyone?

Where were you all before now, *when I didn't have a vampire locked in my kitchen pantry*?

Okay, in my defense, I never watch horror movies. I prefer my entertainment light and feel-goodish. Sue me.

Who doesn't enjoy curling up under an afghan with some comfort food and *Yentl* on Blu-Ray, I ask you?

Obviously not my best friend Colin, that's who. He came over two nights ago and literally *ripped* the bag of Juanita's tortilla chips from my moisturizer-gloved hands and announced, "Seth, we're going out."

"We who?"

"We *us*," Colin said. "Out. In public."

"Do I have to dress up?" I asked, pulling my comfy sweatshirt tightly around me. One of the sleeves suddenly ripped off at the shoulder seam. Okay, so maybe I'd been hibernating too long.

"I don't care if you go stark naked," Colin said. "In fact, that might be preferable. At least then you'd be showing off the goodies, which, need I remind you, haven't had a good airing in about six months."

"Nine."

"Nine months?" Colin sniffed. "Good grief. If your celibacy were a fetus, you'd have given birth by now." I never take offense to Colin; his bitchery comes from a good heartspace. "Dare I ask how many times you listened to Cher sing 'The Way of Love' today?"

He knows me all too well.

I admit it, I'm a sucker for a diva with a broken heart. Lately, though, the heartbroken one had been me. Compounded by the fact that last month I had turned—gay gasp!—forty-one. I was not merely forty anymore, but *in my forties*.

"Three times."

"Three's, like, a half-dozen less than yesterday." Colin sat on the couch and put his arm around me. "Come on, Seth. I know it's been rough, but you need to get out of the house."

"I'm fine."

"That's some fabulous denial you're wearing."

"Thanks, bought it at Macy's."

He cocked an eyebrow at me; wit only goes so far with Colin.

I sighed, nestling against him. "I can't believe he dumped me after five years."

"And four of those years were good." Colin gave me a jostle. "Now let's go see who else is out there."

"I'm not ready to date yet."

"Who said anything about dating? Did I say date? I said let's go look."

"Looking is fun, I guess."

"With the added bonus of, we get to judge!"

"I do like judging."

"Well, hello! Here's my best friend! Where's he been lately?" He kissed my cheek. "B-T-W, don't shave, that stubble makes you look super-hot. But, Seth. You're not really wearing that out in public, are you?"

If I'd just said no and stayed in with Juanita and Cher and Barbra and my unraveling sweatshirt, perhaps I wouldn't be standing in my kitchen right now wondering how long it would take me to whittle my solid walnut Lostine rolling pin into a stake.

***

"Seth?" says Larry, his voice muffled from behind my pantry door. "I'm sorry about earlier. I swear I'm not going to bite you. Please open the door."

"No."

"It's dark in here."

"Oh, the vampire's afraid of the dark, is he?"

"Quit calling me that."

"You tried to bite me!"

"Seth, it was a joke. To make you laugh."
"Deny it all you want; I saw your teeth!"
"They were fake! I'm not a vampire."
I remain unconvinced.

***

"Anywhere but the Strip," I told Colin, who pretended he couldn't hear me over the music, which was thumping at a volume usually reserved for interrogations at Guantanamo Bay. Even after living in Las Vegas for a decade, I've never developed a taste for the sensory overload of the Strip. Colin merely grinned.

Oh, well. Maybe it wouldn't be so bad, just for an hour or so. Some drinks, some dancing, some judging. There are far worse things in life than a friend who wants to see you happy.

I told myself that I'd pretend to be happy, for Colin's sake.

He cut across Harmon Avenue and down a little side street.

"You're gonna love this."

We stepped out in front of a little hole in the wall.

Intemperance was written in a fun, retro font above the door. I'd never heard of it. How long had I been out of commission, that Colin knew about a nightspot before me?

***

I'm trying to remember where I last saw the crucifix that I'd received for First Communion, when a loud crash comes from the pantry. Then silence.

"Larry? You okay?"

"Why would you possibly care?" Larry sounds like he might cry. (Side note: Do vampires cry?) "It's dark,

I can't see."

"Well, the light switch is out here, so you'll just have to sit there in the dark and think about what you've done."

More silence.

"Larry?"

"My ankle is a little tender. I may have sprained it."

My mother was so excited when she gave me that crucifix, but it was gaudy. And *gold*. Even at the tender age of eight, I knew sterling silver was classier.

Whatever happened to it? My mother probably has it at her place, no doubt in some special memory box she keeps to remind her of her children's shortcomings. Heaven knows, she can recite our flaws like the rosary. How's she gonna feel when her only son becomes one of the undead? I can just hear her now: *I knew he'd come to no good, that one, always with the snooty attitude about gold jewelry and my K-Mart housecoat.*

If she'd just bought me the silver crucifix *like I wanted in the first place*, I'd probably have it in my hands right now, instead of my phone, which I am using to Google "How to destroy a bloodsucking fiend."

"You need to open the door, Seth."

"I know."

But I can't seem to muster the courage to do it.

***

Intemperance was a tiny bar-slash-casino that looked like it belonged in a 1950s Technicolor melodrama. Satellite chandeliers, cocktail tables with brightly-colored boomerang Formica. Sleek croupiers in tuxes and slicked-back hair dealt cards to well-heeled gamblers. The only thing missing was Bette Davis swathed in mink. I was in heaven.

Like I said, Colin knows me all too well.

We ordered Manhattans at the bar, because they seemed ironically old-timey, then wandered over to watch the gamblers.

And that's when I saw him, at the other end of the table, dice in his hand.

Not the most handsome man, but oddly hot, in a granddaddy-ish sort of way. There was something so... elegant about him, so dashing. He was debonair, a word I have heretofore never used in my entire life. Everything about him drew my attention: the shock of thick white hair, the dark eyes, his Roman nose. And yes, unnaturally pale skin, a red flag I may have overlooked. He appeared to be sixty-five if he was a day—though I realize now, my math was off by about, oh, two hundred years.

"Hold on, Madge," Colin said, handing me his cocktail napkin. "Somebody's drooling."

"Am not. Just staring."

"Look at you checking out the old guy!"

Colin laughed, a bit too loudly, and that caught the stranger's attention. He smiled slyly and, without taking his eyes from mine, tossed the dice over his shoulder.

"Seven!"

He winked.

So out of practice was I in the fine art of flirtation that I actually did that spin-around, look-behind-you thing, to see who he was winking at.

No one there. It was me.

I couldn't flee back to the bar fast enough.

Colin and I were finishing another round of

Manhattans when our server, in '50s prom queen finery, sat one more down in front of me. "From the gentleman at the bar." She snorted. "I love saying that!"

The gentleman in question gave us a stylish demi-wave—you know the little shake of the index finger?—and started walking over. I tossed down half my drink, Novocaine for the nerves.

"Hello," he said. "May I join you?" He had a slight but unplaceable accent.

"Please!" said Colin, offering up his chair before discreetly meandering off with a wicked grin.

"Good evening." He actually gave a little bow, so help me, and introduced himself as Lawrence Van Somethingforeign.

"Hi." I held out my hand and I swear I thought he was going to kiss it, like I was Marlene Dietrich.

Debonair. There: now I've used it twice.

"I'm Seth." It seemed hard to pronounce, suddenly. "Seth," I said again, slowly. What a funny name I had; sounded like lisping.

Another couple of drinks later, and my name became downright *hilarious*.

***

"This isn't funny," says Larry, from inside my pantry. "Please open the door."

"I can't. I'm afraid."

"We're all afraid, Seth."

***

Alcohol reintroduced me to Flirty Seth, whom I had forgotten existed. "Isn't it past your bedtime, Larry?" I allegedly may have drawled at him seductively.

"I'm a day sleeper."

(*Well duh*, I hear you all say. But I didn't think about it at the time, being deep into round whatever of cocktails.)

"Sleep all day, gamble all night?"

"Not every night, no. Though I am a professional gambler."

His intense gaze was discomfiting. Was it the bar lighting, or were his irises ringed by a razor-thin line of red?

"I thought you were gonna say it's because you're a vampire. Are you a vampire, Larry?"

Larry looked me dead in the eyes. "Yes!"

We laughed and laughed.

"So, are you really a professional gambler?"

"I am." That stare again. "Seth, I'd love to teach you how to gamble sometime."

***

"This situation is out of control. Nothing's going to happen if you let me out, I'm just going to go home."

"How do I know that?"

"You don't," Larry says. "This is where you have to take a gamble. Have faith. Look, I could have called the police a long time ago, Seth; I've got my phone in here."

He makes a good point.

"I know you're scared. And not just about tonight. I saw in your eyes at the casino how lonely and unhappy you are."

What?!

I brace myself for battle, grabbing what weapons I have at my disposal.

Because I'm no longer afraid; now I am *pissed*.

***

Inviting Larry over seemed a harmless way to dip a toe back into the pool. I wasn't planning to make him my rebound boyfriend or anything, and I sure wasn't gonna sleep with him. (Definitely not. Well, probably not. No, definitely probably not.)

When he called me last night, I invited him over, for dinner and gambling lessons.

He insisted on eating late, of course, long after sundown.

Ever the gentleman, he brought an expensive bottle of wine.

I thanked him with a peck on the cheek. It was meant to be innocuous, but I'm sure he saw me trembling like an amateur.

"Would you like a glass?" I said.

"I never drink... wine." Larry snickered.

"Oh. Vodka?"

"That's a line from *Dracula*."

"From *Dracula*? Sorry, I'm not...?"

"The other night, the whole vampire thing?"

I mumbled vaguely. The whole Night of 100 Manhattans was a blur, honestly, though I remembered laughing so hard at one point that I nearly toppled out of my chair.

Suddenly, Larry was in front me, arms raised as if in attack. His eyes were ringed in red, I hadn't imagined it. But my eyes were locked onto his huge white fangs. He got right in my face and, so help me, he *hissed* at me!

You'd think my instinct would be to curl up in a fetal position and scream, but sometimes I surprise even myself. Instead, I smacked Larry hard in the chest with the wine bottle, full-on kung-fu-kicked his ass right into the pantry, slammed the door, and locked him inside.

Who knew my inner diva was such a tough broad? And *then* I curled up in a fetal position and screamed.

***

"Lonely and unhappy?" I throw open the pantry door. "Just what do you mean by *that*, Larry?!"

He blinks at the bright lights in the kitchen.

"Seth, what are you doing?"

"I'm fending you off."

"Is that supposed to be a crucifix?"

"Does it repel you?"

"No. Because it's a spatula and a turkey baster."

Why hadn't I thought to get out the shish kabob sticks? Such a better weapon. They could even double as a stake if it comes to that.

"Back off!" I push them closer to Larry's face, like a threat.

"Put those down. I can't talk to you while you're flailing around playing Buffy the Vampire Slayer."

Larry grabs my weaponry and throws the pieces in the sink. His flesh doesn't sizzle, so I guess maybe it has to be a real crucifix to work.

I cover my throat with my hands, aware that my relatively taut forty-something neck might be deflowered at any moment.

"Listen to me," Larry says gently. "I had fun the other night. You can't imagine what it meant to an old man like me to flirt with a cute younger guy who didn't look right through me like I wasn't there. But your sad eyes, Seth. They always turned away first."

"That's because your eyes are too intense," I say,

unable to look at them even now. "Like you're trying to hypnotize me, so you can bite me."

"Fine, sure," says Larry, shrugging. "Why argue? You're right, Seth: I'm a vampire. *I'm a vampire and you're a happy, carefree man.* Let's both pretend nothing's wrong."

Suddenly I don't feel quite so banter-y.

"You're quick with the jokes and the camp and the humor, but they're walls you're building. I think you're really hurting."

"And *I* think you should leave now, Larry."

"Of course. I told you I would." He gives me that formal little bow. "Thank you for letting me out."

I turn away so he won't have the satisfaction of seeing me cry, and face the wall until I hear the front door close.

I dry my eyes and wonder, *What Would Lana Turner Do?* Because channeling someone else's heartache is so much easier than examining your own.

I take a deep breath and hold my chin up until I can work myself into a proper snit of righteous indignation.

Who does he think he is?
Walls? I'll give you walls!

Larry left behind the bottle of wine, so at least the evening isn't a complete bust. Maybe I'll get drunk and forget the entire last year ever happened. Boy, will Colin get an earful tomorrow; he had assured me there would be no dating.

I flick on the pantry light to see if Larry's crashing around has broken anything.

There they are on the floor, looking pitiful: a set of plastic vampire fangs, the kind you used to buy for

Halloween as a kid. Larry must have gone to a lot of trouble to hunt them up, all so he could play a little joke and make me laugh.

What have I done?

I race for the front door, knowing I'm probably too late to catch him, but hoping against hope that he's still on my porch. I'll invite him back in, ask if we can start this whole evening over.

But Larry's not on my porch. There's no car in the drive.

What an idiot I've been. He's simply a nice, lonely old man, and I just kicked him in the heart. Or to use his words, looked right through him.

Suddenly, out of nowhere, a huge bat comes divebombing down from the sky. It turns a few fancy flips above my driveway, like an Olympic diver showing off, then flies right up in my face. It spreads its wings and hisses, flashing those red-ringed eyes at me, before zipping away into the night.

You don't think...

No, surely not.

It couldn't be Larry.

It must be a coincidence, right?

Right?

Anyone?

THE DARKER SIDE OF US

BY CLARENCE CARTER

"*Hey everyone, I'm Vic.*"
"*And, I'm Vanessa!*"
"*This is our YouTube channel. If you're a subscriber, then you may have heard, we have a new project. It's much different from this. I'd venture to say it'll be quite terrifying,*" Vic said, posing for the audience with his perfect teeth.

The two of them sat behind the wheel of their red Chevelle, where they recorded many of their vlogs.

Vanessa took over. "*Without spoiling too much, we're starting a vlogumentary called 'The Darker Side Of Us.' We start shooting tonight, although we don't have an exact release date yet.*"

"*It'll give you a thrill,*" Vic said before ending the video.

I scrolled through the comments, which acted as a cesspool of hilarity. More often than not, guys commented about how hot Vanessa looked and how they wished they had their money. Vic & Vanessa had been a successful YouTube channel for about three years. They were rich, entertaining, and not bad looking. They had a following of about three million subscribers and growing.

Vic Holland had gone into acting since the success of the channel, landing small roles in TV shows and movies. He prided himself on his acting career. Periodically he'd talk about it at length, even giving behind the scene footage of sets and time-lapsed videos of himself in a makeup chair. At the beginning of the channel, he'd done skits where he'd played characters, dressing up and acting. The skits weren't half bad.

Vanessa Holland, dubbed the queen of makeup tutorials, had gotten a contract for a couple of commercials. In exchange for a few thousand, she'd pitched makeup to braindead tweens with immense success. She too could be entertaining, although I didn't watch the makeup stuff.

I'd been a follower from the beginning. I enjoyed the videos when they'd been original. The skits had been my favorite, but some of the adventure stuff entertained too. They'd gone everywhere on their show, from China to London. Since becoming famous, their channel, in my opinion, dropped in quality. They did vlogs where they sat behind the wheel of their car and talked about their projects more than anything else. The original content had become sparse and practically nonexistent.

I clicked on the comment bar. *"Your videos aren't funny anymore. You lost your touch. I bet your next project will suck, too!"* I typed. Trolling them had become a hobby of mine, probably because I didn't have anything better to do. I got bored often. I'd been a fan in the beginning, before they got millions of subscribers and started cashing in. The reason I continued to watch was that I hoped they'd return to the original content.

Before I got out of bed for dinner, I looked at the comment I'd posted on their video, and it had already gotten fifty thumbs up. I wasn't the only person who thought the quality of the channel had gone downhill.

On the other side of the door, walking toward me, came my brother. "David, let me watch TV in your room," he griped.

I put my hand up, blocking him. I pushed him hard enough to get the point across. He walked backward a couple of steps, my hand still on his chest. I pushed open the door to his bedroom. "Look at that. You can watch TV right here. It's even clean for once," I said.

"Your TV is bigger," he said.

"Everything about me is bigger," I replied.

My brother and I had a good back and forth. Things could get depressing around our house, so I tried my best to make him laugh. Admittedly, some of my stunts went too far. It was a flaw of mine. I didn't know when to turn it off. Our mother worked two jobs, so she wasn't around much. Our father had cheated on her and lived a double life for the better of a decade. He had two families. He had a little girl we didn't know existed until a bill came in the mail for her braces. My mother had opened the letter.

Pranks were the only thing that made my broken home feel okay. My brother Ryan, often the butt of the joke, insisted I start a channel of my own. I'd contemplated it but couldn't imagine being on camera. I didn't think I could handle the scrutiny of an audience. Honestly, I couldn't handle comments like I'd used against Vic and Vanessa. When I pulled my pranks, only he and my mother would witness.

Ryan must have heard their videos playing on my phone because he began talking about YouTube again. "Dude, I'm telling you—you need to make a channel. You're way funnier than that dumb channel you watch. What the hell is it called again? Vic and Vaccine?"

"Vic and Vanessa," I raised my voice.

"She's as fake as Barbie," he chuckled. "They're both made of plastic."

The scent of homemade spaghetti sauce and garlic bread drifted through the air. It wasn't uncommon for my mother to cook Italian food. She'd worked as a cook when we were kids, and she'd learned from the best chef we knew, our grandfather.

"It smells good in here, Mom," I said, taking my place at the table.

"Yeah," Ryan agreed, sitting down too.

She lifted her glasses, which had slid down her nose. "You boys need to get your grades up," she said. "I saw those report cards. You can do better. I work my butt off at two jobs. The least you can do is pass all of your classes." A deep frown creased her face.

"Mom, you don't understand. Mr. Vaughn hates me."

"Yeah, okay," my mother said, shutting down my brother's excuse instantly. "You could do better too," she said, staring at me, fanning herself with her hand.

We lived in Nevada, so naturally, it was hot. The

small air conditioner could never keep up with the oven. We cooked inside our tiny trailer. My mother and brother always fought over the temperature.

Ryan claimed he knew when I thought about doing a prank. He said that I had a look. Ryan stared across the table at me. He must have seen that look because a smile crossed his face.

I didn't want to listen to any more of her lecture, so I shoveled spaghetti in my mouth, making obnoxious grunting sounds, spilling sauce all over my shirt. As I shoveled the strands in, I grunted like a pig. I could feel my mother's scowl hot on my skin.

"Stop it, right now, David." My mother shouted. "You're disgusting." She stared at me over her thick frames.

I shoveled more in my mouth then swung the spaghetti around in a circle, whipping sauce in all directions. "Luk ah me, Imma helllicoper," I said. As I flung the spaghetti round and round, I could feel noodles slipping from my grip and launching across the kitchen. I tried my best not to laugh.

My mother jumped from her seat. "David," she shouted.

Ryan held his stomach, roaring in laughter as he watched my performance. For a moment, I thought he would join the fun, but he looked at my mom and laughed even harder.

The wall to my left looked like it had been painted red with bits of tomato sauce dripping down to the floor. The top of the table had bits of spaghetti lying like pale snakes.

"David, you stop that this instant," she shouted, her face turning beet red. "I'm going to count to three, and if you haven't stopped, you're grounded for a month."

My mother began to count. As she counted, milk shot out of Ryan's nose, which made me laugh even harder. I couldn't take my mother's counting seriously. It had worked when we were younger, but now as young men, counting didn't scare us any longer.

The kitchen looked demolished. Spaghetti sauce covered the table, floor, and left splatter marks on the ceiling. I didn't want to stay there any longer, so I excused myself from the table and ran down the hall to my room, trying to contain my laughter with my hand.

"You're going to clean this up," she shouted after me.

After removing my stained shirt, I flopped on my bed. I'd gotten out of there in time. My mother hadn't collected her thoughts together enough to take my phone yet. *That was a good one*, I thought to myself. For a second, I considered what my brother had said about making my own channel.

"It's not over," she shouted in my direction.

I scrolled through the videos of Vic and Vanessa, the older ones. I picked one of my favorites. Their dad had just bought them a restored Chevelle. What a beautiful car, nice color too. The paint glimmered in the California sun, bright red. They both ran, camera jostling in Vic's hand, to hug their father. Vic went on to do a small monologue about the car. He opened the doors showing off the interior and popped the hood to look at the engine. Vanessa explored too, without much input. Her jaw on the ground.

"I wish I had a car like that," I grunted. I didn't have a car. My mother loved to say she worked two jobs to make ends meet. We didn't have the luxuries Vic and

Vanessa did. Sometimes I would get lost in their videos wondering what it might be like to be them. They went on adventures, and in the beginning, Vic could be funny. He would tell a joke on the Great Wall of China or dress like Mario when they went go-karting. They had some great adventures together, which made for good content.

For nearly three hours, I lay in bed, flipping through videos. Somewhere they'd gone sour, but I hadn't figured out where. Luckily for me, they had three years worth of material. They had hundreds of videos in their archive, and I'd seen all of them at least once.

My eyes grew heavy as I flicked from one video to the next. It didn't take long before I yawned several times and struggled to keep my eyes open.

Something went bump, jolting me from my bed. I looked around, but the room had become too dark to see anything. Usually, that's how I liked it, but not now. I looked to the right, by the door and thought I'd seen something moving. I opened my mouth, but before I could scream, a wet rag covered my face. My eyes got huge, and my breathing grew heavy. For a couple of seconds, I held onto my consciousness and tried to fight them off.

In that dizzy, void of darkness, I thought I heard two people talking. Who could it be? I wondered, trying to keep from vomiting. The world spun, and I didn't dare open my eyes. That sounds a lot like Vic, I thought. Had someone been playing their videos on my phone? Had I forgotten to shut them off? I tried to open my eyes, but I lost consciousness again.

The wind whipped my face as I pried my eyes open. That dizzy feeling stuck like paste to the inside of my

skull. It felt worse than the only hangover I'd ever experienced. My lungs ached like I'd smoked a pack of Marlboros back to back. What the hell happened? I wondered as the world came together in puzzle pieces.
"There you are sunshine," a familiar voice said.
A shadow covered their faces until we drove under a streetlight. Instantly, I recognized Vanessa Holland staring back at me, blonde hair flapping in the breeze. A white tee shirt with the logo of their channel on it. They were available in the merchandise section of their online store.
What the fuck? I tried to ask but realized something blocked my mouth. I looked down, noted the seatbelt pulled tight across my chest, and my arms tied behind my back. The vibration of the car and the wind whipping in my face felt too real to be a nightmare. *Oh no*, I thought. Shards of light swept over the car with the passing of every streetlamp.
"Welcome aboard Captain," Vic said, looking over his shoulder. "Don't panic, we haven't done anything to you, yet." With this witticism, he chuckled. His blonde hair and sharp jawline barely visible from the short strips of light.
The window whirred as it rolled up. Vanessa's blonde hair, which had been dancing in the breeze, immediately fell flat. In the dark cover of shadows, they didn't look like twins, aside from the color of their hair. She didn't look as pretty as she did in the videos, either.
My mind scattered, thinking through all the reasons they might have kidnapped me and settling on the obvious. I'd sent them a lot of hate mail through the comment section, especially him. I'd voiced my

distaste in their changes to the channel often, without shame. I never thought they'd go this far.

The black eye of a lens stared back at me as if looking through my soul. They'd been filming me the entire time, I thought. A red light blinked. With some sort of brace, they'd attached it to the dashboard. My face suddenly felt flush. I didn't want to be on video, tied, and gagged. What kind of sick jollies are they getting out of this?

"We've been keeping tabs on your comments," he said, shooting daggers through the rearview. "It wasn't a hard decision when it came time to pick our victim." Vic laughed.

Vanessa looked back with a smile. "You didn't know you'd be the star of our new vlogumentary, did you?"

All the emotions caught up to me, and I felt unable to hold myself up. I thought I'd flop on the floor in a giant, weeping puddle. Visions of my mother and brother's faces crossed my mind. I would give anything to see them again, and I had to fight the urge to crumble into tears.

Vanessa moved the camera closer. "There he is, David Cutler, the internet troll." A hint of snark passing through her voice.

The camera stayed only inches away from me, watching, staring. There wasn't anywhere to hide. I regretted every horrible thing I'd said on the internet, not just to them. My face felt hot. When I'd had enough, I closed my eyes, trying to wish it all away.

"This is juicy," Vic said, fire in his eyes. "It isn't going to be anything like our old content."

The viewfinder of the camera snapped shut. I

breathed an ounce of relief. For the moment, I didn't have to worry about *that*. I told myself, if I got out of this, I'd have to destroy the camera. There were a lot of things I'd do differently if I got out. For starters, I'd apologized profusely to my mother.

After a lull in the excitement, Vic announced he needed a break. He steered in the direction of a truck stop, firing off a handful of warnings. He made it clear something would happen if I put their operation in jeopardy.

"Lie down," Vanessa said. "We don't need to get caught."

Vic parked the car under a large, neon sign. I lay down on my side, feeling the belt jabbing at my ribs. We were parked far enough out of view. Vanessa looked sharply around the parking lot, making sure we weren't going to get spotted.

I flashed back to a better time.

Once, while my mother went out of town, I'd planned an attack on my brother. He'd been sitting peacefully on the sofa, watching TV. He had a bag of microwave popcorn in his lap. The best part was he didn't see it coming. I'd walked past him into the kitchen and fetched the fire extinguisher from the cabinet. I pulled the pin like a grenade. "You're on fire, Ryan," I shouted at the top of my lungs. I blasted him, spraying tiny chunks and foam everywhere. At the time, I'd found it hilarious. In retrospect, it destroyed the couch.

"You want anything?" Vic asked Vanessa.

"Snacks, I'm starving."

After going through the truck stop store for what seemed like half an hour, Vic returned with a pile of junk food. Among his choices, Red Bull, Slim Jims, chips, and mixed nuts. He handed the bags off to his sister, and I couldn't help watching her flick through it like a kid at Christmas.

"We should record a little more before we get back on the road," he suggested, slugging down a mouthful of Red Bull.

Vanessa took the camera, flipped open the viewfinder, and pointed it at me. "How do you feel?" she asked, taunting me. "I know you can't talk at the moment. You're a little tied up." She laughed at her joke. "If you could talk, would you say our content is getting better?"

As an attempt at retaliation, I kicked the back of her chair, shaking the camera. I mumbled indistinguishable gibberish. If not for the rag in my mouth, they would have caught my wrath. To put it mildly, I told them to relocate the camera to a certain orifice that didn't see much sunshine.

Vic and Vanessa shared a good laugh at my expense. They performed a small monologue about me in the viewfinder. I tried to block out the things they said, hoping one of them would drop dead. The worst thought crossed my mind then, my mother seeing the footage of her son tied up in the back of a car. My lip quivered.

The sun broke through the windshield, reminding me how long we'd been on the road. A series of yawns passed through the car before a stretch of silence. The type of silence in which nobody had the energy to talk, and everyone was a warm glass of milk away from slumber.

The rattle of a wrapper broke the silence as Vanessa

munched on a Twinkie. I expected her to say something about it going to her waist, as she sometimes did in the videos, but she didn't. I found it odd that Vanessa shoveled the trash into the glovebox. She could kidnap me, but heaven forbid she littered.

As the ever growing light illuminated the interior, I noticed a black pistol sitting between the seats. I hadn't anticipated that and felt stupid for not thinking of it. Of course, they had a gun. Why wouldn't they? If I'd known about the gun, I might not have kicked Vanessa's chair.

Vic looked through the mirror at me. It felt as if he were staring through me, straight into my soul. He had a scowl on him that could scare a demon straight.

As I sat in the backseat, tied and gagged, I thought about my mother. I'd put her through hell, and now I regretted it. I'd done it all to be funny, but she didn't share my sense of humor, not as my brother did. Such stunts as the bean slip and slide had only been fun to us. We'd gotten in tons of trouble for that one too. We'd gotten grounded for three months and washed the kitchen floor several times. I also thought about the Christmas we didn't have a tree. I'd thought it would be funny to yell commentary from professional wrestling and tackle the tree like an opponent. I could still remember the devastation on her face when she walked in. What remained of the tree, dilapidated, leaned against the wall. When I told her Ryan did it, she believed me and grounded him instead.

Either I'd gotten used to being a hostage, or I couldn't keep my eyes open a second longer because I drifted off.

"If we don't get to sleep, neither do you," Vic

shouted, waking me.

"I have to pee," Vanessa said.

After gazing at signs for nearly two miles, Vic pulled into an abandoned rest stop. The engine shut off and Vanessa climbed out of the car. At this point, Vic's head was on a swivel. He looked in every direction, assuring nobody would pull up next to us.

The knot which held my wrists in place wouldn't open. I attempted to pry it with my fingernails but couldn't get under the first layer. With my eyes on Vic, I tried to wiggle free from the ropes, but whoever had tied them did an incredible job.

"You think our channel has gone downhill?" he asked, looking at me through the mirror. I stopped moving the rope. "What do you think about my acting career? That makes interesting content, right?" He stared back at me as if I could respond.

I shrugged my shoulders.

Are you kidding me? I thought. Seriously, he'd kidnapped me over a handful of comments, and now he wanted to know what happened to his channel. Where did it all go wrong? I didn't know the answers. Even if I did, I didn't think I'd tell him the truth with that gun sitting beside him.

Vic continued rambling about getting a part in a movie starring next to B-list actors I didn't know. As he spoke, I felt around behind me. I couldn't feel anything but the rope and the leather seat. I turned and found the seatbelt clasp and unsnapped it, careful not to make noise. I clutched the belt between my knees and chest, lowering it a little at a time.

The whir of the window opening drew my attention. A pack of cigarettes came from Vic's pocket, and he slapped one out against his palm. "Don't mind if I smoke, do you?" Vic chuckled at his wit and took a lighter from the pocket. Blue fumes clouded over his head, seeping out the window.

My hand felt around hard plastic in search of the latch. Getting out without being caught seemed impossible. Once I tucked my hand safely under the handle, I waited for the opportune moment. Vic continued to ramble, looked up at the restrooms, and I snapped the door open. I hadn't prepared for the repercussions. My weight leaning against the door made it fly open and dumped me on the ground.

"Oh shit," Vic shouted, tossing his cigarette and clumsily falling from the car.

Time felt dangerously thin. The thump against the pavement did numbers to me. Getting to my feet seemed impossible with my hands tied behind my back, but like a gymnast, I sprung to my knees first and then to my feet. The fall shot hot tendrils of pain up and down my shoulder.

My knees ached, as did my back, but I managed to get moving before Vic ripped around the corner. I didn't dare look back, but I could hear him huffing and puffing as he trailed behind me.

From the rest stop, I could see the highway. I planned to get as far down the exit as possible and hope someone saw me running and stopped. As we progressed down the exit, I could hear Vic's sneakers slapping the cement. It wasn't going to work. I could tell. His shadow sprawled below my feet, and I braced myself for impact.

Vic threw himself into me like an NFL player. I wondered how he'd hit so hard for such a little guy.

We both thumped on the ground. Vanessa must have come out of the restroom during the confusion because I heard the car pull up behind us. It didn't take long before Vic tossed me back inside.

"Son of a bitch," he grumbled, taking the passenger's seat. They hadn't bothered buckling me back in. We couldn't stay any longer in case someone saw. Vanessa pushed the accelerator down and got us back onto the highway.

"You shouldn't have done that," Vanessa grumbled.

Vic grabbed the camera, flipped open the viewfinder, and began filming. Clearly, out of breath, Vic began to speak. "David here almost got away. He managed to unhook the seatbelt and open the door. He flopped out on the ground, found his feet, and managed to run maybe three hundred yards toward the highway before I caught him."

"I was in the bathroom at the time," Vanessa chimed in.

"Luckily, he didn't manage to untie his rope." Vic stopped the recording, closed the viewfinder, and looked back at me. "That's a cute stunt you pulled, don't do it again."

All the aches and pains from my fall caught up to me. I wished I had a Tylenol or something to take the edge off, but they wouldn't allow that. They probably wanted me to feel the pain.

The red bull can came into view as Vic tipped it up, emptying it in a chug. He paused for a second, turned to me, and let out a long, obnoxious burp, making the backseat reek of energy drink.

The chase must have bothered Vic more than it did

me because he sparked another cigarette and inhaled deeply. As he chain-smoked, his hands shook. He looked out the window and huffed. "We could have gotten caught. Son of a bitch," he said, slamming his fist against the door. "If someone, anyone, had been in that rest stop, we'd probably be in cuffs right now."

"It didn't happen, though," Vanessa reminded him. For the first time since the beginning of this kidnapping, Vic turned on the radio. He blew another plume of smoke out the window and looked back at me spitefully. He gritted his teeth as if he had things to say, but decided to bite his tongue.

We drove for a while, listening to classic rock. After half an hour or so, I heard someone's stomach rumble. I looked from Vanessa to Vic, wondering who's belly I'd heard. Vic kept his face in a knot, staring out the window.

"I'm starving," Vanessa said.

"We're almost there." Vic looked down at his phone, which I assumed had a GPS. "We will be there in two and a half hours."

"That's too long. We're gonna have to stop for food. We've been on the road all day. Besides, we don't want David to starve to death." Vanessa chuckled, stealing a glance in the rearview.

Food, I thought greedily. Other than my freedom, nothing sounded better than a greasy cheeseburger and fries. I didn't even care if I had to be hand-fed by one of these assholes. The thought of food made me drool, which made the rag in my mouth soggy.

"Fine," Vic said sharply. "We'll pick up some food, drive-thru only." He flicked the butt out the window and rolled it up.

A smile crossed Vanessa's face, and I remembered why all her male followers loved her. She looked beautiful for a kidnapping psychopath. "Perfect," she said.

Massive trucks covered the back parking lot of the service station. Their engines rumbled over the Burger King speaker. Vic and Vanessa both ordered Whoppers and a Whopper junior for me. They pulled up to the window where Vanessa paid, and Vic kept his eye on me through the rearview. He had a look about him. A look that said, if you say anything, I am going to break your teeth.

It seemed strange how quickly they could go from super polite to heartless. I'd underestimated Vic's ability to act. He could turn it on and off like a light switch, which impressed me. Vanessa passed the bags to her brother and pulled away. The teenager at the window was clueless. They hadn't even seen me through the dark tint.

We were on the road in a hurry, wind whipping the scent of fresh burgers throughout the car. My stomach growled. Vic unwrapped the burger for his sister and offered her a handful of fries.

"I'm going to take off the gag," Vic said, unbuckling himself. "If you try to bite me… so help me God." He lifted the gun from the space between the seats. "No pleading, no crying, just eat." He leaned between the seats.

I nodded my head in understanding. I don't know for sure, but I think Vic took pleasure yanking the tape from my mouth. I spat the gag into my lap and began flexing my jaw, which felt like rustic hinges.

"Eat," he said, holding out the cheeseburger, fingers

tactically pulled back.

It felt humiliating eating from his hand like an untrustworthy child. Clearly, by his expression, Vic didn't like feeding me any more than I did. I kept an eye on his fingers and contemplated taking a chomp, but the gun between the seats kept me honest.

The first bite of the cheeseburger tasted better than anything I could recall. It felt, for a second, like I'd regained my freedom. I closed my eyes and pretended I was on a road trip with friends instead of tied up in the back seat of a muscle car in my worst nightmare.

"Don't go wasting my time," Vic said.

"Let him eat," Vanessa interfered.

Vic held out a bottle of water. Without a flick of emotion, he said, "drink."

The water wasn't cold, but it felt good against the back of my throat. It had been nice being free from the gag for a few minutes. I flexed my jaw while Vic grabbed the tape and the gag. He worked quickly, securing the rag in my mouth, taking pleasure in my temporary asphyxiation.

"It won't be much longer," Vanessa said.

Instantly, Vic gave her a look. That look told me everything I needed to know. Vanessa was the more compassionate of the two. Vic treated me like gum on the bottom of his shoe, and he wished she'd treat me worse.

The car pulled to a stop in the parking lot of a big hotel. It looked less like a hotel and more like an office building from the exterior. The parking lot had a bunch of cars, but none of them seemed occupied. Just as a precaution, Vanessa told me to lie down.

"You sit tight," Vanessa said as if I had any choice.

She looked herself over in the mirror, touching up her lipstick while Vic exited the car.

The back door swung open, and Vic got to work, speaking to me with a brash tone. "You're going to be on your best behavior," he said. He yanked the tape from my mouth. "You will walk with us up to the room." He pushed me forward with no regard and untied the knot. "Trying any more cute stunts could be a hazard to your health, understand?"

I agreed.

"Vanessa is going to take your hand to make sure."

My legs felt wobbly as I stood, rubbing the impressions where the rope had been. It didn't feel like the end of my life. It wouldn't make much sense for them to drag me out here to kill me. "You guys aren't taking me up there to kill me?" I mumbled. I wasn't proud of my voice.

"Are you ready?" Vanessa asked, extending a hand like a date to prom.

"You guys aren't taking me up there to kill me, are you?" I asked again, this time louder.

"If we planned on killing you, we would have done it back at your house. It would have saved us gas and time," Vic said.

"I don't..."

"Be quiet," Vanessa added, nudging me in the ribs.

We walked together through one of the side doors. A cleaning woman stood in the hall, shuffling through a cart. "Good afternoon," she said with a wide smile.

"Hello," Vic replied.

The bite of Vanessa's nails in the soft flesh of my hand jolted me. I forced a smile at the woman. Even her nails piercing my skin didn't hurt as bad as the impressions on my wrists. What were we doing here? I wondered.

Impatiently, Vic hit the button calling the elevator. He shuffled nervously on his feet, eyes shooting up and down the hall. He'd never done this before, and it showed, which made me feel better about my situation.

We didn't share the elevator with anyone. My hands were sweating profusely, and I imagined Vanessa noticed. The floor indicator turned painfully slow from one to two. Awful music, or what passed as music, played over the speaker on the elevator. As we reached the third floor, I realized they hadn't brought any luggage up.

The third-floor hallway looked precisely like the first, except for a turn at the end. Vic led us down a corridor with ugly red carpet and generic pictures of waterfalls and flowers.

We paused in front of a door, and Vic knocked.

I wondered who on Earth could be on the other side of the door and what they wanted to do with me.

The door swung open, and there she was, my mother. "I got you," she shouted.

My heart skipped a beat. I hadn't even noticed Vanessa let go of my hand, or that they'd both turned to me with huge smiles on their faces. Everyone around me laughed hysterically. The words caught in my throat like a traffic jam of disbelief. What the hell had just happened?

"What?" I asked, looking at them all in confusion.

In gasps of air between laughs, my mother said, "You've pranked me a million times." She paused for another healthy spatter of laughter. "I figured out a way to get you back." She pointed at Vic and Vanessa, face red, tears strolling down her face. "I hired them." Ryan, who'd leaned against the bathroom door to keep from falling over, tried to catch his breath. "She got you good bro."

Vic, who'd broken his kidnapping persona, spoke. "Your mother messaged us a couple of weeks ago telling us you were a fan. She asked if we could help her come up with a plan to prank you."

"We went back and forth with her for about a week when she suggested we kidnap you," Vanessa added.

Reality hit me like a ton of bricks. I wrapped my arms around my mother, allowing the humiliation and anger to fade. I'd never been more grateful to see that woman. Even Ryan, who reserved hugs for weddings and funerals, wrapped an arm around me. I'd decided I wasn't going to prank them ever again. Some of my stuff had gone too far. This prank had gone too far as well.

"You mean to tell me," I pointed at Vic. "That was all acting."

Vic pulled the gun from his waistband and squirted me with two spritzes of water. "Bang, bang," he said.

Again, they all howled in laughter.

All the information felt like too much at once. I walked deeper into the hotel room and plopped down on a chair. My legs felt weak from all the excitement. I took deep breaths, trying to bring myself down. My heart had finally retreated from my throat.

"I was never in any real danger?" I asked.

"The only danger you were ever in was when you ran for the road," Vic said. "You could have gotten hurt."

"You know what's the best part of this whole thing?" Ryan broke in. "We have it all on film."

HIGH TECH CLOTHES RACK

BY MARK MCLAUGHLIN

Abel Clover wanted to rent a nice place near his college. He didn't want to stay in a dorm room any longer because he could afford to do better—or rather, his wealthy parents could afford to do better *for* him. He wanted to work on his homework without all the noise interruptions. He also wanted to work out and be able to concentrate on the exercises. In the dorm, his desire to exercise was mocked by the fat, lazy frat boys.

He looked at apartment listings online and found out about a large house, a few blocks away from the college, with three available units. He made an appointment to look at the largest unit.

It was a clean, attractive house with wood trim painted dark reddish-brown. The unit he wanted, No. 3, was on the second floor. The woman who showed it to him, Mrs. Olivant, was a fortyish woman with hair dyed purple. He asked why the apartment included an enormous exercise treadmill with padded side rails. It even featured a built-in video screen. He loved it, but he didn't tell her that.

According to Mrs. Olivant, the previous renter had brought in the treadmill in parts and assembled it in the room. He disappeared about a week later. She left the treadmill where it was, because she had no idea how to disassemble it. Plus, she figured that some renters might like it. As far as she was concerned, he could use it as much as he pleased. If he didn't want to exercise on it, he could use it as a high-tech clothes rack for all she cared.

She explained that the first-floor area under the treadmill was the house's communal kitchen and, next to it, the laundry room. So he didn't have to worry about the use of the treadmill at night, if there were other tenants in the house. Its vibrations wouldn't bother any downstairs tenant directly below. But, if he watched anything on the video screen at night, she would appreciate it if he used earphones, if another tenant was living on his floor. The first floor included a unit, but it was currently empty and located on the other side of the house.

"Why are all three units empty?" he asked. "Is there something wrong with the house that made the other tenants leave? Like, is there a meat-processing plant nearby and the place smells like dog food every day around 3 p.m.?"

"The guy who lived in the largest unit took off, after only a week," she said. "He brought up that huge, crazy treadmill and then abandoned it. I asked the other two tenants to leave because I caught them smoking pot when I stopped by one day. The whole place smelled like the inside of a bong! Not that I actually *know* what the inside of a bong smells like ... but you get what I mean. At any rate, I've decided to hire a carpenter to do some work on those other rooms, but that won't be for a while. You'll have the whole place to yourself for at least a few weeks."

He agreed to take the apartment, and asked if there were any exercise DVDs that went with the video monitor, since there was a slot for them. She told him there were DVDs in the cupboard next to the treadmill, but she'd never looked at them.

"So the guy who used the treadmill, what was he like?"

"His name was emphatically *William*," Mrs. Olivant said. "William Frumos. If you ever called him by the wrong first name, he'd launch into a tantrum to let you know, his mother didn't name her baby *Bill* or *Will* or *Billy* or *Willy*. He *was* very smart and super-fit, and his mind was always going. I often wondered if he was 'on' something—hormones or uppers or those hepped-up crazy caffeine pills."

"It sounds like he was high-maintenance," Abel said. "You're better off without him."

"I suppose," Mrs. Olivant said with a sigh. "Still, he seemed like an interesting person, and I was sad when he took off. He simply left, without taking any of his belongings. Not even his tighty-whities! I have no idea where he went. But, you're free to use that treadmill, so his loss is your gain."

It took a while to settle in, and during that time, Abel did indeed use the treadmill as a high-tech clothes rack while he figured out where to put things.

Eventually, most of his belongings were tucked away and he was able to start using the treadmill for

HIGH TECH CLOTHES RACK

exercise. The machine was in excellent condition and ran smoothly and quietly.

One Sunday afternoon, he remembered that the cupboard next to the machine held DVDs. He brought them out and gave them a look. Oddly enough, none of the discs had labels on them. That made him wonder if there was something sketchy about them. Maybe they were actually porn movies. He put on a t-shirt and sweatpants and slipped one of the DVDs into the player.

The video presented point-of-view scenes of a runner briskly hiking along a mountain lane. The words *The Village In Spring* appeared across the screen, then slowly faded away. The sweet tones of song birds filled the air. He hoped all the DVDs were meant to be used with the treadmill, like this one. Abel enjoyed the cheerful fantasy of running in this quaint nature setting.

He soon heard the soft female voice of the narrator. "Welcome to *The Village In Spring,*" she said. "Truly, there's nothing more energizing than a peaceful run along a mountain lane. We're approaching a charming village, so make sure you watch where you're going. You don't want to run into a villager or trip over a baby goat."

The run lasted about forty-five minutes and was very informative. The village looked like it was located in Germany, Austria, or some other European locale. Strangely enough, the name of the community was never given. The buildings in the village were all made of brick, with slate roofs. The clothes of the villagers were poorly sewn and void of style. Burlap seemed to be the fabric of choice. The people there talked, but always in the distance, so he couldn't tell what language they spoke.

As he moved through the village, the narrator sometimes told him to slow down, so he could take in various details.

Near the end, the narrator said, "In other DVDs in this series, we'll learn about some of the charming farms in this area. We'll also visit a wonderful castle with some amazing secrets!"

Suddenly, in the distance, he saw a handsome, black-haired man in bright-green sweatpants, running across the landscape. The young man extended a thumbs-up before he disappeared in the distance.

In the week that followed, Abel exercised his way through six more DVDs. It was quite a learning experience, finding out about the various aspects of life in the village. At one point, he even ran past a farmer delivering a calf. The female voice told him he could stop and rest nearby for a minute or two, if he wanted to watch the procedure in action.

Near the end of each DVD, he saw the handsome, black-haired man in bright-green sweatpants, running in the distance. Each time, the young man would extend a happy thumbs-up before he ran off.

Even though the DVDs weren't numbered or labeled in any way, it seemed as though he was watching them in the order they were produced. When at last there was only one left to watch, he knew it had to be the DVD that paid a visit to the village's castle.

He wasn't sure that he wanted to watch the final DVD. He was curious about it, but still, he was beginning to wonder about that black-haired man in bright-green sweatpants. His very presence in the videos was problematic.

Abel wondered if he was being led into some sort of trap—in which case, watching the last video alone could lead to his undoing. Surely it was unwise to follow a total stranger who kept giving him such a disturbingly perky thumbs-up.

***

One day, Mrs. Olivant stopped by to drop off some furnace filters for the house. "How are you liking the treadmill?" she said.

"It's great!" Abel said. "The DVDs are incredible. I only have one left to watch. So have you heard from that previous tenant yet? The guy who used to live here?"

"Nope! I suppose he just moved on. That's how young people are, these days. They just do what they want to do."

"What was his name again? I remember you said he was picky about it. Was it Charles?"

"No, it was *William*." With that, Mrs. Olivant flashed a thumbs-up. "He ended every conversation with a big thumbs-up."

"*Really?* I have something I think you ought to see." So saying, Abel went to the treadmill, turned it on and popped in one of the DVDs. "There's a guy giving a thumbs-up on all these exercise DVDs. He's young and has black hair, and he's wearing bright-green sweatpants—"

"That *sounds* like him," Mrs. Olivant said. "He had black hair, and he was always wearing sweatpants. I once came over while he was sorting his laundry, and all his sweatpants were different shades of bright-green."

Abel wasn't paying too much attention to what Mrs. Olivant was saying. He was more concerned with what was happening on the treadmill's screen. The video that popped up had nothing to do with a village in spring. This one showed a variety of young people using treadmills, while the female narrator presented exercise suggestions. There was no sign of the black-haired man in bright-green sweatpants.

"I don't see William anywhere," Mrs. Olivant said. "Did you put in the right DVD?"

Abel popped in a different DVD. Again, no village in spring. Just another group of young people on treadmills, with the same female narrator offering a new round of suggestions. The black-haired man in bright-green sweatpants was nowhere to be seen.

"I don't understand," Abel said. "I've already watched these DVDs and they showed a mountain village, with William running in the distance at the very end."

"A mountain village?" Mrs. Olivant said. "Is it in Romania?"

Abel was curious about his landlady's response. "I don't know. Did William have some kind of connection to Romanian villages?"

Mrs. Olivant shrugged and laughed. "I suppose! It's a strange connection, though. He used to brag about the fact that he was a distant relative of Dracula. In all those old black-and-white horror movies, Dracula's castle was always uphill from villages. William said he was a descendant of Dracula's brother, whose name was... now let's see if I can remember it..." She thought for a moment. "Radu cel Frumos! Yes, that was it. He said that name so many times, I couldn't forget it for long. He said it was Romanian for Radu the Beautiful."

Abel was amazed by this bizarre revelation. "So this William thought he was related to vampires? Maybe he ran off to join a vampire cult."

"Good Lord!" Mrs. Olivant said, making the sign of the cross. "I'd hate to think I'd been renting property to some sort of supernatural devil-worshipper!" She looked around the apartment, as though trying to spot some evidence of past evil-doings, like bloodstains or pentagrams. "I wonder if I should call in a priest?"

Abel tapped at the rail of the treadmill. "You know, I think it's behaving differently because you're in the room."

Mrs. Olivant stared at him, perplexed. "Seriously? I don't think that's possible."

"Well, you yourself said we might be dealing with the supernatural," Abel said. "I don't think you'd want to call a priest. That would probably get back to the media. Then the place would get so much bad publicity, *no one* would want to rent a room."

"That's a good point," the landlady said. "Those news reporters, they love talking about ghosts and hauntings and whatnot."

Abel came to a decision. "I only have one more DVD left to watch. I was going to skip it, because I didn't want to watch it alone. Could you leave for about an hour, and then come back and check on me? I'd feel safer, knowing you were keeping an eye on the situation."

"That makes sense. Hopefully you can figure out what's going on, and we can fix it somehow." With that, she headed toward the door. "See you in an hour."

After his landlady left, Abel changed into his exercise clothes. He then inserted the final DVD and began his exercise session.

Sure enough, *The Village in Spring* returned to the monitor. At this final phase of the adventure, the point-of-view runner was leaving a pig farm. "Weren't those piglets adorable?" said the female narrator. "We've sure learned a lot about animal husbandry. Now it's time to visit that wonderful castle, a few miles outside of town. Get set for an invigorating run!"

Abel stepped up his speed, and before long, he saw the castle, set atop a towering mountain ridge overlooking the ocean. He wouldn't have guessed that the village was located so close to an ocean, but then, it was just a video—anything was possible.

Soon he was running up a mountain lane, toward the castle's huge metal doors. "Don't be intimidated by those doors—just keep running!" the narrator said. "When the time comes for you to enter the castle, the doors will open automatically, and you will witness the wonders to be found within that majestic structure."

Within a minute, the doors creaked open. Abel ran inside and proceeded down a torch-lit hallway. At the end of the hall, he found himself looking down into an abyss that held a mad tangle of overlapping stone stairways, integrating layers of overpasses and underpasses. And on those stairs, hundreds of runners trotted up and down the stone steps.

The runners all looked exhausted, dripping sweat and panting like thirsty dogs who'd been locked inside hot vehicles on a summer day. Many were running barefoot, no doubt because their shoes had fallen apart long ago. Some were limping along on broken feet with missing toes.

Abel tried to turn around and jump off the back of the treadmill—but he could not. He was no longer *on* the treadmill. He was actually inside the castle and he had no control over his legs, which were carrying him into the twisted, multi-level labyrinth of stairs.

In his mind, the female narrator continued to speak in her soft, sweet voice. "You have reached your destination! You are now a resident of the castle of William Frumos. Here you will spend the rest of your short life, along with all the others who have discovered and decided to try out his Treadmills of Death, as well as his *The Village in Spring* DVDs. Your blood will energize and nourish the almighty William Frumos! Thumbs-up to our beloved master!"

Up and down the stone stairways Abel ran, surrounded by the sweat- and blood-streaked hordes of other exhausted runners. He had to wonder: How many other treadmills were stationed in vacant rooms and other indoor spaces around the world? Dozens? Hundreds? *Thousands?*

Up ahead, Abel saw the back of someone who ran with much more gusto than all the others. His hair was black and his sweatpants were bright-green. Abel realized with a jolt of horror that he was just a few feet away from the evil William Frumos.

With a cry of triumph, William jumped on the back of a heavyset male runner in a torn, navy-blue jumpsuit.

"No you *don't!*" Abel cried. He rushed ahead and

managed to wrap his arms around the dark-haired young man. William managed to hang on to his victim as he turned to look at Abel.

Now that William was just a few inches away, Abel could see that the vampire had beautiful eyes, full lips, and stunning features. William looked young, but then, he was a vampire, so there was no telling how old he really was.

William grimaced, exposing long, snow-white canines. "Let go of me!" he shouted. "If I can't feed off the fat guy, I'm going to feed off you!"

"I'm not fat! I'm big-boned!" cried the man in the navy-blue jumpsuit. He punched William in the forehead, squirmed free, and hurried off. Abel twisted William's arm and managed to sit on top of him, so that the vampire couldn't move. ABEL!

Suddenly, William felt an odd sensation, like he was flying through the air at incredible speed. Then he passed out.

When he woke up, he found himself sprawled in the middle of his apartment, next to his treadmill. He was surprised to see that Mrs. Oliphant was sweeping the floor with a broken broom.

"What's going on?" he said, struggling to his feet. He still felt groggy, dizzy, and a little nauseous from his bizarre experience.

"I came back after an hour, like you asked," Mrs. Oliphant said. "I knocked, but you didn't answer. I let myself in and found you, running on the treadmill in some sort of zombie trance. You had a sort of blue glow around you, and so did the monitor. So, I looked on the monitor and you were wrestling with that William guy, and he was talking about how he wanted to feed on either you or some fat guy. That guy really wasn't all that fat. I'd say he was just heavyset. Anyway, I figured you needed help, so I grabbed you by the leg and pulled you off the treadmill. You were holding William, so it pulled him through, too. You were both unconscious when you got here."

Abel looked around. "So where's William?"

"Well, he'd been talking about feeding on people and he had those crazy teeth, so I figured he was a vampire. I mean, what else could he be? A stenographer?" She held up the broken broom. "So I snapped your broom in half and stuck the other half in his heart. I'll buy you a replacement broom later this week. William turned to dust in just a few seconds. Even his unholy clothes! That's what I'm sweeping up. The dust. Do you have a vacuum cleaner? I think we should vacuum, too. If you don't have one, I can go fetch mine from home."

"You saved my life!" Abel said, tears of gratitude streaming down his cheeks. "If it weren't for you, I'd be a forgotten husk in a castle of nightmares. You're the best landlady a guy ever had. Thank you so much! And yeah, you should definitely fetch that vacuum cleaner. I don't want dead-vampire dust all over the place."

RETAIL HELL

BY AMANDA CRUM

Leah pulled into the mall parking lot and wound slowly around the aisles, wishing she had a cigarette. Ten years. Today marked ten years that she had worked retail, a decade of Black Fridays and aching feet and Karens demanding their money back on items they'd already used up. Jars of face cream, perfume, body scrub, lotion bottles with crusty lids. Once, a pot of lip gloss with a pubic hair stuck inside, like a garnish. Leah had called corporate that day and demanded they change their policies on what could be brought back, but corporate didn't have to deal with customers face-to-face, so it meant nothing to them. She had taken to wearing plastic gloves to handle returns.

The lot was filling up fast, with the lunchtime crowd queuing up at the food court and stores luring people in with fall sales. Leah sighed and circled back around, flipping on the radio to keep her company.

"Our top story today comes from southeastern Kentucky, where an interstate pileup that took eight lives this morning has police and rescue crews working overtime," a reporter was saying. "Sheriff Tony Anderson says an accident reconstructionist has been brought in to determine exactly what caused the massive crash, which involved sixteen vehicles and a tanker truck carrying an unidentified substance."

Leah snapped it off. Depressing shit. It seemed like every day there was some new and horrible thing befalling the people around her. It was too much.

Finally, a spot opened up. She pulled in, grabbed her bag from the front seat, and decided to take the food court entrance. Too many employees were gathered around the loading dock, smoking while they scrolled through their phones and avoided eye contact with one another. The smell of tobacco was too tempting, even from where she was. Besides, it was too hot to waste time outside. Fall in Kentucky often meant extreme temperatures well into November, which was utter bullshit. It used to be Leah's favorite season, but now the heat just blurred the line between summer and autumn. She hated overly warm weather.

The corridors of the mall were bustling with activity: shoppers hustled with oversized bags, seniors speedwalked in little groups, baristas steamed milk and filled cups. When she reached Pretzel Pete's, Leah looked discreetly behind the counter, but saw only a teenage girl with thick glasses and a constellation of zits on her forehead.

The usually frigid building wasn't much cooler than the parking lot. By the time she reached The Powder Room, Leah was sweating through her black work shirt.

"Happy tenth!" Sylvie said as she walked in. The store was dead and Sylvie was taking advantage of the lull by copping a squat on the stool behind the register. She was petite, plump, and 49, and she was Leah's best friend despite their 19-year age difference. Something about her Eastern Kentucky drawl and irreverent love of profanity was comforting, like a mixture of a favorite aunt and a high school best friend.

"You remembered," Leah said, giving her a sarcastic smile.

"Of course I did! I even made cupcakes."

"You're shitting me."

"I shit you not," Sylvie said, pulling a tray from beneath the counter. "And I was up after midnight making frosting, so you better eat at least one, you skinny bitch."

Leah plucked one from the tray and gave her a hug. "You're the best. Even if this day makes me want to pop into a hot bath and open a vein."

"You hush your mouth with that talk! Why are you so cranky?"

"Because it's hot as dog balls outside and because I've been working at the fucking mall for one-third of my life. It's depressing. I always thought that by the time I was thirty, I'd have something to show for my time on Earth besides a crappy car and a lot of debt. Something besides a thankless job in retail."

Leah hung up her purse in the miniscule back room and pinned her nametag to her shirt.

"Is it really so bad?" Sylvie asked. "I've been here for six years myself, and it could be worse. I mean, look. We've got a Pretzel Pete's twenty feet away! I would do illegal, dirty things for their caramel butter pretzels. Speaking of, is your little friend working today?"

Leah shook her head. "I didn't see him."

"Has he talked to you at all since…"

"Since the night I gave him a mind-melting blowjob behind the loading dock? No. He hasn't."

Sylvie gave her a sympathetic look. "Then he's an asshole."

A woman wandered in and began sniffing the trial bottles methodically, one after the other. Leah and Sylvie both ignored her.

"Yeah," Leah sighed and bit into her cupcake. "Or I am. Either way, it's gonna be Tequila City, population "me" tonight. You feel like getting blackout with me?"

"I'm too old for blackout," Sylvie said. "Which reminds me, you're gonna have to get into the display windows today and change the signs. I can't do it. My knee's still messed up."

"Oh, come on!" Leah cried, spraying cupcake crumbs. "You know I hate doing the windows!"

"I'm sorry, but I can't climb in there with my knee all swollen!"

"It's not my fault you fell," Leah pouted. "I told you not to climb up on the sink."

"I couldn't help it. I can't hold it like I used to and I'd just had 32 ounces of sweet tea! We were too busy to close down the store so I could go all the way down to the mall bathrooms and I hate using the one inside Downing's. All the little old blue-hairs that shop in there take their morning shits at the same time and the entire place smells like prunes and vitamins."

"Fucking mall," Leah said darkly. "I can't believe it

was legal for them to just take our bathroom when they were doing renovations."

"They must have offered corporate a truckload of money," Sylvie said, biting into her second cupcake.

"Well I'm telling you, you're gonna have to either stop drinking so damn much sweet tea or start wearing an adult diaper. One of these days you're going to really hurt yourself."

"You think I wanted to pee into a Pretzel Pete's cup? It was humiliating. I got piss all over myself when I fell!"

"What I don't understand is, why did you have to climb up on the sink?"

"I don't know, it just felt right," Sylvie said. "I didn't want to just squat in the backroom in the middle of all those boxes."

Leah sighed heavily and threw her cupcake wrapper away. "Fine. I'll do the windows. But you better watch it with that chocolate. You know too much of it gives you the squirts."

"Yeah, remember your birthday last year? Whoo! All that cake just about turned my brown eye blue!" Sylvie said, throwing her head back to belt out a cackle.

The woman who had been smelling the trial bottles suddenly pivoted on her heel and left.

***

While Leah was in the window, Sylvie decided to run over to Pretzel Pete's for some cold drinks.

Leah's one-night stand was there, leaning against the counter as the manager read him the riot act. Sylvie approached the kiosk across from it and pretended to be fascinated by a bejeweled purse that read "MILF" in sparkly letters, keeping one ear cocked as she did so.

"Seth, I'm trying to be cool," the manager was saying, "But you've gotta work with me, here. You asked for a little more responsibility and I gave it to you, but I can't have you speaking that way to customers."

"Hey man, I'm not going to put up with people talking down to me," Seth said. "I'm not a fucking servant."

"I know it's frustrating. Hell, I've worked here for seven years. I've seen just about every kind of customer there is, including the ass—" He paused there, looked around to see if anyone was listening, and continued at a lower volume. Sylvie shuffled a little closer so she could hear him over the hum and whine of the pretzel ovens. "The assholes. There's one on every shift. I get it. But you can't curse at paying customers."

"I didn't curse at her," Seth argued.

"She said you told her to gargle your balls."

"And I don't regret it."

The manager sighed. Sylvie rolled her eyes. How did Leah find these yahoos?

"Just please, for my sake, pretend the next difficult customer is your elderly grandmother. Or better yet, walk away and ask someone else to take over."

Seth nodded as the manager left, then made a jackoff motion with his hand. Sylvie saw her moment and sidled up to the counter.

"Hey, Handsome," she said. "Think I can get a couple of cherry sodas with lots of ice?"

"Sure thing," he said. "Hot as shit in here, isn't it?"

Such a charmer. "It sure is. Wonder why?"

Seth shrugged. "Something about the A/C units not

being able to keep up with the heat outside. They're probably older than me. This place is a dump."

"You're telling me? They stole our bathroom when they started renovating," she said, jerking a thumb over her shoulder at The Powder Room.

"Is that legal?" Seth asked. He pushed two large cups across the counter at her.

"I don't know, I guess they can do whatever they want if there's enough money involved."

He shook his head. "Gotta love these big corporations. Greedy bastards. We should revolt, you know? Climb up to the top of those ivory towers and cut off some fuckin' heads."

Sylvie studied him for a moment. He was kind of cute, in a stoner-boy kind of way. She could see why Leah was tempted. Dark, curly hair, deep brown eyes, and full lips that had likely distracted Leah from his personality, which was garbage.

"Listen," she said, leaning forward conspiratorially, "So long as we're friends now, I gotta speak my piece. My friend Leah deserves better than to be—ghosted? Is that what you kids say these days?—and she sure as hell deserves better than anything you can give her, but she likes something about you so I'm gonna let you in on a secret. The way I see it, you have two options. One, you can man up and ask her out on a proper date. Two, you can take her back to your place and give her a little oral pleasure."

Seth blinked. "What?"

"Well it's only fair, isn't it? One good turn deserves another, my mama used to say. But if that's the option you choose, you really need to put your back into it. I mean, attack it like a spider in a bathtub. After that, if you need to go your own way, at least you'll have given her a little thrill in return for her selfless act."

She took the drinks and left him speechless, dropping him a wink over her shoulder.

***

"You said what?" Leah asked. Her butt was immediately swampy with anxiety-sweat.

"I just told him he needed to do right by you. Wait and see, he'll probably ask you out."

Leah closed her eyes, suddenly feeling light-headed, and stepped down out of the display window. "I can't believe you did that. What the hell, Sylvie? He probably thinks I'm a total psycho now!"

"So? What do you care what he thinks? He's a loser, honey, not your future husband! Just let him grease your monkey and move on!"

"Oh my God."

"Don't be so sensitive," Sylvie said. "In this life, you have to go after what you want and take it before someone else does. I was just giving you a little push, like a mama bird."

"You are not my mother," Leah said, grabbing her purse from the backroom. "Even she wouldn't have embarrassed me like that."

"Where are you going?"

"I'm taking a break. I can't deal with this right now."

She stalked out, ignoring the look of hurt on Sylvie's face, and slipped into the stream of shoppers in the main corridor of the mall.

Leah fumed as she walked, oblivious to the crowd around her. She couldn't believe Sylvie's nerve. Seth was probably texting all his friends at that very moment, telling them about the crazy girl who'd gone down on him and then sent her friend to give him shit for not reciprocating. What a fucking mess.

She made her way to the loading docks and stepped outside the double doors, where a girl she didn't recognize was smoking and scrolling through her phone. The sun was a bright, hot button in a cloudless sky, the heat unforgiving.

"Hey," Leah said, giving what she hoped was a kind smile and not a grimace. "Think I could bum a smoke?"

The girl lifted her head, squinted at Leah. Her makeup was thick but perfectly applied, winged eyeliner and contoured foundation. Her black apron gave her away; she was a Saffron girl, peddling high-end makeup from behind a counter at Dillon's department store. Not well-known as the nicest people on the planet when they weren't trying to sell you something, but this one must have been feeling charitable.

"Sure," the girl said, holding out her pack. "They're menthols though, sorry."

"That's okay," Leah said. "I just need something to get me through the next few hours."

The girl nodded and passed Leah her lighter. "Hotter than a bitch today, ain't it?"

Leah lit up, took a long drag, and leaned her head back against the concrete wall behind her. "Yeah. I'm over this weather."

They stood in silence for a few moments, each thinking their thoughts, and then Leah heard the girl say, "What the..."

Leah opened her eyes and squinted; across the parking lot, an ice cream truck was careening wildly through the aisles, sideswiping cars as it went. The driver was leaning on the horn as he swerved between a parked school bus and a pickup. As Leah watched, a black Mustang roared up the main stretch in front of the mall and t-boned the ice cream truck, sending it spinning. It came to a rest on the curb in front of the loading docks with one deflated wheel hanging out to the side like a lazy dog's tongue. A heavily-tattooed girl with half her head shaved jumped out of the Mustang and ran toward Leah and the Saffron girl, legs pumping hard.

"Run!" she cried, shoving past them to get to the double doors.

"What the hell?" Leah said with a frown, following the girl for a few steps. "Hey! You can't go in there! Are we being filmed for a prank show right now? I mean, she knows those doors are for employees only, right?"

She turned back to the Saffron girl for confirmation, but the Saffron girl was missing half her face. A bald man—the driver of the ice cream truck, judging by the vehicle's open door—clutched her to him in a lover's embrace, noisily chewing on her nose. The girl's eyes rolled back in her head as blood gushed forth, spraying the sleeve of Leah's shirt. She watched in abject terror as the man began slurping and realized he was trying to suck her brains out through her nose.

Behind him, more people were slowly climbing out of the truck, some of them with dried blood crusted on their faces and clothing. One woman was missing a shoe. Leah watched as she limped forward in her sensible business suit and battened onto the Saffron girl's face, taking her share.

On legs that felt like two clumps of oatmeal, Leah

turned and ran toward the double doors.

***

Sylvie was half-heartedly dusting the shelves when Leah barreled into the store at top speed, skidded into a lotion display, and turned around, reaching for the gate that hung suspended over the doorway.

"What the hell are you doin'?" Sylvie asked.

"Shut up and help me! I can't get... this... fucking thing," Leah grunted, stretching as far as she could and coming up short.

"Why are you closing the gate?"

"I don't have time to explain right now," Leah panted. She spotted a familiar shaved head bobbing through the food court and jumped up and down, waving to get the girl's attention. She zeroed in on Leah and changed direction, heading for The Powder Room and garnering more than a few confused looks.

"Here," Sylvie said dazedly, handing Leah the pole they used to pull down the gate. In her panic, Leah had forgotten about it.

They waited a moment for the girl with the shaved head to run inside, then all three of them yanked the gate down. Leah turned the handle that locked it and ran to the backroom for her phone.

"Is someone gonna tell me what the hell is going on? We're gonna get fined by the mall if we keep the gate down during business hours," Sylvie said.

"Some crazy assholes are attacking people outside the mall," Leah said, trying to steady her shaking hands enough to text Seth. She hadn't seen him behind the counter at Pretzel Pete's when she ran by. "I just watched a Saffron girl get her face eaten."

"What?" Sylvie cried. "Is it bath salts? Oh my God,

I knew that shit was gonna end up here, I just knew it. Why can't kids these days just do whip-its like we did?"

"It's not bath salts," the girl with the shaved head said in a monotone. "This is nothing we've ever seen before. I'm Eugenie, by the way. Genie for short."

Leah looked up from her phone. "I'm Leah. This is Sylvie. How do you know it's not bath salts?"

Genie looked past the gate, where cries of confusion were already beginning to ring out down the corridors of the mall.

"Because I saw someone get shot dead by the cops and then get back up."

Sylvie looked at Leah, then back at Genie. "What makes you so sure he was dead?"

"I watched his brains fly out the back of his head," Genie said matter-of-factly. She pulled a revolver from the waistband of her jeans and tossed it on the counter. "Guess this won't do me any good now, unless you have some bullets on you."

"What the fuck?" Sylvie cried, backing away. "Why do you have that? Leah, who is this girl?"

"I have this because I picked it up after a dead guy dropped it," Genie said. "I didn't think he'd mind, since he had three different people chewing on his face. Listen, we've just effectively trapped ourselves in here unless there's a back door in this place."

Leah gestured around the tiny, windowless backroom, which held a postage-stamp sized desk and a ladder that led up to the loft area, where they kept their stock. "This is it. I figured we'd at least be safe in here until the police come."

"Aren't you listening?" Genie cried. "The cops

aren't going to help us! I was on the interstate when that truck tipped over and spilled chemicals all over the road. I saw what it did to the people in its path. They went crazy and started attacking people, and when they were put down by the cops they stood right back up! We need to get out of here. Now."

The crash Leah had heard about on the radio. She'd totally forgotten about it. "You're saying that guy outside... he followed you here?" Leah asked with a frown.

"He sure as hell did."

"So, you saw all this madness going down and led him right to a crowded mall?"

Genie narrowed her eyes. "Yeah, I guess I did. I was just trying to get to someplace safe. I panicked."

The confused cries in the mall's main corridor were quickly becoming screams of terror. The women could see people running past the gate, pushing past one another to move faster. One of the Biters was chasing a teenage girl, who was sprinting down the hall and screaming at the top of her lungs.

"I'm not going out there," Leah said, flipping off the lights inside the store. "This is the safest place for us to be. We'll wait here until help comes."

"I don't like this," Sylvie said. "We're sitting ducks in here."

"No one can get in," said Leah. "If we go out there, we'll have to run. Can you run, with your knee all jacked up?"

"Shit. I can't run with two good knees," Sylvie murmured.

"Fuck ya'll," Genie said. "I'm not staying in a tiny room with only one way out."

She walked purposefully toward the gate, swung it upward, and stepped outside, slamming it down behind her. Leah and Sylvie watched as she joined the throng, slipping into the stream of bodies effortlessly. In a moment, she was gone.

***

Sylvie sat at the desk, eating one of Leah's anniversary cupcakes and trying not to think about how badly she needed to pee. She looked over at her friend, who looked miserable in the corner.

"Did Seth ever answer you?" she asked Leah.

"No, and my battery is dead, of course. The one day I forget to bring my charger to work."

"He might have gotten out," Sylvie said kindly. "I bet he got off work early and doesn't even know what's happening."

They sat in silence for a moment, listening. Beyond the store gate, the mall was deadly quiet.

"Try the store phone again," Leah said.

Sylvie picked it up, listened to the busy signal, and replaced the receiver. "Nope. I hate to say it, but I think that girl was right. Help isn't coming."

"Why did you say all that stuff to Seth?" Leah asked suddenly.

The change in direction threw Sylvie off. She put down her cupcake and looked at Leah. "Huh?"

"Why did you embarrass me like that? I know you don't approve of me messing around with him, but that was just cruel. Why'd you do it?"

Sylvie sighed. "Leah, it's not that I don't approve of him. I don't care what you do, as long as it makes you happy."

"Then why?"

"Because you were going on and on about how much you hate your job and it pissed me off!" Sylvie cried.

Leah recoiled. "What?"

"You're always saying how you thought you'd be more successful, how much you hate working here, like it's beneath you. Well I work here, too! I've been here a long time, does that make me a moron who can't do better?"

"No," Leah said quietly. "That's not what I meant, I..."

"I thought you liked working with me."

"I do, of course I do! I'm sorry. I didn't mean to hurt your feelings. All that crap about wanting something else... that's my mother talking, not me. But I still shouldn't have said it."

"Okay."

They sat in silence for a beat. Sylvie finished her cupcake and picked up her Pretzel Pete's cup.

"So if we're all good, does that mean I can pee? My eyeballs are floatin'."

Leah laughed. "Sure, go ahead. I'm going up front for a minute. I can't sit back here in the dark anymore."

"Be careful. Stay away from the gate."

The store was eerie in the near-darkness; bulky displays hunched in the shadows like something trying hard to hide from sight. The mall's emergency lights illuminated the corridors outside the gate, casting a sickly yellow glow over everything. The space in front of the store was empty; no one moved.

"See anything?" Sylvie asked, emerging slowly from the backroom.

"No," Leah whispered. "It's really quiet. Maybe

everyone was able to get out."

"Or maybe they're hiding in the dark like us."

"I think we should try and make a run for it. I'm parked on the food court side."

"Leah—"

"I know, your knee. But there's something out there that can help you."

"What?"

"You know! What's sitting right beside the food court?"

"Hell, I don't know, there are a lot of options," Sylvie hissed. "I found a human turd over there once."

"The scooters! Those little motorized ones they keep for disabled people! There's a bunch sitting right beside Burgers & Brews, I can see them from here."

Sylvie squinted. "Oh yeah. But are they charged? What if we get over there and they're all dead?"

"Then I'll carry you on my back," Leah said determinedly. "Grab something you can use as a weapon."

"Oh Jesus, Leah, I don't think this is a good idea!"

"What are we gonna do? Sit in the dark until tomorrow comes, waiting for someone to save us who might never show up? Or are we going to save ourselves?"

Sylvie sighed. "Alright. I get it. I was a feminist once too, back when my tits were perky. But if I die, you have to do right by me. Don't let them give me an open casket funeral. I don't want people lookin' down on me and this one long chin hair that won't leave me alone."

"You got it," Leah said, and laughed shakily. "Come on. We can do this."

Sylvie switched on the light in the backroom and

looked frantically around for something she could use as a weapon; in the end, she grabbed her Pretzel Pete's cup. It was better than nothing.

When she walked back to the front of the store, Leah was holding the pole that pulled down the gate, wielding it like a baseball bat.

"Alright. Count of three, we open the gate, make a beeline for the scooters, and get out to the parking lot. I'm parked in the center row, about halfway down."

Sylvie nodded, afraid that if she spoke, she'd throw up.

Leah turned the handle that unlocked the gate and slid it up slowly, wincing as it whined a complaint. They stood still for a moment, listening.

"Really? You're bringing your pee cup?" Leah asked.

"I couldn't find anything else!"

"I can think of three things you could kill someone with on the desk alone! There was a box cutter laying right on top!"

"Well I'm sorry I'm not the stone-cold killer you are, Leah!" Sylvie hissed. "I just grabbed the first thing I saw that I could throw!"

Leah sighed. "Alright. Let's go."

They stepped cautiously into the mall, scanning for movement. There was a faint thumping noise from somewhere on the right, but that was all. The women moved in tandem, with Leah taking the lead.

"Eyes open," Leah whispered. "You see anything moving, you holler out."

"Shh. Listen."

The thumping sound was louder now. It was coming from Pretzel Pete's.

They walked slowly toward the counter, which was lit up by the neon sign below. Behind the cash register sat darkened shapes: the drink fountain, glass cases full of pretzels, and a bulky oven that smelled like something inside it was on fire.

"Christ, it's hot in here," Sylvie said, fanning the top of her shirt.

"Oh my God," Leah whispered, her gaze focused on something that was moving slowly behind the counter.

It was Seth. Half his head was caved in; Leah could see bits of brain and bone poking through the skin of his forehead. Below it, his right eye hung from the jelly of its socket, glistening in the pink neon lights. He was walking dazedly into a shelf full of pretzel toppings, bouncing back, and walking forward again.

"Seth?" Leah said softly.

He turned his head with a creaking noise and smiled at her; she could see dark gaps where some of his teeth had been knocked out. Drool gathered on his chin, dripping silvery strings onto the front of his uniform shirt. He moved toward the counter and tripped over something on the floor, falling headlong into the side of the pretzel oven. Leah watched in horror as the door of the oven popped open, revealing the manager's severed head. His hair was on fire; his eyes had melted into tarry goo.

"Oh, fuck," Sylvie said. "Oh fuck, oh fuck, oh fuck."

Seth regained his balance and looked down at what was left of his manager's body, which was what had tripped him up. Leah began moving backward, reaching for Sylvie's hand.

"Come on," she said softly. "Don't make any sudden movements. Just walk."

They moved backward for a few moments, keeping an eye on Seth, then turned to face the food court head-on.

At least fifty biters were wandering around, bumping into things, tripping over the bodies of those who were unable to get back up. The floor was littered with them. One shopper was missing both legs and lay on his back, reaching up toward Leah and Sylvie with a groan. The whites of his eyes had turned crimson, either from the trauma to his body or from popped blood vessels.

Fifty feet ahead, Burgers & Brews sat silent and dark. Three scooters waited patiently beside it, like dogs wanting to go outside.

"Okay, so we just have to get through a minefield full of crazies and hop on a scooter that may or may not be charged," Sylvie said. "Piece of cake."

"Why are they moving so slow?" Leah asked softly.

"What do you mean?"

"When I was outside earlier and that truck pulled in, all the infected people came bursting out of it, running at top speed. Now they're barely moving and bumping into shit like they don't even see it."

"Maybe they're wearing down," Sylvie said hopefully. "Or maybe they've had their fill."

A popping sound jerked Leah's head around just as something whizzed white-hot past her ear. She ducked and turned in time to see the top of a nearby female biter's head go flying in a spray of red and white. Sylvie screamed as the woman kept moving forward, seemingly intent on getting her mouth on one of them, and threw the contents of the Pretzel Pete's cup in her face.

The biter paused, eyes closed, as warm urine ran down her face in rivulets. Leah and Sylvie watched as she sputtered, blinked, and sat down hard, legs splayed forward.

"Huh," Leah said incredulously. "I can't believe that worked."

"Could you guys make *any more noise?*" asked Genie from behind them.

Both women whirled around to see her standing there with a gun locked in both hands, looking for all the world like a post-apocalyptic badass. She even had the right haircut.

"Where did you get that gun?" Leah cried.

"Took it off some dead guy upstairs. I think he was a security guard. He was covered in blood though, so I couldn't tell."

"Yeah, there's a lot of that going around," Sylvie said, gesturing to the food court floor.

"They've slowed down a lot," Genie said, eyeing the biters as they wandered aimlessly around them.

"We were just talking about that," Leah said. "When those people first arrived, they were in an ice cream truck, weren't they?"

Genie nodded. "Yeah, I saw the bald guy commandeer it, and a bunch of the people he turned got inside with him."

"It's the heat," Leah murmured. "It's hot outside, so hot the mall's air conditioning can't even keep up with it. Whatever's wrong with them, the heat makes it worse."

"Listen," Sylvie said, cocking an ear. Outside the mall, sirens were wailing in the distance.

"About time," Leah said.

"Even if they're coming here to help," Genie said, "How long do you think it will take to explain to them what we already know and then persuade them to do what needs to be done?"

"Too long," Sylvie said, looking around the food court at the shambling dead.

"You were upstairs," Leah said to Genie. "Anyone alive up there?"

"Not that I saw. Once that first group got in, it was just a matter of minutes before they had a fucking army. We're only alive because we had a head start."

"Then let's burn it to the ground," Leah said gravely.

Three of the restaurants in the food court had gas ovens; the stationary store at the edge of the corridor provided plenty of kindling. The women moved quickly and efficiently, dodging the biters, looking past the vicious eyes and the gore that awaited them at every turn.

***

After, they stood outside together and watched the flames from a safe distance. Columns of smoke rose to the sky, but the sirens had stopped. The entire city smelled of smoke.

"Thanks for helping us commit felony arson," Leah said to Genie.

"No problem. It's the least I could do, considering I led them here. Sorry about that."

"I guess we start looking for new jobs tomorrow," Leah said, smiling as tears streamed down her face, cleaning double lines through the soot. "Maybe the Galleria in Greensboro is hiring."

Sylvie curled her lip. "Fuck the mall."

BEST INTENTIONS

BY COLUMBIA STOVER

"Are you sure this isn't some super fancy assisted suicide?"

"Yes," I sigh as Maggie looks over the brochure for CRISPR Advancement Institute while sitting on the bed next to my suitcase. "The science is sound," I say for the hundredth time.

"The science is voodoo."

I raise an eyebrow at her and she raises both of hers in innocent response. Wide-eyed purity.

Maggie can't pull it off though. She has one of those faces that would make Satan himself wary. Her whole vibe is kind of "Blonde Elvira." She's intriguing, amusing and arousing, yet it's obvious at a glance that she'll eat you in your sleep.

"I've never been to Massachusetts," she says, looking at the map on the back of the pamphlet.

"Neither have I." The clinic is just outside of Salem, on a former estate; hundreds of private acres on which to convalesce. I've been saving for a year. The Institute is a cash only affair; since its treatments aren't 100% authorized by the Food and Drug Administration.

"Don't they talk funny there?"

I look at her deadpan, hoping that she'll realize our accent isn't exactly normal. Our Appalachian drawl is an anomaly, even in the South. Especially hers; sometimes, even *I* don't know what the hell she's saying.

"What?" Again with the wide eyes. "Hey are you taking your lucky socks? Or are you going in with the appearance of not being a nut job?"

Reaching over, I pull back the lid of the suitcase and reveal a pair of red and black Harley Quinn socks. These socks have been through thick and thin with me. I won my first Best in Show at an art exhibit wearing these socks. I found my dog at the shelter in these socks—an article of clothing that helps one find their soulmate clearly has some juju.

"Sage, socks are not magic," Maggie says, frowning at me and pointing the brochure at me like an admonishing finger.

"But if socks were magic, Salem is where they'd be most magical."

***

I pull out my itinerary as we're landing. The creases are fragile from wear and tear. A car is supposed to be waiting for me, then it's an hour ride to the clinic.

I'm met by a black SUV, secret service style. It feels like I'm going alien hunting rather than getting medical treatment. Maybe this is the real Area 51 and I'm going to be flayed and dissected like a grey being ET is dead. ET remains dead. And Science has killed him. Nietzche would have probed the alien matter, for sure. *Out of this world philosophy.*

Sage giggles to herself. Maggie is right. I'm a nerd. The driver's name is Kip. He, too, looks like the secret service type... except his name is Kip.

He takes my bags and ushers me into the backseat where water and snacks are loaded in a basket like it's Easter. I pick out a Whatchamacallit and a Twizzlers and we're on our way.

We take back roads, and the scenery is much better than I had expected. In my mind it was all urban nightmare. But I'm pleasantly surprised to see farms and forests. I may not get so homesick after all.

"We're here." It's the first peep out of Kip since Boston.

I look up, and through the windshield I see molded concrete gate posts and an automated iron gate. Lions have little lanterns hanging from their jaws and I think of "Great Expectations." The driveway leads through a little forested alley before opening up onto a vast lawn clipped down with diamonds, like they do at ball parks. The house that contains the clinic is one of those old stone mansions. It's been added onto over the years, but still maintains that air of Georgian style.

We pull into the circular drive in front of the house, and possibly the ugliest gnome I've ever seen perches on the front steps—generally I like gnomes, but this one is just creepy; no apple cheeks, no cheerful smile. It's squat and grimacing, and its eyebrows are knitted up close. The longer I look at it, the more I think the poor little critter is constipated. Evil constipated gnome.

As I get out of the SUV, Kip fetches my bags and

places them at my feet. Two women exit the house to greet me. I nervously pick up one of the suitcases. They are both dressed in soft pink scrubs and have name badges that read Marta and Kate. They look identical, and when they see me staring, they laugh.

"You weren't expecting twins?" Marta says in a velvety voice, no accent.

"I suppose not. I'm Sage," I reply and hold out my hand as I switch my suitcase to the left, thinking of those twins in that horror movie, standing there, side by side.

"Kate, bags," Marta orders before shaking my hand and then stepping out of the way for Kate to take my luggage. I hesitate a moment before giving it up.

"Please," Kate says, "It's all part of the service. Don't think you're imposing." I let go of the handle, she collects the smaller duffle, and they lead me up the stairs and into the house.

The original wood and plaster walls embrace me like a warm hug. The cavernous entry hall is softened by huge mismatched rugs, and people are lounging on tufted couches and reading in armchairs by lamps like old Hollywood film lights. Little tables scattered around the room hold tea sets, and I can see the steam rising from the spouts. It smells like a café.

"This way, Sage. We'll get you signed in while Kate takes your bags up to your room," Marta says holding out her hands like Vanna White.

I follow her into a cozy room off to the left that was probably once a gentleman's study. It's full of books and tables and squishy leather office chairs. At a desk at the end of the room in front of the fireplace sits the most attractive woman I've ever seen. Her dark hair is pinned up in a ballet bun and her white coat has a smudge of something pink under her name tag. I realize as we get closer, that it's icing, a half-eaten cupcake sits by her phone. I am with my tribe.

"Doctor Smith," Marta whispers as the woman continues to scribble furiously. I giggle. Marta looks at me curiously.

"Doctor Smith... Doctor Who. It's a thing, sort of. Never mind." My cheeks turn red and I look down at my fidgeting hands.

"I am not a Time Lord, miss," the doctor says without looking up or stopping her writing. "But I am out to save the world." She finally looks up, almond eyes crinkling at the edges. "You must be Sage. Welcome."

CRISPR sounds like a candy bar, but it's actually highly advanced genetic engineering. It has revolutionized biomedical research and provided cures for diseases never thought possible—all with a simple snip of DNA and then letting it repair itself. The process uses enzymes that make cuts in the sequence and can, if necessary, make space for a corrected gene to be added. Where the controversy lies is that whole new genes can be added. This has led to super babies in other countries; embryos that have been genetically altered to be "superior," and the reason the Food and Drug Administration is reluctant to give it the stamp of approval. Earlier attempts at germline modifications had Third Reich written all over them.

I am here for what they call "regenerative medicine." Stem cells will replace the portion of my motor system damaged by Multiple Sclerosis.

The unfortunate part is that first, they have to shut

down my immune system.

My room is a soft yellow, like real butter, with a big bed and a desk by the window. The drawers are built into the wall, and oddly, Kate has unpacked my things and refolded them to her liking. My soaps and lotions are on a glass shelf above the sink in the bathroom. A clawfoot tub has, of all things, a flamingo shower curtain on the ring hanging from the ceiling.

There's a gentle knock at the door. I open it to find another pastel-clad woman with a name tag reading Tiffany. And she is just as her name implies: blonde and bubbly.

"I'm Tiffany," she nearly squeals. "I'll be your PA during your stay."

"PA?" I ask.

"Oh, yeah. PA, personal assistant." She smiles, so many teeth.

"Ah," I say, "I see." Not seeing at all.

But Tiffany is quick on the uptake and explains to me that, as my treatment progresses, I'll become weaker and weaker, probably more muddled as well. Until then, she'll just be my tour guide and companion. They've thought of everything.

"Happy hour is at 6, she says, pulling a binder off the desk. She hands it to me. "Your schedule and a list of events and tours we'll be taking. There's also hiking, if you like. Most people look forward to the trip to Old Town Salem. Witch houses, and whatnot."

"It's like a resort," I whisper as I page through the binder.

"We try," too many teeth. "Tonight is orientation. We'll all meet in the library after happy hour and doctors Smith and Tygart will go over what to expect out of your stay."

I snap the binder shut, making too much noise. "Great."

I am not naturally a joiner. Most of my life is spent in my comfy chair ignoring Maggie and her need to narrate her own life. In song. Off tune. So, going to this mixer is not high on my want-to-do list. But, it looks like there's going to be a lot of joining expected of me over the next couple of months.

I dawdle, hoping that if I get there late I'll have minimal interaction. But no such luck. I'm swarmed by smiling faces, hands outstretched. *Oh, my God, she's a hugger—oh, and now we're rocking back and forth. Okay.*

I tuck my hair behind my ears and stand awkwardly as they all rush to introduce themselves. "I'm Sage," I say quietly as I'm inspected, up and down. Thankfully the doors open and we're ushered into the library for the longest orientation ever conducted.

This is what I get out of it: Donor cells; Trips to Salem; Ice Cream; Isolation tanks. I zone out during the whole chemo section, preparing for the procedure, dead immune systems, blah, blah. It's hard to stay awake. Especially when others start snoring around me.

Luckily, unlike orientation, the following weeks fly by. We take day trips to Salem, buy souvenirs at the witch museum, take pictures at Tygart House, and eat horrible meat pies. 1692 was not a good year for gourmet cuisine.

But, one by one, our numbers decrease, as chemo eats away at us. Fewer faces are seen in the gardens and at the nightly ice cream socials. Out of sheer stubbornness, I am one of the last holdouts; insisting on taking my book, which I can barely lift, out to the oak tree by the fish pond. Soon though, even that is too much.

The day of surgery comes, and I truly don't recall much. I only remember waking up. Groggy. Bleary. And unable to speak.

"Sh... sh..." Tiffany whispers and pats my shoulder. "You should sleep."

I point to my throat. "Sh..." And I close my eyes and sleep.

The next morning, I wake alone. The nest Tiffany had built herself in the chair next to the bed is empty. I try to sit up, but dont' have the strength. I try to call out to Tiffany, but I still have no voice. Not so much as a squeak. I reach for my call button and Tiffany walks in carrying water and hurries over to me. She helps me sit up and take sips of water. I point to my throat again, and this time she says, "No, it's okay. That's what happens."

Had I missed that in orientation?

She fluffs my pillows, asks if I need anything, then leaves with the pitcher and empty cup. "I'll bring you back juice. You like strawberry, right?" I nod.

Being too weak to move makes for a boring day. So imagine the week of silent immobility I have to endure. The doctors come in daily to check on me. They nod and whisper and pat my legs. I still have no voice. I'm beginning to worry. They just smile and nod.

Gradually, I start to get some strength back. I take to reading my Kindle in bed, then the chair by the window, then I even get out of the hospital gown that had become part of my own skin and get into pajamas and real socks. Not those fuzzy slipper socks. My skin is terribly dry, scaly, almost. I mime for Tiffany to bring my lotion. She smiles and brings me cocoa butter from the bathroom.

It's so quiet. No one is in the halls laughing. No one is yelling at the TV. It feels unnatural.

The doctors continue to whisper and nod and not give me any real information. So I take it upon myself to check on my progress.

Our charts are just outside our doors, in little boxes. I pry mine open and take out the folder. The photo attached is horrible. The spreadsheet tracking my weight is horrifying. Blood type... height... all the normal things you expect to see. Donor type: D. Donor name: Allu. Donor world: Balberith? *What the hell?*

I read the notes the doctors have been scribbling. Voice deactivation successful. Subject seems to be accepting DNA without ill effects. Side effects: weakness, scales on extremities, mucus production has increased. *Well, I suppose I am a bit phlegmy.*

I poke my head out into the hall again to see if anyone is around. Seeing no one, I tiptoe down the hall to the next door, pry open the box and look at the file. It's Shay's, and she promptly sticks her head out her door at the noise. I hold my finger to my lips. She signs that her voice is also gone. I open the file and flip through it and point to her donor: Preta. Donor world: Rahab. She grimaces. I flip to the notes, which are similar to mine. Only she doesn't have excess snot or scales. She is developing horns. She reaches up to the top of her head and gasps.

We go down the hallway, one by one rousing our fellow patients. Derrick, Cari, Leta, and George. Each one a demon donor. Valac, Ordog, Leyak. All from the two demon worlds we've already discovered.

We get to Mara's room. There's no answer at her door. I open her box. The folder is red. The notes say she is rejecting the donor DNA. She's dying.

Shay pushes open the door. Mara is pale and small. Sweating. Her eyes are glazed and she doesn't even know we are there. Her breath is a raspy, shaggy whistle. Shay takes her hand and looks at me. I shake my head, then motion everybody out. We need to move.

We work our way through the hallways as quietly as a mob could move. People are in the vestibule, milling around. Staffers and nurses. Not to be trusted. We keep going until we come to an iron spiral staircase, and I lean over the railing looking down. Not a soul to be seen. Our stocking feet don't make much noise, but the weight of thirteen malnourished patients is still enough to make the metal groan.

The alcove we alight into is rimmed with arched doorways, all marked with staff only signs. Derrick points at one that seems to be buzzing. We shuffle over to it. The air around it hums. You can feel the wrongness. We exchange looks and step back. Shay taps my shoulder and points to the floor. There is more wear there. The knob on that door is shiny from use. Cari looks at me, reaches over, and slowly turns the knob, opening the door. It's like a scene from Scooby Doo, all of us standing in a huddle, staring into the darkened room.

I inch forward and feel inside for a light. Bookcases fill the room. An old blocky computer with a floppy drive is in one corner. Shay walks the perimeter with her finger grazing the spines of the leather tomes on the shelves. She stops and pulls one down. The Prophecies of Leyak. It has a red ribbon bookmark and she opens it to that page. The frown on her face deepens until she looks like a cartoon character. I stand behind her and read over her shoulder. It's instructions on opening portals to demon worlds.

Cari bangs on the desk behind us, making us all jump. She's gotten into the ancient computer, finding a file listing demon lords, demon worlds, and requirements for their slaves. The top request being "silent."

She throws in another disk, this one containing what appears to be Tygart's research notes, going back to 1692. *They've been doing this since the witch trials?*

Cari pages through, pointing out passages. Slaves don't last long in the demon worlds. Slaves have their tongues cut out. Demand is higher than ever. Dr. Smith discovers that introduction of DNA from the demon worlds extends the life of microbes in the foreign environments. We are not the first.

A siren rings out. The power shuts down and red emergency lights kick on. We've been made.

I shoo everyone out the door and back up the staircase. We split up, half one way, half another. Maybe it will give us a chance. Shay, Derrick and I are in one group, Cari leads the other. It's not long until we hear the thunder of feet behind us.

We're all still weak. And running is torture. I grab Shay's arm and motion the others on. We will hold them back as best we can.

The orderlies reach us in no time. They laugh when they see us. Two frail skeletons, trying to be a wall.

They run at us and Shay swings a hidden fire

extinguisher with all her might. The momentum lifts her off her feet. The orderly stands for a minute, stunned, and then falls forward, nearly on top of Shay. Meanwhile, pausing only a moment in shock, the other orderly comes at me, barreling into my guts—full football tackle. We hit the ground hard, knocking the wind out of me, but not my wits. This girl was all county wrestling. We grapple, and I end up behind him, choking him. He sputters and claws at me behind his back. I tighten my grip. His flailing becomes feeble swats, and slowly, his head becomes heavy and his chest stops heaving. And still I hold on.

Shay shakes me and I fall back off him onto the floor. She sits across from me, a quizzical look on her face. She mouths, "Is that a sock?" and points to her foot. I hold it up, Harley Quinn's manic smile glowing in the emergency lights, and shrug. *No such thing as magic socks, my ass.*

We pick our way carefully along the ruddy hallways. Watching. Listening. Footsteps are coming.

I quickly shove Shay into a room. And there, like a beacon of hope, are huge, white French Doors, the garden just beyond. I can see my oak tree.

The doors are locked, but the beauty of French Doors is that they are ninety percent glass. I grab the bust of Sigmund Freud off a table and smash through the panes. Glass flies and I pound away until I have a hole big enough for us to get through. The footsteps, however, have quickened.

We start to run. Gravel, then grass, under our heels. But months of inactivity and illness have made us too weak to keep it up. Shay falls. I pick her up. She falls again. I can see the orderlies. I try to pull her up, but she's spent. *Run, God, Sage, run!*

I run. As best I can, as long as I can, I run. And steps from the oak tree, I am taken.

The orderlies carry us like potato sacks back to the mansion, through hallways and into the alcove with the spiral staircase. I try to make a mental note of which door we come through, but my attention is drawn away, to the fact that we are being hauled straight to the humming door.

The humming becomes melodic, the farther down we go. I realize it's not humming at all. It's chanting. At the bottom of the stone stairs, Shay and I are unceremoniously dumped onto the floor with our fellow escapees. Thirteen. They've gotten us all. *Damn.*

Robed figures stand in a semi-circle in front of a stone archway. Dr. Smith has a laptop sitting on the edge of an old well. She looks up at us, lovely as ever, and wags a finger at us.

One of the robed figures turns and lowers his hood. Tygart. "You should know that it's true what they say about curiosity," he admonishes. "If you had just been patient, this could have been easier."

Someone snorts. "Patient patients." Tygart frowns.

"Your shenanigans have moved up the timeline, which is unfortunate because it means that most of you will not survive your new lives." He walks to the well and draws a pail from it. Doctor Smith curls her nose and backs away with her laptop. Tygart then returns to his place in front of the arch, and the chanting grows louder.

One of the orderlies pulls me up and shoves me forward. Tygart breaks from the chanting and in a booming voice says, "Ouvrez la porte `a Balberith!"

and throws the contents of the bucket forward.

I catch the stench then, as the muck from the well flies through the air onto the stones. As it slides down the wall, fire follows it, creating a doorway of flames.

Tygart reaches back and the orderly shoves me into his arms. He pulls me forward and presses his thumb to my forehead. "Putain cette fille," he says slowly, and pushes me into the flames.

The flames are like ice; the world melts around me like a Dali painting. I stumble as the ground below me becomes solid and fall on hard packed earth. Large boots before my eyes. I look up into the black eyes of what can only be described as a Sleestack with giant, nasty teeth.

"Welcome, slave," it slurs and hisses. "Welcome to hell."

POTION

BY TIMOTHY C. HOBBS

Most city folks consider potions and spells nonsense. But here in the Great Smoky Mountains, we hold a right passion for such things. We even got our own favorite go-to witchy folk, mainly Buford Grubbs, Sadie Mugford, and, the most desired and successful, Hattie Mae Poe.

Hattie Mae is skinny and old. She's bent and wrinkled like bark on an ancient tree. Her filthy hair is long and stringy, and she secretes an indescribable scent—kinda like polecat mixed with mountain heather. Hattie's the one I went to for a love potion. Her shack is deep in the forest. To get to it, you have to cross an old rickety bridge built across Bear Creek and, let me confess, it's a frightful place sunshine or eventide. But when you're stricken by a desire like I had for Sue Ducat (her family's suppose to come from France) fear don't enter into the equation. At least not at first.

POTION

That Sue, first time I laid eyes on her, I knew she was the one for me. She lived a few miles over in Little Elm while I was in Bear Creek (the afore mentioned place where Hattie Mae Poe lives). There's one common church and school house for both them communities. That's where I first met Sue. There's eight grades in that school, kinda bleedin' over into each other. Anything higher up, a person has to go down to Buford, which is too far to travel every day. You'd have to stay with someone or the whole family would have to pull up roots and move, which don't hardly happen. So after eight grades (no matter how many years it took to get through them) folk pretty much settled right where they were, either in Little Elm or Bear Creek. And I figured to do my settlin' with Sue even though she was one grade ahead of me. Yes sir, I figured it when I started seventh grade and saw her standin' out by the next classroom door. She come to Little Elm the summer before. Folks said her Pa got into some kind of trouble with the law about a still he was hiding. Didn't matter to me how she got there, some things were just meant to be.

I think my jaw dropped enough to come unhinged when I saw Sue. And she looked back, flashing eyes so blue they took my breath away. I was right spellbound. The teacher, Mr. Rumford, had to yank me out of the doorway and into class. "What's wrong with you boy? You addle headed or somethin'?" That got the other kids to laughin' and me to blushing, but her blue eyes made that embarrassment short lived.

I brought the matter up to my Ma. She just hemmed and hawed, "Well whatever you think is best, son. Wish your Pa was here to advise you on your dilemma, but..." She drifted off then as she often did. Ma hadn't been the same since Pa fell off that cliff hunting. Broke his neck. How he made it home before dyin', no one could figure. I should have known my love life would be left up to me, but I wanted to get Ma involved. Yet broken hearts just take all the fight out of people sometimes.

Course there's always the big subject of funds. A place ain't no concern as we can live right where I am with Ma. Got plenty of room in our cabin, but funds is another thing. Folks in Bear Creek mostly raise goats, pigs, and chickens. Pigs are hard to keep healthy for some reason. Some of us can corral wild hogs, but it's a dangerous proposition. Goats are a might easier on the nerves. There's this fella from down at Buford comes up a few times a year and buys some of our livestock. Don't garner a whole lot, but it's enough to get a good stockpile of supplies from Tyson Dodd's General Mercantile, which is located right across from the school down by the crossroads. You know, canned goods, dried meat, beans, taters and the like that keeps us fed for most the year beyond what little we grow in a garden or hunt down or raise ourselves.

So I figured I had more than enough to offer Sue a stable and prosperous life. Any young'uns later on could be handy for chores and the like. It was with this confidence that I decided to pop the question to her one day after school, as she waited on the old dilapidated bus that took her home to Little Elm.

There she was, raven black hair below her shoulders, a little breeze making it dance, her eyes lookin' out blue and glistenin'. Her body all relaxed and buddin' everywhere it should be and me with a lump the size of a dirt clod stuck in my throat.

Well, here goes I told myself. "Hey, Sue. Got a minute?"

She spun around and saw who it was talkin' to her and a big grin lifted her lips. Heck, it wasn't a secret I was sweet on her. Everybody in school knew that.

"Well, hey yourself, Newsome!"

(That's me, Newsome Bailey).

Smiling even wider she walked over to me. "What you want? Better hurry though, bus is almost here and my Pa gets awful fidgety if I'm late."

I'm not one to beat around the bush. "Look here, Sue." I tried then to swallow that lump away, but it wouldn't go. So I kinda pulled my shirt collar away from my throat and continued, "You know I'm fond of you, and I don't see no earthly reason why we shouldn't get married and make a life for ourselves right here in Bear Creek."

She looked surprised all right. "Why, Newsome, that is such a sweet thing to say."

Sue was in full blush by the time I added, "As I see it we're both young enough to get a good start forward. My cabin's more than ample, and my Ma ain't no trouble at all."

She was a bit taller than me, and had to bend to plant a warm kiss on my cheek, which just about stopped my wild heart. "But I just can't entertain such a proposition," she whispered and raised up. "Pa wouldn't hear of it."

I said I didn't understand what her Pa had to do with it. I was fifteen and she was sixteen. Both of an age to do what we wanted.

"Well, that's hardly what's stoppin' me. I'm old

enough to choose who I want."

"So what's wrong with me? I ain't tall but I'm stocky and can work and hunt and provide good as any man around Bear Creek or Little Elm."

She looked sad then and lowered her head. "It's just that Pa made a deal with Tyson Dodd."

"A deal? What kind of deal?"

"Well, you know Pa keeps a still hidden. Everybody knows that. Tyson sells the hooch for him." She was right about everybody being aware of it. Me and Ma kept a jug at the cabin for toothaches and the ague that comes around every fall and winter. "Tyson told Pa he'd only take a quarter profit if Pa would give me up to him as a wife."

Of course that hit me all wrong. Tyson Dodd, was a greasy lookin' weasel of a man, and old enough to be her Pa and then some. "He's too old for you, Sue." I was getting redder and redder at the thought of those skeletal old hands exploring Sue's pink flesh. "He ain't got no business even thinkin' such thoughts about you,"

The bus come over the hill then and Sue looked at me with tears in her eyes. "Got to go now, Newsome," she said, runnin' away. I think she said "sorry" but I can't say for sure as she was already too far gone.

I stood stock still. My legs didn't want to move. "Tyson Dodd?" I heard myself whisper. It was then somebody said, "What you need is a love potion." I thought I'd imagined the voice until my vision cleared and I found Ethel Burtchell standin' right in front of me. "A what?" I asked.

"I heard you and Sue talkin'. She sure is pretty, ain't she?"

POTION

"Huh? What'd you say I need?"

"A love potion." She came closer and said real soft like she didn't want nobody to hear. "That old witchy woman Hattie Mae Poe, folks say she makes a powerful love potion. Now Buford Grubbs or Sadie Mugford, they do the same, but those spells ain't near as dark."

"Dark?"

"You know. Callin' on spirits and other things. Makes her potions more powerful."

"I don't know as I want to get involved with witchery, Hattie Mae Poe or not. Sounds like too much of a risk to take."

"You remember my brother Clyde, don't ya, Newsome?"

"Yeah, went on down to Buford to the High School, didn't he?"

"Uh-huh. Got into to weldin' and working on cars. Why he..."

I had to stop her there. Ethel had a way of driftin' off from a topic. "But what's he got to do with what we was talkin' about?"

She had a sudden look of clarity then. "Oh yeah. Love potions. He got one."

"And?"

"He was sweet on Linda Purvis. You remember Linda don't..."

"Yeah, yeah, Linda Purvis, so what about the potion."

"Well, Linda wouldn't give Clyde the time of day, so he went and got one of them love potions from Hattie Mae."

I shrugged my shoulders, "And?"

"Well they been married now for, oh about four years I reckon and got five kids. See they started on that part right after he got that potion."

"I don't know, still seems like a perilous venture, witchery and all."

Ethel smiled and shuffled her feet, kickin' up dust. "Tell you what, Newsome. You ever change your mind about that Sue Ducat, I'd be willin' to hook up with you as wife and all. I always thought you was a looker." She ran her tongue over her lips and giggled. "You and me could have some fun times. Yes sir, some fun times."

That took me aback. I mean, Ethel is pretty, put together, and beyond her age. I have to admit, what she said appealed to me. Momentarily that is. "I appreciate that, Ethel. But right now I got a mind to get connected to Sue."

She tossed her head a bit, letting that dirty blonde hair of hers bounce around, then threw me a come hither look from her green eyes. "Just you recall what I said about you and me. Sue don't work out, I'll be a waitin'." She waved the fingers of one hand and then walked away.

My blood was rushing by then, but I knew I had to hold steady to what I wanted and not be tempted.

I headed on home, thoughts of spell casting and potions mixing in with the womanly traits of Sue and Ethel. Lord but womankind is surely a mystery.

***

After a night of tossing and turning, I came to a decision. Before I ventured into the dark arts for help, I was goin' to confront the problem head on. Have a heart-to-heart with that weasel Tyson Dodd.

Before school the next mornin', I eased into his store, finding him behind the counter with a cup of steamin' coffee clutched in his claws. He looked a little perplexed to see me. "Hey there, Newsome, what can I do you for? Don't get many from school in the store this early. Ain't got no breakfast items other than," he said, pointing to his cup, "this old chicory."

I felt a little uneasy but mad at the same time. "I'm just gonna come out with it, Mr. Dodd. I aim to make a life with Sue Ducat."

He put his cup down on a wooden counter top populated with the ghosts of hundreds of old coffee cup rings. Then he ran a hand through his greasy black hair. "Do tell." He kinda snickered. "Best be gettin' that thought out your head, Newsome. Me and Paul Ducat have come to an understandin' concerning the future of that lovely Miss Ducat. Mainly, that she'll be with me." He held up his hands and added, "All legal and proper mind you."

"Legal and proper?" I got that angry rush again. "You're old enough to be her Pa. Ain't got no business doing what I know you want to do with that young a girl. She's my age and I aim to marry her."

Tyson looked a little skittish then. Like I said before, I ain't tall but I'm stocky and rock hard from all the work I do keepin' up the cabin and the livestock. It must of crossed his mind that a skinny, bent over varmint of a human bein' as himself might be in peril. "Now hold on, Newsome. Don't be judging me so harshly. I got nothin' but the deepest respect for that young lady. Besides, she'd be a right comfort in my old age." Something dirty must have crossed his mind 'cause he snickered again.

I balled my fists and stomped towards him determined to wipe that nasty look off his face when I was gripped by a hand of iron on my shoulder and spun around as if nothin' more than a wisp of smoke. And there, hovering above me, was Paul Ducat. He was scowling. One of the biggest men I've ever come across, 'bout as thick as a tree trunk and a good six foot seven. That scowl on his stubble heavy face put my bladder in danger of lettin' go. But I stood my ground as best I could. "Mr. Ducat, I ain't being disrespectful to you, I just don't see that old man cuddlin' up to Sue." I tried not to squirm, but it was a difficult proposition for certain.

Paul Ducat's scowl vanished and he threw back his head and hooted a big old laugh that I knew was nowhere close to complimentary. He then loosed that grip and let me go. "Cuddlin'?" he heehawed again and pointed at Tyson. "This man here is pledged to my Sue, and I hope he has a mind to do a right more than cuddle."

Tyson joined in the merriment, no doubt gaining confidence with a giant there to protect him.

"What a nasty thing to say about your daughter." That just kinda came out and didn't land well. Paul Ducat grabbed me by the scruff of my neck and rudely escorted me out of the store, tossin' me in the dirt.

He stood there towerin'' over me and roared.

"You stay away from Sue, you little piss ant. She told me all about your love sick proposal yesterday. Even had the gall to ask me to break my arrangement with Tyson." He threw back his head and guffawed again. "Well let me make it crystal to you, Newsome Bailey, she's gonna do what I say. You're gonna look for some other little pigeon to roost in your coop or I'm gonna bust you up like a chord of wood."

He turned and walked away, just moseyed back to the store like nothin' had occurred. I sat there flat on my rear feeling useless. Tyson Dodd and Paul Ducat were havin' a good chuckle at my expense, and I could hear it. I got up and dusted away the dirt and happened to look over at the school. There stood Sue and some others. I didn't know if they was plumb shocked or maybe wantin' to laugh themselves. So I headed away, my tail between my legs, with the intention of goin' home. The farther I walked, the more incensed I felt at my mortification at the hands of Paul Ducat. And before I knew it, my feet were goin' in a whole different direction.

***

It was almost high noon when I got to that rickety old bridge. I crossed it with trepidation, the sound of Bear Creek running slow and peaceful beneath. It almost convinced me to swallow my pride and go back home. Because on the other side of the bridge, the forest didn't appear peaceful at all.

Spring was about to give way to summer, and the woods across that bridge were so overgrown with trees, kudzu, thick bushes and nettles, the sunlight just up and disappeared. Like I said earlier, didn't matter what time of day a person ventured into this forest, darkness ruled. I can't imagine braving this place after sundown. There was a narrow meandering path, but I was convinced I'd get lost and that would be the last Newsome Bailey was ever heard of. Somehow after what seemed hours of walking, that treacherous trail led me to an open area of rocky ground without a sprig of grass to be seen. Recessed on the rear of that space stood a dilapidated shack. What was open space quickly disintegrated into heavy forest growth again, and most of the vines and tree limbs covered that shack like the wild vegetation was holding the broken down hovel together. I stood there for a long time, Ethel Burtchell's words about Hattie Mae Poe ringin' in my head. I have to admit, the choice Ethel had offered of taking Sue's place in my heart was beginning to look pretty good about now. An eerie whistling noise came from the trees then, sounding just like I imagined a tortured soul would. Must have been a gust of wind, but it spooked me. I shook my head and started to turn around and get out of that desolate, gloomy place when I heard soft footsteps behind me.

"Well, looks like company," a voice croaked. "Newsome Bailey, ain't it?"

And there she was, the witch herself.

Hattie Mae Poe looked to be nothing more than skin and bones. Her long hair was matted and scraggly, falling down her twisted back below her waist. She wore some kind of old country dress that appeared as ancient as Methuselah. Dirty, torn and tattered, it scraped the ground as she ambled toward me. Whatever colors and patterns were once there had long washed out to a filthy gray.

"We ain't never met," I told her with a knot in my throat. "How is it you know my name?"

She moved her short, humped form closer. "Why, I know all the folks in Bear Creek and beyond," her yellow eyes twinkling out from a cragged, eroded face. She hesitated a moment, then added, "Best git inside my home, Newsome Bailey, and tell me what you want from old Hattie Mae."

Well, I wasn't about to stick around after seein' this grisly ghoul. "No, Ma'am. I just got a little off the path and ended up here by mistake. Sorry to have worried you any."

I made to veer around her when a withered arm came out of that old dress's sleeve and grabbed me.

"Now you know that ain't true. You came here for some kind of potion." Her claw-like fingers tightened around my wrist with unexpected power. She looked me up and down, considering me like I was something for supper. "Mmmm. Yes, I see it your eyes, Newsome Bailey." A big, mostly toothless grin spread over that haggard face. She tapped a finger on a pointed nose and said, "Love potion, ain't that right, Newsome Bailey?"

Before I could protest, she yanked me toward her shack where a door stood open and waitin' like a ravenous beast.

Once I crossed the threshold, a stench like an old root cellar hit me, the inside of the place dark and murky. With only a few well-worn candles burning, I couldn't tell for certain, but I swear the back walls were nothin' but earth, like the floor. It looked like it only had a front and short sides and must have been built into the side of a cliff. There had to have been a chimney present because toward the back was a fireplace large enough to hold a big, steaming kettle, the smoke from which was definitely escaping up and not into the room. And that was what the entire spot seemed to be—just one large room.

Hattie pointed out a decrepit chair beside a large,

wide table that was the only existing furniture. As I wondered where in the world she slept, she said, "Sit down and take a load off." I had no intention of staying, and the chair didn't seem stable. "No thank you. I really need to git on home."

She smirked a bit and slid off toward the cookin' pot in the fireplace where she stuck in a crooked finger, pulled it out and run it over a knobby tongue. "Is that potions cooking?" I asked while backing up toward the door.

"Potions? Course not. This here's supper." She grinned and licked the residue from her finger. "Squirrel liver stew with some wild onions and herbs." She winked then and added, "And a touch of garlic for good measure." She took a ladle hanging on the crude mantle, dipped it in the pot, and came my way. "Like to have a taste, Newsome Bailey? Ain't nothin' like squirrel liver stew to give you what you need if you get my love potion." She cackled a sullied, wicked laugh and continued coming closer. "Young randy buck like you needs all the energy he can muster to keep a girl satisfied long enough to stick by you."

Inappropriate as that statement was, it sent a shiver of bewilderin' passion through me. Enough to make me freeze in my tracks and open my mouth. She put that ladle on my lips and tilted it so the slimy juice slid right in.

I couldn't believe I actually let her do that. She said it was stew, but who knew what dark innards it really held. And yet, I swallowed the stuff, the concoction slammin' my stomach like a ball of fire. I doubled over and went to my knees, everthing spinnin' around in a dizzy whirl. Last thing I knew I was falling in slow motion to the dirt floor where old stale dust curled into my nose.

***

"Say her name."

The words floated over me like a mist.

"Say her name."

I was starin' straight up as my eyes tried to focus. Wind chimes were hanging from cross slats on the ceiling. My head was still spinnin' so it took a while to realize them weren't wind chimes at all. They was dried and mummified critters. I couldn't swear by it, but some of them sure looked to be things I ain't never heard of. Parts of one critter mixed with parts of another kind. There was also a lot of stringy roots and dried up flowers.

"Say her name." Hattie Mae glared down at me, her mouth a tad open, her lips lookin' wet, repulsive, and greasy, makin' me wonder just what she done to me while I was knocked out.

"What was in that stew?" I asked over a thick, disorderly tongue.

"Somethin' to prime you up. Now, say her name."

"Who?"

She bent close enough to make me shiver. "That gal you want. The one gettin' my potion."

It all came back to me then. "Sue. Sue Ducat."

A smirk came over her and she rose up and snickered.

"Why's that funny?"

Hattie Mae snorted a little more before saying, "Well, somebody else done beat you to it, Newsome Bailey."

"What?"

"Older man come by a few days ago and got a potion for that girl."

I was wide awake now and scrambled up to my feet. "Who?"

"Can't give no names of customers out. Bad for business."

"I wanna know who," I said, clenchin' my fists.

She noticed this and snorted again. "Try violence on me boy and you'll rue the day."

I swear her eyes gleamed an even darker yellow then, like the inside of a candle flame. My stomach cramped as my fists relaxed. "No, Ma'm, I ain't mad at you."

She walked over to that long table, bent down, and brought up a pouch. She opened it and a dead frog plopped out. "Like I said, can't tell you no name… unless you tell me one yourself."

Didn't take me a second to answer, "Tyson Dodd."

A sly grin creased her face again. "That'd be the one."

Well, I felt plumb disheartened, especially after goin' to all the risk of meetin' up with a follower of the black arts. "I suppose that's that then."

She chortled a wicked laugh. "Not necessarily, Newsome Bailey. Unless you ain't interested in somethin' a little more potent than what I give him. Come on over and take a look see."

And I soon found myself driftin' over to her despite an inner plea not to.

Hattie's eyes went wide and she said "Ah ha! There's my little devil." She stuck her fingers in the frog's mouth and came out with something that evidently pleased her 'cause she grinned from ear to ear. "Look, Newsome Bailey."

I didn't see nothin' but slime at first, but then discovered she held an object between her index and forefinger; a small, reddish brown pebble-like thing. "Potent. Very potent." She held it under her long nose and took a deep breath. "Bout ripe too."

The possibility of my upchuckin' was eminent, so I turned away and took some breaths of that stale room air to try and quell it.

Hattie chuckled. "Tender ain't ya, Newsome Bailey?"

"I surely am, Ma'am."

"Well, this has to dry out and be pulverized into a powder for me to make what you need. Unless you changed your thoughts on that Sue Ducat."

That took my nausea plumb away. "You mean, I can still get her? What about the potion you gave Tyson Dodd?"

Rollin' that object over her fingertips, Hattie said, "Always somethin' more powerful out there. But it comes with a high price too, much higher than what that Tyson Dodd was tallied."

"Well, I ain't got that much coin, not with me and Ma just makin' it when that fella from Buford buys some of our goats." I felt defeated all over again. "I guess this time that is that."

Hattie gave me a stare that curdled my blood. "Ain't money, I want, Newsome Bailey. Ain't money at all."

When she said it, I saw what looked to be tiny lights flicker on the back wall. I took a harder look and saw jars outlined by short spurts of illumination, sort of like fireflies was trapped in them.

"Are them fireflies?" I asked, pointing at the little

bursts of sparks.

Hattie's mood darkened, her face caught in shadows as she turned around to look at what I pointed to. And without taking her eyes off the jars, she said, "That they are, Newsome Bailey. And somethin' else besides."

***

Now how was I supposed to get some blood, BLOOD, from Sue Ducat? "Hey, Sue, next time you cut yourself or have a nosebleed, would you kindly save some drops for me?" just didn't sound like something appealin' to most folks, much less a delicate female like Sue.

"Ain't nothin' to it" that old crone had told me when I left her shack. "People bleed all the time. Just see you bring me some of her blood before the next new moon or Tyson Dodd gonna get the gal you want for sure."

I left that witch's den around twilight and heard things rustlin' around like I was being watched and followed all the way till I crossed back over that rickety bridge. But even then, night terrors followed me to my dreams the next week—scary things trapped in jars all dead but still wigglin', and some of them frogs hoppin' around. Worst of all, one night I felt a cumbersome weight on my chest and when I opened my eyes there was this scrawny black cat sittin' on me trying to suck out my breath, and that cat's face looked all too familiar, them yellow eyes alive with wickedness.

Course that horror faded away as soon as I woke up for real. But it left me chilled even with the sun pourin' in my window.

The nightmares soon paled, and I found myself counting the days till the next new moon, which, according to Ma's Almanac, were thirteen, the same number of days left till the end of the school year.

I tried and tried to come up with a plan to get some of Sue's blood without her thinkin' I was some kind of half-ass vampire, but nothin' held water. The closest I came to anything sensible was making up some wild tale about us cutting each other's palms and mixing the blood together. Blood brothers don't you see. Just didn't seem right though. Seemed more of a boy's thing.

With two days of school left, Sue came up behind me to see what I'd been so low about the last few days and tapped me on the shoulder. Well, I was so preoccupied with my growin' misery that her action started me and I turned round so fast we bumped faces, smashing our noses hard enough to bring blood. She laughed but I could see she was hurtin', I know I was, 'cause ain't nothin' as painful as a smashed nose. We were both apologizing so much I dang near forgot to get some of her blood, but then it came to me. I pulled out my handkerchief, which was sure embarrassing 'cause it was pretty stiff with old snot. She didn't seem to mind much and held that hanky around her nose until the bleedin' slowed. Even offered to take it home and wash it, the idea of which I stopped in a hurry. I stuck it in my back pocket. We laughed a little more about it until the bus come to take her home, her wavin' with one hand and pinching her nose with the other as she hurried down the hill to catch it. I was watching her go when she suddenly stopped and yelled somethin' to the driver and then ran back up to where I was and gave me a kiss straight on the lips.

"I don't want no Tyson Dodd, Newsome. I want you." She then ran back and jumped on the bus which had already started a slow crawl down the road.

Well, I wasn't about to go straight home after that revelation, no sir! I headed on through the woods to get to that old bridge and across it to Hattie Mae's as quick as I could. It was late afternoon and I should have been spooked by the surroundings like I was on my first visit, but I still felt Sue's warm lips on mine, could still taste a hint of salt from her nose bleed. And I was ready to get my claim in motion no matter what frights awaited me on the other side of that bridge.

***

Hattie Mae was right pleased with that snotty, blood soaked handkerchief.

"Good work, Newsome, Bailey. Good work." She held up the hankie to get a better look at it in the candlelight. "It'll do nicely, indeed." She set it down on her big table and picked up a small pouch drawn together by leather straps. "Two days ahead of schedule too," she said, handing me the pouch.

"Is this…"

"Yes Newsome. It's ready."

"But don't you have add that blood I brought you? To make the potion work?"

"I gave Tyson Dodd a potion. Yours is more of a spell. Blood's not for the spell, Newsome Bailey. Blood's the recompense for me to do with as I see fit."

"How does the powder work then? Do I blow it on her?"

Hattie Mae's eyes twinkled and she said with a snort, "If you want her to think you're an idgit you do."

"What do I do with it? I mean how…"

She walked behind the table and picked up the handkerchief, rubbing the fabric between her crooked fingers. "That fiddler man still come around Bear Creek from time to time?" she said with an odd distraction.

"Who?"

"When your communities get together for a shindig. Does that fiddler still come around and raise the roof so ya'll can shake a leg?"

"You talkin' bout Cyrus Crow?"

With a sigh she set the hankie down and came back to where I stood holdin' the pouch. "The very man." She touched the pouch and grinned. "I'm guessin' your commune still throws a get together the last day of school for them that's seekin' higher learnin' down in Buford? Cyrus is usually there, ain't he, to fiddle for dancin'?"

I nodded yes.

"You go to the dance and give him this pouch. He'll resin up that bow of his with the powder and let her rip."

"But ain't that the night of the new moon?"

"Don't fret so, Newsome Bailey. Old Hattie Mae got a way of arrangin' things. Things like love, hate, vengeance... and the hour you need to beat, that being the stroke of midnight."

Before I could ask anything else, she added, "Me and Cyrus go back a long ways. He made a few deals with me, pacts you could call 'em. Just hand him the pouch and say Hattie Mae said to resin that bow of his and he'll do it without question or qualm."

"But..."

"She put a finger to her lips and shushed me. "Trust

old Hattie Mae, Sue Ducat will be there with Tyson Dodd. When she hears Cyrus spin the spell, she'll be yours forevermore."

***

And sure enough, there was a shindig at the Pentecost Church's Parish Hall the night after school let out.

I made a point to get there early, but seems most folks had the same notion because the Hall was pretty full when I arrived. They'd already set up the long tables and had most of the food out by the time I came in. The weather was getting pretty steamy this close to summer, so the fares were mostly light ones like melons, berries and nuts. A few baskets of fried quail and some vinegar and wild grape pies also filled out the cuisine.

Ma didn't come with me, which was no surprise. She'd been feelin' poorly lately, but besides that, she stopped attending any such gatherings after Pa died. She said it just wasn't the same doin' such things without him. I was meandering around when one of my school chums brought me a mug of somethin', giving me a sly wink so I guessed right off it was probably some of Paul Ducat's hooch, which it was. I went to one of the rows of chairs someone arranged in a semi-circle toward the back of the hall and sat down and sipped at that fiery brew, waitin' for Sue and Tyson to show up.

A crowd had gathered on the dance floor because Cyrus Crow had walked in and went around the room laughin' and shaking hands before he got up on the raised stage to pick and tune his fiddle. There was no Sue or Tyson, even after a couple hours of dancing. The longer the night grew, I knew the new moon was risin' toward that midnight hour and a certain doom for my love affair.

And then, a little after Cyrus started his third set of reels and waltzes, in they walked big as day. Tyson grinnin' like a possum eating scraps and Sue looked sad and out of place hanging on his arm. She didn't see me at first, but when she did it looked like she tensed up and whispered somethin' to Tyson, who looked my way, chuckled and then laughed while escorting Sue onto the dance floor. It wasn't long till they was spinnin' and movin' with rest of the dancers, and it didn't appear to me Sue was as unhappy with Tyson as she'd confessed to me that day when we bumped faces and her nose bled. It hit me then that the midnight hour was fast approaching. His love potion, you see, was startin' to work its magic. There was no time to waste on my part.

I went to the bandstand about the time Cyrus Crow was startin' his final set of songs for the night. If any name fit a person, it was his. He was thin and spindly, his back humped a little under his neck, and his face possessed a pointed beak-like nose too big for the space it occupied. He saw me come up and glared at me with sweat rollin' down from his flat, black, greasy, thinnin' hair. "Well?" he asked flatly.

I handed him the pouch and said, "Hattie Mae Poe said to resin up your bow with this here powder."

His expression went from one of antagonism to that of sheer terror as he took the pouch from me with a shaky hand and opened it. He gazed in it briefly, then held his bow underneath and poured the powder on it in one dusty move. Cyrus said not one word more to me but straight away started fiddlin' a tune I knew well—Fox in the Hen House. One of those old folky tunes about a travelin' tinker who stopped by homes when the man of the house was out huntin' or workin' and then proceeded to mend rusty holes with a good blockin'.

I didn't think that jingle quite appropriate for a Pentecost Parish Hall, but the crowd didn't seem to mind at all. In fact, the faster Cyrus fiddled, the rowdier the crowd got, whoopin', shaking, and grinding on one another like a renegade orgy was about to commence. I glanced at Cyrus and caught him glowerin' at me, sweat pouring off his forehead, his eyes big and hellish. There was something that sent a chill to my backbone—smoke was rising between the fiddle's strings and bow, curlin' up in what looked like a shadowy, demonic countenance.

I turned to flee from that horror when I saw Sue and Tyson spinnin' madly in front of me. Sue's head pulled away from Tyson, her eyes locked on mine as she pushed Tyson away and took hold of me, pulling me close and pressing her body next to mine while she kept dancin' to Cyrus' maniacal fiddling. Fire rushed through my veins and I wanted her right then. I was so caught up in the wildness, I never saw Tyson come up behind her. All I noticed was somethin' shiny travel across her throat.

Sue stopped dead still, her hands grabbing her throat as a line of red started to flow through her locked fingers. I was dumbstruck, watching her slow descent to the floor, helpless at the moment to catch her. After she fell, I discovered Tyson Dodd standin' there, a knife still clutched in one hand.

"Thought you could one up me, did you?" His face was expressionless. "I been keepin' an eye on you. I seen you hand the pouch to that fiddler. Suppose you thought you could get a better potion from that damned old crone."

He lunged at me, but by that time the crowd had broken up and some men grabbed him and wrestled him to the ground, leaving me to kneel by Sue, watchin' the blood gush out of her slashed throat with every beat of her heart... until her heart beat no more.

***

Little Elm didn't have a church or cemetery. Folks from there always used the graveyard behind the common Pentecost Church close to Bear Creek. Brother Starling, the preacher, didn't come round but every other month for Sunday services much less funerals. So unless word got to him about someone being buried, it fell on the loved ones of the departed to see it got done. And Paul Ducat done just that. Most of us who knew Sue came, although Paul didn't seem too pleased to see me in attendance. But I must have appeared so heartbroken he didn't stir up no fuss with me.

I heard a few days later someone got in the Buford County Jail where Tyson Dodd was waiting for a judge to try his case. Folks say whoever it was came carryin' a hammer, some ten penny nails, and a crowbar. They said every time Tyson Dodd passed out screaming his assailant splashed icy water on him and started all over again until there weren't much of Tyson left to maul.

Course we all knew it was Paul Ducat that saved Buford County the expense of a trial. Paul had a lot of secret doings with the law in regard to his moonshine business—payoffs to some deputies and the like. And after Tyson Dodd met his fate, Paul Ducat was never heard from or seen again. Vanished, just like a puff of smoke.

As for me, I took Sue's death hard, couldn't sleep or eat right. On them long sleepless nights I would ponder such things as spells and potions. I concluded they was all deals with Old Scratch even if his name never came up. Deals that don't ever turn out as planned for people like Tyson Dodd or me. I imagine Cyrus Crow will have to pay for his pacts too one day, all paying recompense to Old Scratch's book keeper—Hattie Mae Poe. I wondered if she'd ever have to pay. Maybe she already has, livin' in all that darkness with things stirrin' around her. And maybe she don't care about being damned 'cause in her blackest of souls she feels about Old Scratch the way I felt and still feel about Sue Ducat.

However, I will give Hattie Mae credit for some bit of honesty. She said Sue would be mine forevermore. And she weren't fibbin' neither.

You see, them long nights I lay fretting after Sue's death, well sometimes I'd kinda drift off into a half dream world, seein' disturbing visions, especially one with them little jars holdin' what looked like fireflies in the back of Hattie Mae's shack. Only them bugs all had tiny human faces, twisted with pain and suffering like they was caught between this world and the after one in a kind of cruel limbo.

One night the visions were so life like I jumped out of bed screaming. Ma come in lookin' all pale and shocked wondering what was goin' on, and I finally convinced her it was only a nightmare and walked her back to her room and to bed. When I returned to my room, I saw somethin' sitting on the ledge of my open window. Yes sir, it was one of them jars, sittin' there as plain as could be. Not no dream for sure.

I picked it up and saw there was a piece of old, yellowed paper around it. I slid the paper off and saw writin' on it. I gazed at it long and hard, not believin' what I made them scribbles out to say. They was fragments, but I got the point.

> "When Lite flickers
> Crossroad by church graveyard
> Watin' in moonlite"

I waited for near a month, until one late night I'll be damned if that thing in the jar didn't start flickerin' a light. I was a little unsure if I should try out those written directions or not but soon found myself slidin' out my window and heading down the hill toward the crossroads by the Pentecost Cemetery.

Autumn was on us then, and the night held a crisp brittleness as I walked on under a high, cold moon. The closer I got to my destination, the brighter and steadier the light in that jar glowed.

When I arrived at the crossroad, I stopped short at what was waiting for me on the cemetery side. A figure sat there on one of the few crumbling benches by the cemetery walls. The hair on the nape of my neck bristled and I suddenly felt queasy and weak kneed, the figure on the bench beckoning with one hand in an abnormal and uncoordinated movement.

Even though I didn't believe it, I thought all of this might be some extended weird dream, I guess I knew in my heart it was true 'cause I went across the road and stood there lookin' at Sue Ducat.

She was in a grave shroud gone moldy gray after these months she'd been in the ground. She looked at me and in that jerky motion of hers pointed to a place by her on the bench, and I sat down without hesitation. By now decay had progressed, her mottled skin dotted with a greenish blue mold. Her hair, somehow grown longer but still a deep, luxurious black, was clumped with erratic clods of earth. I took her hand and was shaken by the icy feel of it, the lifeless weight of it, her long fingernails cracked, wet dirt trapped under them from her diggin' out of the grave.

None of those horrors really bothered me. What chilled me to the bone was her eyes. Those deep blue eyes now a sick, milky consistency, staring out dully from her other world.

She jerked her head toward the jar I held and put one shakin' finger on the glass. The look that spread on her face then was one of utter misery, an anguish so deep I could of sworn I heard a moan rise from deep inside her. But the expression soon faded and she slumped slightly, still holdin' my hand.

The night passed and the light in the jar dimmed. Sue released my hand and stood and turned and walked an unsteady gait back in the direction of the cemetery. I did not follow but instead lingered until the moonlight paled and the first dim light of morning appeared.

I wondered how long her crumbling form would stay together. How many moonlit nights would we meet this way—the land of the living sharin' a silent night with the dead. Would she eventually be nothin' but a skeletal shroud makin' her way to that bench, waiting for me? Would the bones someday detach and somehow still wander across the cemetery to find me?

How long?

But I guess it really don't matter none, 'cause you see, anytime that light in the jar starts to flicker, I'm goin' back to that cemetery bench come rain or shine, sleet or snow, hell or high water 'cause I still have a passion for her deeper than any grave. Yes sir, that Sue Ducat, first time I laid eyes on her, I knew she was the one for me. And always will be. Forever and ever more.

AN OLDER LADY

BY NICOLE M. WOLVERTON

I didn't mean to start an uproar, Sheriff. Honestly, I didn't. An older lady can only take so much, but I never dreamed the Women's Auxiliary at church would report me.

This whole business started after the church bake sale a few months ago. I sat there for hours, smiling over lumpy cakes, cookies as crumbly and parched as the Sahara, and the most anemic pies I ever did see. No, of course none of them were mine. You've had my apple crumble. It won a blue ribbon at the North Georgia State Fair. It could make a grown man cry. You shed a tear or two over it yourself. Don't tell me you haven't.

No, I don't have a pan of it in the kitchen right now. Sorry, Sheriff.

Yes, of course. Back to the bake sale. I did my duty for the Women's Auxiliary, I really did—I didn't complain once. Not even when that Ginny von

Foofenheimer showed up and dressed me down for not selling her ridiculous whole wheat prune bread.

Whole wheat prune bread. God in heaven, what kind of person wants to eat *that*?

Truly, Sheriff, I *am* giving you the condensed version of the story.

Now, where was I? Oh, yes—of course. Ginny's prune bread. Well, I smiled at her, right enough, but she frosted my fiddlesticks. Everyone knows I'm a good volunteer. I give blood—why in my seventy-three years I've donated sixty gallons. Those nice Red Cross people mailed me a letter about it. And goodness, I brake for pedestrians and ducks. But like I said, an older lady can only take so much. So when I came home and those kids from that other church rang the front bell, well, I wasn't at my best.

No, I *do* remember it all perfectly. Fresh-faced and sweet, the both of them. Identical smiles, Sunday best clothes. The girl—pretty blonde thing—she held out a pamphlet and asked me something about discovering the secret to eternal life.

And then, it just popped out of my mouth, easy as pie. Good pie, that is, mind you—not that gummy Shoo Fly from the bake sale. Anyway, I said, "No, thanks, but I'd love to tell you about Satan. Would you like to come in?"

Why? I really couldn't say *why* I said it. I just did. I might have been thinking uncharitable thoughts about Ginny at the time. I admit that, and I prayed on it. A lot.

Oh yes, the girl. Well. She clutched the little round collar of her blouse, while the boy she was with sputtered like I'd jabbed him with a hat pin. His holy book hit the ground—and me, I couldn't stop grinning. I thought my dentures would fall right out of my head. I remember doing this thing with my hand, like a game show host showing off a car, except it was more like I was inviting those kids in for tea and the dark arts. Turn the letter, win a prize.

No, Sheriff. Of course not. You see me and my Edwin every week at church. I'm a good God-fearing lady. It was just... well, like I said, I was not myself. Not at all. Maybe Ginny drugged her awful prune bread? I do admit I tried a bite. It was as terrible as it sounds.

Right, back to the story. Did I mention the tulips were in bloom? These gorgeous Queen of the Night tulips that I bought from... well, the only reason I bring it up is because tulips bloom in the spring. So all this was in April. And it was just chilly enough to need a shawl.

I'm just trying to help you establish that this happened in the spring. Perry Mason calls it establishing timeline. You don't have to get so huffy.

Yes, of course. Well, the boy nearly fell off my porch. His eyes went big, and he made these wheezy sounds. Maybe he thought Satan was playing pinochle in my pantry. Whatever that poor child thought, he didn't say a word—just bolted right down the three steps to the sidewalk and ran off. Left that girl there by herself. Maybe an older lady like me doesn't *look* dangerous, but I could be. I *was* wearing that racy red dress with the lace around the sleeves that day, and it's not as if I don't know how to use rat poison. Why, who knows what I could have done to that girl if I were a nasty type. Truly, is chivalry dead in young men these days?

Merciful heavens!

The girl, at least, had some manners on her. She picked up the book the boy had dropped, thanked me for my time, and went on her way. Nice girl. Didn't even start running after I yelled about Satan's orgies. I admit I got a kick out of the idea. What, with Edwin's model train set up in the living room, I don't know where we'd fit enough people for an honest-to-God orgy.

Yes, that's his train set over there by the side window. You see how I decorated the parlor to match? Those drapes are the same blue as Edwin's locomotive! No, I guess that's not really relevant to the story, but—

What's that?

Rat poison? I'm sure I have some in the house *somewhere*. My Edwin usually takes care of that kind of thing. Why do you ask? Oh, well sure, I understand—but you know I didn't actually mean that I would have poisoned that dear girl. I was just making a point.

Next thing you know, you'll be asking me if I was serious about the orgy.

Sheriff Timmons! Do I have to remind you that I know your mother? I'll call her right now—you know very well I wasn't serious. Well, no, I told you I don't know why I said it in the first place. It was as unplanned as spilled milk.

You know, I still think maybe Ginny put something in her prune bread. The marijuana, maybe. It's a gateway drug, I hear. You should write that down on your pad, mister. I remember back in the day that Ginny ran with that hippie crowd who protested the war.

Medications? Yes, I take pills for my blood pressure

and some lady problems that I do not see fit to tell you about. Nothing that would make me say things. No, nothing like that.

Right, so I'd forgotten all about those kids, and a few days later I'm sitting on the green flowered couch in my front room, knitting a baby blanket for that new couple at church, when the phone rings, and it's that nice reporter from the local paper. I remember because the light shining in those big, broad windows made the yarn look extra yellow. The reporter asked for Mrs. LeVey, which I thought was a funny-sounding name.

"No, no," I said to him, "this is Mary Levan. *Levan*," and he chuckled, so I thought he found it a funny name, too. *His* name was Bert, that reporter. I thought maybe he was going to ask me about how I keep my rhododendrons looking so beautiful or where I got my lovely tulips, but he said he'd gotten a tip that I was Satan's bride—and he wanted to know all about Satanism for his column on religion.

This real funny picture jumped into my head. You've seen my wedding photo of Edwin—it's that one over there on the credenza by the stairs. Your mother was at my wedding, did you know that? Well, all of a sudden I imagined the Devil's head on my Edwin's body—red, shiny skin and black horns; a neat little black van dyke on his chin. Oh, I laughed something awful over the idea of it. Edwin can't even grow sideburns!

Now, Sheriff, I'm right with the Lord—I've been a Lutheran my whole life, and I'll die one, too. But that nice Bert started talking about how the people of this town just aren't too accepting of Satanists, and that just struck me as plain un-Christianlike. Isn't it my duty as a God-fearing woman to stand up for people of different religions? Do unto others and all of that? I felt like I had to do *something*.

So I told him what I knew about Satanism. That's not much, mind you.

Well, of course. If you want to get to the heart of it, I don't know a thing, so I admit to you that I made up a few things. The proper way to pray to Beelzebub and the spell you need to say before slaughtering babies for sacrifice. The fact that the Dark Lord prefers freshly grated Parmesan on his spaghetti and meatballs. That sort of thing.

But that's when it all started going funny. My paper boy blessed himself when he dropped off the paper the next day. Wouldn't even say hello. Trampled some of my tulips, too. Write that down.

I looked like a real lady on the front page of the paper, if I do say so—I sent Bert that portrait the church took for the directory, the one where I'm wearing that darling pink sweater set with the pearl buttons. I was even wearing my gold cross necklace. But lordy, that headline! "Local Woman Says Satan is Her Co-Pilot." I never said such a thing. I even thought about complaining, but what's done is done, I always say.

Now, my Edwin wasn't so excited about the article. I told him I was just trying to be a good Christian, but you know him. Maybe he had a point, though, because a few minutes after that, someone yelled "Baby killer!" from outside the house. It sounded like that Lori Gerber from next door.

I thought maybe she was practicing for picketing the Planned Parenthood and Women, Infants, Children offices again. There weren't any signs in her yard, but that was definitely her blue Buick cruising down the street after all that screaming. I was still standing outside, wondering what in heavens was going on when Lori drove by again. She stopped this time and threw an avocado at me! It bounced right off the hat of my littlest lawn gnome and into my flowers. The ones that weren't trampled.

It never occurred to me that it might be that darn article in the paper that caused the ruckus until she started shrieking about cavorting with heathens and blasphemers and devil worshippers. Why, I told Lori I was going to call her mother and tell on her for disrespecting her elders. It's bad enough to throw things at an older lady, but wasting fruit like that? Her mother would be appalled. Besides, why an avocado? Are they supposed to be the devil's fruit?

No, Sheriff. Avocados are definitely fruit.

Right. So Lori was going on and on, and, well, an older lady can only take so much. It just came out of my mouth: "I've cursed that avocado for you, you know. I'll be making Beelzebub's guacamole with it, missy." That's where the idea for my guacamole recipe came from—the Devil's Guacamole just sounds so... festive and fun. I just can't believe the Women's Auxiliary took issue with the idea and reported it to the authorities. Did they call 911? Don't they know 911 is for emergencies? Well, I never!

I'm sorry, Sheriff. Of course—back to Lori. I yelled after her to slow down when she sped away. She was driving like a maniac, and there are children in this neighborhood. She could have killed someone. Merciful heavens!

No, I haven't seen her since that day. I thought

maybe she was too ashamed to show her face after that display. I tell you, Sheriff, kids today just don't have any respect at all. And Lori's in her forties, too—I would be ashamed if she were mine.

That wasn't the only incident, mind you. There was the fire in the shed out back—you didn't hear this from me, of course, but I saw Ginny herself running away from that one. I'm telling you—you really should investigate her. A few other incidents happened, too.

Yes, I'll report it good and proper after we're done here.

It wasn't all bad, though. A few days after that, the sweetest group of black-haired boys and girls asked if they could join my church. I thought they were talking about the Lutheran church, but can you imagine—they were talking about the Satanist church the paper made up. I guess they like fresh Parmesan.

Well, I couldn't bring myself to say no, could I? They were so polite. Real ladies and gentlemen. So I told them they could just take the church over as long as they left off with the baby sacrificing. It seemed like the Christian thing to do. I'm pleased as punch to say that The Fourth and a Half Church of Lucifer lives on, even today. It's the only one in Georgia, I'm told. The new High Priest called me just the other day to give me an update on their fundraising. Bless his heart.

I bet no one tries to sell whole wheat prune bread at their bake sales!

Yes, things did calm down a bit after that. Why, of course it did—that's right about the time the Mayor accidentally posted photos of himself online diddling that honor student at the high school. Satanists aren't big news in the face of something like that.

There *is* no more story, Sheriff. I swear it. Well, right up until the Women's Auxiliary got huffy. It's not against the law to take the Devil's Guacamole to a potluck dinner—what did they expect me to do with all those avocados? Zack and the congregation have a crate delivered to me every month. I tell you what *should* be against the law—Ginny's prune bread.

Oh, Ginny's *missing*? No, I haven't seen her lately either.

Yes, of course you can look in my pantry. The basement? Well, surely, but my Edwin may have just spread rat poison. He said something about it yesterday.

No, Edwin is off for his tee time.

Do you really think the rat poison could have worked that fast? Those little things are just cute as a button, and it did hurt my heart so to think of them dying down there. But surely, you could be right—that might be what smells so funny.

Do hand over my cane, Sheriff, and I'll lead you to the basement stairs. You're welcome to check, but my arthritis pains me a bit today. If you do see any dead rats, leave them be. My Edwin will clean up when he comes home. He's a dear like that.

Do you like this tissue box cover? I crocheted it myself. I have an extra—I'll give you one. They're so decorative. A real conversation starter, too. The light switch is just inside the stairwell there. Lean in just a little farther—you'll feel it along the wall.

Oh! Sheriff, are you okay?

Are you… can you hear me? I daresay, I think I heard some glass break as you fell. Did you bang into my preserves shelf on the way down? Oh no, I hope you didn't get my honey-soaked peaches—they're a real treat, and I was saving those last jars.

I do apologize that it's come to this.

You're bleeding, are you? And you can't move? Hmm. I'll check back in an hour or two to see how that's coming along for you. Do watch out for the other bodies. I meant to clean up after myself but this darn arthritis really is such a nuisance—you really should take care of yourself, Sheriff. Getting old does sneak up on you. Luckily, Edwin is such a dear.

Well… you certainly can't blame me for pushing you. I *did* warn you. Merciful heavens! An older lady can only take so much.

JACK IN THE MORNING

BY WADE HUNTER

I woke to a noise that sounded like a dog choking on a squeaky toy. My head throbbed with the mother of all hangovers. I didn't have a dog or a squeaky toy. I ignored the sound. It came again. I propped myself up on an elbow and peeled open an eye.

A monster sat at the foot of my bed, glaring at me. I should have been scared, but it was easier to believe that I was still drunk from last night's whiskey binge than to believe that I out bid everyone on eBay for a two foot gargoyle that would watch over me while I slept.

"About time you woke up," the monster said.

I looked at this strange, little, alcohol induced dream and kindly said, "Bugger off, it's Saturday."

"Insufferable fool!" it growled.

I rubbed my eyes. This was a dream. There was no doubt about it. It had to be a dream. Yet, a small part of my mind was trying to convince me that I was awake and I needed to have my wits about me. I looked again at the thing perched on the end of my bed. Nope, this had to be a dream. I must still be drunk. I needed to go back to sleep. I laid my head back down.

"Get up!" the monster yelled in a voice that sounded like a Doberman talking.

I groaned and pushed up onto an elbow. I looked at the monster with what I hoped was a reproachful stare. "Dude, you wake me on Saturday morning at..." I looked at my clock. My jaw dropped. I snagged the clock off my bedside table and thrust it at the red eyed, leathery skinned monster sitting at the end of my bed. "Dude, it's five in the morning! You woke me at five in the morning on a *Saturday*, and you're calling me insufferable?"

A snot bubble popped in the monster's pig-like nose. "Pathetic whelp," it snarled.

There was nothing for it, I was going to have to deal with this, dream or not, if I wanted to get any sleep, and I desperately wanted more sleep. I rubbed a hand across my face. "I thought all whiskey induced hallucinations were regulated to the form of pink elephants. You're not even pink. Come back when you're pink and elephant shaped."

The monster truculently flapped its wings. The force lifted the strange beast a foot into the air before it settled back down. It pointed a finger at me. "Punishment!" A blue bolt of electricity shot from the little bastard's hand and nailed me in the chest. My muscles spasmed. I grunted and fell back on the bed. I may have peed a little. "Stick that in your pink elephant," the monster said as I lay there spasming.

After half a minute, the spasms abated. I gingerly sat

back up. The little monster glared at me with a look of superior grandiose. I promptly kicked him hard enough to propel him across the room and into the opposite wall. He hit with a smack and crumbled into a heap on the floor. I pulled the covers back over my head. I was almost asleep when weight settled on my chest. I peeled the covers from my face and glared. My little winged bully was back. One of his eyes was swollen shut. I sighed. Apparently, I was getting up, regardless of how bad my head hurt or of my desire to crawl into a dark hole and die.

"Dude, what's your deal?"

The little monster pointed a clawed finger at me. "Your soul belongs to me now. You should not have struck me. "

I rubbed a hand through my hair and gave a pull. Mental note—*lay off the whiskey*. I pushed myself into a sitting position, forcing the little monster to shuffle back onto my legs. "Umm, what?"

The little monster laughed. It sounded like he had a chest full of phlegm. "You don't remember." He rubbed his hands together and smiled. "That makes it so much better. The suffering tastes so much sweeter when they don't remember."

I sighed. "Listen, little man, unless you want me to thump you again, I suggest you either explain, or go look for the One Ring somewhere else. "

The monster gave a quizzical look. "Ring?"

"Golem? You're stealing his act. There's copyright laws, you know."

"No."

I huffed. "Never mind. Just tell me what it is you're doing in my room, and why you think my soul belongs to you."

A slippery, little smile spread on the monster's face. I suddenly understood the term devilish grin. "William Robert White, I have granted your greatest desire." He stretched the word *greatest* out in a sensual seductive group of syllables. It sent a ripple through me. I shook it off.

"Obviously, it didn't have to do with a little pig-faced lizard guy and a blender. What are you talking about?"

The little monster smiled. "You signed a pact with me, William Robert White. Last night, you received your greatest desire, and now, your soul will become mine."

I rolled my eyes. "When did this happen?"

The monster licked its lips. "Couple hours back."

I thought about it. I'd spent the night drinking on the couch and playing Ultimate World War on my gaming station. My girlfriend, Charlene, broke up with me over dinner. She said something about me needing to grow up. She said I was a professional now, a lawyer, and I needed to act like it. She said she was sick of dating a little boy, that I spent too much time drinking and playing video games. Then she left me, sitting there to pay the bill. I mean come on, Charlene, if you're going to dump a guy over dinner, don't stick him with the tab. That's just lemon juice on the cut.

So, what then? I finished my steak. There was no need wasting a piece of art like that. I paid the tab—*thanks a heap, Charlene, you bitch*. Then, well, then I proved her right. I came home, spun the cap off a bottle of Jack Daniels, dumped some ice in a thirty-two-ounce mug, and mixed the golden joy juice fifty-fifty with Mountain Dew. That done I moseyed over to the couch, picked up my game controller and fired up the latest Ultimate World War game. The whiskey flowed. Virtual enemies died. I swiftly pickled myself over my lost girl. At no point did I remember seeing this creepy little guy join my pity party.

Maybe I was still drunk. That (at least) would help explain what was going on.

The monster scuttled forward and pinched my leg to wake me from my reverie. "Moist and juicy. I will eat your flesh, then grow it back. The pain will be exquisite."

I was *soooo* not in the mood for this. I backhanded McCreepy off my legs. He flew over the side of the bed and landed with a groan and a muttered curse about hellhound balls slapping my face. I sat up, rubbing the palms of my hands into my eyes. It was time to wake up for real. I heard a fluttering of wings and a weight landed on my bed. I gave the persistent little shit a glare through my fingers.

"Punishment!" the little monster barked. His barbed tail whipped around and stung me on the left shoulder. It hurt like a sonofabitch. The muscles in my arm went numb. Okay this was not good.

The monster's tail reared back again. I caught it with my right hand just before it plunged into my neck. I can only imagine what would have happened if the strike found home. My left arm was on fire at this point. I yanked and hoisted until I had the monster hanging upside down by the tail.

The little guy flailed, but my reach was longer than his. He couldn't get me.

"Put me down!"

"No."

He snapped at me with pin like teeth. "You'll pay for this!"

"Stop squirming," I admonished. "Let me think."

"I will eat your innards for lunch!"

"This is getting us nowhere." I had to find some way to control this guy. I thought about twirling him around my head and seeing how my wall looked splattered with monster brains, but something stopped me. I looked at the little monster. Its eye (the one that had been swollen shut just a minute ago) was perfectly fine now. My arm was not. If this wasn't some whiskey-soaked attempt of a joke by my brain, then I needed to proceed with caution.

"Scoop out your brains and wipe my ass with them!"

"Dude, not sanitary at all."

I stood, holding the monster at arm's length so that he couldn't rip into me with his flailing claws. I lifted him so we could look each other in the face. "If I put you down, will you explain what happened last night?"

"After I rip open your scrotum and play Ping Pong with your balls!"

I raised an eyebrow. "Tempting, but no."

"Your soul is mine, human scum. I demand you release my tail so that I may flay the meat from your bones. Punishment!" Electric blue light started to glow around his hand.

I shook him until I heard his cheeks flapping. The blue light faded. I looked around and saw what I wanted thrown across the chair in the corner. It took some doing, but I managed to get the heavy sweatshirt over the monster's head. The shaking addled him. I took advantage of his rattled state to get the job done. I got his head poking out the head hole of the sweatshirt. I used the drawstrings on the hood to tighten it around his neck enough so he couldn't squirm his head out the hole. I wrapped the arms of the shirt tightly around him once, pinning his tail and his arms to his sides, then I tied the sleeves in a knot behind him. I carried my little monster out into the kitchen and set him on the table. I noticed the bottle of Jack Daniels sitting on the counter. It was full last night. Now? Not so much. No wonder I felt like the top of my head was going to explode, and, oh yeah, I had a monster tied up on the table. Maybe all that missing whiskey helped explain that little tidbit.

The monster came around from his shaking and growled. "Release me!" He did not look happy. Too bad.

"First, coffee," I said. Ever the host I asked, "You want some. Good shit. High end bean." I held up the coffee grinder. "Freshly ground."

"Yes, minion, I desire your Earthly coffee."

I sighed. "Dude." I stopped, looked at the little beast sitting regally, as if he wasn't tied up in my college sweatshirt. I took the high road. "Okay, if we are going to have an actual conversation, I can't keep calling you *dude*. What's your name?"

The little monster glared at me, but one eyebrow (okay, one heavy fold of lizard skin) raised in interest. He took a second to consider, nodded. "You may call me Master."

"Yeah, okay. I get that. Signing of a treaty and all, but until we get to that point or at least until I have had two or three cups of coffee, what can I call you?" I dumped beans in the grinder.

"Do you think I'm a fool?"

I almost took a picture with my phone to show him how he looked in a sweatshirt straight jacket, but I refrained.

"Names have power, I will not give you mine."

I rubbed my hand over my face. This headache wasn't going away. I needed coffee, and I needed it ASAP. I poured water into the coffee machine, and much to my dread hit the button to grind the beans. The noise was like needles in my brain, but I told myself it was a necessary evil. I heard 'Master' groan behind me. I looked. His eyes were closed, and he shook slightly. Normally, I would have screwed with him by starting and stopping the grinder, but the noise was hurting my head just as much as it was hurting his.

"Stop that incessant racket," the little guy demanded.

I stopped. The beans were done anyway. The monster slowly opened one red eye and made a very sad attempt at a glare.

"Okay, so you won't give me your real name, and I refuse to call you Master."

His eyes flared. I raised my hands. "I know. Contract. Sold my soul. Eat my innards for breakfast and regrow them. Sounds like my relationship with Charlene, but here's the thing, until I read this contract and determine the nature of its binding on me, I refuse to call you Master."

He glared. I sighed. The blissful sound of the coffee maker producing drops of sweet nectar filled the kitchen. I looked at the monster. "Cream? Sugar?" He searched my face with his beady red eyes. I noticed for the first time that they were red because they were bloodshot. I imagined mine looked much the same. He stared at me a moment. His gaze drifted over to the bottle of whiskey on the counter. He looked back at me and flipped his head in the direction of the bottle.

"Hair of the dog?"

He closed his eyes and gave me a small nod. Was this monster as hungover as I was? I had to be dreaming. My hand went to the shoulder that got stung. It was just now returning to normal. That had hurt. I wasn't sleeping.

The aroma of the coffee was amazing. Deep. Dark. Delicious. I dumped some sugar in mine, opened the refrigerator to get creamer and thought maybe my houseguest was right. I closed the fridge and grabbed the bottle of whiskey. I examined the label.

"Jack," I said as I poured a hit into each cup. "That's your name now." I slid the cup in front of the monster.

"You dare name me?" The little guy hissed.

I nodded. "Yep. I name you, Jack. You're in my house, drinking my expensive coffee, mixed with my alcohol." I took a sip. "Be happy I'm not calling you Shit Face McGoo. How'd you like going around with that one for eternity."

"Actually, I know a Shitface McGoo. Real jackass." Jack looked at his coffee and back at me. He huffed and his shoulders sagged. "As far as tortures go, this is a very nice one. I may have to use it on you every morning for the next twenty years." His voice lacked some of its evil superiority.

"What do you..." I realized what he meant as I

caught him looking longingly at his hot brew. I had Jack's hands tied up. He had no way to get to his coffee. He was right. It was a pretty nice form of torture. I took a long, slow sip of my coffee, smacked my lips in delicious delight, then got up and retrieved a straw from one of the cabinets. I plunked it into Jack's cup.

"You could untie me."

I nodded, sipped. "I could, but I won't. Not until you've had your coffee and we've talked. I don't need another lightning bolt to the chest or stabbed in the neck."

Jack huffed in reply as his lips encircled the straw. His eyes slid shut in ecstasy as he slurped up coffee. He drained half his cup and sighed.

"Told you it was good shit."

He opened one eye and looked at me. A smile slid onto his face. He nodded. Jack finished his cup before I was halfway done with mine. He looked at the empty cup mournfully.

"Seconds?" I asked. The little guy had relaxed noticeably. He nodded. "I'll even untie you if you promise to behave and talk to me. No attacking me until we have this pact thing understood. Deal?"

Jack's eyes went from my face to the mug in my hand to the empty mug on the table. He nodded. "Done."

"That a boy." I finished my cup in two quick swallows, grabbed Jack's mug, and filled them both. I set the mugs down on the table, reached behind the little monster and undid the knot in the sweatshirt. "Up and over." I grabbed the hood and pulled. The sweatshirt only gave mild resistance as it caught on Jack's wings. He wiggled and came free. I sat down as

Jack stretched.

"Okay," I said, but Jack held up a hand, one finger pointing skyward in the universal (and apparently trans-dimensional) gesture for *wait-a-second*. I shrugged and sat back.

Jack wrapped his hands around his steaming mug and inhaled the aroma. This time he drank in little sips, savoring the morning bean juice and whiskey. When Jack was done making love to his drink, he set his cup on the table and gave me a sideways glance. "When this is done and you are my servant, you will make this coffee for me."

I nodded and took a sip of my coffee. "About that. I wish to review my contract."

"It is not customary," Jack said. He took a long slow sip of coffee. His eyes closed in pleasure. I was suddenly worried what would happen if he had too much caffeine.

"Well, thing is, Jack, I don't remember signing this contract. The first time I remember seeing you is at the foot of my bed. You could be trying to trick me. I may never have signed anything. I don't even know what you are, where you came from, or how you ended up in my place."

Jack rolled his eyes. "You're one of those humans, the inquisitive ones. Just my luck." He muttered something to himself that was too low for me to hear. Staring into his mug, he growled, "It's all that she-beast's fault." He swirled the contents of his drink like they were a fine wine. "Stupid, hellhound screwing wench."

Seems like I wasn't the only one to have a throw down with the opposite sex recently. "Jack, you're muttering to your coffee." I almost asked about the hellhound screwing she-beast but figured I'd save that part of the conversation until after we cleared up the whole soul selling issue.

Jack gave me a sour glance. "You ask a lot of questions."

"I have a lot of questions. I'm a lawyer. It's how I'm wired, and I've never had a..." I rolled a hand at him and made a questioning face.

"Fourth Level Imp."

I raised an eyebrow. "Did I fall into a Dungeons & Dragons game or something?"

He pointed a warning finger at me. It crackled with blue light. I held up my hands in acquiescence. "Sorry. It's not a slight. I love D&D." Jack shook his head, sipped his coffee.

"Okay. I've never met an Imp before."

"Fourth Level Imp," Jack said. It seemed like a conditioned response, like he had to constantly remind people of his station.

"Fourth level. What comes after that?" I was curious. I mean how often does one get to ask these questions right from the source.

Jack drained his cup. He wiggled it with a hopeful look on his face. I smiled, grabbed the cup and filled him up. He nodded thankfully when I set the full cup down on the table. I wondered where he was putting it all for such a small guy.

"Minor demon," Jack said. His words seemed clipped.

"And that's something you can aspire to?"

He glared this time. I let it drop. "So how did you end up in my house?"

Jack took a sip and shrugged his shoulders. "You were asking to make a deal. I took a shot."

What in the world would I have asked for? Surely not... "Charlene? I don't remember." My eyes drifted to the bottle of whiskey on the counter.

Jack shook his head. "Mentioned her in passing. That was it."

"What then? I have no clue."

Jack waved a hand. A sheet of leathery parchment appeared on the table in front of me. "The Contract."

I felt the parchment between my fingers. "Odd paper."

"Flayed skin."

I dropped the parchment. "Yeah, that's gross."

Jack settled back onto the sweatshirt, making a pillow of it. "Not a lot of trees in the Underworld. Lots of people, though. Don't worry. It grows back once it's ripped from their body."

"How comforting."

Jack smiled. "Oh, I wouldn't use the word comfortable in any fashion."

I swallowed. Steeling my nerve, I reached for the piece of dried up human that was my possible future. I read. "It states here that you need to enslave a human soul to reach minor demon."

Jack nodded, sipped.

I raised an eyebrow and kept reading. "You've got to be shitting me!"

Jack set his mug down and cocked his head. I shook the parchment at him. "Are you telling me that I sold my soul to become better at a video game?"

Jack smiled. "Not just better. The best." He made jazz hands.

"So, you're telling me I traded eternity of having my skin flayed from my body to become the best Ultimate World War player in the world?"

"Yep."

"Bullshit." My eyes drifted from Jack to the bottle on the counter. I'd been known to make some rash decisions when I drank.

Jack stretched his wings, flapped, and flew to the counter. He examined the level of coffee in the pot, looked at me and gave the pot a little wiggle in my direction. I walked over and extended my cup. Jack poured. "So, I am now the best player in the world, but am bound to serve you for all eternity?"

"Humans make rash decisions."

"No shit. I don't believe I could be this stupid, though."

Jack dumped three teaspoons of sugar into his coffee and topped it with whiskey. He stirred the steaming brew with his tail. "Go check."

I walked into the living room, fired up the game console, and checked the rankings. "Son of a bitch!" I looked at Jack sitting on the kitchen counter all smug. He raised his hands in an *I-told- you-so* gesture. I scowled and reached into my pocket for my phone. I took a picture of the screen. I mean, come on, best Ultimate War World player in the world? I had to snap that shit out. Maybe I could look at that picture everyday as my skin was flayed from my body to remind me of how stupid (and okay, how awesome!) I was. But did I really want to spend all of time having my face peeled off. No. That sounded like it would suck. Jack seemed like a nice enough guy, once he had a cup or four of coffee in him, but a denizen of hell is just that. You can put lipstick on a pig, but it's still a pig. I'm sure he wouldn't always be so cheerfully non-aggressive.

"Satisfied?" Jack asked. He flew back to the table to lounge on my sweatshirt.

"Hardly." I snatched the contract. At least at first glance, it was pretty straight forward. I had to think. I'd read enough fantasy novels, played enough games. There were always things the dark forces failed to mention, rules that they had to follow.

I looked at Jack. "I signed this under the influence of a lot of whiskey. That makes it an invalid agreement."

Jack snorted. "It is not one of your stupid human contracts. This is a demonic contract. Most of which are signed during high states of emotional distress and brewed in alcohol. It's how we roll."

"It's how you roll?" I shook my head. Jack was right. I was sure. I lifted the paper to look at the signature. It was sloppy, but it was mine. "I thought these contracts had to be signed in blood."

Jack sipped, shook his head. "Blood for blood. If you would have traded your soul for the life of another then we would have used blood. You wanted to be the best Ultimate World War player in the world, so we used that special edition Mountain Dew to sign. Elementary spell-craft. Use a component related to the desire."

I glanced over my shoulder. Sitting on the counter was an empty two-liter bottle of Mountain Dew with the image of a soldier on it. I rubbed a hand through my hair. Things were not looking good.

"Do you want to start your service by rubbing my feet?" Jack stretched and wiggled gnarly, hookedtaloned toes. I cringed.

There had to be a loophole. There was always a loophole. I looked at the contract again. There was no loophole in what was written. Wasn't there always something? My mind churned. There was something that Jack said earlier sticking in my mind, waving frantically at me. What was it? *Last night, you received your greatest desire, and now, your soul will become mine.* He said your soul *will become* mine, not your soul *is* mine. I read over the contract again. Then, I saw it. There was a space at the bottom of the paper, three inches with no writing. I looked at Jack. He tried to look casual, but the look was forced.

I walked into the living room.

Jack sat up. "What are you doing?" Tension strained his voice, making him sound more Chihuahua than Doberman.

I turned out the lights, walked to the far wall, and clicked on the black light mounted there. I looked at the contract. There was writing in that open three inches of space at the bottom of the contract.

Jack flew into the living room. "Hey, what do you think you're doing?"

I turned and smiled. "Fine print, Jack. Every contract has it. What's the saying? The devil is in the details, right? That's the fine print. It's a weapon, one I'm skilled at using. I'm a lawyer. We live by small print. It's how we roll."

Jack muttered a profanity. It was something about a donkey-dicked medusa. I'm not sure.

I held the contract up and read. "It says I have the right to challenge you to *combat of my choosing* before the fall of the dusk until the contract becomes final."

"You can ignore that."

I gave him a look. "I don't think so. Listen, Jack, I kinda like you in some weird, bent way, but I don't want to spend eternity as the ball boy for Scrotum Ping Pong."

Jack's lizard eyes darted back and forth. "Okay, ignore that last statement—the one you weren't supposed to read, and I promise no flaying of skin."

"Wow, Jack, that is kind of you, but I think I have to invoke my right to combat."

Jack's face hardened and his tail came up to wiggle above his head. A drop of venom dripped from the end of its scorpion point to sizzle on my couch. "Such action will make your time as my servant worse."

I held up a hand. "Hold up with the fire and brimstone." I looked at the paper again. *Combat of my choosing*. I smiled, walked around the couch, and sat down.

"You are wise to yield."

I patted the couch beside me. "I'm not yielding."

"You only felt a small dose of my venom. You will suffer." He flapped down to the seat cushion opposite me on the couch. His tail rattled in anticipation of the strike.

"Put that thing away." I grabbed a game controller off the coffee table and pushed it in his direction.

Jack looked confused but took it. "What's this for?"

"I'm challenging you to *combat of my choosing*." Jack stiffened. His tail shot up. The controller bounced off my forehead. I patted the air with my hands. "Ouch. Easy big guy. It's *combat of my choosing*. I'm not going to fight you physically, even though I kinda already kicked your ass." Jack's eyes narrowed. "Even so," I placated. "I have no doubt that if it came down to it, you would beat me in a physical contest. One little bolt of lightning, and a shot to my neck with your tail and I'd be done."

Jack eased a little, but just a little. "What then?"

I bent, picked up the launched controller, and handed it back to him. I rubbed the rising bruise on my forehead and grabbed a second controller. "I challenge you to combat via Ultimate World War. Twenty kills wins. You beat me, I'm yours. I beat you, the contract is void."

Jack's eyes grew wide. He looked from me to the TV. The world rankings were still on the screen. My name beamed, sitting king of the hill as Grand Kill Master of the planet. Jack looked at the remote in his hands. He made a small choking noise, before looking up with a crazy little glint in his eyes. "It has to be physical conflict."

I held the contract up and pointed to the small print. "Sorry, buddy, it doesn't say *physical* combat. It says *combat of my choosing*. Combat is any contest or struggle. I've made my choice."

Jack rubbed a hand across his scaly face. He looked back at the TV. "But... uhm... but... ahh... oh, shark toothed demon twats."

Twenty to two kills later (I felt bad and let Jack get a couple in right at the end), I raised my hands in victory.

Jack slumped back into the cushion of the couch. "I'm screwed."

I kind of felt bad for the little guy. "Don't take it so hard, Jack. I'm sure you can get another sucker to steal a soul from. You just have to watch your choice of words on the contract."

Jack looked at me with baleful eyes. He looked at the controller. His fingers worked the joystick and the buttons. He shook his head.
"How about more coffee?"
"Yeah," Jack said. His voice was deflated. "Yeah sure. With a good hit of whiskey. I'll need it."
I had to grind more beans and brew a fresh pot. When I walked into the living room with two steaming cups, Jack had joined a multiplayer game. I set the coffee and whiskey on the table in front of him, walked around the couch so as to not disturb his game and sat.
"She's going to kill me, you know?"
I looked at him. "Who?"
Jack killed a player on the screen. He really wasn't bad. "My demon of a wife."
"She made demon?"
Jack chuckled. "Oh yes, and trust me when I say that not a day goes by when I don't hear about it, about what a disappointment I am. She comes home all the time smelling of hellhound, doesn't even bother to roll in the sulfur pit to cover the smell anymore." Jack's player in the game took a sniper round to the head. He took the opportunity to swallow a hit of coffee.
I felt bad. Jack was a likable sort when he wasn't trying to steal my soul. "Sorry to hear that, Jack. You really think she'll kill you?"
Jack laughed. "Yep. Her last words before I left were 'Don't come back empty handed, or I'll have your guts for supper.'"
"And you think she was serious?"
Jack gave me a look as if I had just clucked and laid an egg.
"Wow, what a bitch."

"Cha."

I sipped my coffee. I had an idea. It wasn't like I had a roommate or a part time roommate for that matter now that Charlene was gone. It was partially my fault Jack had to go home empty handed. "You can hang out here if you want."

Jack sat up in a surprised rustle of wings. "No shit."

I shrugged. "Why not? There'd have to be some ground rules. Mainly, no trying to entrap or enslave me."

Jack nodded. "Wouldn't be able to anyway. I would be bound by the protection of your hospitality and could not act ill towards you."

"Well then you're welcome to hang out until you figure out what to do." I looked at him. "No killing the neighbors or any crazy shit like that."

Jack wrinkled up his lizard face. "I never was into slaughter all that much."

"Good to know." Jack's game ended. He set his controller down and picked up his coffee. I did the opposite, joining a game that was about to start.

Jack motioned at the television with his coffee mug. "Enjoy it while it lasts."

"What's that?" I asked as I picked a player off.

"The number one world ranking."

I stole a glance at him. "Since the contract was voided?"

"Nah," Jack said. He sipped his coffee. "I'd say the top hundred made a deal of some sort to get there. Eventually, today, tomorrow, a week from now, another gamer is going to offer up his soul to be the best in the world. Video games are a cash cow for souls."

"Wow. That's scary, but maybe you'll get another shot then."

Jack slumped. "I'll slip to the bottom of the call list."

"There's a call list?"

"Yep. Could be years."

"Ouch."

"Yeah, tell me about it. Now do you see why I don't want to go home? Even if she didn't eat me, it would be years of torment, and she'll get a call before me. I can't even imagine the humiliation of falling two levels behind her."

"No line skipping then."

"Oh, you can, but then you have to survive. Everyone you skip would be gunning for you."

"Loopholes. You guys love loopholes. There has to be one."

Jack's face twisted as he thought. "I suppose, if I don't go back then it's still my turn, but something would have to fall into my lap."

"Well, you never know."

Just then my cell phone rang. I looked at the screen and let out a groan. Jack looked over. I showed him the display. "Charlene. Calling me at six in the morning. Not good."

"You gonna answer that?" Jack asked.

I shook my head. "Nah. It will just be drunk ranting. Typical behavior for her. Drink all night, get blind drunk, then call and give it to me for one thing or another."

Jack wiggled clawed fingers at me. "Give it."

I handed it over.

Jack answered the phone. "Yo! Jack here."

"Speaker," I whispered. He nodded, and switched

my cell to speaker mode.

"Who the hell is Jack? I called William's cell. I know I did. Says so right here on my screen. So put that piece of shit on the phone, Jack!" Her words were slurred. Yep, she was sloshed.

Jack raised an eyebrow and gestured towards me with the phone. I shook my head.

"He's not here, ever."

I suppressed a laugh, gave a thumbs up, and went back to my game.

Charlene growled. "Aaaaaahhhhhhh! I'd give my soul to forget I ever met his sorry ass."

Jack looked at me and winked. I fist bumped him and mouthed, "Bingo."

Jack's smile widened into a shark's grin. "Well, Charlene, I might just be able to help you with that."

AGNES AND THE GHOST IN WHITE

BY GEORGE TSIRAKIDIS

I am wearing everything exactly like I'm supposed to. Woolen pink suit and matching skirt, silk white top with a rosy floral design, same color pumps with the shortest heels possible, a pearl necklace, and of course, my small hot pink hat. A proper eighty-year-old lady. Yes, you heard right, I turned eighty just two days ago. I despise my birthday. Stopped celebrating it years ago. My birthday week is my personal Passion Week.

I'm walking down the street before my house in Chelmsford on a marvelous May morning, dressed exactly as I described above, confident about myself—I can dupe anyone—when suddenly, I see them in front of me.

Holly fucking Parker and Grace Rose wend their way toward me. I don't know if you've ever been to Chelmsford, but it doesn't have many alleyways to take cover from two irritating jades when you need to. Trapped as I am on the pavement, I don a bovine expression on my face—easy stuff if you've been practicing for the better half of your life—and wave to them in the majestic way of the Queen.

Holly Parker, the accursed mummified bigmouth, speaks first, of course.

"Agnes, my dearest, how are you today?"

That's a shock, Holly. You usually try to unearth gossip with your very first question.

"Praise God"—I never actually praise Him, believe me—"I am fine, my dear Holly. How about you?" I smile broadly, giving myself more wrinkles in the process, to pacify these bitches. As if I haven't gotten enough from eighty years of a shitty life.

"We are marvelous, praise God. And where are you going, all alone and dressed so exceptionally?"

Damn, Holly, you never disappoint.

"I'm a widow, Holly. Loneliness is my nature nowadays." Fuck me, I am spectacular.

"Forgive me, Agnes. I didn't wish to bring your spirits down on such a lovely morning." Of course you did, you morose harridan. Your sole purpose in life is to make everyone as miserable as you are, you viper.

"You didn't upset me at all. Don't worry." I would never indulge you. "I am expecting you tomorrow afternoon for our usual tea, girls." I have no clue why we insist on calling each other 'girl.' Look at us for Christ's sake!

They both nod with pleasure. They are not about to miss the highlight of their week, being two gossiping viragos who love nothing more than to make passive aggressive comments, when they in fact deserve to be locked away and spew their hatred in private. Holly Parker more so, since Grace Rose is the quietest person

I have ever known. So quiet that I almost like her. Almost.

I keep walking after another gentle queenly wave, making my way to the local market and, after that, to the town square to get myself something fresh for dinner and something green for dessert. There's no need to start a real conversation; tomorrow we'll have our fill of each other.

I don't give a single shit if you think badly of me. I hate my friends. They are all churchy pretentious hags who feed on the pain of others. None of them can make peace with the fact that they've lived a miserable life and are trying to make sure—before their ridiculous lives are over—that everyone feels as wretched as they do. So I permit them a favor every Friday afternoon. We gather in my garden, drink tea and list our laments. But I am not like them. I do it out of pure boredom. What else is there to entertain me at eighty?

I return almost an hour later—it takes me an hour just to shop, what a degradation!—and I take off the uniform. I throw the skirt suit on the floor, the hideous hat on the sofa, my pumps under the stairs, the pearls on the wooden lowboy with the abhorrent doily and the second-best tea set. I feel like I can breathe again, now that I'm rid of these dreadful clothes. I plug the earphones into my phone.

You see, it's risky blasting David Bowie on the speakers. I don't want anyone in this neighborhood to know who I truly am. They would never understand.

I plop myself on the couch, push the piles of clothes to the floor—I have to clean up before the old biddies get here tomorrow—and dig between the pillows of my yellow checkered couch. Everything in my home has been wisely chosen to fit the charade.

My fingers grab the joint I rolled last night, praise the kids from the square. I place it between my lips, take the lighter from the table and, with the exquisite sound a flame makes when it bursts into life, I light up my consolation.

I lay my head back on the arm of the couch and close my eyes. Dizziness embraces me and David's voice in my ears soothes me even more. Life is sweet, if you know what to do with it.

I don't even know how many hours have passed when the alarm clock rings my head off. Bloody thing, it cut off my song. I glare at the screen and the reminder to take my blood pressure pill. Sunlight has ghosted the sky as day gives its place to dusk. My favorite hour. Neither morning, nor night. Bittersweet.

I struggle to get up. My head is spinning. I walk through the piles of clothes to the kitchen. Bloody pills.

When I reach the door, my eyes spot a figure standing on the first step at the top of the stairs. I grasp the baluster, a scream escapes my mouth and I stare, terrified, at the gargoyle.

On the top step stands the unmoving figure of a man under a white sheet, like a little kid dressing up on Halloween. I freeze, gaping at the figure. It does not stir or talk. Only the white sheet sways as if lured by a light breeze.

"I'll call 911," I scream but I know it's a fool's errand.

The figure doesn't respond. My heart is bouncing in my chest. I have no desire to have a heart attack when I am awake. I don't mind if it happens when I'm asleep.

I'm sweating like a pig, but I still can't move. I just look at the intruder. No eyeholes on the fabric, like the trick-or-treaters usually make. Just a white sheet blowing on a phantom wind.

"Are you Death?" I shout. "Is it my time?"

No answer. The Ghost in White is inertia itself. I can feel my blood pressure rising. I need my pills.

I begin walking towards the kitchen, panting heavily. I can sense the Ghost's gaze on my back as I reach for the kitchen cabinet where I keep my pills. Glancing over my shoulder every few seconds, I swallow one for blood pressure and one for my heart—I'm not dying today, Satan!

I grab the rolling pin from the countertop. I haven't made a single pie for thirty years, I just have a rolling pin in a visible spot in my kitchen so the old crones think the pies I serve them are homemade. I move back out to the staircase and look for the mysterious ghost, but it has disappeared.

I stand alone in the dark, wondering:

How shitty was the weed these fucking brats sold me?

My heart will need a good few hours to return to normal. Thankfully, I care about death as much as Holly Parker cares about me. Which, believe me, is as low as my red cell count.

Friday dawns and I hear the alarm clock shouting at me, once again, to take my pills. I swallow so many pills every day that it makes me nostalgic for my youth. Particularly the summer I met my husband. Sometimes, when I swallow a pill, I find myself smirking at the memory of our nights on the beaches of South Italy and our vacation to the Greek islands. Different kind of pills then, if you get my meaning.

I've already started tidying up the house. The hens

must find it in impeccable condition. Each dolly in its place, my porcelain knick-knacks straightened on the mantel, the framed pictures of my 'cats'—never had one, always hated them—hanging above it. The garden table set, cookies and scones and tea all laid out. The good tea set to pretend I'm the perfect hostess to my not-friends. Sitting at the garden table, I can see the top of the staircase through the open doors. It makes me think of the figure standing there last night; a shiver runs through my body. Am I losing my mind?

When this fucking tea date is over, I'm going straight to the town square and telling off these goddamn kids that sold me skunk and almost sent me to Hell long before I was due. I'm not going to lose my mind because of their bullshit. I only hope they give me some good stuff for free to properly show their remorse.

There they are, my dear frenemies, landing in my garden like vultures. Holly Parker leads the pack, of course, the general of this little army of Jesus Christ, our lord and savior. Voiceless Grace Rose follows, and the marvelous duo of Muriel Greenwood and Constance Castle bring up the rear. Muriel has got early dementia, which makes her far more entertaining than the others, and Constance always has a crooked smile on her face, a parting gift from the stroke she had last summer, which reminds me again of my husband on that trip to the Greek Islands.

They flail their arms in hello and each takes her place around the garden table. I take up the innocent face I know so well and tap the kettle to show them all is ready and waiting for them. As I serve, I lay out my usual lies.

"My dears, what a blessing this sunny day is. You know how I love to have our tea dates out in the garden!"

Holly is prepping her poison, I can see it. She exclaims, "Of course, dear, we've all heard how much you loved the outdoors when you were younger."

Fucking adder, don't you ever rest?

I serve them elegantly—alright, my hand shakes a little but fuck you for thinking it before I said it—and I sit back down, shifting my attention to the inside of my house.

"How are you all?" I ask, even though I don't care in the least.

"Well," Grace Rose answers. It will be the only word that comes out of her mouth today, I'm sure. On the rare occasion when she does talk, she barely opens her mouth. Her face muscles must hurt from disuse.

"I'm packing for our trip to Venice with my husband next week," Muriel says.

Her husband died ten years ago. She's been mentioning him a lot lately, but none of us bother to tell her he's dead. Can you imagine the drama we would have to deal with? We glance at each other conspiratorially; Holly answers:

"That sounds terrific, my dear Muriel. Don't forget to pack your Sunday best."

The viper strikes again! I glance back at the house. It looks different every Friday, all tidied up like this. Like a hospital.

At the top of the staircase, though, I spot the discord to my perfect charade. The Ghost in White. I can hear my heartbeat in my neck. I haven't smoked at all today; this is not an illusion. The Ghost is there, as real as the old hags before me. Motionless, chilling, otherworldly. Am I getting what Muriel has? Or, worse, what Constance has?

"Girls," I say, my voice breaking, "can you tell me what you see at the top of the stairs?"

"Where?" Constance asks through her crooked smile.

"On the top of the stairs," I insist.

"Dust," the sleezy Holly Parker replies.

"Nothing," Constance answers.

"Nothing," Grace Rose confirms. A second word today, she must be exhausted.

"I can see the lovely home of a hostess filled with energy and joy," Muriel adds happily. I must start taking whatever she's on.

But I see the Ghost clearly, standing on the first step at the top of the stairs. Or the last step, depending on where you're standing. I can feel it looking at me, even with no eyeholes. It's watching me. It freezes my blood, steals my voice. I'm dizzy, I'm losing my mind. I'm not scared of death, but I want to be sane till the last breath I take.

"I think teatime is over, girls," I say. There it is again: 'girls.'

"Over? Already?" asks Holly Parker, visibly excited to tell everyone she knows how I kicked them out after barely a quarter of an hour.

"Forgive me, I'm not feeling well suddenly."

"Can we help, darling?" Grace Rose asks me with earnest concern. I have never heard her speak so much in my life—she'll have to crawl home from the exertion.

"No, thank you." I get up and lead them away.

They kiss me goodbye in turn, wishing me to get well, soon, and all that mumbo jumbo.

"Have fun in Venice, Muriel," I tell her and slip back into the house.

The Ghost is gone. I breathe deeply, holding my chest.

"What do you want?" I scream with all my might.

Silence.

And suddenly all the objects on my walls drop loudly to the floor and shatter. The framed pictures of my 'cats' over the mantel, the porcelain knickknacks, the grandfather clock in the hall. The knives and ladles hanging over the stove clatter down in unison.

The sound reverberates through my skull. I scream and cover my ears.

"Show yourself!"

The blinds on every window bang closed and seal with a loud click.

Darkness envelops me.

I shuffle to the closest light switch. I flick it. Nothing. Still dark.

Focus, Agnes.

A soft breeze wafts around my ankles, coming from the kitchen. I turn and see it there. The Ghost in White stands still. The pristine white sheet is the only thing I can see in the darkness.

I move towards it. I want to touch it, pull the sheet off and see who's hiding underneath. I approach slowly, as slow as my shaking legs allow, and come to a stop before it. I reach out with fingers that tremble from age and fear both.

"Remember now, Agnes?" it whispers in a voice straight from Hell.

And disappears.

I cry out in horror. I can see nothing. I fumble blindly, guided by memory alone. I keep my arms stretched in front of me. I can see it moving in the living room before the fireplace.

"What do you want me to remember?" I ask. "Who are you?"

I move towards it. Fear won't stop me. I can beat it.

"Guess," I hear it whisper in my ear before it disappears again.

I fall to my knees and cover my face with my hands.

Am I dead? Is this death? Is this damnation and eternal punishment?

I sigh. You won't break, Agnes. Not now.

"Do I know you?" I ask, trying to buy time.

"Yes," it whispers in my ear.

"Are you... my mother?" I ask the air. "Did you not torture me enough while you lived?"

No reply. Wrong guess, then.

I raise my head to see it. My father died right after I was born. Why haunt me now? My sister ran away when we were very young, she's definitely met more interesting people than me to haunt.

No one else has known the real me. No one knows the real Agnes. Only the walls of this house and its silent furniture. No one but...

I make myself speak what I never wanted to.

"Thomas, is it you?"

A burst of light chases away the darkness. The Ghost in White stands on the first step at the top of the staircase again. Or the last, depending on where you're standing.

"Is that why you stand there?" I ask.

No answer, but I know now.
I understand.
I remember.
I never actually forgot. But why now? After all these years? Is it my mind, slowly slipping away? Or is my life going to end soon and I need to face my darkest secret? Is this my last birthday in this world?

Maybe Thomas has always been here and I couldn't see him until now.

I hide my face in my palms and cry through the night.

***

The sun struggles through the shut window blinds. I get off the floor where I fell asleep and open them wide. A wonderful day greets me. The cherry trees in the neighborhood are blooming.

On the top of the staircase, the ghost of my dead husband is still there. As unmoving as yesterday. I take a deep breath.

"Good morning, Thomas," I say. "I hope you burn in the deepest pits of Hell."

I put on my pink suit and matching skirt. My shirt with the flowers, the pearl necklace, my hot pink hat, my pumps. I've got milk, bread, two bottles of pills, and more weed to buy.

I walk down the street with my head held high. There they are again, the obnoxious mummies on their morning stroll. I nod hello.

"Girls,"—of course, 'girls,' the return of a dead husband doesn't change customs—"tell Muriel and Constance tea is rescheduled for today, same time. I woke up feeling marvelous."

I don't wait for their reply. They gape, Holly

Parker's mouth is wide open as I walk past them.

An hour later, I'm home, ready to tidy everything up and welcome them with open arms. Thomas is on the stairs again—what an asshole!

Holly Parker, Grace Rose, Muriel and Constance arrive on time, sit in their usual seats, and I pass the same tray around, sip tea from the same cups, wearing the same clothes I do every time. But this will be the last time.

I sit back down in the empty chair and stare right into Thomas's ghost watching me from the house. As I pour tea, I ask them the question that popped into my mind the minute I opened my eyes this morning.

"Girls, what's your opinion of your husbands, really? I have never asked."

They glance at each other.

I go on, "All of us besides Constance have been widows for years. We can tell each other the truth, for the first time." I stop. "Not you, Muriel. Your husband is taking you to Venice next week, you don't have to tell us about him."

"But he's wonderful," Muriel answers like she didn't even hear me. "Wonderful and silent, like I've always wanted him."

He better be silent.

"I had to work for my marriage," Holly Parker begins. "No marriage is constantly happy. No husband and no wife are perfect."

A diplomatic answer. I expected nothing less from the queen of gossip.

"My husband loves me," Constance says. "He's the only one that takes care of me after my stroke."

"Mine was a drunk and a womanizer," Grace Rose

says, shocking even Holly's marble exterior.

"Yours?" Holly asks me, knowing I started this conversation to talk about Thomas.

"My husband," I say, "wanted to change our lives and our personalities the moment we got married. He insisted we had to fit in. He insisted so much that often he had to convince me using his open palm."

"Poor Agnes," Muriel says in one of her odd moments of lucidity. "What did you do?"

I shrug.

"Nothing," I lie.

I killed the fucking bastard. I killed him on the first step at the top of the staircase, or the last, depending on where you're standing. And now he has appeared again, on that precise spot, so I can never forget.

"That's why," I go on, "you won't ever see me in these clothes again. Or see my house like this again. From this day on, you will meet the real Agnes and I hope, from the bottom of my heart, that you will continue to come to tea every Friday."

None of them answer, but I'm not giving up.

"Also, in the living room between the pillows of the yellow checkered sofa, I've got three joints all rolled up for us and ready to blaze."

I look up, at the top of the staircase, where the figure of the Ghost in White has already begun to fade. You won the battle, Thomas, but I'll win the bloody war.

Fuck all the way off, Thomas. Fuck off, nasty clothes. Fuck off, prim-and-proper house.

Welcome, Agnes!

TV SPIRITUAL GUIDE

BY ZACHARIAH STANFIELD

Max poured milk into a bowl of Raisin Bran and floated his spoon off the rim. A Saturday habit that changed about as much as Max's apartment. Unmoved drab brown fixtures highlighted the understated space. Complemented with milk and raisins, he might stomach poverty better. The breakfast of champions.

The cereal bowl was a new addition to his apartment, a recent purchase at a local thrift store. Max frequented the place and a few others to furnish his home needs, but mostly, he collected niche items from his childhood to add a touch of color and bring life into his home. The bowl fit that description, thermochromic plastic—just add milk—with a cast of early 90's cartoon characters displayed inside. They were vibrant, emoted through their individual styles and looked as though they could tell a story. A modern patera for hapless twenty-somethings.

Max's method for consuming cereal involved time

and the absorption of milk to soften things up. Eating quick left the roof of his mouth raw, and he'd spend the day tonguing at the sore spot. Five minutes was all it needed and that gave Max some time to set up.

He grabbed a TV tray from the closet and laid the remote in the seat of his chair. Not sure what to watch, he turned on the TV and just selected one of the shows he needed to catch up on. Binging television was the social connection at work, a new "keeping up with the Joneses." Watching one episode week-to-week risked being left behind. From *The Real Housewives* to midwest serial killers, it changed day-to-day and was always time sensitive. No one in the office wanted to talk about last week's episodes, and forget about cartoons. Max didn't understand or even care for the shows, but grew tired of never having anything to say. It worsened during an election cycle.

Max paused on the Looney Tunes icon, wanting the exploits of Wile E. Coyote over modern issues, then started up something Bill mentioned Friday at lunch, *Dasvidaniya: Dangers of the Beluga Caviar Trade*. The narration for these documentaries always had some poor man's Attenborough leading the charge. It never worked.

Max checked on the cereal. The milk-logged flakes disintegrated into a soggy mush. He swirled the milk around the bowl then plunged in for a bite.

"Ow!"

Max dropped his spoon and sloshed some milk onto the tray. He looked around for the voice.

"Hello? Who's there?"

"No one, idiot."

The words gurgled up from the cereal. Max thought

he might be hallucinating the cartoons to life, or worse, in desperation, conversing with inanimate objects.

"Um. Hi." Max stuttered. The milk swirled and began rising up the rim of the bowl and out of it. Raisins sank down the bulbous white fountain and the liquid took the shape of a head with bran flake eyes and a raisin mouth.

"You couldn't eat Froot Loops?"

"What?" Max asked.

The head repeated. "Should I talk louder? The cereal, Froot Loops. Why couldn't it be something I like? Raisin Bran, seriously? What are you, sixty? Need to be 'regular'"?

The disembodied milk head was female, her voice was a bit older and judging by the milky visage she was Max's age.

"I do have Life cereal, if that's better?"

"No, it would not be. I'm dead and bathing in Life wouldn't make me feel better."

"I didn't know you were dead. Why are you in my bowl of cereal?" Max asked.

"Isn't it obvious? I haunt this bowl."

"Who are you?"

"Shannon."

Max tightened his lips and just looked on in amazement.

"You plan on telling me your name or are we just going to sit like this for a minute?" she continued.

"I'm Max."

"Hi, Max."

"Hi?"

"Don't look so stunned. I don't understand the physics of this sort of thing. You're eating out of my favorite bowl, which I am clearly still attached to, so, here I am with all my supernatural quality. Not exactly a science, but that's the best I could come up with on short notice."

"Metaphysics," Max corrected.

"No one likes a know-it-all. Do you want to be the first guy to make contact with the dead or the first to *correct* them? Don't be that guy, Max."

Max shook his head in agreement.

"Do you normally communicate through cereal?" he asked.

"Nope. Just got tired of the crap you're watching."

"It just started."

"More to my point, really. Do you always watch this kind of thing, because I don't know if I can take a lot more of this. You should really return me to the thrift store if this is going to be my afterlife." Shannon laughed at her pun.

"I don't really watch this stuff. I just do it to keep up with my co-workers."

Shannon leaned over the tray and into Max's face. Some milk dripped in his lap.

"You let your coworkers decide what you're going to watch? That's sad."

"Okay, they don't decide what I watch. I watch what they're watching so I can talk about it with them."

"You can't talk about what *you* watched?"

Max didn't say anything.

"I mean, you do suggest things for them to check out, right?"

"Not really."

"That might be a problem, Max."

Max stood up from his seat and paced.

"You know, you're pretty hostile for a milk ghost thing."

"The only *friendly* ghost is a cartoon one."

"Do you know something good worth watching?"

"Being dead, I don't exactly have my finger on the pulse of pop culture. Also, I was shelved for a few years in a thrift store."

Shannon turned and took in the apartment. Max lived in a small studio, and all of his knickknacks and furniture were cloistered together, making the space appear even smaller at first glance.

"Nice apartment, a touch small, but I've seen worse."

"You live in a bowl. Don't complain about my place."

Shannon's head turned to Max and grimaced. The milk and cereal collapsed in a splash, covering the tray and leaking onto the floor.

"Shannon?" Max flicked the bowl a bit to move it and dabbed at the puddle of milk with his finger.

"Hello?" Max sat back in his chair, upset that he insulted her. He wondered why she showed herself to him in the first place and what her presence meant for him. She didn't give many answers during her brief appearance.

The television flickered, changed to static and then searched through the icons by itself. It stopped on Looney Tunes and began to buffer content. An animated girl stood in a nondescript desert on an endless highway. The road wound off into the horizon, probably to some ill-fated cliff. She was lanky in her shorts and tank-top and had her hair pulled back in a ponytail.

"I haunt the bowl, but I'm not chained to it. I have boundaries, so, the bowl is more like my point of origin."

She vanished, turned on his lamp and reappeared. "See?"

Max didn't see much of anything. The whole mess had dropped on him before breakfast. A breakfast which now dripped on the floor. Max lived a quiet, solitary life. A mouse could shake up his existence and that paled in comparison to a haunting. Shannon babbled on about being animated, but Max failed to listen to any of it. Stuck between curiosity and annoyance, he wondered about the best way to remove a spectre.

"I think I'm gonna clean up this mess. Just make yourself, um, comfortable or find something to watch."

Shannon danced around, humming to herself. Max wiped down his tray and took everything to the sink. He considered his position. A ghost haunted one of his newfound trinkets, not a particularly pleasant ghost, who also possessed his television and took up residence in a Road Runner cartoon. He examined the bowl and its cartoon characters. Max couldn't imagine being eternally bound to some beloved object. He was never much attached to anything in his life.

He turned on the hot water faucet and plugged the drain. He sprayed the purple liquid dish detergent in and watched bubbles foam up. He placed the detergent bottle at the back of the sink and read over it—*Cuts tough grease. Removes tough stains.*

Up to this point, Max never fancied himself spiritual, which limited his exorcism options. He vomited in church once, but that seemed to point toward it not being his thing. So, praying over the bowl to bless it was out. Most of his success came from hard work. *Maybe just washing the hell out of the bowl would eliminate Shannon?* It was a better idea than no idea. Max pulled out his sponge and a Brillo pad and set to work on the bowl.

He scrubbed the bowl with vigor. He worked the sponge all over, applying more detergent and lathering until the bubbly foam was everywhere, then he rinsed the bowl to the point of exhaustion. He grabbed the Brillo pad, hesitated for a minute, then put it in the bowl. He knew the steel wool would mar the faces of the characters. He was proud of this find, even with the accompaniment of Shannon.

"You're working away."

Max was startled by the words. Shannon's face, outlined in the detergent bottle, was watching him clean the bowl.

"Lot of work for one bowl. Are you Obsessive-Compulsive or something?"

"No, I'm just thorough."

Max lifted the bowl out of the water and showed it to Shannon.

"Are you using a Brillo pad on my bowl?"

"Yes."

"Don't! It will ruin it."

Max submerged the bowl and pad to begin again. A loud crack sounded and Max grabbed his cheek. A wet dish towel floated beside him and wound up again for a second strike.

"I said DON'T!"

Max pressed on, but a second pop struck his leg. He

grabbed the dish towel and tossed it at the wall. Max reached for the sink but an R2-D2 stein he found at a garage sale clocked him in the jaw. The faucet hose turned on and sprayed down his pants.

"So scared you peed yourself?"

"I did not!"

"You totally peed yourself."

Max screamed and snatched the bowl and Brillo from the sink. He avoided several assaults from tin lunch boxes as he dove over his chair. The lights dimmed and flickered and the apartment vibrated. Shannon yelled for Max to give up the bowl, but he was determined to finish up. Shannon's energy bounced around different objects, turning them over or launching them at the chair. She appeared in the television, this time not as a cartoon but as a news anchor.

"This just in, local apartment tenant dies under odd circumstances. Let go of my bowl!"

"No!"

"I've had that since I was a girl. Do you know how many proofs of purchase I had to save? My grandmother helped me!"

The chair lifted from its spot, exposing Max who huddled to protect himself from the short ranged attacks. The chair had remained in the same place since Max moved in, now it was being hurled through his bathroom door.

"Had enough?"

"That just cost me my deposit. I'm destroying this bowl, I don't care if it kills me!"

Max felt himself rise off the floor. He tried forcing the Brillo into the bowl but his arms were splayed out.

Nothing he tried loosened Shannon's grasp. The bowl ripped out of his hand and was set gingerly back down on the kitchen counter. Shannon viewed on from behind the anchor's desk. She stacked some papers, moved them to the side and folded her fingers. Max levitated closer to the television.

"So Max, any last requests?"

In his wildest dreams, Max never saw himself getting a last request before dying. Even more confounding, it was at the hands of a ghost.

"Your spooky TV gag is so original. Poltergeist sucks by the way."

Not the brightest idea to get in a last minute dig, but Shannon smirked so he continued.

"Not a lot of time to come up with one last request."

"At least I am giving you one."

Nothing within reach satisfied his last moments alive. Maybe he should keep it simple. Max sighed. "Can I watch Fantasia? It's my favorite movie."

Max drifted back to the floor. Shannon relinquished her grip on him, and he moved back, a bit hesitant.

"I love Fantasia."

"Really?"

"Yes, really. I've watched it so many times. I know every color and musical cue. It's perfect."

"Would you like to watch it with me?"

He tried a last ditch olive branch to sate the ghost. Shannon didn't say anything. The chair from the bathroom floated back to its spot, and the television blinked to black. Max sat in his chair and could sense Shannon. Her translucent form floated longways as she cupped her chin in her hands and watched the screen. The black divided and orchestral shadows found their places on stage. Shannon smiled and turned to Max.

"What do you want to watch next?"

ALL THE DEVILS ARE SINGING

BY E.J. SIDLE

There's a demon in my apartment. Which is good, because I'm not sure what I'd do if the Summoning had called something else. Demons are at least a predictable entity. Some of the other creatures out there are not.

Or, demons are *usually* predictable. This one is a little less so, since he's completely naked. Although, it's clearly true what they say about demons because *wow*.

He almost looks too human to be from the Otherside, but there's a little something sinister about the ooze of his power. Definitely something sinister about the size of his... claws.

I'm distracted, and it's a mistake. He moves across the ritual circle like a striking snake, vicious and economical. It's a good circle, I drew the wards myself, but it's an untested one. I can feel his power, feel his momentum, and I'm going to be too slow to get out of reach.

The wards shudder but stay firm, sigils flaring around the circle. He's caught in place, claws extended and hovering inches from my head. I breathe out, long and slow.

The demon gives me a resigned look. "Well, that's done it."

"It worked?"

"Step into the circle and find out," he says. I don't move, and he shrugs. "Can't blame a demon for trying. Who are you, then?"

"Fontaine," I say.

"I knew a Fontaine once," he says, giving me a careful once over. "Few hundred years ago. Although, she was a woman."

"It's a family name." I resolutely keep my eyes from wandering, instead glancing between his face and the book in my hands. "This says your name is… Raymond?" I blink. "*Really*?

"It's a family name," he says, eyebrows arching. "Why am I here, Fontaine the Summoner?"

"I'm a PhD candidate."

"Ah yes, academia," Raymond interrupts. "Truly the best reason to Summon a demon."

"*Demonology* PhD candidate, asshole," I snap. "You think all this fancy new warding designed itself?"

"You performed a Summons to test your ward designs?" he asks.

"How else will I know if they work?"

"And this is your ritual space?"

I shake my head. "Usually I'd run a Summons in the lab, but I'm not the only PhD candidate and I don't want them seeing what I'm working on. How am I supposed to get grant money if they steal all my ideas?" I shrug, giving him a quick smile. "Academia is a contact sport. It's why we make the best Summoners."

Raymond doesn't smile back. "Really? Because you used a Life Contract. I'm here until you give me a soul. Are you planning on feeding the other candidates to me?"

"Well, I've definitely got a scumbag ex you can have. Trust me, no one will miss him if you… suck his soul out, or whatever. Contract fulfilled," I say. "Of course, none of that matters if you don't leave the circle. Contract doesn't fully form until I release you, and I won't be doing that."

"Then why am I here?" he growls.

"I told you, to test the ritual warding," I say. "It clearly works, which is great news for me. Give me ten minutes to get the banishment sigils organised, and you'll be back where you came from."

"Will I now?" Raymond says softly. Something tenses low in my stomach, a flutter of discomfort. Raymond's eyes track down to my abdomen, then back to my face. "Read me the Contract."

"What?"

"The Summons you used from the book," he orders. "Word for word."

I glance at the book. "It's like… four pages long. In Latin."

"Just the last line," he says. "Now, please."

"Fine!" I squint at the translations in the corner. "Something about honouring the commitment, then it's 'until the death do us part'. So, the Contract is over once you devour a soul." I close the book with a soft snap. "But you'd have to get out of the circle first."

Raymond sighs. "Give me the book." He holds a hand out expectantly, fingers staying within the wards.

"Uh, no!" I say. "Never give a demon a book on demon rituals! That's rule one."

"Rule one is don't attempt a Summons when you're ill prepared!" Raymond says. "*Give me the book.*"

"Sheesh, okay!" I open it back to the right page and hold it up for him to see. "Look with your eyes. It's not going into the circle."

He leans forward, squinting. It's small text, and the light from the ritual candles is subpar. I almost feel sorry for him. Then, he giggles.

There's no other word for it. A grown-ass demon, naked in my shoebox studio apartment, trying to smother a decidedly undignified giggle.

"What?" I ask.

"Fontaine," he says carefully. "Did you translate this?"

"Some of it," I admit. "But my ritual Latin is a bit… rusty. I used Google."

"Did you check it over?"

"I was going to!" I say, closing the book. "But I ended up watching Netflix, and… I mean, it clearly worked! You're here."

"That I am," he agrees. "But that last line is wrong. It's not 'until *the* death do us part'."

"What is it, then?" I ask, curious.

"'Until death do us part'," he says. "Fontaine, you married us."

***

I throw up in my bathroom. Twice.

Raymond's power is still there, thick and fluid in the back of my mind. My stomach hurts, my eyes sting, and I spit more bile into the toilet bowl.

Has a Summoner ever accidentally married a demon before? There are rituals for a more deliberate marriage, for joining demonic covenants and communing with the Otherside. All those rituals end with the Summoner tied to an altar having their heart cut out.

Can the Summons be undone? Has it even fully taken hold, if Raymond hasn't been released from the circle? Will my soul be forfeit even if I perform the banishment? Does it have to be consumma—*nope*.

All I can do is send him home. Contracts aren't supposed to fully form unless the demon leaves the circle. It's why my new, stronger warding will be such a hit with the grant committees, and why I'm still safe. Even an accidental marriage has to obey the laws of demonology.

I rinse my mouth out and splash water over my face. My stomach churns, an uncomfortable tension seeping out from my navel. This time there's no nausea, and I straighten my shoulders before leaving the bathroom.

Raymond isn't how I left him. He's fully clothed, looking even more human in jeans and a shirt. They're not mine, and I stare at him for a few seconds before moving further into the room.

"Where did you get the clothes?" I demand.

"Demon magic," he says.

He's not in the circle.

"Oh *shit*," I breathe.

He's fast, he's so fast. I stumble, back hitting the wall, and he's already *right there*. One hand clamps over my mouth, claws scraping against my skin. The other pushes hard into my gut, holding me in place.

"I'm not going to hurt you," Raymond promises softly. "But I can't have you using any Summoner tricks. No spells, okay?"

I nod. The hand covering my mouth moves away, and then Raymond takes a step back. I slump a little, bracing against the wall to stay on my feet.

"What the fuck?" I gasp, voice rougher than it should be, stomach churning. "I don't understand."

"The Contract formed," Raymond says, surprisingly gentle. "You can feel it. Once it took hold, the circle couldn't contain me. Not even with your additional wards."

"Feel what?"

"Have you ever held a Contract before?" he asks.

"No!" I laugh, sound a little too loud. "Summon and banish. I've never wanted to let a demon out of the circle."

"Well, this is what a Contract feels like," he says, twisting his fingers.

My stomach heaves, a thrill of discomfort that has me clutching at my abdomen. Something expands, sinking into the space between my organs, threading tendrils out beneath my skin. It's too much, and I feel like I'm about to be torn in half.

The pressure lessens suddenly, dropping back to a dull ache. I'm on my knees, sucking air through my teeth in a way that's perilously close to sobs. Raymond's crouched a few feet away, watching me with a sympathetic expression.

"I remember my first Contract," he says. "They're not all so overwhelming." He pauses. "Although, since this is a Life Contract, I don't suppose you'll ever experience a second one."

"Are you going to kill me?" I demand, dragging myself to my feet. My knees wobble, but I stay upright.

"I can't hurt you, Fontaine," he says, also coming to his feet. "Not deliberately, not while the Contract is active." He gives me a long, considered look. "Not unless you ask me to, anyway."

"I'm not asking!" I snap. "I'm never asking. We clear?"

"Of course."

He leaves me leaning against the wall, moving instead to pace around the remnants of the circle. I watch in silence as he plucks one of the candles from the floor, snuffing it with his fingertips. The box I keep them in is still open on my desk, and he packs the candle away with careful, practiced gestures.

"You've taken a ritual down before," I say softly.

"You're not my first Summoner, Fontaine," he says, methodically snuffing the next candle. "Unplanned house fires really ruin a nice meal." He glances over at me. "Although, most Summoners use white church candles. Sometimes red. Why are yours mismatched birthday ones?"

"I never get around to replacing the proper ones once I use them up," I mutter, cautiously stepping away from the wall. I'm unsteady but stable, and I keep moving until I can collapse onto my bed. "Don't judge me, Raymond, I'm having a bad day."

"Perhaps, if you had used traditional candles, there wouldn't have been any confus—"

"I don't think the *candles* are the problem!"

He's quiet for a long moment. "I have something for you."

"Annulment paperwork?" I ask, sitting up. "Tequila?"

It's a ring. A gold ring.

"I understand it's tradition for married humans to have rings," Raymond says, shrugging. He drops it onto my bedside table. "I thought perhaps you might appreciate it."

"Where did you get it?" I demand.

"Same place I got the clothes," he says. "Demon magic."

"You know we're not... *really* married?"

"We are until the Contract ends," he says placidly.

"That's a cheery thought." I scrub a hand across my face, slumping back down onto my pillows. "Right. Okay. I have a plan."

"Do you, now?"

"Campus archives," I say. "Full of old magic and even older rituals. I bet there's something there I can use to break the Contract."

"Ah, because accidentally marrying a demon is a common problem?" Raymond says.

"Are all demons assholes, or is it just you?" I stare at the ring for a moment before dragging the covers over my head. "Turn off the light."

"As you wish."

I don't move from beneath the blanket. "Did you just *Princess Bride* me?"

The light flicks off, and he snorts. "I'm a demon, I haven't seen that movie." There's a long beat of silence. "Buttercup."

"No, we're not doing this!" I snap, resolutely staying beneath the covers. "I'm gonna go to sleep and pretend none of this is happening."

"What do you want me to do?"

"Go away?" I ask hopefully. He scoffs, and I sigh. "Fine, get some rest then."

"Where?"

"What do you m—" I live in a small studio apartment. No bathtub. No sofa. One bed. "On the floor, Raymond. On the fucking floor."

"Of course," he says, grin in his voice. "As you wish."

***

I try to sleep, but I can't. I can feel Raymond's presence in my room, surprisingly unobtrusive but still there. And, low in the pit of my stomach, the Contract keeps throbbing.

There are hundreds of first hand Summoner accounts, and I've read most of them. Some are more detailed, outlining every moment of the experience. Others end abruptly, undoubtedly bloodily, when I assume the demon claimed what was due. None mentioned the Contract as such a physical feeling. Then again, none mentioned marriage, either.

The Contract pulses again. I wince, shifting awkwardly to ease the pressure. It's not painful, not exactly. Instead, it feels like the Contract is pushing and expanding, pooling into the crevices of my body.

There's another throb, this time with a sting of discomfort. A flex of power.

Demons can break Contracts. Test them for weaknesses, then shatter them. Maybe this is what it feels like, having a demon work to devour you. Maybe when the Contract splits me open, Raymond will be there to eat what's left.

The Contract tenses, stretches a little more. This time, it hurts.

"Raymond!" I hiss. "Are you doing that?"

"No," he says.

He's closer than I thought, and I fight the urge to panic. "Yeah? Who is, then?"

"You opened yourself as a demonic conflux."

"Excuse me, what?"

"You performed a Summons and reached out," he says. "I'm not the only thing that reached back, Fontaine. I was just the one who got here first."

Something shifts out in the dark, and the Contract expands a little more. It aches, deep and low, and I inhale sharply through my nose. "Great. That's just great."

"They see you as an entry point to this plane," Raymond says. "Put the ring on, Fontaine."

"What?" I demand, sitting up. "Are you serious right now?"

"It marks you as mine."

"I'm *not* yours."

"But I have claim on your soul," he says. "Put it on. Then everything else on the Otherside will know not to break you open for a feast."

I reach for the ring. "That's disgusting."

As soon as I have it in my hand, the Contract goes still. It flutters, a slightest hint of feeling somewhere below my navel, then the throbbing eases. I let my head fall back against the pillow, tension draining from my body. "Oh."

"Yeah, 'oh'," Raymond says. "You're welcome."

***

The next morning, I find the bruises blooming across my abdomen. In shades of yellow and black, they look disturbingly like fingerprints. Beneath them, the Contract churns. I keep the ring in my hand while I shower, then slip it into the pocket of my jeans. Just in case.

Raymond makes coffee and French toast while I get ready. He stays out of the way, thumbing through my ritual books with obvious distain and unobtrusively tidying the stacks of research papers strewn around my apartment. It's surprisingly companionable, and I can almost forget that I want him out of my life.

Almost.

I don't want to take him to the archives, but he refuses to be left behind.

"There are literally thousands of Summoners on campus," I argue, already pulling on my coat. "What if they realise you're a demon?"

"No one will, not unless I want them to." He conjures himself up a leather jacket, shrugging it on. "Besides, do you really think there aren't already demons here? This place is a buffet of mages ripe for the taking."

"No way. Someone would notice if students were vanishing."

"Humans, always so focused on instant gratification," he says, holding up my keys when I start patting down my pockets. "Think of it like this—find a few promising candidates, respond to Summons, form a Contract. A bunch of souls ready to harvest, give or take a few decades."

I swallow. "So I'm not the only one?"

"You're the only one for me," Raymond says.

"*No*, no." I yank the door closed with more force than necessary. "Absolutely fucking not. Turn it down, Raymond, this isn't a game."

He smiles, sharp and dangerous and definitely not human. "As you wish."

***

Most days I walk to campus. There's a shortcut through the woods, an overgrown trail that takes maybe twenty minutes.

Raymond laughs when he sees the trees. "A forest? Really?"

"The Necromancer kids like it for rituals," I say, shrugging. "There's a few good picnic trails. I'll show y—uh. I'll show you photos."

We walk the rest of the way in silence. It's a comfortable silence though, with moss squelching underfoot and the soft rustle of wind through the pines. The Contract still throbs beneath my skin, but it's background noise to the peace of the forest.

"You like it here," Raymond observes.

"I do. The forest is one of the reasons I chose to pursue my PhD here," I tell him honestly. "A walk in the woods is a great way to start your day."

Beyond the trees, the main campus is busy. Exams are looming, and we see increasing foot traffic as we emerge from the woods and make our way towards the archives. No one gives Raymond a second glance, and I stop worrying that we'll be outed by an observant demonologist.

The archives are humming with activity. The first few floors are full of undergraduates, all hyped up on caffeine and blasting Summoning music from their phones. Raymond scowls at them, following me as we make our way towards the upper levels.

"This floor is reserved for faculty, PhD candidates, and invited scholars," I explain, digging through my pockets for my swipe card. "If anywhere has answers, it'll be here."

"You have a lot of faith in an old library," Raymond says. I shrug, holding the door open. He steps past me and goes still. "Oh."

"Yeah," I say, following him in. The stacks reach up towards the roof, shelves spread out in all directions and bursting at the seams with books. I inhale the smell of parchment and aging magic. "'Oh' about sums it up."

***

We spend all morning holed up in an alcove, searching without success. Raymond vanishes into the stacks, emerging with books bound in human skin and carved from bones. He piles them up beside me, watching as I gingerly turn the pages. Sometimes, he flicks through the volumes I bring back, snorting in disgust and tossing them aside at random intervals.

"Dude!" I hiss when one bounces off the floor. "Can you be gentle with these please? They're irreplaceable."

"Even if they're incorrect?" he says snidely. He doesn't throw the next one, though.

In the dying hours of the afternoon, I find something promising. It's a small, weighty tome, handwritten in sprawling Latin.

"I can only read maybe half of it," I say, three additional books open beside me to help translate. "But I think it'll work. Most of it is about nullifying lesser Contracts, but I think the last ritual is for a life bond. I'll need to do some more translating."

"Without Google this time," Raymond suggests.

"You could help!" I retort.

He makes a non-committal sound, already skimming through another text. "I could teach you how to do these rituals, you know. Better than any long-dead Summoner."

"Summoners don't generally take lessons from their demons."

"Or maybe they just didn't write about it," he says.

He's not wrong. Why would you admit to taking direction from a demon? It's one thing to Summon them, another entirely to collaborate as equals. Or to enjoy having them around.

"Your clothes," I say, drumming my fingers on the table. "Not all demons can conjure things like that."

"And not all humans can Summon," Raymond says, looking up. "You know, I might be able to teach you demon magic. You could conjure your ritual supplies instead of substituting them."

"That would make one hell of a PhD."

He smiles. "That it would."

He has a nice smile.

The Contract pulses, sharp and uncomfortable. I blink, shutting my book with more force than necessary. "Uh… I think that's everything we need." I tuck the books into my satchel. "Let's go."

There's no one else on the floor, and we make our way back through the stacks in silence. Before we can reach the door, it swings open with a soft click.

"*Shit*," I whisper, recognising the new addition. "Hide!"

"Why?" Raymond asks, not moving. "We've already established that no one can tell I'm not human."

"It's not that!" I hiss. "Damn it, Raymond, would you *move*?"

But it's too late, because the figure entering the library grins. "Hey there, Fontaine!"

"Hi Mike," I say, throat dry. I rub my hands on the back of my jeans, watching as his eyes drop down to the gesture. I want him to pass us by, but he changes trajectory and suddenly he's close, too close.

I don't step back. It's a near thing, though.

"Been missing me?" he asks, low and affectionate and not at all like the man who spent our entire relationship sleeping around.

Raymond's arm settles over my shoulders, warm and solid. "Who's this, Fontaine?"

"Mike," I say stiffly. "And Mike, this is Raymond. He's my... uh—"

"Husband," Raymond supplies, just as I say, "friend."

Mike stares between us, then gives Raymond a knowing look. "Gotta watch him, Ray. You know what they say about Summoners."

Raymond grins, but it isn't a nice one. There are too many teeth, and claws prick against my shoulder blade. "I know what they say about you, Mike."

"Don't," I say quickly. "Raymond."

"Fine," he mutters. "Fine! As you wish, Buttercup. Let's go."

We leave Mike standing there. I can feel his eyes on the back of my neck, but Raymond's arm stays around my shoulders.

"Scumbag ex?" he asks, once we're alone on the stairs, warm and solid beside me.

"Scumbag ex," I confirm.

"I'm sure I know someone who'll eat him as a personal favour to me," Raymond says.

I snort. "He'll give them food poisoning. Don't worry about it, Raymond. I had it covered long before I fake-married a demon."

He doesn't respond, and I gently shrug off his arm when we get back to the main floor.

By the time we reach the woods, I'm feeling more relaxed. The books are a comforting weight in my satchel, and the early evening light speckles through the mossy trees. Beneath our feet, the path squelches welcomingly, and I sigh softly.

Soon, it'll all be over. No more demon marriage. No more Contract. Just the promise of a highly successful career in academia. Exactly what I've always wanted.

Then why do I feel so nauseous?

The Contract shudders, a deep burning pull that has me on my knees. I retch, coughing and choking, agonising pressure building beneath my skin.

I fumble for the ring in my pocket, clutching it desperately in my fist. This time, it doesn't help.

"Fontaine!" Raymond hits the ground beside me, and I have an absurd moment of concern about the damp ruining his jeans.

I laugh, low and pained. "Assume this isn't you?" I choke out.

"No," he confirms. His hands pull at my jacket, my shirt, smoothing along the bruises below my navel. I hiss, twisting away, and he frowns. "Someone close, though. Too close to be on the Otherside."

"W-what?"

"Stay here," he orders, already on his feet. "Stay here, keep a hold of the ring. I'm going to make it stop, Fontaine, understand me?"

"*Yes!*" I snap, but he's already gone. He's so fast, I keep forgetting that he's so fast.

I stay where I am, arms wrapped around my abdomen and head spinning. I focus on breathing, on the wind in the trees, on the damp moss staining my knees.

Slowly, the pressure lessens. It's barely noticeable at first, but then all at once my skin stops feeling like it's stretching, and the churning in my abdomen settles to a low ache. I let myself fall forward, exhausted and elated and gasping for air.

I'm not alone.

There's a certain feeling that comes from being alone in the woods. I relish it in the early hours of the morning, or at the end of a long day. I've walked the woods in all weather, in light and dark, when I've been too drunk to stand up straight. I know what it feels like to be alone with the world. And right now, I'm not.

The wind still shifts through the pines, and somewhere distantly there's the low hum of traffic. Gingerly, bracing against a tree trunk, I pull myself to my feet. I can't see anyone around me, no eyes flashing in the dark. Still, the hair on the back of my neck prickles, and I tentatively take a step forward.

I don't run. I'm not sure I could, even if I tried. Instead, I take steady, rolling strides towards home. One foot in front of the other, listening to the moss squelch beneath me with each step I take.

Trees rustle somewhere off to my left. There's a flash of movement, something else in the woods, and I suddenly can't swallow past the terror rising in my throat.

Turns out, I can run.

Branches whip across my face and I stumble over slippery logs, through sucking mud. There's crashing behind me, branches groaning and breaking, and I can hear my breath gasping too loud in my own ears.

Never thought I'd die in the woods. I wonder if I'll feel Raymond taking my soul. Or, maybe it won't matter, if it's another demon that guts me.

I stumble and nearly fall, but hands grab the back of my shirt and haul me upright. I lash out, trying to break free.

"Steady Fontaine!"

I recognise the voice. "*Mike*?"

"What the hell happened to you?" he demands, taking in the stains all over my jeans. "Why're you running from me?"

"R-running from *you*?" I ask.

"Yeah," he says. "I've been trying to catch you since you stood up. You always been so quick on your feet?"

"You *chased me* through the woods?" I snarl, twisting out of his grip. "What's wrong with you?"

"Didn't mean to scare you, Fontaine, just relax," he says, reaching for me again.

I bat his hand away. "Fuck off, Mike. I thought you were... I—"

"Shh," he says. "You thought I was what? A demon?"

He smiles, wide and bright and with too many teeth.

I back away, but there's nowhere to go. "You're not Mike," I accuse.

"No," the demon agrees. "I'm just wearing his skin."

"Don't," I say, flinching as clawed fingers smooth my hair away from my face. "Is Mike… did you kill him?"

"I did," the demon whispers, stroking my cheek. "It was easy. I didn't think it would be so easy. Just a *twist* and the soul comes right out."

"Why?" I ask.

"He Summoned me, but he never sent me away," the demon says, still tracing my cheek bones, unblinking eyes level with mine. "I was happy to wait for his soul to grow. But then I saw your—what did he call himself? Your *husband*."

"He's not my—"

The demon slaps me. It hurts, a sharp agony that takes me by surprise. He hits me again before I can recover, then once more. My head snaps to the side with the force of it, blood flowing from my nose.

"Your husband," he continues, as if I'd never interrupted. "He and I have unfinished business. I think ripping your pretty little soul to pieces right under his nose might help settle it."

I try to force a laugh. "We're not really married. It's not like that."

"He called you 'Buttercup'," the demon hisses. "Do you think he has pet names for all his Summoners?"

"That's just a stupid joke," I say. "He's not going to care if you eat me!"

"He'll care that I'm taking what's his!" the demon roars, claws closing around my throat. He shakes me, rough and cruel. "He'll care when he sees what I've done to you!"

He tightens his grip, crushing my windpipe in his hand. I scratch desperately at his wrist, trying to find purchase, but he lifts until my toes kick uselessly at the ground. The Contract screams and chokes, trying to keep itself alive. Or, maybe that's just me, tears streaming down my face and every banishment spell I know dying on my lips.

I try to kick him, try to pry his fingers from my skin, but it's not enough. My vision goes blurry, the pain in my chest becoming a dull, distant roaring.

I always knew there was a chance it would end like this, with a demon in the dark. Never thought it'd be the *wrong* demon, though. Never thought I'd have a preference for the hand around my throat.

Then, I'm falling. It lasts forever, my body collapsing in on itself, the wet moss stretching up to catch me. It hurts, I know it hurts, but it's only a small spark of discomfort that barely breaks through the haze.

Around me, there's movement. Branches creak and groan, but the moss stays wrapped around me like a blanket. Nothing else can touch me anymore, just the forest standing vigil. It's a comforting thought, and I don't want to open my eyes.

Gentle hands smooth over my face, shifting hair from my eyes. Fingers press against my throat, careful but firm, looking for a pulse.

"I'm alive," I manage, slurred and broken, eyes still squeezed shut,

"Then breathe like you are," Raymond orders. "In and out, Fontaine, like you mean it."

"Is this you taking my soul?" I ask. It's hard to talk.

"No, not today," he says. "I'm going to move you, Fontaine, but I'm going to knock you out first."

"I... uh," I mumble, head spinning. "Pass out. I'm gonna... yeah."

"It's okay." He brushes his fingers against my temples, a caress that turns into pressure. There's darkness at the edge of my vision again, welcoming and warm. I close my eyes and let it have me.

***

I wake up in my bed. Everything hurts. My throat feels raw, eyes scratchy, and the Contract throbs deep in the pit of my stomach.

"Ugh."

"Sit up slowly," Raymond advises. "I healed you a little, but demon magic can only do so much for weak human bodies."

"Fuck you," I manage, voice rougher than it should be. Still, I take my time, manoeuvring until I can lean against the headboard. "What happened?"

"You almost got eaten," he says. "That demon... he's an old acquaintance. We had a disagreement a few centuries ago."

"And he thought killing me would fix it?"

"He thought killing you would hurt me," Raymond says with a sigh.

I swallow past a lump in my throat. "He killed Mike."

"He did. I tried to heal him, but there are limits," he says. "I'm so sorry, Fontaine."

"So am I," I whisper. "Mike was... he wasn't good to me, or for me. He wasn't a friend. But he didn't deserve that."

"I know," Raymond says gently.

I glance over at him, and for the first time realise he's in the middle of a ritual circle. "What are you doing?"

It's a complicated circle, unfamiliar and sprawling. Sigils loop out from the edges, dark and unknown. It's not complete, not yet, and I feel a warm rush of relief when Raymond carefully steps over the markings.

"I'm nearly done," he says, peering at one of the books strewn across my desk. "I translated it myself. You Summoners do love obscure Latin dialects."

"It'll break the Contract?"

He nods. "As soon as you activate it."

"You shouldn't know how make a circle," I say, frowning. It's expertly done, too polished to be from a book.

"But I do," he says, digging a box out from beneath the books. "Here, I got you something."

"It better not be more jewellery," I warn, reaching out for it anyway.

It's a nice box, surprisingly solid. Inside, it's packed with proper white church candles. Good ones, too, far better than what I'd usually buy myself.

"Thank you."

Raymond shrugs. "Thought it might be better not to chance your birthday candle substitutions again."

Demons aren't supposed to be like this, they're not supposed to understand magic and give you gifts. They're not supposed to draw their own banishment circle and willingly step inside it.

"Will it hurt?" I ask. "Breaking the Contract. Will it hurt?"

"No," he says, then winces. "Not much. You'll feel a tug and some pressure, but it'll be fast. Promise."

I shake my head. "No, will it hurt *you*, when it breaks?"

"Maybe," he says. "Without a soul to anchor me, I'll return to the Otherside. It can be a... process."

"So," I say, carefully putting the box of candles on my bedside table. "What if I don't break it?"

Raymond blinks. "Then I stay. And, eventually, I rip your soul from your body in a way that will most definitely sting."

"Which could be decades from now," I continue. "But in the meantime, we can find the other demons on campus. Banish them before they eat anyone else."

"Fontaine, they've operated like this since your institution began," Raymond says gently. "You can't change it. Demons will always be drawn here."

"Maybe, but I'm not going to know if I don't try it."

"You're still a conflux, that won't end until the Contract severs," he warns.

I shrug. "You've managed to keep me breathing so far. We'll work it out." I grin. "Plus, this'll be an *amazing* PhD, you have no idea."

"This is mostly for the PhD, isn't it?"

"Yeah," I admit.

"Academics," Raymond says, exasperated but surprisingly fond.

"So," I say, quick and fast, before I can change my mind. "This whole marriage thing wasn't really what I had in mind, right? But, I suppose... it's not... it's not *all* bad."

"It's not," Raymond agrees.

"Well, I'm not feeling very magical right now," I say. "So you might as well clean that circle off my floor."

He moves, fast and fluid, crossing the room to kneel beside my bed. I startle, tensing as he hooks a careful hand under my knee, dragging me closer.

"Hang on!" I protest, but I don't try to break free.

"Relax, Buttercup," he says gently, letting me go. "I have something else for you."

It's the damned gold ring again.

"Where did you even find it?" I demand. "I dropped it, I think, when the demon… in the forest."

"You did, and I called it back. It can still protect you," he says, not looking away from my face. "Put it on."

"Can't we use a necklace or something?" I whisper. "A watch, maybe?"

"No," he says. "It's not just about shielding you, Fontaine. You know it's not. So put it on."

"It doesn't mean anything," I protest softly. "You know that, right? I'm not saying it never will, but right now it doesn't *mean* anything."

"Fontaine," he says. "Put the ring on."

I hesitate for a moment, then reach for the gold band. "Okay, Raymond. As you wish."

A VEGGIE TALE

BY RICHARD LAU

(A Rap-scallion Tribute to Richard Matheson's Horror Classic, "I Am Legend")

Roger Nielsen looked at his watch. He had about three hours of daylight left. Then they would return. Forty-five years ago, Nielsen's mother Barb had told him to eat his vegetables. Now, though he did not rhubarb's advice, the vegetables were trying to eat him.

Most of the world had become vegetarian, and not in a good way. A pandemic of unknown origin not only killed whomever it befell, but also mutated and reanimated the victim after death as a curious hybrid of human and vegetable. A hybrid that not only spread the virus, but also hungered for human flesh.

As part of his daily routine, Nielsen inspected the defenses he had set up around his home. He checked the salvaged blenders, mixers, and food processors daisy-chained by linked extension cords encircling the house. He made certain the generator, safely sheltered in the garage, had enough fuel to power the devices overnight. The mere sound of the whirring blades seemed to agitate and keep the veggie people away. He glanced at the timer that controlled the whole system. It would kick on soon.

Three months ago, the plague seemed so far away, in someone else's state, in someone else's county, in someone else's city, on someone else's block.

He remembered the day he saw his first actual plague victim. Nielsen had been talking to a neighbor, Choy Chee, about restoring classic taxis. Chee had been saying, "In determining the value of the taxi, like the history of any other car, you must first consider the cabbage."

Nielsen found the information fascinating, but then he heard his landline ringing. "Thanks shallot for the advice. I'll be right bok, Choy," he had said. And when he returned, he had found the bodies of Choy and his wife, Kim. Choy was still in the garage, slumped over his workbench, no doubt looking through some of the old car magazines he always had strewn about. Kim was in the side yard, the pool of water surrounding her from a still-flowing garden hose indicating that she had been lying there for some time.

He had hurried home, called 911, and proceeded to take a hot shower to clean off whatever germs he may have picked up. When he came out of the bathroom, his wife Flora was curled up on the sofa watching a Presidential address on television. Broccoli Obama, sporting a calm countenance with a slightly unhealthy green tinge was saying, "Greetings and salad-tations.

As your President, I rutabaga your patience and confidence as we fennel all available resources into fighting this pandemic."

He remembered Flora saying, "I don't carrot all for what he had to say," as the briefing ended with a hearty rendition of "Kale to the Chief."

By nightfall, no emergency personnel had arrived for his neighbors. And he realized none was going to.

He had been watching the Chee house from his living room window when he saw his neighbors come out, as casually as if they had just been taking a napa. But their bodies were now rounder, with layers of greenish white veiny leaves bunching and protruding through their clothes.

Too late Nielsen realized he should have put some sort of warning in front of their house or at least bound up the bodies.

Gus Russet was jogging down the street with his six little children, vainly all named after him and numbered, running in front of him. Russet had played football at King Edward College in Idaho and was even drafted professionally to the Yukon Gold. He considered himself quite a spud. He was probably returning from the nearby park with his little ones. Nielsen watched as the Chees and another neighbor named Artie, who now resembled a stumpy green acorn, attacked the ex-footballer.

Russet's six-foot frame collapsed like a sack of potatoes, as his kids screamed and scattered. As he saw Artie choke Russet, Nielsen could stand by no longer. He ran out his front door, grabbing a nearby garden hoe. Artie and the Chees backed away when they saw Nielsen swing the hoe over his head. He chased them down the street, yelling like a madman, "Beet it, you Fruit of the Loom rejects!" Eventually, they split up and disappeared into the shadows and bushes of the neighborhood, and he lost track of them.

Winded, he returned to the scene of the attack only to find a worse carnage going on. Thinking it was safe, Russet's children had returned to their fallen father's side, and the former football player was grabbing them up and munching on them like Super Bowl snacks.

Nielsen marveled in horror at how quickly the transformation had begun. Gus Russet's brown skin was darker and rougher, his previously athletic body lumpier and more asymmetric.

"You monster!" Nielsen raged. "How could you do that to your children?" Nielsen pointed at the crumpled tiny bodies who were all named after their murderer. "All of those Guses! Why couldn't you a-spare a Gus? Have you no mercy?"

"I yam what I yam!" yelled Gus Russet, his new thickening skin beginning to flake off as he flexed a bicep and postured. "And I'm even more a-peeling!"

The tots at Russet's rooting feet reanimated and began crying that they were hungry.

"What are you bothering me for?" roared Russet. "Mommy's at home. Go home and edamame! Besides, Pappy has some unfinished business."

Nielsen didn't like the way Russet was eyeing him, with the twenty-or-so eyes now covering the big man's body.

Nielsen quickly realized the danger he was in. Compared to Russet's bulk, the hoe in his hands was a toothpick. Out of the corner of his eye, he saw Artie coming back down the street from one direction and

Choy and Kim Chee from another. He was about to be outnumbered and overrun.

He ran back to his house, saturated in a toxic shroud of grief, shame, and disgust.

"What's wrong?" Flora had asked. "You look like you went to the edge of the roof and did an endive!"

He told her of the horror he had witnessed. They quickly began fortifying their house, moving bookshelves in front of windows and propping pieces of large furniture against the doors.

Exhausted from their efforts, but trying to ignore the screams and chaos of the less fortunate outside of their shelter, they had made sweet, desperate love.

That night seemed so long ago, but it still caused Nielsen to produce a shudder. To distract himself, he focused on the present, keeping his mind and hands busy, cleaning the sensors of the motion detectors and the panels of the solar-powered spotlights. The lights not only illuminated his yard but also the large cardboard cut-outs of the Easter Bunny and other rabbits he had looted from nearby stores. They were beginning to show their wear, along with the stacked cookbooks focusing on vegetarian recipes. He added "paint more bunnies on wood" to his mental checklist and hoped his artistic skills would suffice. As an afterthought, he also reminded himself to check the neighbors' attics for those animated deer folks used as Christmas decorations. He would try anything that stood a chance of repulsing the nightly harvest of ravenous veggie people.

Finally, as the sun was setting, it was time to retire inside for his usual reward, a stiff shot of whiskey, the first of many in the passing night. Nielsen knew he had been drinking more lately, but he didn't count, and he didn't care. Alcohol was plentiful and easy to find. The mutants didn't drink it, and for a while, Nielsen amused himself with the thought of "stewed vegetables." But the amount of surplus made Nielsen even lonelier, realizing he must be the only remaining human around in the immediate area.

It hadn't always been like that. As the empty shot glass slammed down on the kitchen counter, he thought again of Flora.

The day after his encounter with Russet, Flora slept in. He had taken a cautious reconnaissance outside. The few veggie people he saw appeared to be in some sort of coma and had planted themselves partially in the ground. He whacked one like a golf ball with the garden hoe, and it still remained unconscious. The steady rise and fall of its leafy chest indicated he had not killed it, and, for some reason, Nielsen was relieved. He would probably feel differently once night had fallen, and the thing with the split head was pounding on his door, demanding a piece of him.

While Flora slept, he had further improved the defenses of their house, boarding up windows, reinforcing doors, affixing barbed wire around the roof in case any of the veggie people could somehow get up there.

The hours passed quickly and, as dusk began to set, he noticed a stirring in the street. The veggie people had begun to move. He quickly put away his tools, took one last look around, and retreated into the safety of the house.

Flora was now awake but still in bed. She was weak, suffering from fever and chills. Both of them knew what it meant, but both pretended it was nothing to worry about. After she had some vegetable broth soup, she fell asleep again.

That was the first night since his college years that Roger had drank through the night. He made sure he didn't get soused, for he wanted to be alert with the veggie people wandering outside, thumping on the doors, windows, and walls trying to get in. But he wanted the alcohol to take some of the edge off the guilt that he had brought the virus into his home.

They had received a set of Ginsu knives as a wedding present. Nielsen busied himself making a harness out of an old belt to hold several of the larger knives and cleavers.

The night passed slowly. Nielsen tried not to watch the clocks, for their numbers and hands seemed frozen. The tension made the surrounding air as solid as a block of wood and just as difficult to inhale.

Once in a while, Flora would awaken and call to him. He'd read to her from a book by her fava-rite mystery author Celery Queen or the latest non-fiction by media personality Dr. Root Westheimer, as recommended by Okra Winfrey.

Sometimes they just sat in silence; other times Flora would somehow find the energy to try to cheer him up and pepper him with playful questions: "Do you love me from my head tomato?" He would reply, "I'll always love you. If you be true to me, I'll beetroot to you."

They would reminisce about happier times. "Remember that two-piece swimsuit I bought in San Diego? The bikini with the zoo animal pattern?"

"That zucchini was two sizes too small and fit perfectly!" Roger gushed, and Flora blushed at the memory.

And even with the wailing and banging outside, she'd fall asleep again.

At these times, Nielsen would go into another room. He'd pound back on the walls. He'd rage to himself, "They can't come in! We can't go out! Why can't they just lettuce alone?"

When the sun rose, and he was certain things had quieted down, Nielsen set his alarm clock to allow him a quick nap to not waste more precious daylight. He then got into the routine of checking the outside of the house for damage and exploring other houses for what helpful and handy things he could find. At first, he didn't venture very far, but as his confidence grew, he was able to travel farther, even driving his truck when he had the fuel. He avoided Russet's house, fearing what he might see inside.

Day in and day out, Nielsen felt it was important that he kept to arugula schedule. But Fate kept changes in the wind.

It was on a day with a sunny sky and temperate weather when Flora would have been normally tending to their garden. Instead, later that same day, she died. He would never rue Flora leaving him in such a manner. The choice wasn't hers any more than it was his, and throughout her illness, their relationship had romained rock salad.

He buried her in that same garden. And that night, she had come back to his door.

His wife had always been a beautiful woman, but when she appeared at their door again that night, with her red rounded curves and green offshoot hair, she looked absolutely radishing.

It took a strength of will Roger knew he would never have again to slam the door in her face, to throw the bolt and hook the chain, to ignore her pleading through the walls and scratching at the boarded windows. He cranked the stereo up loud, playing Cornie Francis's "Who's Sorrel Now" over and over. He tried to read. He tried to make lists. Mostly, he cried.

The next morning, he found her. True to her helpful nature, she had conveniently replanted herself back in the garden. He had to do something. He wouldn't be able to pass another night without taking her back in his arms.

The radio had been broadcasting the locations of public fire pits, after scientists determined it was the best way to dispose of those who had died of the virus as well as those who had mutated. During the daytime, survivors lined up, bringing bodies for disposal. Enough fuel and other material were added to keep the fires burning throughout the night.

The nearest official pit was three hundred miles away, by a major metropolitan city. Making such a journey just wasn't feasible. It was too far away. In addition to the long road trip, who knew what he might encounter. And at the destination, there was probably a long line of cars full of distressed and possibly infected people.

He wasn't worried about getting sick. He felt fine. For some reason, he had been blessed with the curse of immunity. But still he'd find the queue cumbersome.

He was in a pickle. He couldn't stand the thought of his wife burning among the other chard bodies. But at the same time, no matter how much he grieved for her, how much he missed her, he couldn't have her returning every night.

Then he remembered the geyser.

There was one at a state park only two hours away. It had been one of their favorite places. The boiling water should kill the virus as well as fire, and it seemed somehow more appropriate, less disrespectful.

With tears stinging his eyes, he dressed her for the last time. He carried the world to his truck that day, refusing to put her in the bed but securing her in the passenger seat. If not for the garnishness of her transformation, she could have simply been dozing on one of their many day trips.

He arrived at the fenced-in dirt lot of the state park just in time to see the geyser erupt, recalling the many times he and Flora had watched the watercress into the sky. After about ten minutes, the spout subsided. He had about two hours before the next burst. It would only take him five minutes to pick up her body, walk out to the hole of still-boiling water and drop her in. He had said his goodbyes on the drive up.

It should have taken five minutes. It probably did. But it seemed like forever. Forever, he clung to her body, as strongly as the wet mud clung to his boots. He convinced himself it was only the rising steam or the floating mist that moistened his face.

And when he couldn't fill his lungs one more time with the sulfur-stained air, he let her go, with his arms, with his heart, with his entire being, with his soul.

There were no words he needed to say; there were no words he could say. Whatever he was leaving behind was no longer the woman he had married. His heart was now stone, and nothing would sprout from it.

He remembered little of the trip back home, except arriving before dark and being tempted to leave the door open, welcoming whatever came.

How long ago had that happened? Months, years? Calendar pages had long withered into meaningless squares and numbers. He was barely aware of the graying hair on his face and the stink of unwashed clothes on his body.

Memories deteriorated into hazy shadows of light and dark reflected in the glasses and bottles he emptied. His mind was permanently banked with pea-soup fog.

Living alone, he didn't need mushroom. Still, he grew restless, pacing in the confined space at night like a trapped lion. Alternating thoughts of self-loathing and self-preservation made his head spin and ache, and when the spinach was finally overcome by drink, he fell into troubled sleep.

One day, Roger Nielsen awoke as a very different person. Gone was the rational, frightened man who had struggled to keep his body and his sanity safe. He might have cracked. He might have given in to the madness that surrounded him. It might have been like those tales where one had fallen so deep into the Earth, one came out the other side, emotionally scarred and physically disfigured from the journey. He just knew he was not the same man he was when he had fallen asleep.

He no longer sought peas of mind. He no longer fought and rebelled against what had become the reality of his present. One could not change the past any more than one could yawn and then try to onion.

Roger Nielsen declared war and decided to eggplant his flag right then and there. From that day forward, Roger Nielsen would be a warrior, a deity, a demon, a blunt instrument of vengeance and justice. Broken as he was, he would rule this broken kingdom.

He looked forward to the daylight hours, not as a respite from the horrors of the night, but to create a few horrors of his own. He strapped on his belt of Ginsu knives and then stopped by the garage for the pruning shears and hacksaw.

"It's harvesting time!" he bellowed, as he rushed out the front door, thrilled for the first time to see so many of the veggie people planted in his yard.

With the seriousness of a surgeon turned demented serial killer, he pruned and parsnipped the still-human limbs off of the vegetable torsos.

When he felt the urge, he crudely unzipped his pants and took a leek on some of the slumbering sonovabitches.

That night, he laughed sadistically, watching and cheering as the amputated and mutilated veggie people struggled in their plots in the dirt, managing only to roll and wobble side to side in their shallow graves.

The next day, he ran outside again, this time with the battle cry, "Who ya gonna cauliflower? Veggiebuster!"

He no longer worked gingerly and mustard all the strength he could to inflict as much damage in his limited time of daylight.

That evening, he toasted his savage triumph, lifting a glass to a silver-framed photograph of Flora, lounging in some tropical paradise that must have only existed in a fairy tale long, long ago. Though she was smiling in the picture, her ice-blue eyes did not look happy. They were accusing.

"What have you done?" her photo seemed to ask him. "These are not the actions of the man I married."

Before he answered, Nielsen poured himself another stiff one. Then he slurred, "Soybean bad. So what?"

He resented his dead wife trying to squash what small pleasure he was able to find left in the world.

These creatures, for Nielsen no longer considered them remotely human, even with their vegetable-shaped torsos possessing four human limbs and a head, had swarmed the neighborhood. They mostly invaded from within as new victims mutated and sprouted from the depth of each night like the zombie plants they were. From the beginning, they had been merciless, crowding and choking his life like unforgiving weeds. It was now their turn for a similar cocktail, a concoction of a tiny dash of watered-down misery mixed with three strong shots of furious vengeance. Just add a veggie garnish. Nielsen snickered.

Still respectful, still caring, he gently placed the photograph face down and continued celebrating alone.

A week later, feeling especially arrogant and cocky, he stepped outside on the porch and took a deep breath of night air. The sense of risk was invigorating and the aura of power intoxicating. Excitement was pumpkin through his veins. Keeping watch for anyone roaming around, he poured cooking oil into the veggie mouths of the limbless, delighting in their spitting and coughing and cries of "Yuca!"

Several more days passed, and there were no new veggie people self-planted in his or the neighboring yards, just his old immovable victims. It was time to get rid of them. The neighborhood was soon filled with the smoke of dozens of small fire pits.

But still no new veggie people showed up. Could word be getting around? Could they be warning each other? Well, if they wouldn't come to him, he would go find them.

He would do his scouting during the day when his prey was most vulnerable. And after sundown, he would gratefully accept the challenge of the hunt with his targets being at their most plentiful and dangerous.

Three blocks over, he found Lionel Hummel. The retired army kernel liked to take walks, and if Nielsen was watering his lawn, they'd often have a chat. True to being a soldier, the old man had planted himself at attention, almost straight upright, like a scarecrow turning into a corn plant. A developing cob of corn created an inappropriate bulge in Hummel's trousers. At least Nielsen hoped it was a corncob.

"Don't ask, don't tell," Nielsen muttered.

Hummel's sleeping, age-spotted face was still recognizable, but his previously stout body had grown rod-thin and reedy. Leaves resembling broad spear tips unfurled from the top of his balding head down to his upper thighs.

Nielsen began to sweat and garlic his lips in anticipation. He would return home, pick up some more equipment for the hunt and turnip a little before dark.

Hours later, with the setting sun still reddening the sky, Hummel began to stir.

From his hiding place behind a street-parked car, Nielsen muttered, "Always an early riser, eh, old soldier?"

Hummel stiffly pulled one foot and then the other out of the ground. He was barefoot, his toes turned into thick, pale roots. Hummel shook his leaves loosely and then ambled toward the nearest house.

Nielsen began to stalk the corn man, keeping Hummel in sight while at the same time keeping his distance. Hummel crouched at the base of a tree, inspecting a small cage. The clever old soldier had been laying traps for the small critters still in the neighborhood!

Giving in to his anger and irrational jealousy at Hummel finding an alternative food source, Nielsen moved in quickly and collard the old man, lifting him up, amaized at how weightless the mutated reanimated corpse seemed to be. He flung the corn man against the tree before it could bite him. Nielsen wasn't worried about becoming infected, but the idea of being bitten revolted him.

"Sorry for the tassel," Nielsen punned, in true James Bond fashion, for that is how he viewed himself now. "Care to lend me an ear?"

"Stand down, soldier!" the former army officer ordered, as if he still held his rank and stature as a human. "What's this nonsense you're trying to bamboozle me with?"

"Can bamboo shoot?" Nielsen asked, and not waiting for an answer, he continued. "Well, I certainly can!" He pulled out the flare gun he had recovered from Russet's house and pulled the trigger.

The corn man burst into flames, crackling and popping, reminding Nielsen of how long it had been since he had been to a movie theater. He scooped up some freshly popped kernels, tossed them into his mouth, and chewed with satisfaction. His eyes gleamed while enjoying the spectacle of Hummel's burning foliage mixed in with the soundtrack of the old soldier's leaf-shuddering, raspy profanities.

The commotion would attract attention, and Nielsen didn't want to push his luck and get surrounded or trapped. Still trying to emit some measure of pride and joy, he strutted back home to his den, a happy hunter, a dandelion.

Once there, he skipped his collection of bottles and reached for something stronger. There was almost an electric shock as his fingers touched the silver frame.

"Flora?" he asked the photograph, raising it to face those piercing eyes again.

"What have you become?" she seemed to say. "Do you think the violence cassava your problems? Are you salsified?"

And though he had sworn never to do so again, Nielsen searched deep into himself. "I've bean there, done that," he said, resisting, but finally giving in.

The words didn't belong to Flora. She was long dead and gone. He knew that. He bitterly accepted that.

Nielsen admitted and submitted to the turmoil that bubbled within him, like the boiling water of a geyser.

In spite of his efforts, he was alone. And because of his efforts in killing the veggie people, he ironically grew more alone every day. Because of his immunity, he would never become one of them.

Although he had immunity, he also was a carrier. He could go in search of other human survivors, but he wouldn't want to infect them, and any he found would probably be happy to take precautions not to be infected by him. He was not ready to kill other people, even in self-defense.

But worse than the veggie people, even worse than being physically separated from his fellow humans, somewhere along the way, he had lost his humanity.

And being no longer human nor vegetable, he was stranded in isolation on a desert island of suffocating inbetweeness.

His house was his pod. His skin was his shell. His soul was the meat rotting within. He had literally become a human bean.

Roger Nielsen slumped into a padded easy chair whose cushioning refused to comfortably accommodate his kidney-shaped body. He muttered to nobody in particular, "I am Legume."

ABOUT THE AUTHORS

RICHARD LAU

Richard Lau is an award-winning writer who has been published in newspapers, magazines, anthologies, and the high-tech industry. Several of his plays have been produced or performed as readings. He does not maintain an online presence, but may be reached at readers2rlau@gmail.com. He wishes to thank Barbara for her punderful attitude in reading his punny stories.

ANGELIQUE FAWNS

Angelique Fawns is a speculative fiction writer with a background in journalism. She turned her pen to horror, sci-fi/fantasy two years ago, and has short stories in twenty or so anthologies. She lives with her family on a large farm north of Toronto with horses, cows, chickens and a large obnoxious Boer goat. You can see more of her work at www.fawns.ca or connect with her on Twitter at @angeliquefawns.

ALEX COLVIN

Alex Colvin is a Canadian humor writer who dreams of being immortalized in Wikipedia. He's been published in magazines and anthologies. You can find more of his silly stories on his website:

https://alexcolvinwriter.com

KEVIN M. FOLLIARD

Kevin M. Folliard is a Chicagoland writer whose fiction has been collected by The Horror Tree, Flame Tree Publishing, *Hinnom Magazine*, and more. His recent publications include "Halfway to Forgotten," featured on *The No Sleep Podcast*; the *Short Sharp Shocks!* Halloween tale "Candy Corn"; and his 2020 horror anthology *The Misery King's Closet*. Kevin currently resides in La Grange, IL, where he enjoys his day job as an academic writing advisor and active membership in the La Grange and Brookfield Writers Groups. When not writing or working, he's usually reading Stephen King, playing Super Mario Maker, or traveling the U.S.A.

JOHN KISTE

John Kiste is honored to have his tale included in Coffin Blossoms. He is a horror writer who was previously the president of the Stark County Ohio Convention & Visitors' Bureau and a Massillon Museum board member. He is an organ donation ambassador, a McKinley Museum planetarian and an Edgar Allan Poe impersonator who has been published in *Third Flatiron, With Painted Words, A Shadow of Autumn, Modern Grimoire, Dark Fire Fiction, Six Guns Straight from Hell 3, Theme of Absence, The Dark Sire*, NonBinary Review's *H. G. Wells and The Odyssey* anthologies, and whose work was included in Unnerving Press's *Haunted Are These Houses*, and Camden Press's winner of the 2019 Preditors and

Editors readers' poll for best anthology, *Quoth the Raven*.

MARK McLAUGHLIN

Mark McLaughlin is a Bram Stoker Award-winning author of fiction, nonfiction, poetry and more. His latest releases are the huge story collection, *THE WEIRD WORLD OF MARK McLAUGHLIN MEGAPACK®; HUMAN DOLL*, a novel of suspense set in the entertainment industry; and *THE HELL NEXT DOOR*, a novel of horror and the supernatural. McLaughlin is also the author of numerous works in the literary tradition of H.P. Lovecraft, many co-written by his best friend, Michael Sheehan, Jr.

R.A. CLARKE

R.A. Clarke is a former police officer turned stay-at-home mom living in Portage la Prairie, MB. She survives on sloppy toddler kisses, copious amounts of coffee, and immersing her mind in fantastical worlds of her own creation. Whenever not crafting short stories, she keeps busy working on her novel, or writing/illustrating children's literature. R.A. Clarke's work has been published by the *Writers Workout*, *Writers Weekly* (24-hour contest 1st & 2nd place winner), *Sirens Call Publications*, and *Polar Borealis* Magazine.

She can be found at: www.rachaelclarkewrites.com, or on twitter at @raclarkewrites.

ROBERT P. OTTONE

Robert P. Ottone is an author, teacher, and cigar enthusiast from East Islip, NY. He delights in the creepy. His collections *Her Infernal Name & Other Nightmares* and *People: A Horror Anthology about Love, Loss, Life & Things That Go Bump in the Night* are available now wherever books are sold.

He can be found online at SpookyHousePress.com, or on Instagram (@RobertOttone).

JOHN WOLF

John Wolf is a librarian lurking in the Pacific Northwest. When he's not shelving books or processing holds, he likes making things up and putting them on paper. A graduate of Washington State University—Vancouver, John has been writing and publishing for eight years. His work has appeared in *The Wicked Library*, *Electric Spec*, *Bards & Sages Quarterly*, *Silver Blade Magazine*, anthologies from *Deadman's Tome*, and others. He subsists on a strict diet of coffee, bad movies, and good podcasts. You can follow his Twitter @JohnTheEngMajor.

JUDITH BARON

Judith Baron is a fiction writer. Her short stories have

been published in *Canadian Dreadful*, *Handbook For The Dead*, *Animal Uprising*, *The Sirens Call eZine #47: Deeds Most Foul and Unnatural*, *Future Visions Anthologies: Volume 2*, *Horror Bites Magazine Issue #8*, *The Poet's Haven Digest*, *Deadly Bargain: A Colors in Darkness Anthology*, *Trembling with Fear: Year 2*, *Spadina Literary Review*, and *Accursed* by Jolly Horror Press. She has a degree in Political Science from the University of Western Ontario and currently lives near Toronto, Ontario.

MYA LAIRIS

Mya Lairis has a thing for monsters, and always has since watching *Clash of the Titans* and *Godzilla* back when she was a wee one. She enjoys crocheting, painting, reading military horror and bio-thrillers but will read anything. While she began writing paranormal and fantasy shorts, she enjoys composing horror shorts. Mya lives in Maryland with her two furry kids, the diva Zoe and Cougar the devious.

CARINA BISSETT

Carina Bissett is a writer, poet, and educator working primarily in the fields of dark fiction and interstitial art. Her short fiction and poetry have been published in multiple journals and anthologies including *Arterial Bloom*, *Gorgon: Stories of Emergence*, *Hath No Fury*, *Mythic Delirium*, *NonBinary Review*, and the *HWA Poetry Showcase Vol. V* and *VI*. She teaches online workshops at The Storied Imaginarium, and she is a graduate of the Creative Writing MFA program at Stonecoast. She is a member of Codex, SFWA, SFPA, and HWA. Her work has been nominated for several awards including the Pushcart Prize and the Sundress Publications Best of the Net. Links to her work can be found at: http://carinabissett.com.

LIN MORRIS

Lin Morris lives and writes in his hometown of Portland, OR. His work has appeared in *Unlikely Stories, Trembling with Fear, Flumes Literary Journal/The Haberdasher,* and in the anthology *Flash of Brilliance*. His short novel *The Marriage Wars* is available on Amazon. Despite the strenuous efforts of his parents to reverse nature, he remains defiantly and irrevocably left-handed.

CLARENCE CARTER

Clarence Carter is a Maine based author, writer of the crime fiction novel *No Honor Among Thieves*. He's also been published in an anthology called *The First Stain*. He's currently putting together a collection of short stories called *Shadows & Keyholes*.

AMANDA CRUM

Amanda Crum is a writer and artist whose work has appeared in publications such as *Barren Magazine* and

Eastern Iowa Review and in several anthologies, including *Beyond The Hill* and *Two Eyes Open*. She is the author of three novels, *The Fireman's Daughter*, *Ghosts Of The Imperial*, and *The Darkened Mirror*. Her first chapbook of horror-inspired poetry, *The Madness In Our Marrow*, was shortlisted for a Bram Stoker Award nomination in 2015; her story *A Shimmer In The Parlor* was a finalist for the J.F. Powers Prize in Short Fiction in 2019. She currently lives in Kentucky with her husband and two children.

COLUMBIA STOVER

Columbia Stover lives in a valley, surrounded by trees. She has two dogs, both of whom are bigger than she is. She grew up with books. Books everywhere. And this is why she writes.

TIMOTHY C. HOBBS

Timothy C. Hobbs is a retired medical technologist living in Temple, Texas. His story *Moon in Submergence* was published in the 2013 Sirens Call Publications anthology *Fear of Water*. His short story collection, *Mothertrucker and Other Stories* and a novel *Veils* were published through Publish America in 2008. His novels *The Pumpkin Seed* and *Music Box Sonata*, and a novella *The Smell of Ginger*, were published by Vamplit Publishing in the United Kingdom A novella, *ED*, was published in 2014 by Visionary Press. A collection of flash and short fiction, *In the Blink of a Wicked Eye*, was published March 2015 by Sirens Call Publications. The horror story *Open, Locks, Whoever Knocks*, was included in Disquieted Dreams Press's *Best Horror Shorts 2015* publication. A short story, *Trust*, won the Golden Stake award at the 2017 International Vampire Film and Arts festival in Transylvania.

NICOLE M. WOLVERTON

Nicole M. Wolverton is a Philadelphia-based writer of fiction and non-fiction for adults and young adults. Her short fiction has appeared in *Aji* magazine, Jersey Devil Press, and elsewhere in various anthologies and literary magazines; she is the author of *The Trajectory of Dreams*, a psychological thriller published by Bitingduck Press. When Nicole is not attempting to make people laugh uncomfortably, her voice is often heard echoing down the Schuylkill River, issuing commands to a crew of cancer survivors and caregivers as the assistant coach and steersperson of the Power Over Cancer dragon boat team. She also loves to travel but is much quieter on airplanes.

She can be found at www.nicolewolverton.com or www.prettyasanairport.com, or on Twitter at @nicolewolverton.

WADE HUNTER

Wade Hunter is an author of dark fiction and horror. In his early teens he was introduced to J.R.R. Tolkien's

The Hobbit and became lost in the visions of the fantasy world. As he grew older and his imagination found new depths, Wade immersed himself in a world of books, movies, and comics. His latest work *Sin Eater's Journal* can be found on Amazon. Other works by Wade include *Harvest Moon, Judgment, Dark Glimmers, Shadows of the Soul, I am Fish Slayer,* and *Creeper*. He converted his story *I am Fish Slayer* for Short Stack's first comic anthology. He also writes young adult and children's stories under the name Aaron Buterbaugh. Wade lives in Weirton, a small town in the northern panhandle of West Virginia with his wife and two daughters.

Follow Wade on Instagram @WadeHunterStories

Come play in the dark.

GEORGE TSIRAKIDIS

George Tsirakidis was born in Thessaloniki in 1992. He studied political sciences and recently completed his Masters in Communication and Culture. He has worked at the Cinémathèque and at the Cinema Museum of Thessaloniki. His first novel, *O Kipos*, was published in Greece in February 2020.

ZACHARIAH STANFIELD

Zachariah Stanfield is a writer from North Alabama. His fiction has appeared in *Shotgun Honey* and *Out of the Gutter* magazines respectively. Zachariah is currently working on his first novel.

E.J. SIDLE

E.J. Sidle is an Australian who currently finds herself living in Scotland. She has a day job that takes up too many hours, and likes to spend her free time with her dog, Bullet. E.J. also enjoys travelling, playing video games, and drinking ludicrous volumes of coffee.

ACKNOWLEDGMENTS

It takes a lot to produce a book. First of all authors, then artists, and then editors. We have all spent countless hours working on this. I think it turned out fabulous.

There are a few people I'd like to thank. I had an idea for a skull with flowers, and I asked Amanda Crum (I had seen her posting sketch after sketch online) if she could give me a sugar skull, or a skull with flowers. After some back and forth, she nailed it.

Once I had that, I passed it to the wonderful cover artist Eloise J. Knapp, who took the art and made it into this great book cover. I'm super happy with it. I'd like to thank both Eloise and Amanda for the cover.

I hired Autumn Miller to read the initial submissions and make recommendations. She likes the same kind of horror/comedy as I do and we've often talked about shows and books in the genre. She was in the Jolly Horror Press inbox every day rejecting stories or forwarding to me those she thought had serious potential. I doubt you will find another small press that makes a decision on a story in a day or two. That's all down to Autumn. After the super job she did, I hired her as an actual editor and she did great work on a few stories.

I can't forget Lori Titus. Lori was more of an advisor to Jolly Horror Press this go around. Life intrudes you know. There are many things we seek her advice on. She is always available to be the tie breaker. When Autumn and I disagree, which isn't often but does happen, Lori is decisive for us. And we take her judgement to heart.

ACKNOWLEDGMENTS

I'd also like to thank T.J. Tranchell for his excellent work guest editing a few stories. Neha Rautela for her exceptional advice, Michelle von Eschen for continued guidance, and John Wolf for helping me write the back cover verbiage.

If you've reached this part of the book and are still reading, it's time for me to thank you, the reader. Thanks for supporting our little press. It means the world. Hope you enjoyed reading our third collection. There will be many more. Next up, *Fornever After: A Tragic Love Anthology.*

-Jonathan Lambert

Printed in Great Britain
by Amazon